The Button Box Series
Book III

The Silver Concho

Life Is a Rub-Board

By Sandy Jones

PublishAmerica
Baltimore

© 2009 by Sandy Jones.
All rights reserved. No part of this book may be reproduced, stored in a retrieval system or transmitted in any form or by any means without the prior written permission of the publishers, except by a reviewer who may quote brief passages in a review to be printed in a newspaper, magazine or journal.

First printing

All characters in this book are fictitious, and any resemblance to real persons, living or dead, is coincidental.

PublishAmerica has allowed this work to remain exactly as the author intended, verbatim, without editorial input.

All scriptures quoted from the Authorized King James Version of the Bible

ISBN: 1-60703-768-8
PUBLISHED BY PUBLISHAMERICA, LLLP
www.publishamerica.com
Baltimore

Printed in the United States of America

Dedicated to
Robert (Bob) Slayden
(One of the last of a breed: a 'Real' cowboy)

Acknowledgments

It is good to have friends who lift you up and encourage you; someone who is honest, kind, and enthusiastic with their comments and advice. I have such a friend, her name is Margaret Davis, Security person at the College (Jacksonville College) where I work. This woman has been a publicity 'team' all by herself. Thank you, Margaret for always being sensitive to my hopeful efforts and for believing in me.

Another such special friend is Diane Spriggs, Editor of the Baptist Trumpet in Arkansas. Diane has spent much time pouring over my manuscript, trying to help me 'undo' some of my punctuation and grammar 'bloopers'. I didn't get the complete manuscript to her in time to do as thorough a job as she wanted to but, "Thank you, Diane, for trying to help my writing to be of a better, more professional quality— If you will help me again... I promise to get the newest manuscript to you in time."

Thank you both,
Sandy Jones

FOREWORD

I have always enjoyed reading, especially historical novels that take me back to "a better time and a better place." But since I became the editor of a weekly religious newspaper (the *Baptist Trumpet*) and am called on to read a large quantity of printed material on a daily basis, my "recreational reading" had become almost non-existent…and I missed it.

All that changed when I received a copy of Sandy Jones' first book, "The Brass Button (No Return-No Regret)." It was one of those "can't wait to see what happens next" and "can't put it down" books and I thoroughly enjoyed it.

I knew the book was the first in a series; but, to be honest, I didn't see how she could top it. Then came her second book, "The Pearl Button (Meant to Be)" and that was exactly what she did because it was even better than the first! I found myself retreating to a quiet place at home and reading until my eyes began to cross, forcing me to put the book aside and go to sleep.

Now that I have read and enjoyed "The Silver Concho (Life is a Rub-Board)", I no longer wonder "if" she can top it, I just can't wait until she does! I am already looking forward to the next one.

Sandy shows an uncanny insight into the hearts and lives of her characters. Her dialogue and nuances work together to make every character real and believable; and her descriptive narration of the events as they unfold take you back in time and make you feel like you're right in the middle of the action.

These well-written, spell-binding books are love stories, to be sure; but they're so much more. They are filled with humor, action and, most of all, they are written from a Christian perspective and are testimonies to God and His interest in every area of our lives.

In a day and age when so many of the new books are worldly and cause the reader to blush, Mrs. Jones' books do just the opposite—they will lift your heart and spirit to greater heights and leave you with a smile on your face and a song in your heart.

I'm sure you will enjoy reading this book as much as I did and will join me in encouraging Sandy get the next book in the series out as soon as possible.

—Diane Spriggs, editor and business manager, Baptist Trumpet

INTRODUCTION
Granny's Visit

Granny hurried into the front hall. She removed her rain-cape and shook the water off as much as possible. Hanging it on the hall tree, she called, "Hello! Andrew; are you here?"

Granny had come to visit with her grandson, Andrew, who was home from college for a few days. Everyone else was out of the house for a day-workshop at the church.

From the bedroom, she heard, "I'm in here, Granny. Come on back. I'm folding my clothes in preparation for returning to school next Monday."

Andrew's big brown eyes, sparkled when he saw his grandmother. "What are you doing out in this weather," he questioned.

"I couldn't miss a chance to see my 'handsome' grandson; weather or no weather. It is terrible out there, I hope it doesn't totally ruin your weekend with the family.

"It won't ruin this day, if you will tell me one of your famous button stories," he said hopefully.

Granny had a collection of buttons in a carved wooden box on her treadle sewing machine at home in the country. They were buttons, clasps and fasteners of varied shapes, sizes, colors; and assorted materials. There was a story connected to each one. The children and grandchildren of Granny's family delighted to hear those stories.

Smiling at her grandson, she reached into her pocket and produced a silver disc about the size of a fifty-cent piece. It was smooth, thin, and embossed with intricate designs. There were black leather strips laced through star-shaped holes at either side of it.

"Do you know what this is," she asked.

Andrew stared at the disc for a moment. "I think it's some sort of clasp, or catch, or decoration used in Texas. I've seen them at rodeos and in western movies."

"A silver concho," Granny explained. "I had this one in the bottom of my button box. It has a very special story about a very special kind of man attached to it.

"Sit down and make yourself comfortable. You will hear about one of the toughest, yet kindest men I have ever heard of. He was an uncle to our family—the brother to your great, great, great grandfather, Matthew Galloway."

"Oh yes, I remember the story about Grandpa, Matt." Andrew's eyes twinkled. "He was a U.S. Cavalry officer, wasn't he?"

"Yes, he was, but Jacob 'Jake' Galloway was the brother who stayed home and ran the ranch in Texas—The Silver Concho."

"I've named this story, "Life is a Rub-board". Listen and you will see why. I also want you to listen for a lesson regarding the rub-board. It is the key to the story of a real man."

PROLOGUE
He's Coming Home

"Carrie! Carrie!" The sound of boots, pounding across the front porch, and the excited voice of her husband, Jake, brought Carrie Galloway rushing from the kitchen. Her face was a picture of fright as she ran through the house. "What? What's wrong, Jake?" she cried, placing her hand over her rapidly beating heart.

Jake let the front door slam behind him. He came to an abrupt halt just before running over his wife. Reaching out, he threw his strong arms around Carrie's waist and swung her around and around, laughing hilariously. "Nothing's wrong!—Everything's right!" he said between kisses to her forehead and cheeks.

"Put me down! Tell me what you're so excited about," she demanded. There was a half-smile on her face, and a twinkle in her eyes at Jake's shenanigans—coupled with bewilderment at what could have him in such a dither.

"Matt's coming home!" He waited for a moment to let it sink in. "Did you hear me, Carrie? Matt's coming home for good! He's decided that he wants to bring Dimple back to Texas. He says he plans to make a life here because he doesn't want the military life for Dimple…and their kids, someday."

Carrie leaped back into his arms. "Oh Jake; our prayers have been answered!" She kissed him soundly. Then, as was natural for Carrie, exclaimed, "Oh! My goodness! When will they get here—I've got to get the house ready!"

Jake grinned at her womanly concern. "Calm down, Honey. It'll be months, possibly a year. The important thing is that they're coming back to Texas to stay."

He lowered her feet to the floor. "Matt said he'll muster out of the Cavalry sometime after October of this year—Maybe even wait until next spring. You'll have plenty of time to get ready for them."

Carrie's brows came together in a frown, her disappointment evident. "Why is he waiting so long? Won't the Cavalry release him before then?"

His smile became smug. "It seems he has a little problem; if you want to call it that. Dimple is expecting a baby in September. Naturally, Matt won't try to make the trip before she and the baby are strong enough to travel. Add to that, Dimple's father and his new wife, Anne, are also expecting a baby in November."

Carrie squealed, "How wonderful for them!—Imagine a second family."

"He'll have to consider the weather too. If winter comes early this year, they'll wait until next spring."

Carrie's mouth fell open then snapped shut. She was both elated and disappointed. Dimple was such a sweet girl. Carrie just knew they would become close…maybe as close as sisters.

She would never say anything to Jake about it, but she missed having another female to talk with. The Galloway ranch, the Silver Concho, was several miles from the town of Llano, where her father practiced medicine. The only time she saw most of her friends was when they went to hear the circuit riding preacher on the first Sunday of each month.

She shook her head. That wasn't quite right. There were trips to town for supplies and occasional holiday celebrations or other social events; but she had no one to just 'talk' to over a cup of tea without riding a good distance to see her best friend, Caroline Marshall. It would be so wonderful to have Dimple close by.

"Will they live with us—here in the ranch house?"

THE SILVER CONCHO: LIFE IS A RUB-BOARD

Jake watched her face. It was Carrie's way to, mentally work things out ahead of time. He knew she liked Dimple, and he was happy about that. But, he also knew that she was anxious for Matt's plan to become a reality.

Placing his hands on her upper arms, he answered her question, "They have to at first. But, when they were here last fall, Matt made a remark that makes me think that he'll probably want to build his own house. We were near the spot on Comanche Creek where it runs beneath the bridge that grandpa built. Matt sat there on Breeze just looking around. After a while, he said, almost under his breath, 'Jake, this sure would be a nice place to build a house'. I nodded—hoping that he was thinking about doing just that."

Carrie listened happily, as tears formed in her eyes and ran down her cheeks. This was a dream come true for Jake. She was so thrilled for him.

She reached up to wipe her eyes. "Go get Collin…I think he's riding his stick horse in the front yard. Supper's ready."

CHAPTER ONE
Remembering

Jacob 'Jake' Galloway turned twenty-nine years old in the spring of 1875. Like his brother, Matt, he was a handsome man. He grinned each time his pretty wife told him so, but discounted the knowledge as unimportant—except to Carrie. He was tall: six feet-four inches, broad shouldered with dark hair, and possessed a square, manly jaw, and wide forehead with deep-set, cobalt-blue eyes. Years of hard ranch-work had added muscle to his rather large frame.

* * *

Jake was so excited at the prospect of Matt's return that his appetite had completely deserted him. Carrie watched him push the food around on his plate. She nudged him beneath the table with her foot, and spoke for their two and a half year-old son's benefit, "Jake, how in the world am I going to talk Collin into eating properly, when you won't do so yourself?"

Jake cut his eyes at the boy who was watching his father expectantly. Collin was notorious for eating only favorite foods while pushing the rest aside.

"I'm saving the rest for So'jer," the boy explained, as if that settled the matter.

"Soldier gets plenty to eat without your help, Son. I'm surprised we have any more jackrabbits on the whole ranch. He's so fast, he catches *at least* one a day," Jake chuckled. When father's eyes met son's, undeniable pride twinkled in them.

"Papa, when will Unca Matt come back? I want to see him. I want to look at his so'jer suit some more," Collin declared.

Jake smiled. "It'll be a little while yet, son. He has some things to take care of before he can come see you again. But, when he comes back, guess what he'll be bringing with him?"

Collin's sky-blue eyes were wide. "What? What will Unca Matt bring?"

Jake slapped the table in front of the curious child. "He'll be bringing you a little cousin."

"What's a cussin," Collin questioned. He had never heard of one and he wasn't sure he wanted one.

"A cousin," Jake paused, "is a little boy or girl for you to play with. They are almost the same thing as a brother or sister." Jake winked at Carrie, and then looked back at his son. "Would you like that?"

Collin's eyes lit up even more. His head bobbed up and down. Suddenly, he turned and looked at his mother. "But I still want you to get me a baby brudder for Christmas."

Carrie looked at Jake and turned pink. She saw the twinkle in his eyes when he spoke.

"Mama and I are working on that.' He winked at her.

"But, no more tricks, young man. You need to eat your supper."

"Are *you* gonna eat all your supper, Papa," the wily little imp countered.

Jake answered, smiling devilishly at Carrie, "Oh yes, I need to be strong—to work on getting you a brother."

"Jacob Galloway! I'll want to speak to you later. You need to be careful about making promises," Carrie chuckled.

Jake's expression rivaled his son's for innocence. "Oh Honey, I don't *ever* make promises that I don't do my very best to keep."

"Eat your supper," she mumbled.

***

Supper was over, and the dishes were washed and put away. Carrie put Collin to bed, and went to join Jake on the front porch. She sat down on the top step beside him.

It was getting dark. April weather in west-central Texas was pleasant in the evenings. Nights brought a symphony of sounds: katydids chirped, birds called, grasshoppers whirred, and in the distance, the howl of coyotes in the nearby hills. Occasionally, the hoot of a barn owl added additional rhythm to the music. Stars were just becoming visible in the early evening sky, and twinkled an orchestration of all the sounds.

Jake sat on the edge of the porch with one booted foot on the ground, and the other on the bottom step.

He was quiet; but when Carrie settled down next to him, he reached out and pulled her snuggly to his side. Absently, he brushed her temple with his lips.

"Hey, that was good," he whispered, and cupped her chin with his big, work-roughened hand to press his lips to hers in a long, sweet, lingering kiss.

When their lips parted, he looked deeply into her eyes. "How long has it been since I tried to tell you how much I love you?"

"Not too long, but I never get tired of hearing it. *Try again.*" She smiled and rested her head against the side of his chest. He held her in the crook of his arm and looked down at her upturned face.

"I *can't* tell you how much I love you." She looked up at him with trusting eyes. He went on, "...because there aren't enough words. At least, if there are, *I* don't know them." He smiled.

"But, I *can* tell you that...if I had everything I wanted in the world, and didn't have you, and your love—I wouldn't want to live."

He paused for a second, "I *know* what I'm talking about, Sweetheart...I've been there."

"But you *do* have my love. You'll have it always," she sighed. "and I have yours."

Reaching around his chest as far as she could, she hugged him tightly and added, "Isn't God good?"

Jake's laugh was a deep rumble in his chest, "Yes, He is—He surely is."

* * *

They sat contentedly for a while. Carrie asked, "What are you thinking about?"

"Oh; I guess the news that Matt will be coming home for good has me kinda reminiscing about the past."

"Want to share your thoughts? You've never told me much about your family's history," she gently persuaded.

Jake dropped his eyes to her face. "You really want to know?"

"Of course—I'm part of it now," she answered sincerely.

* * *

He tightened his hold on her shoulder and looked down the moonlit road, winding its way around a small grove of Pin Oaks to the front of the 'Concho' ranch-house...their home.

Beyond the grove, Jake knew there was a little stone bridge that crossed a creek that meandered through the southeastern corner of their land.

"You know the little bridge over Comanche Creek?—Well, my granddad built that bridge in 1830. He and Big Mama, my grandmother, left Virginia in the spring of 1821, looking to take advantage of land grants offered by Spain to anyone who would settle and prove land in Texas.

"But Mexico was kicking up a fuss about wanting independence from Spain by the time he got here; so, Grandpa just squatted for a while near Nacogdoches. He'd just wait until the Mexicans and Spanish settled their differences.

"The fighting wasn't going on that far to the east and Grandpa Ed had a wife and young son to think about."

Carrie smiled, "Your father?"

Jake nodded, "He was born just after they'd crossed the Sabine River into Texas.

"Anyway…After Mexico won their independence in 1822; Santa Anna allowed immigration from other countries…for a while. He wanted the taxes and prosperity that would come from populating the land.

"A man by the name of Austin had been given one of those huge pieces of land in 1821. He was to see that it was divided among settlers who wanted to come to Texas."

"I've heard about him…Moses was his name; Moses Austin." She grinned, "Kind'a fitting,—don't you think?"

Jake nodded again. "Only he died before he could get people settled on the land; so his son, Stephen F. Austin, took up his dream. All this was going on about then.

"Grandpa pulled out of Nacogdoches in 1827 and drove a wagon west-northwest until he came to this area. He liked what he saw."

Jake exhaled, "According to what I've been told, it took some doing, but he finally got his land…from an appointed Mexican Governor named 'Martinez', around San Antonio.

"The house that we're living in was by no means the first one on this ranch. Grandpa built a small cabin, hardly more than a lean-to, first. It kept the wind, rain and cold off Big Mama and my pa, until he could put up a bigger house.

"By November, the year following their arrival here, there was a much bigger, nicer, cabin with a small barn, a corral, chicken coop and hog pen to boast of. That house lasted for the next eight years, clear through the Texas war for independence.

"But, there was a period of time between 1835 and 1836 when Grandpa loaded Big Mama and Thomas, my father, up in a wagon and, after boarding up the whole place, he took them back to Nacogdoches to stay with friends while he went off to fight alongside General Houston."

"Your grandfather fought with Sam Houston! Was he at San Jacinto?" Carrie's eyes were wide with wonder.

THE SILVER CONCHO: LIFE IS A RUB-BOARD

"Who do you think helped blow up Lynch's Ferry," he chuckled, his face alight with pride.

"Wonderful! That makes me so proud for you *and* Collin; to be descended from a man like that," Carrie exclaimed.

"Yeah,—I'm proud alright; but I plan to teach our boy that every man earns his own reputation. He can't ride on the coat-tails of an ancestor."

Jake was silent for a few moments, and then went on speaking, "When Grandpa and Big Mama were finally able to come back here in the summer of 1836, the house and barn had been burned.

"Some people wanted to blame it on the Mexican sympathizers, but Grandpa said, according to the signs all around the place, it was the Comanches. They were the forgotten people in all this squabbling over Texas. They had been here even before the Spanish.

"Grandpa started over; and this time he built with Adobe and named the ranch, 'The Silver Concho'. What is now the front room and part of the kitchen was the original house."

"When did he add the other rooms," she questioned.

Jake shook his head slightly. "He didn't, my father enlarged the kitchen and added three bedrooms not long after he brought Mama to Texas in '45. Grandpa had passed away and, Grandma lived here, of course, so when I was born not too long afterward he decided they needed more rooms.

"Matt was born just before my fourth birthday; so we *all* lived here with Big Mama until my parents both died. Mama died in the winter of 1856, then dad, the following spring."

Carrie's eyes filled with tears. "How old were they? 'They couldn't have been very old. What killed them?"

"Mama was thirty-one. She died of pneumonia. Pa was only thirty-six. A maverick longhorn bull caught him by surprise when it charged out of some brush, near where he was cutting fence posts. He lived about a year after it happened—gasping for breath."

Jake dropped his head. "After Mama died, I guess he just…didn't want to live without her."

"Oh Jake—I'm so sorry." She said softly, patting his hand. To dispel the sad memories, she begged, "Please tell me about your parents. They must have been special people."

Jake laid his other hand over hers. "Yes. They were—both of them. They were made for each other."

He cut his eyes at her and winked. "Like us."

Carrie bumped his side with her shoulder. "You don't have to convince me. I know it." Her face became serious again. "Now, tell me about your mother and father."

"As you know, Thomas Edward Galloway was an only child. He was the first Galloway to be born in Texas. He grew up in tough times. He knew what it was to fight for what he wanted, including Indians, Mexicans, would-be squatters and land grabbers, weather…and the land itself. He watched his pa, my grandpa, refuse to give up. Grandpa started over several times and each time he built bigger and better."

Jake stared into the darkness for a few moments. "My father was just like him. He refused to let anything defeat him…until Mama died."

"Tell me about when they met." Carrie said, trying to get his mind back on the happy times.

* * *

"In 1839, when Thomas Galloway was eighteen years-old, Texas was a republic and, except for Indian trouble, everything was pretty settled. He decided he wanted to go back to Virginia to meet the only grandparents still living—Big Mama's people.

Of course, it was a joy for them to see their grandson for the first time in his life. They did everything they could to spoil him. And they had it in their mind to talk him out of going back to Texas." Jake chuckled. "I don't think they'd have been successful if it hadn't been for a friend of the family that convinced Pa that he was made for the military.

The man had connections and, before you know it, Thomas Galloway was a cadet at West Point Military Academy.

The fellow had been right. Pa thrived on military life. His instructors all said he had the makings of a long, successful career in the U.S. Cavalry."

THE SILVER CONCHO: LIFE IS A RUB-BOARD

Jake's chest rumbled in a soft chuckle. "That's why I didn't worry about Matt's chances for success in the Cavalry—He's Thomas Galloway's son."

A few seconds of silence followed. "During Thomas's first year at the 'Point', he met a beautiful girl from Virginia…my mother.

"He'd gone down to be with his grandparents during his Christmas leave. Texas was too far away to try to go home for the holidays.

The community where the folks lived held a taffy-pull for the young people every year at that time. When the broad shouldered, handsome young man in uniform walked into the room, my mother told me that every girl and woman between ten and fifty nearly went into a faint."

* * *

Carrie squeezed Jakes bicep. "I can imagine,—especially, if he looked like you." She smiled up at him. "You're the best looking man I've ever seen. I will admit though; Matt gives you a lot of competition. But then, he looks like your twin instead of just a brother." She pulled his head down and kissed him solidly.

"Woman! How am I gonna keep my mind on my story if you keep tempting me?" Jake tried to sound annoyed, but did not succeed.

Carrie's mischievous expression contradicted her answer, "I'm sorry, go ahead. Tell me more."

"Hummph!" Jake huffed, grinning at her theatrics.

* * *

"Thomas shyly ignored all the eye-fluttering and flirtatious remarks. He had been there only a few minutes when he spied the prettiest girl in the room.

Mama told me that she was standing at the stove stirring the buttered molasses. Her back was to the door so she didn't see him come in. When she turned around to spread a ladle of the hot stuff on a platter, their eyes met…and she missed the platter, dumping the whole mess on the table instead.

Her mother scolded, 'Jane! What are you…?' She stopped and followed Mama's stare across the room. 'Oh…' she said when she saw Pa. Her mouth snapped shut.

They were married one month after he graduated from West Point. He and his best friend and classmate, James Spiers traveled to Virginia together for the wedding."

* * *

Jake took a deep breath. He looked down at Carrie. "Do you want to hear anymore tonight?"

"Oh yes! At least tell me how they wound up back in Texas."

"OK. That won't take long."

* * *

"After returning to West Point, my father applied for an assignment in Texas. The Mexicans were trying to back out of the 'Treaty of Velasco'. That's the agreement signed by Santa Anna that he would get out of Texas and stay out. He also agreed that the border between Mexico and Texas would be the Rio Grande River. He didn't want to honor that either.

So war between the U.S. and Mexico was likely. Texas was in the union by then and Thomas wanted to be near his folks when the trouble started.

Then a letter came from Grandma Sally, 'Big Mama' we called her, telling him that his father was dead.

I never knew what killed my grandpa—I never asked. Anyway, she wanted Pa to come home. She could not handle things alone—especially with trouble brewing.

I think she wanted to get him back to his land, Texas, his heritage. Pa resigned his commission and took his new wife of less than a year and came back to The Silver Concho."

THE SILVER CONCHO: LIFE IS A RUB-BOARD

* * *

Jake slapped both hands on his knees and stood up. "Come on, Sweetheart—daylight comes early and I've got a lot to do tomorrow."

CHAPTER TWO
Life Is a Rub Board

"I'm gonna kill that rooster!" Jake mumbled as he threw his legs over the edge of the bed and sat up, rubbing the back of his neck.

Carrie turned on her back and squinted at her husband's broad shouldered outline in the dim, pre-dawn light. "Why would you want to kill old Gabriel? He's the best alarm on the place."

Jake twisted at the waist to look down at her. "He may be the best alarm, but he doesn't have enough sense not to get right under our window to 'blow his trumpet.'" He swung his hand toward the open window. "…and it's not even daylight yet!"

Carrie laughed, "Jake, Gabriel knows that if he ever let you sleep to daylight, we'd be having him with dumplings for dinner."

Just then, Gabriel let fly with another laborious crow. Jake jumped up and moved to the window. He stuck his head out and shouted, "Alright! I hear you—you did your job! Now go bother the hens down at the hen house!"

He pulled his head back inside and shut the window. Turning back to the bed, he bent down, placing his hands on either side of Carrie's head, smiling, "Speaking of bothering the hens…" he growled as he nibbled her neck.

She squealed, "Jacob Galloway! You stop that! You said last night that you have a lot to do today!"

He raised his head still grinning. There was a wicked gleam in his eyes as he chuckled, "I gotta start somewhere…"

* * *

Collin padded into the kitchen in his little nightshirt. The two year-old, like his parents, was an early-riser. He rubbed his eyes with his tiny fists and yawned.

Jake scooted his chair back from the table and patted his knee. The little boy ran to his father and raised his arms to be lifted to his regular morning perch.

Collin's highchair sat in the corner, but it was almost a sacred ritual between father and son that Jake would hold him at the breakfast table.

Carrie set a cup of milk in front of her son and bent to kiss his cherubic cheek. "Good morning, Chief. How's my little Indian?"

Collin chuckled, a sweet, baby sound. "I hungry Mama." He twisted around so he could look at Jake's face. "…And Papa is too."

Carrie set a bowl of scrambled eggs, a small platter of saucer-size pancakes, syrup, butter, a plate piled high with crisp bacon and a pan of hot biscuits on the table. "There you are…let me see you make all that disappear," she challenged.

"Yummm…get us a whole bunch, Papa," the child ordered.

"Don't you worry—I plan to," was Jake's reply. Carrie watched with pleasure as her two 'men' cleaned the plate twice.

Later that morning, Carrie stood in the front yard with a hoe in her hands. She carefully weeded and cultivated the flowers in her jealously tended flowerbeds. Collin played in the dirt at her feet.

Jake rode up the hill from the barn. He and his foreman, Wade 'Cooter' Marshall were heading toward the south pasture holding pen for the day. Joel and Manny, whose name was really 'Manuel', would be working on the pens to the north and east, the other four 'Concho' cowhands were dragging strays out of the ravines and gullys to the west.

Stopping near Carrie, Jake thumbed his hat back on his head and grinned down at his wife and son. "Between the two of you, we've got a fair size dust storm brewing here."

Carrie stopped and leaned on the hoe. "How long do you think you'll be gone, Jake?"

"I can't say, Honey, it depends on what we run into," he explained. His eyes twinkled as he watched her pretty face.

"What you run into? What do you 'expect' to run into?"

Carrie was always cautiously aware of the possibility of Comanches showing up to help themselves to 'Silver Concho' beef.

The Indians were still incensed over their failure, and the U.S. Calvary's refusal to stop the senseless slaughter and waste of their primary food source, the great buffalo herds. There had been a siege by the Indians at Adobe Wells the previous summer. A young, Kwahadis-Comanche chief named Quanah Parker led the attack in an attempt to destroy a nest of white buffalo hunters. Things did not go well for the Comanche, and now some of the war chiefs were calling for attacks on all whites.

* * *

Jake's smile disappeared. He knew what she was thinking. "I only meant that roundup starts in a couple of weeks. Cooter and I, and Joel and Manny have to check the condition of all the holding pens. We'll be fixing anything that needs it. That's what I meant. It has to be done before we start branding calves."

"Oh." Carrie chose not to say anything about watching for Comanches. She didn't want Collin to hear.

"We'll be in before dark. You get your list ready and Saturday we'll all go into town. 'Maybe we could even go on to Llano and visit the Doc for a couple of days. Would you like that?" Carrie's father was the only doctor within a one hundred mile radius of Llano.

Collin, who was busy digging a hole in his mother's flowerbed, suddenly stood up and looked up at Jake. "Papa, can I go help work on the holin' pens? I can ride wif' Unca Cooter in the wag'in."

Cooter, Jake's life-long friend cut his eyes at Carrie and opened his mouth to speak; but Jake cut in before he could say anything. Jake knew that Cooter would never say no to his 'little pardner'.

"I was depending on you to stay here and help your Mama get things done, so we can all go see your Grandpa on Saturday. You *do* want to go see him—don't you?"

Collin's little head bobbed up and down. "Uh Huh...I love 'Gwampa'. He gots a big..." he spread his arms to show how big, "...Candy jar."

"Now Collin, you know that candy jar is for little boys and girls who are not feeling well.

It's to help them get better," Carrie reasoned.

"No Mama..." the tyke answered with authority, "Gwampa' tol' me it's for *me*. He jus' lets the sick kids have a piece of *my* candy." He turned his tiny hands palms up in front of him. "I don't mind."

"Well, I'm proud of you, son. That's real nice of you to share *your* candy," Jake chuckled, as did the other two adults. He turned his eyes back to Carrie. "We'll be back as soon as we can." He winked. "You and I will talk some more about Collin's little brother."

Carrie rolled her eyes and blushed. He added, "Oh, by the way, give old Gabriel an extra helping of cornmeal today. He's the best alarm on the place."

Cooter grinned. He knew there was more to what was being said than what he was hearing.

* * *

The next two days passed swiftly for Carrie. By Friday morning, she was finished in the flowerbeds, so she decided to help Hardtack in the kitchen garden.

Hardtack was the cowhand's nickname for their cook. The jolly, little, good-natured man had once been a sailor. The men loved to tease him about his biscuits being hardtack, like the biscuits eaten aboard ships. He was actually a good cook, but they took pleasure in giving him a ribbing.

About two-thirty, Friday afternoon Carrie was just putting Collin down for his nap, when she heard a wagon rumble noisily past the house. It was heading down the hill, toward the barn.

She went to the kitchen window and peered out expecting to see Jake and Cooter. Cooter was alone. She watched as he drove the wagon into a shed, attached to the side of the barn and jumped to the ground. Unhitching the horses, he turned them into the corral and headed up toward the ranch house.

Stepping out the kitchen door, Carrie waited until he came through an arched gate that led to the patio-courtyard at the back of the house.

"Afternoon, Carrie," he said, reaching for his hat and dropping the hand that held it carelessly to his side.

"Jake wanted me to let you know that he'll be along after while. He decided to go see how much luck the boys were having draggin' those strays out of Chico Ravine." He grinned sheepishly, "I could'a done it, but you know Jake—He's used'ta being in th'middle of thangs."

Carrie nodded and smiled. "Cooter, I just took a molasses cake out of the oven, want a big chunk, and a cup of coffee? There is something I want to ask you about."

"For a piece of molasses cake, I'll answer *all* your questions. Lead the way," the segundo foreman answered.

Once inside, Carrie motioned to a chair at the kitchen table, "Make yourself comfortable while I cut you a piece of this cake."

Cooter watched her, respectfully, as she moved around the room gathering cups, plates and eating utensils. He couldn't help but grin; remembering the day Jake first saw the pretty girl.

Carrie turned and caught him grinning. "Wade Marshall! What are you grinning about? That smile must mean you've been up to something, or you're planning to be."

"No! No! Mrs. Carrie. Don't hang me yet." He said, throwing up his hands. "I was just remembering the first time Jake laid eyes on you. That's the only time in my life I ever saw Jake so tongue-tied and bumfuzzled he couldn't say nothin'."

"He would have probably been more tongue-tied if he had known what I thought of him at the time," she said tartly.

Her expression became more serious. "How long have you known Jake, Cooter?"

"As long as I can remember…my earliest memory is of us playing jokes on the girls at recess at the little school in Mesquite Grove over near the springs. It ain't there no more."

Carrie nodded. "Tell me about Jake when he was a boy. I can't get him to talk about himself very much, but, I've heard some of the older people say that he and Matt had a rough time."

"I guess you *could* say that, but Jake Galloway weren't cut out of ordinary leather."

Cooter forked a bite of cake and washed it down with coffee. As he swallowed, his eyes had a far-away look in them.

* * *

"Jake was born on this place, as you know. His Pa had come back to Texas just out of the Cavalry. He was an officer, graduated from West Point. But Big Mama, Jake's Grandma, called her boy back to Texas when Grandpa Ed passed."

Cooter took another bite of cake and sipped his coffee. "After the war with Mexico was over, things settled down some, and folks got on with their business.

My Pa had come here as a soldier in '45, and he came right back here from Tennessee just as soon as he got out of the army and loaded up Mama and me. I was about three years old. I'm two years older than Jake.

"One day, when I was about twelve, a neighbor came by our house bringing word that Mr. Thomas Galloway had died. It was awful sad news 'cause Mrs. Jane, Jake's Ma, had also passed not more'n three or four months before that.

That left a Grandma and two young boys all alone on that twenty thousand acre ranch. Folks began to wonder if Mrs. Sally Galloway would take her grandsons and go back to Virginia." Cooter laughed, "They sure didn't know that old lady. The family didn't call her 'Big Mama' for nothing...It sure wasn't her size. She weren't big as a minute.

I used to come home after school with Jake and later, Matt. Big Mama would say to me, 'Cooter, you're always welcome—you know that. But if you're gonna hang around Jake, you're either gonna watch him work, or you're gonna roll up your sleeves and help. He's got a ranch to run.'

She'd get cowhands from the community to come roundup the Silver Concho cattle in the spring of every year, and do the branding. Then, she'd pay'em off in thirty head apiece. That way, the herd stayed on 'Concho' land."

He wagged his head. "She must've been the toughest little woman in Texas. 'She was determined to hang on to this ranch. It weren't for herself, neither—it was for the grandsons.

I've heard her tell Jake, time and again, 'This land and this ranch are yours and Matt's heritage. You've got to keep it for yourselves and for future generations'.

She'd put both her hands on his shoulders and look him straight in the eyes and say, 'Jake…you're mighty young to be having to act like a man, but you got it to do.' She'd smile and go on, 'You're Thomas' son; and I got no doubt that you've got th'grit to do it. Your little brother is too young to be much help right now, but hold on, he'll grow to be a big boy like yourself. Together, you'll make a great ranch out of the Silver Concho.'

For four years after Mister Thomas died, Big Mama ran things and kept the boys fed and clothed. There were some bad winters and that cost some of their cattle, but she kept pushing Jake and he kept growing."

Cooter waited while Carrie refilled his cup. She sat back down, anxious to hear more.

"Did you know that your husband was as big as some full-grown men by the time he was fifteen? He was at least five-ten or eleven. I guess that's what saved him. He was big and strong, and not short on gumption and he wasn't lazy neither. He'd get up before daylight and take care of the stock horses and milk cows, then take off for school with Matt hanging on behind him. There were too many on'ry longhorns running free between here and the school to turn a seven or eight year-old loose on a horse. 'Course, by the time Matt was ten, he could handle it.

THE SILVER CONCHO: LIFE IS A RUB-BOARD

After school every day, Jake would come home and work 'til past dark cuttin' summer grass for hay against the winter. Plus, Big Mama always had a kitchen garden—both the boys helped with that. She and Jake also planted a field of corn together. Jake harvested it. Then, there were the hogs and chickens. Matt did a lot of the feedin', but he was still too young to carry much weight."

"How old were Jake and Matt when their Grandmother died," Carrie asked.

Involuntarily, Cooter's head jerked in memory. "That's when things *really* got tough".

* * *

"Jake was fourteen and Matt, ten. What had been, 'you're *gonna have* to be a man', was now, 'you *are* a man', for Jake." He looked at Carrie. "A fourteen year-old *'man'*, Mrs. Carrie.

The whole country knew Big Mama was failing. 'Guess that little woman just wore slap out—trying to take as much load off Jake as she could. 'Doin' work *no* woman ought'ta have to do.

She finally took to her bed, but she put it off as long as she could lift one foot in front of the other. Neighbor women helped out all they could, bringing food, cleanin' the house, do'in washin' and tending to Mrs. Sally's needs.

One day, Big Mama called the boys to her bedside. 'Jake,' she said, 'my time has come. I've got some words for you and Matt. I want you to know how proud I am of both of you. I know your Ma and Pa would be too.

Now, you remember this…. all your days…both of you—Life is a 'rub-board'. It's full of bumps and rough places. All of them can be for good or bad. That's up to you, 'cause; if you're strong enough to last through those bumps and rough places, you'll come out clean and smellin' good, but, if you're not strong, you'll tear up and fall to pieces…and you won't be good for nothin'.

You got a whole life ahead of you. Make the most of it. The way to make the most of your life is to live it in the way Jesus would have you to. Don't ever stop going to meeting and never stop worshipping God.'

She squeezed their hands and said, 'Be a man,'—Then she died."

Carrie's voice was shaky as she said, "A fourteen year-old man… Oh, Cooter, how in the world did they make it?"

Cooter ate his last forkful of cake. Carrie started to rise to refill his cup. He held up his hand. "If you don't mind, I think I'd like to have a cool drink of water."

She nodded and filled a glass from the water bucket sitting on a small table by the back door.

When Cooter had taken a long drink, Carrie scooted her chair closer to the table and asked him to continue.

"I want to hear about those years between the time that Grandma Sally died and when I met him," then she added, "If Jake comes in, we can talk again sometime when he's not here."

CHAPTER THREE
Neighbors, Good and Bad

"After Big Mama's burial, the folks for miles around were real conscious that there was two boys living alone out here, and they did kind, neighborly things…for a while. But you know how it is…people just seem to get careless, not meaning to, but still careless. They go about their own business and forget somebody who's havin' a hard time.

Jake and Matt, who was ten, made their own way and each one did what he could. Because Jake was the oldest and the biggest, he did all the heavy, outdoor work. Matt did his best to cook." Cooter chuckled, "…but, how many ten year-old boys do you know that can cook anything fit to eat? They ate their vegetables mostly raw and their meat, which Jake usually killed and cleaned, was still bleeding when it went on the plate.

I used to come over to see'em every chance I got, but I always made sure it wasn't at meal time." He laughed again.

"One Sunday, six months after their Grandma died, the boys came to hear the circuit rider. The women took one look and were awfully ashamed of themselves.

Jake and Matt were clean—Big Mama had taught them that—but their clothes were a sight. And both of them had lost weight; even though they were getting taller.

Well, the next week, a group of women got together to talk about what they could do. They thought they'd come up with a good idea, but Jake wouldn't have it."

"What was their idea," Carrie asked.

"They sent Elsie Cash and Bea Langley out here to offer taking turns keeping Matt for a month or two at a time each. They thought that'd relieve Jake from worrying about his little brother. Whoever had Matt at the time would see to his clothes and such. They also promised to bring baked good to Jake from time to time."

Carrie frowned. "What did Jake do?"

Cooter grinned. "Turned'em down flat." He explained, "You see, when Mrs. Elsie first started talking, Matt was standin' off to the side, and when Jake glanced his way, Matt was shakin' his head no.

That settled it for Jake; so he answered real respectful like, 'Mrs. Cash, I appreciate all you ladies being concerned about us, but Matt and I are all the family we've got left. We don't want to be separated.' Jake kinda dropped his head and added, 'I know we look sorta throwed away, but we belong on the Concho together.' He looked at the women then and threw another idea at'em. He said, 'Matt does most of the cooking and housekeeping. If you ladies could see your way clear to take turns coming out to the house just once a month and teaching him some things about cooking, and sweeping the house, and washing our clothes, and the linens…I…*we* would sure appreciate that. Oh—and cut our hair too.'"

Cooter cocked his head and chuckled again, "To this day, I suspect that Matt is a better cook than Jake. That was when Jake turned fifteen and Matt, eleven."

* * *

"The next year, there was this sorry, no-account that came out'a nowhere, and called himself, "Joe Washington."

Pursing his lips for a moment, Cooter said, "I imagine ole 'George' would turn over in his grave, if he knew that such'a fella shared his name.

THE SILVER CONCHO: LIFE IS A RUB-BOARD

Well, Joe couldn't keep a job. He was too lazy. Several people in Llano, and around about, hired him to do odd jobs. He'd just half do'em and the people would pay him off and tell him to hit the road—which, I don't think bothered him none, because he really didn't want to work.

I don't know how he heard about those two young boys living by themselves, trying to run the Concho; but Jake told me, that late one afternoon, Joe showed up here at the house. I guess he thought he had him a plan to get in on a good thing.

The boys were eating their supper when they heard a man calling, 'Hello, the house!' Jake told Matt to stay back out'a sight and he went to the front door. He stopped in the doorway—sort-of half-in and half-out. Big Mama had always kept a loaded shotgun standing by the door. 'Course, Joe couldn't see it.

Joe was sittin' astraddle a mule. He grinned, friendly like, but Jake wasn't fooled.

'What can I do for you,' Jake asked.

Now, in the first place, Joe Washington wasn't expecting no sixteen-year-old boy to be six-foot tall—and Jake had a no-nonsense look about him. But I guess he thought it would be easy to fool a young'un.

Washington said, 'I've heard about you boys livin' out here by yore selves...and I figured you probably could use a man to do some of the heavy work.'

What Joe didn't know was that Jake had already been told about a 'good-for-nothin'' that was suspected of stealing anything that wasn't nailed down—too lazy to work. Jake knew he was lookin' at 'im.

'Well, you figured wrong. We don't need any help,' Jake answered.

Joe was surprised at the boy's spunk, but he wasn't gonna be put off that easy. He sputtered, 'Now see here...ain't no sixteen-year-old boy gonna 'bow up' at me!'

He started throwin' a leg over his saddle to get down off his mule.

Jake calmly bent down and picked up the shotgun. He held it loosely at his side,—not aimin' it...yet.

Joe stopped halfway to the ground off that mule. He hung there, sizing up Jake's grit.

'Mister, this shotgun doesn't know I'm only sixteen. It'll shoot as good for me as it would have for my Pa.' Jake raised the barrel. 'I'm about ten seconds away from proving my point, if you don't get off this ranch.'

Jake stopped to let it soak in. Then, he added, '…And don't come back, or next time I won't wait ten seconds.'

"He didn't," Carrie moaned, her eyes shining with admiration for her husband's courage at such a young age.

"Yes, he did. If I'm lying…I'm dying." Cooter winked.

"That ole reprobate jumped on that mule and lit out as fast as he could. He never looked back neither.

Jake told me that Matt had been watching and listening to the whole thing. He turned his eyes to his brother and asked, 'Jake, do you think he'll come around here again?'

Jake was thoughtful for a minute then shook his head, 'No, he's a coward. He's not about to chance facing this shotgun again. But you keep it handy; just in case he comes around when I'm not here.' He looked at Matt real serious, 'I'd hate for you to have to do this…but, if he *does* come back,—don't you give 'im no quarter."

Cooter looked up. "That was when Jake was sixteen and Matt was twelve. It seemed like trouble just came in waves for the Galloway brothers. Something was always comin' up that threatened their ability to keep the ranch goin'.

Cooter took a swig from his glass of water. "I reckon Jake and Matt always kept Big Mama's words about life being a 'rub-board' in mind because they were determined not to fall apart."

* * *

"The next year, Matt was gettin' bigger, and Jake began to put him to doin' things outside the house. By that time, Jake had quit going to school; but he made sure Matt went on.

It was a bad winter that year. When Jake went out in early March to check on how the herd had fared, he found that quite a few had frozen to death, starved, or been eaten by the wolves. He finally decided to do

THE SILVER CONCHO: LIFE IS A RUB-BOARD

as Big Mama had always done; so he hired six or seven men to help gather all they could find. He agreed to pay them one out of ten for all they brought in.

By the middle of April, he had about twenty-seven hundred head accounted for. He told those men to cut out their two hundred-seventy, and then brand all the new calves with Silver Concho's brand.

Next, Jake asked if I would help him and Matt drive a small herd of about two hundred and fifty head up to Ft. Worth. He planned to sell them to one of the big cattlemen there.

We started bunchin' some of the cows with calves about ready to wean, and Jake picked out a few of the young bulls that weren't doing their job yet—getting ready to make the drive to Ft. Worth, the first of May.

One Saturday morning, a week before we planned to leave, we all three got up and rode out to where the trail-herd was gathered. They weren't there!

We could not believe our eyes at first. Jake rode around the perimeter of where they had been a couple of days before. He got down and studied the ground."

Cooter looked at Carrie, his eyes twinkling merrily. "The cattle had been rustled.

Jake grabbed his hat and threw it down. He was so mad, Mrs. Carrie. Jake didn't use cusswords—didn't know many—but that day, he *invented* some.

I asked him if he thought maybe Indians had run off with 'em, but Jake said it hadn't been Indians. Number one; Indians don't herd cattle; and number two, the hoof prints he'd found were shod.

Matt, who was thirteen, said, 'What are we gonna do, Jake?'

I'll never forget the hard look in Jake's, seventeen-year-old eyes, when he answered. He said, 'Matt, *you're* gonna stay here and watch the house—*I'm* going after our herd.'

Matt's head started shaking, but Jake stopped him, 'Don't you know, if word gets around that the Silver Concho is an easy mark because we're young, it won't be long before every rustler in the country will be cutting himself in for a piece of our herd. It could *ruin* us, Matt!'

'But you're only seventeen!' Matt argued.

Jake shook his head. He was not gonna hear that. He said, 'Like I told that sorry Joe Washington, Matt; my six-shooter and shotgun don't care how old my trigger finger is.'"

"Did Jake really intend to go after the rustlers alone?" Carrie sounded incredulous.

"Yeah, he *intended* to; but, when I spoke up and told him that I thought I'd tag along, he sure didn't turn me down.

My folks already knew that I was planning to help drive the herd to Ft. Worth, so I didn't bother to tell my Pa about the change of plans. I just mounted up and took off behind Jake."

Cooter chuckled as he looked at Carrie over the rim of his glass. "Let me tell you, Mrs. Carrie, Jake wasn't gonna let the grass grow under his feet. He took off after his cattle without even going back to the house for a bedroll. He said the tracks couldn't have been more than a day old, and he aimed to catch 'em before he ever had need of a bedroll.

I looked back at Matt, just before we topped a rise, and that little hardhead wasn't headed toward the house like Jake told him to. Instead, he was high-tailing it for Llano! We were to find out later that he was going after the Sheriff. 'It was a good thing too.

It didn't take an expert tracker to follow that herd of cattle. The tramped up ground just kept pointin' the way. Once in awhile, Jake would get off and look at the hoof prints of the horses that were following the herd. It wasn't long before he knew that there was only three riders we'd be dealing with.

We rode hard all day—just stopping long enough to water our horses and let 'em take a breather. Jake and I sat down under a cottonwood while the horses grazed a few minutes. He sat there saying nothin' for a while. Then, he surprised me when he said, 'Cooter, when I get to Heaven, I'm gonna ask the Lord why He took my father, a man who always did the right thing, and let men like these we're following live. It just doesn't seem fair.'"

"What did you say," Carrie asked softly.

"At first I didn't know *what* to say, but then I realized that Jake was coming onto a crossroads in his faith in God. I was a Christian, and I was his friend. It was up to me to help him not to go off in a wrong direction in his thinking.

I said, 'Jake, the Lord is merciful. He knew your Pa was ready to meet him—these men probably ain't...else, they wouldn't be thievin'.'

He didn't say anything else, but I guess I got through to him, because later when we were back on our horses, he said, 'Cooter, I hope I don't have to shoot those men to get my cattle back.'

It was getting so dark that we could just barely make out the tracks when we heard the cattle bawlin'. Jake pulled up on the reins and looked at me.

He got down and came over close to me. Real soft-like he said, 'They've probably got one man guarding the herd while the other two set up a sleeping camp. We'll locate the 'night-rider' and take care of him, then deal with the others.'

The cows were bedded down in a little grassy place between two groves of trees. There was a shallow creek running down the middle.

Jake and I could see the glow of their campfire across the creek, so we knew where two of 'em were.

We tied our horses out of sight and then hunkered down—so we were shorter than the cow's backs—and went looking for that third man.

Well, he wasn't hard to find. He was a fat little Mex on a paint horse. He had him a guitar and was strumming it real soft, trying to keep the cows from spookin'.

We could tell by the sound of the guitar that the rider on the paint was coming our way. Jake motioned to me, and I hefted myself up onto a low limb that the night-rider would most likely pass under. Jake stepped behind the tree and squatted down.

When the fella got right up under the limb, I dropped down in the saddle behind him and put my arm around his throat. Jake stepped out from behind the tree with his six-shooter pointed at the man. Jake whispered, 'Sigue tocondo esa guitarra,'—which is to say, 'Okay, Pedro, keep playing that guitar.'

I stayed on the horse behind the Mex. He was real nervous. He didn't know if I had a gun or not, and Jake was walking along beside us, holding the horse's bridle.

SANDY JONES

The men at the fire could just barely make out that there was a rider out there in the dark playing a guitar; so they thought everything was all right.

We moved slowly around the herd, pretending the rider was just makin' a normal pass. We worked our way closer to the two at the fire.

When we were about a hundred feet short of where they were; Jake broke away and snuck through the little grove of trees at their back.

I made Pedro pull up on his horse and stay back. Like I said, he didn't know whether or not I had a gun, and I wasn't about to tell him that the stick I had jammed behind his ear wouldn't really shoot him."

Cooter hooted, "He was sure put out later when he found out that I'd held him prisoner with a stick."

He continued, "Just as Pedro's horse stopped, I heard Jake say real loud, 'Don't move a muscle, Joe Washington, and tell your friend he'd better not move one either.'

I don't mind telling you, Mrs. Carrie, I was some more scared. I didn't know but what those crooks might pull their guns and start shootin' at Jake's voice, but, thank the Lord, Jake had been right about Joe Washington when he'd told Matt that the man was a coward. Like all cowards, he wasn't gonna fight until he was sure he had the upper hand.

Joe yelled back at Jake, 'Who are you—and what do you want?'

Jake didn't say nothin' for a few seconds. I guess he was thinking over his answer. Finally, he called out, 'I'm the man you stole these cattle from, and, I've come to take 'em back—simple as that.'

Well, Joe's face looked like somebody had stomped the toe of his boot. But, after a minute, it changed to a smart-alec grin. 'Man?—Did you say man? There ain't no *men* on the Silver Concho. I hope you had better sense than to bring your kid brother with you; 'cause I'd sure hate to kill me *two* boys.'

Jake started to answer, but from somewhere on the other side of the grove, another voice broke in. 'He *didn't* bring his little brother, Joe; but he *did* bring *me*. This is Sheriff Briscoe. Throw down your guns...now!'

I guess Jake was as shocked as Joe and his buddy, 'cause he didn't come out of hiding until he saw the sheriff step into the light of the fire and kick those fella's guns away from them.

I poked Pedro in the back with my *gun-stick,* and shoved him into the light. When Sheriff Briscoe saw what I had in my hand, he nearly fell down laughing.

Jake didn't quite know what to say to the Sheriff. 'How did you know,' he asked.

Briscoe smiled. 'Matt came flying into town. He ran into my office begging me to go with him to help his brother catch some men who'd rustled some of your cattle.' The lawman laughed. 'I nearly had to lock him in the jail to keep him from coming into the middle of this. He didn't cry, but I thought he was going to when I told him he wasn't going into a possible gunfight.'

The sheriff looked at Jake, shaking his head. 'He was *real* concerned about his big brother.'

Well, to make a long story short, the sheriff made those three drive Jake's herd all the rest of the way to Ft. Worth. Jake, me, and the sheriff kept our guns on 'em."

Cooter's grin was devilish. "And this time…Pedro knew that it wasn't no stick in my hand."

* * *

Jake stopped in front of the house and dismounted. Collin had just gotten up from his nap and heard his father's voice calling, "Where's the 'Queen' of this palace and the little 'Prince'?"

The door slammed open, and the little prince flew out and into Jake's arms. Carrie glanced toward the front room and then back at Cooter. "Promise that you'll tell me more, next chance we get. I want to understand why Jake and Matt became enemies for awhile there."

"Jake was *never* Matt's enemy, Mrs. Carrie. Matt just *thought* he was."

CHAPTER FOUR
For the Love of My Brother

Llano, Texas was a typical cattle-country settlement in 1875. It boasted of two general stores, a millinery shop, and dressmaker—for those women who could afford to have someone else do their sewing. There was a blacksmith shop, and livery, one saloon, a hotel and café, sheriff's office, and jail. At the very end of town a church building which housed the Baptists one week and the Methodists the next for the first two Sundays of each month. That building also served as the community center and school.

The Post Office sat at the end of Main Street in the middle of the 'T' where Main ran into 'Doc Stoddard Road'; named for Doctor William Stoddard, Carrie's father. There was also a harness-saddle maker and a small bank in Llano.

The town had built a rodeo arena and stands—mainly for the Fourth of July celebration. But, throughout the year, the arena was a favorite gathering place for cowboys who loved to ply their skills in various contests. Of course, the fact that the young men would be there bronc-riding, roping, bulldogging, and the *favorite*, bull riding, made it a popular place with everyone for miles around.

Besides the businesses and public buildings all along Main Street, two crossroads intersected Main. Houses of various sizes and conditions lined those streets.

THE SILVER CONCHO: LIFE IS A RUB-BOARD

The name, Llano, means 'a high plain' and the town was nestled high in the west-central Texas hill country. Llano became the county seat in 1856. The citizens were proud of that fact.

* * *

Carrie's father migrated to Llano right after the Civil War. His wife suffered with Consumption, so William Stoddard thought the high, dry climate would help her. She appeared to improve for a while; but after four years, she succumbed to the disease.

Marie Stoddard died when Carrie was eighteen. A level-headed girl with a generous, easy-going nature, Carrie became her father's nurse-assistant and took over the housekeeping duties. She was of average height with a slim, yet womanly, figure. Her thick, light, golden-brown hair hung to her waist when it was down. Carrie's beautiful emerald-green eyes were a legacy from her Irish, maternal grandmother.

* * *

Stealing glances at her as their wagon moved down the street toward his father-in-law's house, Jake never tired of looking at his lovely wife. After a little over four years of marriage, Jake still felt awed by the fact that she was really his.

Carrie came into his life at a time when Jake was convinced that his very existence was in vain. Not only had he fallen in love with her on sight, but also her quiet faith and gentle understanding had pointed his way back to the Savior's side.

Thank you Lord, for the beautiful woman beside me. Help me to be worthy of her love, Jake prayed silently.

"Are we almost there," Collin asked, rubbing his fist against his eyes. He lay on a quilt at his mother's feet.

"Almost, but not quite," Carrie said softly. "Close your eyes for a few more minutes and the next time you open them, I think we'll be there." The child turned on his side obediently and went back to sleep.

Scooting closer to her husband on the bench seat, Carrie hooked her arm beneath Jake's, and laced the fingers of both her hands over his bicep.

"How did you get to be so big, and strong, and sure of yourself," Carrie flirted.

Jake looked down at her, feeling a little embarrassed and a little pleased at the same time by her description. "Well, my size is probably a direct result of my ancestry. My father and his father were both big men. As far as being *sure* of myself…I don't think that happened until I met and married you."

He continued, "You convinced me that I *must* be worth something because you were able to fall in love with me. Then, when you told me about God's love which—I'll be honest with you—I'd doubted ever since Big Mama died, I came to understand that He had been there all the time. God watched over and guarded two young boys, bringing us to manhood…despite our differences for a while.

Now that I know Christ as my Savior, I realize what the Apostle Paul meant in Philippians when he said, 'I can do all things through Christ, which strengtheneth me.'"

Jake gave her a quick 'peck' on her brow. "Thank you, Sweetheart." Carrie sighed.

After a few moments of comfortable silence, she spoke again, "Jake, I know that you don't like to talk about it, but what happened to you and Matt to cause such a split between you two?"

Jake did not respond, but stared down the road in front of them over the heads of the horses. Carrie nearly concluded that he could not answer her question. But then he raised his arm and dropped it around her shoulders, pulling her closer to his side.

"It took me a long time after Matt left for West Point to realize what went wrong. I know now that we both made some mistakes."

He took a deep breath. "My mistake was in not realizing that Matt didn't understand why I drove myself and pushed him so hard. Our childhoods and early adult years were endless nightmares of, work-eat-sleep, work-eat-sleep. I never took time to be a kid…and I refused to let him be one either.

I look back now and see that Matt was too young to see my

responsibility—that *I had* to hang on to the Silver Concho—for both of us. He was all I had and I was all he had. I knew it was *all* up to me."

Jake turned tortured eyes on Carrie. "I *had* to do it, Carrie! Otherwise, all my grandfather's, my father's, and Big Mama's work and dreams for us would've died. It would have been because "*I*" had failed."

Carrie leaned against him and spoke, "I can certainly see why you felt such pressure. Not many fourteen-year-olds would be mature enough last." She laid her hand on his cheek. "You are one in a million, Jacob Galloway. I am so proud of you."

Jake grinned down at her. "Thank you, Honey, but the truth is; I don't see myself as someone you would have been proud of during those years between the time Big Mama died and Matt left home. Matt was more *sociable* than I was. I can remember an incident when he was about eleven or twelve years old. One of the boys at school was bragging about the litter of puppies his dog had. The boy told Matt and several others that if they would come home with him after school that day and pick out the one they wanted, he would hold it for them until it was old enough to wean.

Well, I had been middle-busting the corn all day, and I was hot and tired. I needed Matt to come straight home from school to weed the kitchen garden before dark. We depended on it to help us through the winter and spring months; besides, we ate from it in summer and fall.

He and one or two other boys went to see the puppies. I guess they played with them for a while." Jake shook his head slightly, remembering his reaction toward Matt. "When Matt came home about three hours late, I was fit to be tied. I told him I didn't want to hear about any 'fool' dog, and that he need not even *think* about taking one of them. He had too much work to do to waste time on a useless pup."

"Oh Jake, he was just a boy," Carrie said sadly.

Jake looked at her solemnly. "So was I, Carrie."

She flinched at the hurt in his eyes and said quickly, "Sweetheart, I didn't mean you were to blame. I was just sympathizing with Matt's feelings too."

Jake nodded. "As time went on, there were plenty of social events and church meetings that we had to miss because we were too busy surviving and trying to keep the Concho from going down. Matt got to where he didn't even ask to go anymore. He knew my answer would be, 'We've got too much work to do.'

One of the worst years between us was the year Matt turned fifteen. He started really noticing the girls and, believe me, they were *noticing* him too. It made for a lot of temptation for him to go off and leave his work undone so he could attend birthday celebrations and such. We almost came to blows over his being bent on going sometimes."

Carrie looked up at him teasingly. "I can't believe the girls weren't *noticing* you too. You're every bit as handsome as he is—and four years older!"

Jake smiled. "The girls never saw me, and I never saw any girls. 'Except on the few trips we made to town for supplies. That only happened when we'd sold some cattle and had the money *for* supplies. Then I'd see a few girls.

Oh, there were a few times when the neighboring women would come out to the house with baked and canned goods and such. They *always* brought their daughters with them." He chuckled. "I was usually so busy working that I didn't stop long enough to enjoy all the eye-fluttering and giggles they threw at Matt and me."

"I'm thankful for that! If you *had* taken time, I would never have had the chance to meet you. I'm *sure* of that." Carrie remarked dryly.

Jake squeezed her against his side. "I'm ashamed to say, but by that time I'd all but quit going to church. I just didn't see how I could trust God—since He had evidently forgotten about me and Matt. I guess something Big Mama said just before she died is what kept me going.

Things got worse and worse between Matt and me. He resented me as a brother-father. Boys, at sixteen, think they are capable of running their own lives. In all fairness, at the time, he was older than I had been when our grandmother died. I guess he thought if his brother could be a man at fourteen then he could *sure* be one at sixteen.

But, there's something about being the oldest son that make you harder than a younger son; especially in our case." Jake bit his bottom lip as he thought about what he was going to say next.

THE SILVER CONCHO: LIFE IS A RUB-BOARD

"It all finally came to a head one hot, August day. I sent Matt to the south pasture to build a holding pen near the creek. We were bunching cattle, getting ready for a late summer cattle drive to Ft. Worth. Matt was working alone, and it was his third day out there.

About three o'clock, I finished building a pen in the east pasture and decided to ride over to see how Matt was coming along with his. As I topped the little rise before you get to the creek, I saw Matt coming up out of the water. He'd been swimming! Actually, he was just cooling off, but I thought he was wasting time—playing.

I was hot, and aggravated with him. He pulled on his clothes as I rode toward the pen. When I got to him, I called him a 'fool' kid and chewed him out for wasting daylight."

Jake grinned at Carrie sheepishly. "I tell you—I was really surprised by what happened next. Matt had argued with me plenty of times, but he had a pretty cool head and didn't lose his temper very often. But that day he did.

Before I knew what was happening, Matt reached up and grabbed my arm, then yanked me off my horse. I landed hard on my backside and came up sputtering, 'Matt! What's the matter with you?'

He had his fists doubled up and he started swinging at me. I threw up my forearms to block his punches and yelled at him to quit before I had to hurt him." Jake's eyes filled with tears as he remembered his brother's next words.

Matt stopped hitting me, but he still kept his fists up. I'll never forget what he said to me through gritted teeth that day. '*You're* what's wrong with me! I'm not taking anymore off you! This is my ranch too, and if I want to go swimming in the middle of the day, then I dad-gum sure will! And don't try ordering me around anymore 'cause I won't be listening. You're bigger than I am now, but I'll catch up in a couple of years and when I do, I'll stomp a *mud hole* in you!'"

Jake was quiet for a long time. When he looked at her again he admitted, "I think that was the first time that I had ever *really* paid attention to my little brother.

Standing there looking at Matt's angry face, all of a sudden the face of a little six year old boy crying for his mama, and just four and a half months later, his papa, came to my mind. I was young too, just ten, but at least I understood what had happened.

Then, I remembered a quiet little eight year old coming home from school and changing into his work clothes and going straight to work in the garden or whatever else Big Mama had for him to do—no time to play…never.

I also remembered Big Mama encouraging me and bragging on me because she knew I was the oldest. She probably thought it was enough for Matt that she kissed his cheek and called him her 'baby'. But it *wasn't* enough. He needed to feel useful and appreciated too. Matt had grown to despise me more every day without me realizing it. He despised my ram-rodding him all the time. I suddenly knew that, despite my reasons for being the way I was, I had lost the only thing of real value in my life…the love of my brother."

Carrie shook her head. "Jake, surely it wasn't *that* bad. Matt loves you now. I think it was always there, beneath his anger and bitterness."

"You're right, but knowing that now didn't make it any easier for us during the next eight years," Jake replied.

"Until the day I got his letter telling me that he'd received Christ as his Savior, and that he forgave me and was asking for my forgiveness, I never knew a moment's peace concerning my brother.

"After the incident at the holding pen, I tried to 'back track' on our relationship. I relaxed on letting Matt go places. To my surprise, he really didn't run the roads that much. He liked the rodeos the neighboring cowhands put together. Matt was a good rider and won some prize money at the Fourth of July rodeo, when he was eighteen.

I didn't try to give him any more orders either; didn't want to fight with him. It surprised me to find out that he would do most anything I asked him to do, as long as he thought it was his choice.

The Smiths, one of our neighbors over near old Mesquite Grove, had a pretty quarter-horse mare. She had been bred to a black Morgan stallion. When the colt was born it was one of the finest little horses I ever laid my eyes on." Jake looked at his wife. "You saw him, Breeze—Matt's stallion.

Well, before the colt was completely weaned, his mama was running across a mesa and stepped into a prairie dog hole; breaking a leg so badly that there was no help for her. Old Mister Smith had to shoot her. It liked to have killed him to do it—especially since she had a young colt.

He tied the little fella to the back of his wagon and led it slowly into Llano. He was looking for someone who had the time and patience to hand-feed it and bring it along until it was old enough to take care of itself. Anyone could look at that colt and see what a fine stallion he was going to make.

This all happened about two months after Matt's 'blowup' out at the pen. I guess I wanted to make it up to him—try to let him know that I *did* love him. So I bought the colt. Mister Smith tried to give him to me, but I thought the gift would mean more if it cost me something.

I can still remember riding down the hill to the barn with the colt following along behind. Matt was in the barn working on a bridle strap. I stepped inside and asked him to come out for a minute, that I had something I needed help with.

He got up from the bench and followed me. When he saw that black colt, it was like a magnet was drawing him to it. He walked over to it and dropped down on one knee. He ran his hand over its nose and head; then on down its neck, withers and forelegs. You would have thought he was its mama—the way he inspected it.

When he got through going over it, he looked at me and asked, 'What are you gonna do with him?' I just raised my eyebrows and answered, 'The question is…what are *you* gonna do with him? He's yours'.

"What did he say? Did it help his attitude toward you," Carrie wanted to know.

"I don't know how to describe Matt's feelings, but I do know it changed him. He put all the love and need for companionship he felt into that colt. He stayed with the little horse every possible minute he could spare. He hand fed it and curried its coat until it shined like a crow's wing."

Jake chuckled, "One night I woke up and looked over at Matt's bed and saw it was empty, so I went looking for him. I found him in the stall with Breeze; asleep on some hay in the corner.

That winter was a fierce one. It was the year Matt turned seventeen. It got so cold that Matt hung blankets over the walls of Breeze's stall. Then he made a 'tent-top' over it because he couldn't stand the thought of the young stallion being cold while he slept in a warm house."

Eyes twinkling, Jake remembered, "I think he would have brought that horse *inside* the house if he could have. Carrie, I don't know how many times I'd walk into the barn to find Matt standing with his elbows propped on Breeze's stall gate, talking to him like a friend."

Jake grinned again. "And, from the look in Breeze's eyes, you'd think he understood every word Matt was saying."

Carrie smiled in response. "Jake, even an animal understands when it's loved."

Jake cocked his head to the side for a moment. "I never thought of that." He was silent for a while, then continued his story.

"I got real sick in January that winter. I think I must have had pneumonia. Mrs. Marshall, Cooter's mother, sent him over to check on me one day. I was flat on my back in bed, sick as a dog. Cooter hung around and heated the chicken soup his mama had sent with him. He stayed by the bedside while I mostly slept. He waited for Matt to get back before he headed for home.

Matt went out that morning to check on our cattle that always took shelter from the winter winds in Chico Ravine. When it got to be four o'clock, the sun was pretty low in the sky and Matt still wasn't back. I was plenty worried. I knew there were wolves and cougars—not to mention, Comanche—roaming the area where Matt had headed that morning. I also knew Matt wouldn't go off and leave Breeze, who was still too young to break.

So I made up my mind to get out of my sick bed and go after him. Somehow, there was a 'gut-feeling' that he was in trouble. Cooter wouldn't hear of me getting up. He said *he'd* go find Matt.

Cooter rode out alone. He reached the mouth of the ravine just as the sun was giving off its last rays. He said later that he picked up on Matt's horse's tracks near the top of the ravine. Dismounting, Cooter followed the hoof prints until he saw where Matt had also gotten off his horse. Matt's boot prints led up the ridge of the ravine and Cooter said his heart almost stopped when he came upon what appeared to be 'intrals and blood' all over a small boulder. But when he took a closer look, there were the forelegs and shoulders of a large cougar that had been gutted and skinned and was lying near-by.

By that, Cooter knew that Comanches like cougar meat, so one plus one meant that the Indians had skinned that cat, and Matt—who we knew was there at the time—was with the Comanches. We didn't know if he'd gone willingly or if he'd been captured. I thought it was unlikely that he went willingly." Jake dropped his head in thought. "I found out nearly six weeks later that I didn't know my brother like I thought I did.

It took me nearly three weeks to get over my pneumonia. I spent the next two and a half weeks trying to get an idea of where the Comanches were wintering. Sheriff Briscoe warned me not to try to go into their village alone. He said, 'Matt is probably okay if he's with them. He's still a kid and Comanches admire courage in young males—Indian or white, but you're big, and old enough to be considered a man by them. They'd kill you before you ever made it to their village. The best thing you can do is to ride to Fort Concho and see if you can go with the Cavalry the next time they ride into Comanche territory.'

After hearing that, I didn't know what to do. I nearly went crazy trying to decide how to find my brother. I'd just about decided to go it alone and try to sneak into the Comanche territory and locate him.

Then suddenly, over six weeks after Matt had disappeared, in early March, I went out to the barn to feed Breeze. He had really missed Matt—to the point that he'd bare his teeth and back his ears at anyone who tried to handle him. As I neared the barn, I heard a voice coming from inside, before I got to the door. I had my six-shooter with me, so I turned my back to the wall and sidestepped to the edge of the door opening. Slowly, I poked my head around the door and there, in front of Breeze's stall, was Matt. His hair had gotten pretty long and, since he had been shaving for nearly a year, he had a short beard. Other than that, he looked fine.

I tell you, Carrie, I didn't know whether I wanted to hug him or kill him. I walked in and Matt turned to look at me, but didn't say a word. We just stood there looking at each other.

I finally said, 'You had me worried, boy. Where have you been all this time?'

He grinned then and began telling me the doggonedest tale about him happening upon a Comanche boy about his age, who was cornered by a cougar. When Matt shot the cat, the Indian insisted on making him a 'blood brother'. Then he wanted Matt to go with him to the Comanche village, as his honored guest. Running Horse was the boy's name."

Jake looked at Carrie with a smile. "When Matt was here last December, he told me he knew his meeting Running Horse was planned by God. He knew because he'd been wounded in a desert fight with some renegade Indians. He couldn't ride and thought he was going to die. His men were on their way back to the fort to get a wagon to transport him. He was alone. All of a sudden, out of nowhere, Running Horse appeared and saved his life." Jake's eyes became serious. "The Lord works in mysterious ways."

"He certainly does," Carrie agreed softly, "But that story is amazing!"

* * *

Just then, Collin awakened again. He propped himself up on one little elbow and squinted up at his mother. "Are we there yet?" he demanded.

Carrie leaned over to pick her son up and placed him on her lap. She pointed down the road ahead of them. "Whose house is that?"

"Papaw's!" shouted the child.

CHAPTER FIVE
It's All Yours, Brother

Doctor Stoddard thoroughly enjoyed the weekend with his daughter and her husband, but he wasn't fooling anyone. One look at the joy in his eyes when his grandson was near betrayed the *real* source of his pleasure.

"Papaw, come play in the dirt with me. Let's build a new corral...and put horses...and cows...and..."

Carrie interrupted Collin's imaginative plea. "Now Collin, you know that Papaw can't build dirt corrals like you can. Do you want him to feel bad? Why don't you do something that he can do best? Why don't you sit in his lap and let him tell you a story?"

Collin studied his mother's face seriously for several seconds, then turned his eyes on his grandfather. "Do *you* know a story Papaw?" William Stoddard chuckled. "I sure do. I know a story about a little boy and a great big giant!"

Collin's blue eyes widened and he gasped, "Really?"

"Really."

Collin eagerly climbed into Papaw's lap and looked up expectantly into the adoring face.

"Before you start, Dad," Carrie spoke. "Jake and I are going for a walk. It has been a long time since I sat under my favorite tree down by the river. You know what usually happens when Collin stays still for any length of time." She was referring to the fact that the energetic child would fall asleep when he relaxed, even for a few minutes. "So, just do what you usually do. Your bed will be fine. We'll be back in a little while."

Jake took Carrie's hand as they stepped off the porch together. The couple knew Carrie's father was happiest when he had the full attention of his handsome, little grandson.

* * *

The Llano River was lined with massive domes of granite. It was said to be an ancient site of 'human sacrifice' by certain Indians. Other legends said its heights made it a 'rallying point' for meetings among the Indians. Still other Indian tales spoke of 'Ghost fires' flickering off the walls of granite at night.

As a young girl, Carrie discovered a huge cottonwood tree on its bank, near her father's house. She found peace and solitude sitting in its shade and listening to the gurgle of water as it rushed over large slabs of sandstone lining the riverbed. The spot was particularly dear to her because it was the place where Jake asked her to marry him.

"Do you remember what happened here?" She teased, as they settled down beneath the tree.

"No—what," Jake asked, his twinkling eyes betraying his feigned innocence.

Carrie, pretending to be hurt by his lapse of memory, held her hands out, palms up. "Think—It'll come to you."

"Ohhh, that," he chuckled and reached to pull her snuggly against his side. He leaned back against the tree trunk then lifted her chin with his fingertip. Lowering his head slowly, deliberately, he kissed her lips with a sweet longing.

"How could I *ever* forget where an angel said she would be mine? This is the most hallowed place on earth for me," he answered huskily.

Carrie stared at him for a long time, her eyes roaming his face. "Jake, how in the *world* did you turn out to be such a wonderful man? I mean…you had such a rough time growing up. It's a miracle that you're not a hard, bitter man."

"It is a miracle, Carrie. A miracle from God. There was a time when I was exactly what you just described; a hard, bitter man."

Carrie snuggled closer to his side. "I really can't imagine you *ever* being that way. Tell me about it."

* * *

"I was telling you about Matt and Breeze yesterday. Well, I guess the next three years were the ones that *really* hardened me."

He stopped for a moment, thinking. Looking into her eyes, he asked, "Do you have any idea of what it's like to want forgiveness from someone and you don't even know what you've done wrong?" Without waiting for her answer, he went on. "That's where I was for those last three years that Matt was at home.

Breeze was Matt's whole world. He spent so much time with the young stallion that I wasn't sure if he even knew I was around any more. 'Fact is, Matt *ignored* me.

He'd take care of his part of the work, but more often than not, he ate his meals with the ranch hands. By that time, I had hired four cowhands, a foreman and a cook." Jake adjusted his position against the tree and reclaimed Carrie, pulling her back into place against the side of his chest.

By then I was twenty-one, and I'd learned that the market price of the thirty head of cattle I had been paying the men to come help me with the roundups and branding was more than enough to pay their salaries for a year—fulltime. That took a big amount of the workload off Matt and me. Of course, we had to build a bunkhouse and cook's shack; but it was worth it."

His chest rumbled deeply. "Cooter wanted to come help me for nothing but room and board. It took my threatening to whip him to convince the 'hardhead' that he couldn't be my foreman if he was just a volunteer. I told him I would feel like I had to hold back on ordering him to do something if he wasn't being paid for the job.

After I convinced him that he *had* to accept pay, he wanted to take only what I paid the regular cowhands. I finally said, 'Ok, Cooter—if you want to just *work* for the 'Concho', Matt or I will have to act as foreman.' He didn't like it, but he finally gave in and agreed to take higher wages.

All this time, I tried to pull Matt into the running of the ranch. But every time I'd ask his opinion on something, he'd say, 'You've always ran things, Jake. Why are you asking me *now?*"

"Oh Jake—that wasn't fair," Carrie commented.

"Fair or not; that's the way he felt," Jake sighed.

"Matt was nearing eighteen and I could see that he was going to be a fine specimen of manhood. It was amazing to watch him grow and become big and strong. At the same time, Breeze was maturing and muscling out, but Matt was very careful not to put too much weight for long periods of time on his back." Jake's chest rumbled again. "One thing for sure—Matt didn't have to worry about anyone running off with his horse—no one else could ride him.

One day Cooter and Manny were going to clean out the stalls. Cooter had a hackamore in his hand to slip over Breeze's head so he could lead him out to the corral while they worked in the barn. Matt was in town with Hardtack, buying supplies.

When Cooter opened the stall gate with a rope in his hand, Breeze backed his ears and charged him.

I happened to be coming down the hill toward the barn. All of a sudden, I heard Cooter and Manny yell at the same time. They came flying out of the door with Breeze right at their heels. Both men vaulted over the fence into the corral. Breeze pranced around like he was making sure they stayed there."

"What did you do?" Carrie was laughing at the image Jake had painted. "Surely they didn't have to stay there until Matt got back."

"No, they didn't. For some reason, Breeze would 'tolerate' me. I guess it was because I looked and sounded so much like Matt.

I walked real slow like toward him, talking soft and keeping my hands to my sides. I told Cooter and Manny to slip out the other side of the corral, then I backed up to the corral gate—still talking to Breeze. When I got it unlatched, I pushed it open carefully and stepped back.

Breeze is an intelligent animal. He watched the gate swing open, then he looked at me.

After a second he pranced, big as you please, into the corral."

"You're kidding!" Carrie was amazed.

Jake's hand went up. "That's not all. You can believe me or not; but I *know* what I saw.

He not only put himself into the corral, he turned around and pushed the gate shut with his nose. That was his way of letting me know that he was in there *only* because he wanted to be."

"Jake! How many people have you told that 'tall tale' to?" Carrie giggled.

"Not many—I didn't have to. Cooter and Manny told everyone in the country about it," Jake laughed. "When Matt came home and heard about it—that was one of the few times I ever saw him double over laughing."

Jake's eyes lost their merriment. "But back to your question about what happened during those three years...

The older Matt got, the more restless he became. He started going into town on any pretence. He'd hang out at the rodeo arena and come home in the wee hours of the morning—If he came home at all. I never smelled alcohol on him, but I knew it was just a matter of time; considering some of the crowd he was running with.

I tried to warn him—talk to him. He told me to mind my own business.

Then, the summer after he had turned eighteen in January, Matt didn't come home one night. Early the next day, Sheriff Briscoe sent word for me to come to his office. I mounted up and rode into town as fast as I could. I was afraid something had happened to Matt.

When I got to the jail and rushed into Briscoe's office, he could tell by looking at me that I was worried. The first thing he said was, 'He's all right. I've got him locked up.'

Well that stopped me in my tracks. I asked, 'What's he done?'

"Nothing—yet." The sheriff scratched his ear looking at me from beneath his hat. He told me that he'd taken Matt into custody under the pretense that Matt was *'disturbing the peace'*. But he just wanted to separate him from that rowdy bunch he was with.

Biscoe went on to say, "Jake, I've watched you two boys grow up out on that ranch all by yourselves. I admire both of you for your grit. You're from good stock and you've made fine men. But even *'fine'* young men can ruin their lives by getting involved with the wrong crowd." He went on. "Matt is at the age when he thinks he has to *prove* his manhood. I imagine it has something to do with being the *little* brother. Now, I'm not smart enough to tell you exactly what you need to do, but I *can* tell you that Matt needs something in his life that will give him purpose. If he doesn't find it quick, he *will* find something else to do, and it might not be for the best."

Briscoe released Matt into my custody. That galled my brother because he knew he hadn't really done anything to be arrested for in the first place.

I tried to talk to him as we rode back to the ranch together, but he let me know that he was tired of everybody running his life and telling him what to do. He said, 'Jake, I'm thinking real hard about just leaving.'

My heart came up into my throat when he said that. I shook my head. 'Where would you go?'

'I don't know—anywhere to get away from here…and you.' Matt's eyes looked like ice when he said that. I felt like a bull had just stomped my chest. We rode the rest of the way home without a word.

For the next few weeks, I was as jumpy as a cat. Every time I couldn't actually *see* Matt, I worried that he'd made good his threat and run off. I couldn't sleep and my appetite left me. Even though I thought and thought about ways to fix our troubles, nothing came to mind. Then one day, out of the blue, an idea came to me. I know now that it was from the Lord.

I was worrying, as usual, about the future when my father's best friend, James Spiers, came to mind. Pa told me all about him when I was eight or nine years old.

James Spiers was a fine Christian, a man's man, and an excellent officer according to Pa. I knew Colonel Spiers' sweetheart had died very young, before they had had a chance to marry. For that reason, Spiers determined to make a lifetime career of the Cavalry. Dad said James Spiers had such a fine, military mind that he'd been commissioned to be an instructor at West Point Military Academy.

When I remembered all that, the idea came to me that he might be able to help Matt and me. I wrote to him, explaining my concerns and asking if he thought my brother might be accepted into West Point.

That was in September of sixty-nine. By Christmas, I had just about decided that the Colonel hadn't been able to get a commission for Matt, so I started trying to think of something else. Then, about a week before Matt's birthday, I went to the post office on the chance of getting mail. We still had distant relatives in Virginia and, every year or two, they wrote to us.

The second I walked in and saw Mister Carson's face, I knew there was good news. He handed me two envelopes—one was addressed to Matt and the other to me. The stationary bore the West Point insignia, so I knew who they were from. I stuck Matt's letter inside my shirt and backed up to one of the benches in the post office."

Jake took a deep breath. Carrie looked up and saw that he was swallowing hard; this was a very difficult memory for him. After several moments, he began again.

"Colonel Spiers' letter began by telling me how *honored* he was that the sons of Thomas Galloway would seek him out. He praised Pa as one of the finest men and dearest friends he had ever known.

Next, he apologized for the delay in answering my letter. He assured me that it was not for lack of interest in my problem. He explained that he had been busy pulling strings and submitting 'proxy' applications for admission to West Point for Matt. He said he was pleased to tell me that he had been successful and was sending Matt a separate letter, offering him the opportunity to follow in his father's footsteps.

The Colonel also told me that he'd made no mention of my involvement. Considering the problems between Matt and me, he thought that would be best."

Jake cleared his throat. "All the way home I wrestled with whether or not to go ahead and give Matt the letter or just tear it up."

"Why would you want to do that?" Carrie's brows came together in a puzzled expression.

"Because; suddenly it occurred to me that this might fix Matt's problems, but what about me? I might never see my brother again, and despite what he thought, I loved him."

"So what helped you decide to give it to him?"

"I had to admit to myself, that no matter what it was going to cost me, he was worth the sacrifice. After he'd been gone a while though, I began to regret that decision.

When I got home, I found Matt, where else, with Breeze. I walked into the barn and handed him his letter. He looked at it and at the insignia. Then he looked up at me with a question in his eyes. I didn't say anything, but turned and headed up the hill to the house.

About halfway up the hill, I heard him give a *Texas yell* and I knew what was coming next.

Sure enough; in a few minutes, Matt came in all excited. He waved the letter at me and told me who it was from and what the offer was. I didn't let him know that I already knew. I just said that I was happy for him and that he would do well in the Cavalry. After all, he was Thomas Galloway's son."

* * *

"Two days later, January of 1870, Matt packed his saddlebags, loaded his rifle and handgun, then grabbed a bedroll and enough cash to get him to West Point.

I stood on the front porch and watched him mount Breeze, who was three years old and a lotta stallion by then. Matt looked at me and I'll never forget the pain his words gave me. He said, 'Well Jake, I'm gone…and I won't be back.'

He tipped his hat to me and added, 'You can have it all—It's all yours brother.' I watched him ride away. I remember whispering, 'All mine?'"

CHAPTER SIX
A Helpless Heart

The Jake Galloways walked up the trail that led from the bank of the Llano River to Carrie's father's home. Neither spoke; each thinking their own thoughts.

Just before they reached the yard fence gate, Carrie stopped and turned to her husband.

"Jake, it still bothers you to think about the problems you and Matt had for a while, doesn't it?" Before he could reply, she continued, "Surely you know that God worked it all out. He had a plan all the time, but you were both too young to understand."

Jake gazed down at her for a moment. Reaching out, he took her in his arms and pulled her tightly against himself. Resting his chin on the top of her head, he answered, "Honey, I know beyond the shadow of a doubt that God brought about a miracle for Matt and me. I have my brother's love and his friendship again. It could *only* have been the work of God. It was such a…a '*sinkhole*'. There was no humanly way out of it. But…"

"But what," Carrie encouraged.

"Sometimes I look back over those years when we were growing up, trying to survive, trying to keep our land, trying to stay together, and I wonder…what did I do wrong? How could the loss of those years that Matt hated me have been prevented?" He shook his head in dismay. "It just bothers me to think that I made Matt so bitter and unhappy when he was a boy."

"Jake, you listen to me...and listen well," Carrie said gently, but firmly. "You did absolutely *nothing* wrong! Was it wrong to obey your grandmother and work your fingers to the bone so that she could die in peace, knowing you were capable, at fourteen, to take care of yourself and Matt? Was it wrong to sacrifice yourself so he could have food, clothing and shelter? In addition, was it wrong to care enough for Matt to lay aside your own feelings to do everything you could to make him happy? Was it wrong, to expect him to help, according to his abilities, in order to teach him to contribute also?

Jake, from what I saw last fall, when Matt and Dimple were here, he is a strong, healthy, well-adjusted, intelligent and capable young man. Who do you think he can thank for those qualities? It can't be his parents, or even Big Mama—he was too young when he lost them.

No Jake; he can praise the Lord that he had a strong, courageous, single-minded brother. You did nothing wrong. You and Matt were victims of circumstances beyond *your* control. You did what you *had* to do and Matt didn't understand...at the time. Now God has rewarded your hard work and love with everything that is good in life."

She came up on her tiptoes and kissed his cheek. "And I never, never, never, never, *never* want to hear you berating yourself over things that are *God's* business! We're all sinners, Jake, but your sin was *not* one of laziness or lack of courage and love for Matt!"

"Wow Lady! Did you ever consider becoming a lawyer," Jake asked with admiration.

"Don't you make light of what I said, Jake. I meant every word."

Jake bent his knees, scooped her up in his arms and whirled her around. "I'm not making light of you, sweetheart—I was just praising God that you always hit the nail on the head."

Early Monday morning, Carrie rousted her *men* out of bed and after a big, hardy breakfast, they loaded the wagon to head back to their ranch.

The adults laughed when Collin declared that he thought he'd take his candy jar home with him.

"But Collin, that jar is also for other children who come to see your grandfather when they don't feel well. Don't you want him to have some candy for them too," Carrie reasoned, casting her eyes at her father.

William Stoddard brushed his hand across his mouth in an attempt to hide his smile. But, *nothing* could squelch the twinkle in his eyes.

Collin became quiet, his little head cocked to one side. After a moment, his blue eyes widened and he looked at William, "Couldn't you get a 'nudder' jar for them?"

This kid is smart'; fast thinking was called for. "But if you take your jar home with you...how will I keep it filled? You live too far," William explained.

Collin's expression became thoughtful again. "Well...ok, I'll leave it here, 'cause I know you always have candy for me."

William was sitting in a chair on the front porch. He spread his arms and Collin stepped eagerly into his embrace. "When you get home, ask Mama for your surprise," he whispered in the child's ear, and kissed the downy-soft cheek.

Earlier that morning, the doting grandparent had filled a small brown bag with Collin's favorite candy treats. "You're in control of this. I know better than to give him the whole bag at once. Too much candy is not good for him. But, every once in a while, give him a stick of it and remind him that Papa loves him," he said to Carrie.

Dad—you spoil him rotten!" Carrie kissed her father's cheek. "...I'm so glad you do. A child can't have too much love."

* * *

The instant Jake arrived on Silver Concho land; he saw that Cooter was already busy. Roundup started the next week, and many preparations were being made. Wood had to be gathered, hauled and stacked near the holding pens. Branding irons, ropes, and leather strips, used to secure the legs of the animals, were stacked on the back of wagons to be kept near the work sites.

Every cowhand had his own ropes and 'pigging' strips as standard equipment; but extras were needed at times. Jake also noted that small bunches of cattle had been herded to the general vicinity of the holding pens. This hastened the work, as it took time to locate the cattle and drive them to the pens.

When the branding of new calves was completed, cowhands would separate the herd into age groups and drive them to designated areas. They would graze there until late July when another roundup would be held. At that time, Jake would have his men to cut out a large herd of about twenty-two hundred head of cattle, ready for market, and drive them to the Ft. Worth stockyards.

On nearly every cattle drive, neighbors who had fewer cattle would add fifty to a hundred head to Jake's herd. In those instances, the neighbor provided a rider, or riders, for his own cattle. Jake was glad to have them along, but was not responsible for losses incurred because of stampedes, Indians, rustlers or other hazards of the trail.

The Silver Concho herd was kept to a maximum of four thousand head at any given time. Most of the twenty—thousand acres was good grazing land, but Jake did not want to risk overgrazing. He sold off just the right number of cattle every year to maintain a balance.

The ranch was home to ten cowhands, Cooter (the foreman) and Hardtack (the cook). They knew they had a job for as long as they wanted one, under two conditions—they did their job, and they maintained their morals (at least, while they were on 'Concho' land).

Jake was good to his men and took care of their needs whenever they were sick or hurt. He allowed no fighting or alcohol on the ranch. If a cowhand went into town on Saturday night and got drunk, that man knew he had better *not* come back to the bunkhouse in that condition.

Profanity or vulgar language was not allowed; especially, if Carrie or Collin were within earshot. More than half the men who worked for Jake now had grown up with the Galloway brothers and held them in high esteem. They were excited over the prospect of Matt's returning soon to help run the ranch.

THE SILVER CONCHO: LIFE IS A RUB-BOARD

* * *

Jake delivered his family to the ranch house, then drove the wagon down the hill to the barn. As soon as he had stowed it, he saddled Guapo (Spanish for handsome), his mustang paint stallion, and led it up the hill to the house. He called from the front yard, "Carrie! Will you come to the front door for a minute, Honey?"

Carrie dried her hands on her apron as she walked through the house. "I'm coming, Jake," she answered. She stepped out the door onto the porch and smiled prettily.

"It's only ten o'clock. I think I'll go find Cooter and the boys, to see what'all they've done so far." He grinned apologetically. "Don't worry about dinner for me—I'll eat off the chuck wagon."

"Are you going to stay out on the range *all* day," she asked. Carrie was used to Jake being gone from sunup to sundown during roundup and preparation for branding.

"No, you can look for me before dark." Dropping the reins, he stepped up on the porch and placed his big, work-roughened hands on either side of her lovely face. He kissed her deeply.

"Think about me while I gone," he whispered huskily against her lips.

Carrie's eyes fluttered open and she gave him a smoldering look. "Constantly."

* * *

It was almost four o'clock. Jake had completed his rounds to the various worksites. The day was warm for that time of the spring. He glanced toward the north and watched clouds on the far horizon moving toward him. A frown creased his brow. "Sure hope it doesn't set in to raining—you can't brand cattle in a thunderstorm," he muttered.

After turning Guapo toward home, Jake's mind went back to the days before Matt left for West Point. Matt had been a 'top hand' with cattle. He squinted his eyes in remembrance of how his brother liked to compete with other cowhands for the fastest time in roping and throwing steers. Matt's muscular arms and back would gleam with sweat, but he never tired of competition. Jake understood now that it was Matt's way of proving he was as *tough* as his big brother.

We had a few good times. It wasn't all bad, Jake thought. His mind moved to the time when he, Matt and Cooter had gone 'Grizzly' hunting.

* * *

A fellow who called himself a 'mountain man' came into the area from up north in the Colorado Rockies. The man came across Concho land looking for the son of his brother. The boy was supposed to be in the Llano area. The mountaineer wasn't too good with cattle, but he sure could spin a yarn.

Jake and Matt went down to the bunkhouse at night just to listen to 'Mountain Jack' talk. The stories he told about his encounters with the great, silver-humped Grizzly bear so intrigued Jake, Matt and Cooter that they decided to go after one.

"One of the biggest mistakes I ever made—nearly got us all killed," he mumbled.

Jake still broke out in a sweat when he recalled his 'run-in' with the half-ton bear. No one bothered to tell them that they didn't have to track a Grizzly. Once you were in his territory, he would find you.

The third morning after they arrived in the Colorado Rockies, they were moving across a meadow where a cold stream ran down off the mountains. All of a sudden, Jake heard Cooter say under his breath, "Would you look at that…"

Cooter pointed toward the lower mountain slope, beyond the stream. Loping down the hillside toward the stream was the biggest animal, except for a full-grown, fleshed-out, Longhorn bull, Jake had ever seen.

The bear saw them just about the same time they spotted him. The huge beast stopped and stood up on its hind legs to take a good look at them. Falling forward, shaking the big silver hump on its back, it roared as it continued on down the hill. The bear was moving so fast that, when it crossed the stream, it appeared to 'part the water', throwing sprays of water high into the air.

Cooter dropped off his horse, grabbing his rifle, and shouting, "Ok, boys—this is what we came for!—make 'em count!"

Matt also jumped to the ground, rifle in hand, and veered to Jake's right. Cooter had moved to the left, leaving Jake in the center. The bear watched them and stood up again.

Jake shouldered his rifle and fired twice; hitting the critter both times, dead-center in its chest—where he *thought* the heart would be. The bear roared again, dropped down on its all-fours, and charged Jake!

Matt and Cooter were firing also, but the bear kept coming! "Shoot 'im in the ear and in the eye every time you can; but shoot'im," Cooter yelled.

When the bear was no more than twenty feet away Jake remembered praying, "Oh Lord, help us!" With no time to aim, he shot the creature in the eye. With multiple wounds, it still took half a dozen steps before it dropped dead—literally, at Jake's feet.

Jake sank to the ground and put his head between his knees. After a full thirty seconds of silence and hard breathing, Cooter said, "You ok, Jake?"

Jake nodded and, in a croaking voice said, "I think I'm about to cry." Cooter and Matt laughed shakily.

Matt asked, "Do you think you'll ever do this again, Jake?" Jake lifted his head and looked at his brother. "Nope—I've had *both* my grizzly hunts…my first *and* my last."

* * *

1875

Good memories… Jake approached the stone bridge and, crossing Comanche Creek, gazed at the pretty spot where Matt would probably build a house. He dismounted and led Guapo up the little knoll. At the summit, he dropped his horse's reins, knowing it would graze near by.

A large Pin Oak tree dominated the little hill. Jake leaned against it and looked at the scene before him. The view from this spot was one of the prettiest on the whole of the 'Concho' ranch. To the south, one could see the meandering path of Comanche Creek with small groves of Cottonwoods, Pin Oaks, Scrub Cedar, and Mesquite trees lining its banks and dotting the rolling hills of that part of Texas.

Turning toward the north, he saw in the far distant northwest, the blue-shadowed outline of the foothills of the Davis Mountains. Jake knew that the further you traveled to the west-northwest, the more desert-like the terrain became. Sandstone bottomed rivers and deep rugged ravines and arroyos filled that land. Grass became sparse, eventually giving way to the sandy, cactus-strewn badlands of extreme west Texas and southern New Mexico.

It had been nearly thirty years since Mexico relinquished all claims to those lands that were now Texas, New Mexico, and part of Oklahoma and Colorado territory. Except for occasional trouble spots with the Indians, Texas was a peaceful place to live and raise a family in 1875.

Jake dropped to the ground with the tree at his back. He drew his knees up, resting his forearms across them, with his hands dangling between. Sitting there in the quiet of the afternoon, Jake began thanking God for all the blessings of life: his beautiful wife and the little son he treasured so much, *and* the restored love and friendship of his younger brother. Also, for Dimple, Matt's sweet little wife. She had been *so* instrumental in their reconciliation

How patient and merciful the Lord was! Jake's heart had been filled with bitterness and rebellion after Matt rode away, yet God sent people into his life to draw him to Himself. Where would he be now, if it had not been for a friend like Wade 'Cooter' Marshall? Or…where would he be if it were not for the love of his precious, Christian wife?

His mind drifted once again to that morning of January 1870.

* * *

Jake stood on the veranda, watching the shrinking images of Matt and Breeze slowly disappearing into the distant horizon. His heart felt as if a 'fist' were squeezing it. The further away Matt rode, the harder the fist squeezed. He had been certain that it would burst and stop at any second.

For days, weeks, and on into months, Jake moved like a man in a bad dream. He made decisions regarding the ranch mechanically, without emotion or real concern. Cooter told him later that he watched Jake go through the *motions* of living without caring.

Cooter also said that he and Manny were observing Jake one day about three months after Matt left when Manny commented, "He can't go on like this."

Cooter said he had decided then and there that, as Jake's best friend, he *had* to do something to help him. The first thing he did was to bathe Jake in prayer. *I know You know how much he's hurtin', Lord. You know what it will take to help Jake snap out of this. I'm askin', Lord, that You draw Jake to Yourself, please Father. That's the real answer for him. If he could just learn to turn it all over to You...well, he could trust in Your love for him. Then he would claim Romans 8:28 and learn to live by faith. Help me to show him by example that none of us are ever out of Your sight or mind. I ask all this in Jesus' name.*

Within a few days after Cooter began to pray for Jake in that manner, Jake's attitude began to change. At first, Cooter was baffled. The 'change' was not what he had expected. Instead of relaxing and settling down to enjoy all the successes that were his, Cooter could see that Jake was becoming more and more hard-nosed and determined.

Jake hit the floor before daylight, barking orders, and pushing himself and his men to work longer harder hours. He was irritable and moody, and the men avoided him when possible. He created deadlines that were not necessary, simply because it gave him something other than Matt to focus on. The feeling of failure and emptiness seemed to fade during the times when he was working hardest.

This went on all through spring. Cooter moved out of the bunk house and into the ranch house. "I think we'd have more time at night to talk and plan, owner to foreman, if I was in the house with you," Cooter suggested. Jake knew what his friend was up to, but said nothing.

Even now, five years later, Jake smiled and whispered, "Thank you, Lord, for a friend that was wise and caring of my needs back then."

CHAPTER SEVEN
My Brother's Love

Jake got up and walked to the edge of the clear, fast running creek. He squatted down to scoop up a handful of the cool, refreshing water and brought it to his lips. Then, stepping over to a large slab of sandstone that hung out over the water, he sat down again. His thoughts returned to the year his brother left to join the Cavalry.

* * *

1870
June of 1870 found the Silver Concho cattle branded and enjoying a time of lazy grazing. Later, August would see half the herd trailing toward the market.

Jake remembered that was the first year he had contracted with some of the farms of south central Texas to buy a portion of their feed crops for his horses and milk cows. He had also enlarged the kitchen garden, added a bigger hog pen and built a new chicken house.

Except for a few food items, medicine and clothing, the 'Concho' produced all it needed right on the ranch itself. Jake blew out a long breath. With all that, he had not been a happy, satisfied man.

His mind sprang back to the present when he heard Cooter approaching.

THE SILVER CONCHO: LIFE IS A RUB-BOARD

* * *

Cooter was hot, tired and hungry—it had been a long day. Tomorrow promised to be even longer. Yet, there was something very satisfying about working for Jake Galloway on this ranch, a sense of accomplishment against big odds.

Mounting his horse, Cooter reined it toward his house. Three years ago, when Jake married the beautiful Carrie Stoddard, Cooter had moved out of the ranch house. Young married couples deserved privacy.

Riding through a small stand of Pin Oaks, Cooter lifted his eyes to the bridge over Comanche Creek. There was his friend, Jake, sitting on a slab of sandstone at the edge of the water. "Wha...what's he doing?" Cooter muttered and lifted his hand in acknowledgment to Jake's wave.

Jake watched his foreman approach with a relaxed grin on his face. Cooter did not bother with the bridge but rode his horse out into the shallow stream. He allowed the horse to stop midstream to drink. "I thought you'd be long-since at the house by now," he commented.

"What ya studyin' about?"

Jake looked intently at the man who had been as close to him as a brother, including Matt.

"Not much—a lot of things," he said softly. "I guess the fact that Matt is coming home for good has me thinking about the past...and hoping for the future." Cooter didn't reply, but pulled up on the reins and nudged his mount up the sandy bank.

He climbed down off his horse and dropped its reins. Ambling over to where Jake sat, Cooter lowered himself down on the big rock. He looked at Jake, a far-a-way look in his eyes. "You know, it's really something how the Lord brought all this about...really something."

"What *something* are you talking about?" Jake's voice held a note of amusement.

"Well...I mean...everything. You and Matt managing to hold onto the Concho, Matt's coming to the point that he thought you were his enemy, him ridin' off to join the Cavalry, you almost hating yourself over it." His eyes began to twinkle, "Then along comes Miss Carrie, and the whole world changed colors." He grinned at Jake, "Didn't it?"

Jake's chuckled deep in his chest, "It sure did. Even though I first thought she'd never have anything to do with me."

Cooter's tone became serious, "Yeah...You sure are one lucky—change that—one *'blessed'* fellow...I remember the day you first laid eyes on her."

* * *

August, 1870

"It was coming up on August round up. We came in one evening from bunching the herd all day when Hardtack met us at the barn complaining about the condition of his cook-wagon. He said it had a broken wheel rim. He demanded that you get it fixed or replaced before we took off for Ft. Worth.

I remember you nearly took his head off. You said, 'Well...what are you telling me for? You know where the blacksmith is—take it to Llano and get it done!'"

Cooter scratched the side of his jaw and raised amused eyes to his friend. "That spunky little, Yankee jumped right back at you. 'That's not my job! I'm ye're cook! I don't have 'nuff time to be a'fedd'n all you gluttoned boys. I shore can't be runnin the roads, hauling wheels to the smith's. If you want me along on the trail ride, ya better be having that wheel fixed so's I won't be deef from rattlin' cook pots at the end of the first day's ride!'

"Your neck and ears turned beet red, but I guess your respect for the old man curbed your temper 'cause you said 'Alright Hardtack, tomorrow's Saturday. Cooter and I will take the wheel into Llano ourselves.'" Jake smiled, remembering...

* * *

Early the next morning, they loaded the broken wheel onto the bed of the supply wagon and drove northeast toward Llano. Cooter glanced out of the corner of his eye at the somber face of his friend as they bounced along the sometimes deep-rutted road. Jake sure was an unhappy man those days, and there wasn't anything anyone could do for him—but keep praying.

"Gonna be a hot one," Cooter commented, looking for something to talk about—anything to break the silence.

"Yeah…It's that time of the year," Jake replied. He said nothing more.

* * *

It was nearing noon when Jake and Cooter reached the outskirts of town. Like most small, western towns in 1870, Saturday was a busy day. The businesses were generally crowded with patrons, and the main street bustled with folks. Cooter and Jake drove along, heading for Abe Mills blacksmith shop. Jake was seemingly oblivious to the excitement of Saturday morning in town. He stared straight ahead, speaking only when Cooter spoke to him.

A group of young women clustered in front of the general store. One of them happened to glance up as Jake's wagon was about to pass by. Cooter watched as their heads went together and she spoke to the others. Suddenly, he and Jake had the full attention of five smiling females.

"Kind of makes you feel like the last piece of chicken on the platter, don't it?" he said to Jake out of the corner of his mouth while grinning back at the girls.

"What?" Jake turned his head to look at his friend. Cooter jerked his head toward the front of the store. Jake glanced at the girls on the boardwalk. "Humph, maybe you do. I feel like I'm probably the 'neck' that nobody wanted in the first place."

He really don't know that he's a good-looking fella, Cooter thought in amazement.

* * *

Carrie Stoddard had risen early that morning, and after finishing the breakfast dishes, she swept the floors, dusted the furniture, and made her bed. She hurried to her room and dressed in a yellow gingham, short-sleeved dress. Sweeping her light, golden-brown hair back to the nap of her neck, she tied a matching yellow ribbon around it. The heavy, shining mass of swirling curls hung down her back to her waist.

"Carrie! Are you ready girl," her father, Llano's only doctor, called as he pulled their carriage up to the front gate.

"I'm coming, Dad! Let me grab my shopping basket, my book, and my bonnet," she called over her shoulder. Running back to the kitchen table, she scooped up the handled basket and tossed in the book she had promised to lend to her friend, Caroline Hartman. She snagged her bonnet from the hall table as she darted out the front door.

William Stoddard was standing by the carriage as Carrie ran down the steps. "You don't need to break your neck, honey—I'm just going to check on old Mrs. West's *dropsy* condition. I'm also going to Sr. Hernandez' house to warn him, *again*, to watch what he eats, or he'll suffer with his gout. Both these old people refuse to listen to me about eating so much salt pork. But I have to try."

Then Carrie accepted her father's hand and he helped her into the carriage. She laughed, "I know, Dad, but it's pretty hard for an eighty-three year old woman to believe that pork is bad for her when she's been eating it all her life."

Half an hour later, the doctor stopped in front of the General Store. Carrie stepped out of the surrey and turned back to face her father. "I have a little shopping to do, and then I'm going to walk over to Caroline's house. When you're ready to go home, you can pick me up there."

The doctor nodded. "Have a good time at Caroline's. I should be there around two-thirty or three o'clock." He gave the reins a snap and moved on down the street.

As she turned to enter the store, Carrie heard her name called. Turning around, she saw three of her friends from church coming toward her on the boardwalk. The girls smiled and exchanged greetings. Carrie noticed their flushed faces and the glow of excitement in their eyes.

"Did I miss a parade," she teased.

Tiny, dark headed Emily Darst shook her head and giggled, "You missed something better."

Francis Caldwell added, "You just missed seeing the most handsome man in these parts—Jake Galloway. He and Wade Marshall drove by here a few minutes ago."

Placing the back of her hand against her forehead, she pretended to swoon. "Ohhh—I thought I was going to faint!"

Carrie drew a blank. "*Who*…is Jake Galloway?"

"Who is Jake Galloway!" the three girls shouted in unison. Immediately, they covered their mouths and blushed furiously, as several passers-by gaped at their outburst. Emily stepped closer to Carrie and said in stage-whisper, "Carrie, do you remember that '*gorgeous*' boy that use to ride in the Saturday rodeos? He won the bronc-riding prize last Fourth of July. His name was Matt Galloway."

Carrie nodded hesitantly, "Y-es…I remember he was very handsome—but I understood he left Texas, heading for West Point Military Academy."

"He did," Florence White broke in, "but, believe it or not, there's another Galloway brother who is just as unbelievably handsome. He's older, and also 'single'…Jake."

"He hardly ever comes to town. That's probably why you've not met him," Emily gushed.

Francis spoke again. "The Galloway brothers own a pretty big spread about eleven miles west of town—The Silver Concho. Their grandfather had one of the original land grants from Mexico. The boys' parents died when they were real young, leaving them and the grandmother. I don't know the whole story, but somehow Matt and Jake were left completely alone when Jake was only fourteen and Matt was ten." She shrugged, "It's amazing that they managed to survive and hang on to the ranch."

She added knowingly, "Despite the fact that he's *breath-takingly* handsome, I heard that Jake is hard as nails and mean as a rattler—that's the reason Matt left home."

Carrie didn't like to judge anyone on hearsay—good or bad. "Maybe he had to be tough '*and*' mean; in order to survive at fourteen."

Emily, the romantic, crooned, "Well, sweetheart...I'd have to catch him in the *very act* of drowning kittens before I'd want to believe anything bad about him. He's just *toooo* good looking!"

Carrie chuckled. "I've never seen a man I would give that much leeway—just because of his looks." She turned to go inside the store.

"Well keep your eyes open. You just might see one today," Emily called before Carrie disappeared through the doorway.

A few minutes later, Carrie left the store, heading for the Hartman home. The hot sun was beaming down, so she reached up with one hand and untied her bonnet ribbons. She tugged it off her head in order to use the brim to fan herself as she walked in the shade of trees lining Main Street.

* * *

Jake and Cooter stood in the big, double-door opening watching Abe work. The blacksmith's brawny arms and shoulders bore witness to twenty years of blacksmithing.

"Do you think you can finish with that wheel today," Jake asked, "Hardtack's foaming at the mouth to start outfittin' the chuck wagon as soon as possible. He's only got ten days to get ready for the trail ride."

Abe wiped his sweaty brow with a forearm. "I'll do my best, Jake, but it'll take a little while. I have to take the rim off the wheel and fire it before I can fix the break. Then it has to be re-rounded before it can be clamped back on." He looked at Jake. "If you have something else you need to do in town today, you'll have plenty of time."

Jake thought for a second, then turned to Cooter, "You hungry?"

Cooter grinned. "Is a pig's eye pork?"

Jake looked down the street toward the hotel café. "I've heard the food is pretty..." He stopped mid-sentence, his eyes fixed on someone across the street.

Cooter saw Jake's mouth gape open and stay that way. Turning his head, then his whole body, he watched a very pretty young women walking on the opposite side of Main Street.

The girl wore a pale yellow and white, gingham dress. Her long, golden-brown hair hung to the middle of her back in curls. She held a bonnet made of the same material as her dress loosely in her hand, and a small shopping basket swung from the other.

Jake felt like he'd just been pole-axed, totally unaware that he was gawking at the girl.

Suddenly, Carrie had the uncomfortable sensation of being watched. She glanced around, looking to see whether the feeling was justified. Her emerald-green eyes collided with a pair of incredibly blue ones. The young man was staring rudely.

She looked away quickly, but not before she saw that this *had* to be the man all her friends were swooning over. He was tall and dark-headed like his brother, and extremely handsome…and he had no manners!

Walking faster, mainly to escape his unabashed interest, she felt her heart thumping wildly—why…she could not imagine. She was not afraid of the man, even if Francis *had* described him as being mean as a rattler.

In the brief moment when their eyes met, Carrie had not detected anything that would frighten her. He was just rude!

* * *

"That's Carrie Stoddard, the doctor's daughter," Cooter whispered.

Cooter's voice yanked Jake back to reality. "What? You *know* her?" He trained his sight anxiously on his friend. Cooter shrugged. "I know who she is."

"How—Where did you meet her," Jake prodded.

"Sometimes I'd see her at the Saturday rodeos, back when I sometimes came in to watch Matt ride. But, more recently, I've seen her in church."

Jake turned back to watch the girl again. He nodded absently at Cooter's words. Cooter and Abe exchanged covert grins. It was plain to see what Jake was thinking.

After a few more moments of staring at Carrie's back, he turned to Cooter, "Come on—let's go get something to eat." He moved down the street toward the restaurant.

Cooter fell in beside him as Jake glanced over his shoulder at Carrie once again.

"Cooter, I must be dreaming." He was silent a moment. "Church, huh?"

Cooter followed Jake into the hotel restaurant without saying a word, but in his mind he was thinking, *could this be the Lord's way of drawing Jake to himself? No matter what the reason—Jake needs to get back to worship. It's the only way he's ever going to find the way to making peace with himself, with Matt…and more importantly, with God.*

As they were being seated at a table near the window, Jake noticed the smug express on Cooter's face. "What are you grinning at?"

Cooter quickly schooled his features to reveal nothing. "I was just thinking. That Stoddard girl is mighty pretty, ain't she? It's enough to make a fella want to go to church every Sunday."

Jake's gaze narrowed. He reached up to rub his upper lip. He wasn't sure, but it seemed to him that Cooter was happy that he might be going to church tomorrow. "I guess it is," he muttered.

The waitress arrived to take their orders. She smiled invitingly at both men. "What'll you two have today?"

Grinning at her, Cooter answered, "Bring me the house special for the day…and a lot of it!" She turned her eyes on Jake. He nodded. "I'll have the same."

Cooter attempted to discuss the upcoming cattle drive while they waited for their food to arrive, but he could tell Jake's mind was somewhere else.

Running through Jake's mind was the picture of Carrie Stoddard moving gracefully down the street. He relived the heart-stopping instant their eyes had locked. Was it really possible that she would allow him to talk to her.and get to know her and eventually?

* * *

Pushing his plate aside, Jake placed his hand on his full stomach and commented, "That was good! Now, I guess we need to go see if Abe has the wheel finished or if we'll have to come back to town on Monday."

He shook his head. "I hate to do that; time is wasting. Hardtack wants to get right on loading the chuck wagon."

After paying for the meals, Jake and Cooter stepped outside the restaurant and were about to cross Main Street when they spied Doc Stoddard's surrey moving in their direction. Jake stopped, watching it approach.

Carrie Stoddard sat beside her father in the surrey. They were talking about one of his patients when the vehicle came abreast of where Jake and Cooter stood. Carrie's attention shifted to the two men…Jake in particular.

For the second time that day, Jake was gawking. To his utter surprise, she smiled sweetly and nodded politely at him.

* * *

When Carrie arrived at Caroline Hartman's home earlier that day, her friend could not help but notice the high color in her cheeks.

"Are you upset about something, or is it that it's hot outside today," Caroline asked. "Your face is flushed."

"It's probably a little of both," Carrie answered as she joined her friend on the settee. "It *is* hot, but I'm trying to decide whether I should be pleased or annoyed."

"About what?"

Carrie smiled sheepishly. "Do you know or know *of* a young man by the name of Jacob Galloway?"

Caroline's eyes widened with delight. "You actually *met* Jake Galloway?"

Shaking her head, Carrie replied. "I didn't actually *meet* him; let's just say I 'encountered' him. He stared rudely at me as I passed the blacksmith shop on my way here."

"How do you know it was him," Caroline wanted to know.

"It had to be him. No one else in town today fits the description given to me by Emily, Marie and some of the other girls I ran into in front of the store this morning," Carrie reasoned.

"Well, I don't know what they told you; but, if they said he is tall, dark haired, blue-eyed and absolutely 'delicious'…they got it right," Caroline said, bouncing up and down on the seat.

"It's been about three years since I saw him last. Mama used to drive out to the Galloway brothers' ranch—You know there are *two* brothers, don't you," she injected. "Jake is the oldest. Matt is the other brother. Both of them are something to behold!

"Anyway, Mama and some of the other ladies around here used to take turns carrying baked and canned goods out to them. First their parents, then their grandmother died leaving them by themselves when they were fairly young.

Most of the time, when it was Mama's turn, she took me with her." She giggled, "I think she hoped I would catch the eye of one of them. It didn't matter which one."

Caroline added dramatically, "But, alas…it didn't happen. I was too old for Matt, and Jake was always too busy to notice me. At least, I'd like to *think* that that was the reason he never looked twice." She sighed. "So what is the problem if he did stare at you? I'd *love* to have Jacob Galloway gawk at me."

"The problem is that one or two of the girls said Jake has a reputation for being *quote*, 'mean as a rattler'. They said he actually ran Matt off the ranch by being so hard-nosed. I don't care *how* handsome he is, I don't want to get involved to any degree with a mean spirited man."

Caroline placed her hand on Carrie's. "Oh, I wouldn't believe that without talking to someone who knows Jake well. Sheriff Briscoe has known him a long time. He could tell you anything you want to know about the Galloway boys."

Carrie nodded absently. "Well, I probably won't ever see him again, but if I get a chance, I *will* ask the Sheriff what he thinks of Mister Jacob Galloway."

* * *

"At least she didn't stick her tongue out at you," Cooter teased after observing the small nod of Carrie's head toward Jake.

"Yeah…well, that's *something*," Jake muttered from the corner of his mouth.

They returned to Abe Mills' shop to find that he could not complete the repairs on the wheel until much later that afternoon. Jake placed a loose fist on his hip and looked away, trying to decide whether to wait all day or come back on Monday for it.

Cooter glanced at Abe before he spoke, "Jake, we were talking about coming back into town to church tomorrow. Why don't we have Abe leave it in front of the shop and we can pick it up on our way out of town?"

Jake looked at Abe, his brows raised in question.

"Sure! I'll leave it against the wall by the front door," the blacksmith answered with a smile.

CHAPTER EIGHT
The Competition

August 1870—Eight months after Matt left for West Point

Cooter grinned, but did not let Jake see his expression as he entered the kitchen. Jake sat at the table with a cup of Hardtack's strong coffee and a plate of pancakes in front of him. That sight in itself was nothing new, but, the way his friend was dressed,, and the way Jake's dark, slightly curly hair was combed back and gleaming was new.

A pair of shiny, black, hand-tooled, Mexican-style 'Botas' (boots), had replaced Jake's worn, scuffed work boots. His dazzling white, long sleeved shirt, with a black string tie almost hurt Cooter's eyes. A pair of 'never worn before' black trousers completed Jakes' new look.

Choosing not to risk embarrassment, Cooter sat down at the table and accepted a cup of coffee from Hardtack before he spoke casually, "I usually leave here on Sunday at about nine o'clock. Church services start at eleven." Silence.

When Hardtack handed Cooter his breakfast, he picked up the honey pitcher and poured a generous amount of the sweet amber liquid over the buttered pancakes. With the first mouthful, he closed his eyes in bliss. "Hardtack, if you were a woman I'd marry you. These are the best pancakes I've had since I ate breakfast with Mama a couple of weeks ago."

Hardtack snorted.

Cooter grinned, glancing at Jake whose eyes were filled with humor and friendly skepticism.

"I hope you're looking for more than a good cook, Cooter."

Cooter looked out the kitchen window for a moment. He pretended to give Jake's question serious thought. Turning back to his friend, he chuckled rakishly, "Yeah—there's *more* to a woman than cooking; but then, I ain't *really* looking—are you?"

Jake squirmed in his chair, but did not turn away. Running his tongue over his teeth, he leaned forward, resting his chin on the heel of his left hand. "I didn't know I was...until yesterday." With that, he placed both hands on the table and pushed himself up.

"You never know."

* * *

The church house and community center buildings were located on Main Street, near the center of town. Behind them was the rodeo arena. Jake glanced at the arena fences. His mind flashed back to the times when Matt had ridden in competition, mostly for the fun of it, but sometimes for the prize money. *How is Matt doing at West Point? Will I ever see my brother again?*

"We'd better hurry, Jake. It looks like we're about the last ones here."

Jake's attention bounced back to the present. He looked toward the front stoop of the church building. A lone man was climbing the steps. As the fellow reached the top, he turned and waved a hand in their direction.

Jake commented, "That's the Wilson's youngest boy—isn't it?" He lifted a hand in acknowledgment of the young man's greeting.

"Yes...and no," Cooter responded. "Yes, he's a Wilson. But no, he's not the youngest. That's Charlie. He's the one that tried to rope Matt into the wild bunch he was runnin' with. It could've meant big trouble for Matt if the sheriff hadn't stuck his brand into the fire."

Cooter shifted his eyes toward his companion. "You remember...the time Sheriff Briscoe sent for you because he had Matt in the 'cahoose' for disturbin' the peace." He huffed at the memory. "Only, he wasn't disturbin' the peace and Matt knew it."

Pulling the wagon beneath the shade of one of the big Pin Oaks dotting the churchyard, they both jumped lithely to the ground. Jake tied the reins to a hitch rope and they walked toward the porch. Charlie waited for them.

"The music is just now starting. It's a wall-to-wall crowd. Let's crack the door open and see if we can spot a place to sit," Charlie whispered.

After receiving a nod, he pushed the door open enough for them to scan the interior. Jake immediately spied Doctor Stoddard and his daughter. They were sitting near the center aisle on a pew mid-way into the sanctuary. There was a vacant seat next to them!

Jake's heart jumped and he moved to claim that vacancy. However, Charlie beat him to it. The scoundrel rudely shouldered Jake aside with a smirk on his face. "Tough luck", he muttered under his breath and proceeded to the seat.

Jake watched helplessly as Doc looked up at Charlie then moved over on the bench enough to allow the man to be seated.

Carrie felt her father's nudge. She turned her head and saw Charles Wilson grinning down at her as he took the seat next to the doctor. Charlie winked…in church!

She pretended that she did not see his blatant gesture and turned back to face the front, but not before she caught a glimpse of a pair of incredible, cobalt-blue eyes throwing fiery darts at Charlie.

Jake Galloway! That is him! This is the first time I've ever seen him in church. I wonder what has gotten into him? She attempted to reign in her thoughts and force them back to the worship service but it was a couple of minutes before the rhythm of her heart settled back down to normal.

Meanwhile, Jake's anger threatened to rob him of hearing God's Word. He and Cooter found a seat on one of the back pews beside three young boys. It soon became apparent to both men that the boys' had chosen that back bench because it was well out of range of their mother's watchful eye.

The boys hand play, spit wads and the rubbing of the toes of their shoes under the pew in front of them added to Jake's irritation, managing to distract his attention from the services.

When Cooter had had enough, he reached across the back of the pew without a sound and 'thumped' the boy farthest away from him on the back of the head. The little rebel's head whipped around accusingly toward the boy next to him. Before he could charge his brother with the 'thump', Cooter caught his attention. The boy's eyes widened as Cooter pointed to himself and with a doubled fist held discreetly low, sent a silent but clear message of what the consequences would be if the youngster didn't 'settle down'. The boy meekly ducked his head. The 'thumping' was repeated twice more. Neither of the boys saw the others get their 'thump' but the pew on which Jake and Cooter sat was completely peaceful for the rest of the service. Of course, Cooter was bluffing, but the kids did not dare test him.

Jake was in a turmoil. He was excited about the prospect of actually meeting and being acquainted with Carrie Stoddard. For that reason, he was glad to be in church services again. However, the training he had received as a child was playing havoc with his conscience.

How long had it been since he had attended God's house? He could not help but recall Big Mama's dying words, 'Don't ever stop going to meetin' and worshipping God.' Jake flinched. He'd certainly failed in that. Would things have turned out differently between him and Matt if they had continued to go and listen to the Word of God?...Probably.

"Time is a gift from God. He wants us to know that. It should be *redeemed* not just *spent* or *used* in a wasteful, foolish manner."

Brother Keller's booming voice brought Jake back to the little room with a jar. He sat up a little straighter and endeavored to listen more closely. *'Lord, I need to hear this. Boy—do I need to hear it!'*

The man of God continued. "I'm an old man now. I've been riding this circuit for over sixteen years and, in that time, I've grown to know most of you people pretty well. I've known two or three generations your families in some cases, including your grandparents. I don't know why but I'm sure *God* laid this message on my heart today. Now look at Ephesians 5:14—17. 'Wherefore He saith, 'Awake thou that sleepeth and arise from the dead...and Christ shall give thee light.

'See then that ye walk circumspectly, not as fools, but as wise, redeeming the time, because the days are evil.'"

Brother Keller paused. "Now listen closely—this is the most important verse for the message today. Verse seventeen: 'Wherefore be ye not unwise, but understanding what the will of the Lord is.'

"As I said before, some of your parents and, in the case of you younger people, your grandmas and grandpas have brought you up under my ministry." He paused and looked around.

Jake flinched under the sweep of Brother Keller's eyes. The preacher's vision did not actually rest on him but, in Jake's mind, it was as if a finger pointed directly at him. Holding his breath, he braced for the next statement.

Brother Keller was known for being plain spoken. He was never cruel or judgmental, but he *was* bold to speak the truth.

"I know you are all good folks; but even good people can get so cold, careless and unfeeling toward the Lord that one morning they will wake up to find weeks, months and, sometimes, years have passed without a thought for God. They have wasted half their life. I am not your judge, but God would have me to press His cause. Listen again to what He is saying to all of us this morning. Verse fourteen; '*Awake thou that sleepeth.*' Verse fifteen, '*Redeem the time.*' Finally, verse seventeen, '*Wherefore, be ye not unwise; but understanding what the will of the Lord is.*'"

The preacher caught his bottom lip between his teeth. He was silent for several seconds; giving time for the verses to sink in.

"Let me ask you this—*how* are you going to know what the will of God is for your life if you don't spend time talking to Him, reading His Word, and listening to His messages?" Keller paused dramatically again. "You are *not*. And—I am sad to say—that as a result, those wasted weeks, months and years will cost you dearly. You see...there is one of God's laws you 'cannot' break. That law is, '*whatsoever a man soweth—that shall he also reap.*' You cannot neglect your service, worship and fellowship with God and go unscathed."

Brother Keller went on to explain some of the things that cause men and women to stray away from a close relationship with the Lord. He concluded his sermon by assuring the congregation that it was never too late to return to the loving arms of Jesus. But, he warned, "Don't harden your heart. If this message has been for you…you know it. The Holy Spirit will see to that. For the love of Christ, heed it!"

The congregation stood and sang a hymn. Afterward, the preacher called on Doctor Stoddard to lead in closing prayer.

Jake had not realized that Carrie's father was a leader in the church…but then he hadn't been attending. A disturbing thought came to him, *Maybe the good doctor won't want his daughter to have anything to do with me.* The possibility shook Jake. What was it the preacher said? *Those wasted weeks, months and years will cost you.* Jake fought the lump that threatened to form in his throat. Wasted weeks, months and years had *already* cost him. He swallowed hard and muttered a prayer, "Never again, Lord…never again."

* * *

As soon as the last 'amen' was said, people began to move toward Brother Keller who stood at the back door smiling and shaking hands. Jake turned toward the aisle. As he did, he flicked his eyes toward Carrie and her father. Charlie stood at the end of their pew, preventing them from moving out into the aisle. He was talking to Doctor Stoddard, but Jake could see that he was staring at Carrie while doing so. Jake unconsciously squeezed his hands into fists.

Since Jake and Cooter had sat on a pew near the exit, they were among the first to leave. A short, stocky-built man just ahead of them gave the minister a gap-toothed grin. He was saying in a semi-joking manner, "Ouch, Preacher! You sure stepped on our toes this morning!"

Keller shook the man's extended hand while laying his other hand on the man's shoulder.

"Well Wallace, I'm sorry to hear that. I was aiming at your heart."

"Uh…yeah," Wallace stuttered and hurried out the door.

"Jake! Wade!—I'm so glad to see you two young men here today!" Turning his eyes pointedly on Jake, the preacher continued, "I hope to see you more often after today." He grinned. "You've always been a blessing and inspiration to me Jake."

Jake nodded meekly. "Thank you, Preacher. I'll be back." He looked away for a second then quickly faced the minister again. "I'm thickheaded sometimes…I learn things the hard way. But I *do* learn."

Brother Keller chuckled and slapped Jake's back as he passed on out the door.

* * *

Once they were in the churchyard, Cooter said, "What do we do now? I saw the wagon wheel sittin' outside Abe's shop door when we passed. I guess we need to go load it up and get home with it. Hardtack's foaming at the mouth for it."

Jake was not listening. His eyes were fixed on the front door of the church building. He answered his friend distractedly, 'Yeah…we'll pick it up on the way out of town; but I'm not ready to leave just now." He turned his face to Cooter, grinning sheepishly. "There's somebody I want to speak to first."

Cooter's eyes twinkled as he grunted, "I figured you might."

* * *

Inside the church, Carrie waited impatiently while Charlie stood at the end of the pew talking to her father. She could not help but glance toward the door. Jake Galloway and Wade Marshall had shook hands with the minister and disappeared out the door. Carrie did not know why, but she urgently wanted to get outside before Jake and Wade left the area.

After all, she told herself, *someone needs to let Jake know how glad we are to see him here today.* She glanced down at the floor, hoping Charlie or her father would not notice her blush with the next thought. *I also want to get his attention before some other girl works up enough nerve to speak to him.*

Carrie's admission shocked her. From what she had been told of

Jake Galloway, she wasn't absolutely sure she *really* wanted to speak to him…no matter how handsome he was.

Jake watched intently as person after person continued to file out the front door. Many called out to others and waved while making their way to a wagon or carriage or to their mount. Several of the older girls nodded at him then turned beet red when he tipped his hat in return. But Jake's attention was not on them.

Doctor Stoddard had parked his surrey under a shade tree at the side of the building. Jake deliberately stationed himself so that the Doctor and Carrie would *have* to pass by him on their way to it.

After several minutes, he saw Carrie immerge. She seemed to be looking around for someone as she descended the steps. Her beautiful emerald-green eyes found his and Jake's heart stopped.

She smiled.

Taking a deep breath for courage, Jake was about to move in her direction when Charlie Wilson darted out of the building and down the steps. He ran quickly around the Stoddards and stopped in front of them. "I wonder if you would mind if I rode along side your surrey, Miss Stoddard? I'd sure like to talk to you some. We didn't have much chance in the church house." He suddenly realized that Carrie's father was listening, Charlie turned to him. "If…if that's alright with you, Doc…ah…I mean Sir."

Doctor William Stoddard was no fool. He knew he had a lovely daughter. He was quite accustomed to fumbling, nervous young men trying to gain Carrie's attention. So far, she had shown no interest in them. But as Charles Wilson was requesting the privilege of escorting her home, the doctor noticed a tall, rather handsome young man standing near the corner of the building. The young man was gazing intently at Carrie. Though she tried to disguise her interest, Doc saw pink spots appear on her cheeks as her eyes darted back and forth between that man and Charles Wilson. Doc would be willing to wager that the 'pink spots' were not for Charlie.

"It's all right with me, Charlie, but that's up to Carrie," he laughed softly. "It's not me you're wanting to talk to."

Charlie turned a pleading expression on Carrie, and though she didn't really want to put up with Charles all the way home, Carrie's good manners came to fore. She smiled graciously. "That would be fine, Charles. Though I can't imagine what you want to talk about that is worth such a long, hot ride out of your way."

"Oh, it ain't out of my way, Miss Carrie. In fact—*any* direction where you're headed is always *my way*."

Jake was standing near enough to hear the exchange. After Charlie's last remark, he turned and walked away. He thought he was going to be sick to his stomach.

Carrie watched Jake turn away and realized she was keenly disappointed.

After loading the repaired wheel into the bed of the wagon, Jake and Cooter headed for the Silver Concho. Jake was silent. Cooter knew why.

"You ought not to give up on meetin' Miss Carrie. She's a smart girl. It won't take her but just a little while to figure out that she don't want to have nothing to do with Charlie Wilson. 'Specially after she hears what folks think of' im." Cooter's tone let Jake know that his good friend was attempting to encourage him.

"And *who's* going to tell her about him? His father owns one of the biggest ranches in these parts. No one will want to get on the old man's bad side by shooting their mouth off about one of his boys," Jake huffed. "And you can bet she'll get an earful of what 'folks'—meaning Matt's old buddies—think of me from Charlie. He took a deep breath and turned his face toward Cooter. "How long do you think it will take her to decide that she wants nothing to do with *me?*"

Cooter's mouth opened then snapped shut. It was not right. Jacob Galloway was, and always had been, the hardest working, most unselfish, decent person Cooter had ever known. He did not try to answer Jake's question.

Carrie endured Charlie's prattle as he trotted his big gray gelding on her side of the surrey. He did his best to impress her with tales of his prowess with horses, guns and of how many rodeo prizes he had won. He went on to brag about a trip to New Orleans he had made with his father and two older brothers when he was sixteen. He told of their ride up the Mississippi River on a paddle wheeler. He did not say what kind of boat it had been, but she suspected that it was one of the notorious gambling boats. She was not impressed.

Carrie's interest peaked when Charlie mentioned the area rodeos again. Matt Galloway, Jake's younger brother, had been a regular participant in them. Carrie had not forgotten for a second the disappointed look in Jake's blue eyes when Charlie had stepped in front of her at church that morning.

"I attended a few of those rodeos, Charles. I used to see a young man by the name of Matt Galloway there. He seems to have disappeared, but I think I saw his brother at church today." She paused, trying to sound casual. "Do you know either of them?"

Charlie stared at her for several seconds. *Why was she asking about the Galloways?*

He made up his mind quickly, *Matt's gone and here's my chance to eliminate the other serious competition.*

"Why yes; as a matter of fact I know both of them real well." He rolled his eyes. "Matt was, 'is' a real nice fella, but his brother..."

Charlie watched to see how closely Carrie was listening. He saw that he had the Doctor's attention also. That pleased him; it never hurt to have *Papa* on your side.

"I don't like to talk about a man behind his back, but Jake Galloway don't deserve no better." He glanced at Doc Stoddard again and noted the man's stoic expression.

"Well...anyway, Matt and me and a few others used to run around together and the things we heard about how Jake treated his kid brother would make the hair stand up on the back of your neck."

"Did *Matt* tell you those things himself?" Carrie questioned.

"No, Matt was not the kind to talk about his problems; but any *fool* could see how he was being treated."

The thought ran through Doctor Stoddard's mind, *It probably was a 'fool' that decided that the older brother was mistreating the younger one.*

Charlie was really into his story now. He continued, "After their grandma died and left just the two of them to run their ranch, it seems that Jake, who was the oldest like I said, was so mean and hard driving that Matt finally got fed up with it. Instead of hanging around 'til he busted loose and killed Jake, he decided to run off to West Point and become a Cavalry officer." Charlie stopped to catch his breath. "To tell you the truth—all Matt's friends decided that that suited Jake just fine. He *wanted* Matt gone all along—so he could have the ranch all to himself."

Charlie straightened in his saddle and assumed a cocky voice, "But he's in for a big surprise if Matt ever decides to come back and claim his half of the ranch. It'll be a surprise because, when the Cavalry gets through with Matt, Jake will find it mighty hard to bully his brother anymore!" Charlie stopped talking, waiting for Carrie's reaction to his spiel.

Carrie was silent for a few seconds. Then she spoke, surprising Charlie, "That's a sad, sad story, Charlie. The worst thing that can happen between brothers is for them to fight over their inheritance. *Nothing* is worth your brother's love."

Charlie didn't quite know what to do with that, but he smiled knowingly. "I think you're right, Miss Carrie… Too bad Jake Galloway didn't see it that way."

CHAPTER NINE
Pyrite or Pure Gold

"Here's your wheel, Hardtack. Cooter and I will put it on the chuck wagon first thing in the morning," Jake said, as they lowered the repaired wheel to the ground in front of the cook shack.

"If you're going to be needing anything else for the trail, I want to know before this weekend. We plan to pull out for Fort Worth early—one week from tomorrow morning."

Hardtack grinned, a wide and toothy grin. "I'm thinking I have most everthang, but I do wish I'da told ya to pick up some peppermint candy yesterday. The boys are easier to keep outta my sugar barrel when I have candy to giv'em."

Jake turned to Cooter. "If you make it back to town this week, pick up a supply of hard candy. Nodding, Cooter jumped back up on the wagon and gave the reins a flick. The wagon bumped and rattled around the end of the barn and into the shed.

Jake headed to the house without another word. He was partly confused and depressed. On the other hand, he was excited and hopeful about the possibility of getting to know Carrie. He had to think.

* * *

Carrie was up early the next morning as was her custom. However, this day she moped around the kitchen, seemingly unable to accomplish the simple task of preparing breakfast. The night before had been miserable. She tossed and turned on her bed, unable to relax. Sleep had eluded her until just before dawn.

Charles Wilson was not the first person to tell her about Jake Galloway's *'mean spirit'*. If he had been, Carrie would have discounted it as a would-be suitor's attempt to discount a man that he considered competition. However, Francis White had said the same thing! Could it be true? She shook her head to ward off doubts about him. After all, Emily, Caroline and several of her other friends had expressed disbelief that the man was as bad as some said. If only she knew someone who *really* knew the Galloway brothers…Jake in particular…someone whose opinion she trusted and valued.

Pouring herself a cup of coffee, she sat down at the kitchen table to wait for the biscuits to bake. Her mind returned to Jake. Why did it matter to her? She really didn't know the young man. And *where* had he been all this time? Was he antisocial, a hermit? She was confused and more than a little disturbed. She couldn't explain why she hoped the negative reports about Jake were unfounded; but, for some reason, she did.

* * *

Monday morning Cooter rode through a little stand of cedars complaining to himself. The day was already hot and it was only seven o'clock. The final gathering and count of the main trail-herd was under way. As Segundo (the Spanish word for 'second' that Texas ranchers in that part of the country used for foreman), it was his responsibility to have an accurate account of all the cattle that would be leaving the ranch. The task was made more difficult by 'rogue' bulls—young bulls who were not content to stay with one of the particular bunches.

He topped a small hill and rode down toward the water 'tank'. Texas ranchers often dug small water holes around natural springs or on runoff paths. These tanks provided drinking water without the cattle having to travel long distances to secure it. They also helped to prevent over-graze near the main water source on a ranch.

THE SILVER CONCHO: LIFE IS A RUB-BOARD

A flash of color near the waterhole drew Cooter's attention. He squinted against the early morning Sun. Jake was standing beside the water.

Cooter heeled his horse and galloped down the hill. He dropped to the ground and let the reins drag. Jake turned at the sound of his friend's approach. "How's it going," he called.

"Doin' right well,' Cooter chuckled and added, "but it'd go a lot better if you would let me make 'steaks' out of a couple of young bulls. Those rascals just plain refuse to stay where we put 'em."

Jake's expression changed suddenly. "Yeah—a lot of young bulls don't want to stay put."

Cooter sensed that Jake wasn't just talking about cattle.

"What are you doing out here this morning? I thought you'd be staying close to the house—get'n ready to leave next week."

Jake didn't answer. Cooter waited.

After several minutes, Jake spoke. "Cooter, do you ever think about what your life is all about? I mean—what do you want—where are you headed?"

Cooter's eyes narrowed. He stared at the man before him. Jake didn't really want an answer.

Jake bent and picked up a small, flat rock. He hurled it skipping across the surface of the water. "I've been thinking all morning about my life...and..." He lifted his eyes. "...I don't like what I see." He turned and stepped to the edge of the water, his back to his foreman. Cooter was silent again for a few moments.

Finally, Cooter said softly, "Jake do you remember when we were kids and we used to skip rocks like that across the tank? We didn't worry about life. It wasn't time yet. Everyone has a few years like that. Sometimes it's good to remember those things."

Jake whirled, his face flushed in anger. "No Cooter—I *don't* remember doing that, because I don't remember being a kid!" He paused. "I realized yesterday, when Brother Keller was preaching, that I've wasted my life so far." Jake's expression became pained. "My problem is...I don't know how to back up and start over."

He reached up and took his hat off. Sliding his fingers through his dark hair, then slamming the hat back in place, he continued, "Maybe it's too late."

Cooter shook his head all the while Jake was talking. "Slow down, Jake! Let me answer your question." He watched Jake's face become guarded. *'Lord help me to say this thing right. My friend needs help…He needs to turn to You. Help me to show him that truth,'* Cooter prayed silently.

"Jake, no one can tell somebody else what they want out of life. That's between them and God. Take me for instance; I just take one day at a time. I stay open and go through whatever door the Lord opens for me. I don't try to second-guess God. He knows what He has planned for my life and I *know that I know* God only wants good things for me. It will all work out in the end, no matter how it looks at the present."

Jake's hands went to his hips. "That might be the way *you* see things, Cooter…after all, your folks lived to see you a grown man. You *could* take one day at a time. You *could* make your own choices, but what about me? Things that *had* to be done were just shoved in my face—I didn't have a choice. I didn't even have time to think! I got up every morning and it was already decided what I *had* to do. Day after day—year after year; this ranch became a twenty-thousand acre prison!" He struggled with his frustration for a moment.

"Here I am twenty-four years old and everything I've ever touched has turned to…dirt!—And I'm dirt too!" Fighting to keep tears at bay, he continued, "I dream of having a family. When I saw Carrie Stoddard pass by Abe's shop last Saturday, I knew she was everything I've ever wanted out of life. She's fine and descent, and looks like an angel. But I'm just kidding myself to think that a girl like that would ever have *anything* to do with the likes of me, Cooter! Too many people knew Matt and they think I ran him off so I could have the ranch all to myself."

Cooter's heart clenched at the hurt he saw on Jake's face. He knew his best friend had the wrong perspective, but he also knew that Jake needed to empty his frustration—so he listened without interrupting.

"Do you know what Matt's last words were to me?" Without waiting for a response, Jake persisted, "He looked down at me from Breeze's back and said, 'I'm gone, Jake. I won't be back. You can have it all. It's all yours brother.'"

Jake jabbed a thumb at his chest. "All mine, Cooter! Even my brother thinks I'm a dirty so-in-so who would steal his birthright! Why should Carrie Stoddard think any different? After all, Matt *is* gone!" Jake turned angrily away again.

Cooter let the silence hang between them for a few minutes, then he said softly, "To whom much is given...of him shall men require the more."

Jake's head jerked around over his shoulder. "What's *that* supposed to mean?"

Cooter inhaled. "It means, Jake that you haven't learned to count your blessings. Everything you said may be the truth...as you see it but it ain't the way it really is."

"What do you mean—'not the way it is'? How is it then," Jake barked.

Cooter flinched, but continued softly, "Jacob Galloway, you were born into a fine family. Your folks were hardworking, brave pioneers. They took their lives in their hands and came west to make something of this land—land that was crawling with Indians and Mexican folks who resented white settlers from the United States. But the Lord blessed them anyway. By the way, my folks only own *one* section of land—one hundred, sixty-six acres, Jake. Your folks and now you own twenty '*thousand*' acres! Your father made a real big sacrifice to see that The Silver Concho stayed in the family. He did it for you and Matt.

"Then there was your Grandmother. Big Mama did the same thing as her son. That little woman sacrificed her life's health to see that you and Matt had a proud heritage. That heritage ain't all tied up in just the land neither. It was in the kind of *people* that lived on this land.

"When Big Mama died, Jake, the keeping of that heritage was passed on to you as the oldest son. You didn't ask for the job, but your pa and your grandma hadn't asked for it either. They just stood toe-to-toe with their duty. Why? Because they loved their family more than they did theirselves.

"Now, as I see it, Jake, you've done the same thing because you're a

Galloway…and Galloways don't quit!" Cooter's eyes softened and he lowered his voice. "Do you honestly think God has been asleep for the past fourteen years…and that He hasn't seen your obedience and sacrifice? Do you *really* think He don't know that you love your brother and you did what you had to do for him as much as for yourself?

"He knows, Jake, and He *will* work things out for your good, if you just trust Him. Believe in Him…don't buckle now, Jake! All the Charlie Wilsons in the world can't keep the Lord from blessing you. Lies can't stand in the face of the truth. One day Matt will realize all I just said is true too!"

Jake was quiet. He stared at Cooter. His expression began to soften and his stance relaxed. "You really believe all that, don't you Cooter?"

"I don't just believe it, Jake. I *know* it."

* * *

Sheriff John Briscoe stood on Doctor Stoddard's front porch. He knocked on the door a second time. From within the house he heard the doctor's daughter, "Coming!"

Carrie opened the door with a friendly smile. "Sheriff! What brings you here? Whatever it is…Dad or I didn't do it," she said with a laugh.

Stepping back to open the door wider, she welcomed him, "Come in, Sheriff. I'll find Dad. I think he's in his treatment room counting pills."

The sheriff grinned, removed his hat and stepped into the front parlor. While he waited, he looked around the room. A few well-chosen pictures hung on the walls, balanced by candled sconces and framed needlework. Cream-colored drapes, bunched with dark-green ties, complimented the upholstered furniture of the same shades of green and cream. A large woven rug of gold and green covered the center of the floor. Carrie's piano, positioned on the farthest wall completed the homey look of the room. A single, gold-framed picture of an older version of Carrie graced the wall above the piano…Marie Stoddard.

"John Briscoe—Carrie already told you we didn't do it—so, what can I do for you?" William Stoddard grinned as he extended his hand to the lawman.

Briscoe shook the doctor's hand. "I'm hoping you can relieve me of some misery."

"What *misery* is that?"

The sheriff glanced at Carrie. "I've got a boil on the back of my…ah…leg. I've tried sittin' in a tub of hot water, but nothing seems to help. Will you have a look at it, Doc, and see if it's ready to lance?"

"Sure! Come on back to the treatment room, and I'll fix you up. Those things can really be painful. How in the world have you been riding your horse with a boil on your leg?"

"It hasn't been easy, Doc." The sheriff grunted as he stiffly followed the doctor's lead to the treatment room.

A few minutes later, the doctor dropped his scalpel into a basin of boiled water and leaned over the treatment table. "Grit your teeth. This will hurt some for a few seconds," he said as he prepared to lift the 'head' out of the lanced boil. "Carrie, have that carbolic acid ready. This is a nasty mess."

Carrie moved quickly to the medicine cabinet to retrieve the carbolic acid and some swabs of clean cloth. She grimaced with sympathy of the sheriff's pain as her father completed the procedure.

The sheriff's face was pale, but he smiled weakly with relief, as he stood bandaged and clothed once again in the front room.

"John, you'll need to give the wound site about a week to heal. Stay off your horse. It shouldn't bother you anymore, but sitting in a tub of warm water is still a good idea. Just make sure you dry it off well. Wash it everyday with this carbolic acid and keep this black salve on it." Doctor Stoddard patted his patient's shoulder and handed him the medicines while he spoke.

Carrie stood behind her father watching. Suddenly, she remembered. "Sheriff Briscoe, do you know a young man by the name of Charles Wilson?" The lawman stiffened almost imperceptibly. Carrie didn't miss his reaction.

"Yes, Miss Stoddard, I know Charlie. Why?"

Carrie stuttered, "Uh…uh, before I say anything else, I want to know if you also know Jacob Galloway?"

The sheriff nodded slowly. "Yes, I know Jake too. Why do you ask?"

Carrie didn't quite know how to phrase her question, but she lifted her shoulders and plunged in, "Would you mind telling me about them? What do you think of them—their character? I value your opinion."

The sheriff smiled. "Miss Carrie, I don't usually make a habit of telling all I know about folks around here. I know you understand."

Carrie's breath caught. He didn't want to say anything bad about Jake. "I understand, Sheriff, but…" Briscoe interrupted, "Let me ask *you* something. Do you know what 'Pyrite' is?"

Carrie looked blank. She glanced toward her father. The doctor smiled. "Pyrite, Carrie, is a mineral that looks like gold. It's sometimes called 'fool's gold' because it deceives people when they first see it. It's worthless." Carrie turned back to the sheriff, confusion evident in her expression.

Briscoe spoke again, "All I'm gonna say about Charles Wilson and Jake Galloway is that I've known both boys since they were nine or ten years old. My honest opinion is that Charles Wilson is pyrite and Jake Galloway is "Pure Gold."

Carries mouth formed an "Ohhh".

Doctor Stoddard watched as he and John Briscoe exchanged knowing smiles.

* * *

Later that morning, Carrie was once again in the treatment room changing linen on the treatment table and returning unused bandages to the cabinet. Having performed the tasks so often, she could do them without concentrating. It was a good thing, for she was completely preoccupied with thoughts of Jake Galloway. The man was a mystery. It seemed that all her friends had known 'about' him for years. How was it that she had just first laid eyes on him three days ago? And, only two people that Carrie knew were personally acquainted with him: Sheriff Briscoe and Wade Marshall…and Caroline, a little.

The lawman had made it clear that he thought highly of Jake. That was encouraging. She determined that she was going to talk to Wade Marshall also, the first opportunity she had. She wanted to ask Wade what had *really* happened between the two Galloway brothers.

CHAPTER TEN
Rodeos and Women

Thursday morning, Cooter left Hardtack working on the almost loaded chuck wagon and headed for the ranch house to see Jake. When he entered the kitchen through the back door, he found his boss sitting at the table, a ledger and several invoices lay out before him. An open cashbox was also there.

When the door opened, Jake lifted his head and grinned. "Good—I'm glad you came back to the house before you took off for town. I have something I want you to do while you're there."

He stared at the invoices for a moment then went on, "I don't see any reason for Claude Porter at the general store, or Abe Mill and two or three others, to have to wait for another five weeks for *their* money. Especially since I have it right now."

Jake counted out the cash, then handed Cooter the money and invoices. "While you're in town, take care of these bills for me…and Matt."

"You *and* Matt huh?" Cooter looked at him thoughtfully. *Him 'and' Matt.*

Jake grinned at his friend. "Yes, me *and* Matt." His eyes shifted back to the metal cashbox. It was built with a divider down the center. "It's half his, you know. I split all profits from the ranch fifty-fifty; and when I pay bills, I pay them fifty-fifty also. Someday when…" Jake glanced at Cooter. "…*if* he comes back, he'll have his share waiting for him."

"He'll come home again," Cooter said with quiet conviction. Jake exhaled. "We'll see."

* * *

Llano was located in southwest Texas 'cattle country'. They loved their cowboys. Rodeos were regular events during good weather. The largest, county-wide, rodeo occurred in connection with the Fourth of July celebration.

However, the final community rodeo took place each year in the middle of August. It was a well-attended, local affair; and most of the contestants were from the surrounding ranches and homesteads. Friends and neighbors were eager to cheer their favorites before the late summer cattle drives to the Fort Worth market began. None of the area's young people would willingly miss this opportunity to mingle with others of their age group. The fall, church-wide, picnic was the only other 'outdoor' social event left for the year.

In the past, several weddings were the direct result of the rodeo official's practice of letting young, single women present prizes and certificates to event winners. It seemed that cowboys liked girls better than prizes. Romance often blossomed.

To help raise prize money, young ladies participated in a bake sale held on the day of the rodeo. Cakes, pies and cookies were auctioned to the highest bidder, who did so in the name of one of the contestants. The girl whose cake was purchased in that contestant's name was the one to present his prize or certificate of participation. There were no unhappy cowboys at the end of the day—win, lose or draw.

Whatever their reason for participating; the girls looked forward to meeting a cowboy in the center of the arena. They blushed prettily amidst the cheering and teasing of the crowd. A few the men winked or bowed, and some of them even did a little 'jig', according to their nature. Others were as red-faced as the girls were.

* * *

Carrie could hardly wait for the coming weekend. The rodeo would begin at ten o'clock in the morning and last until sundown. She wondered if Jake Galloway would participate this year. His brother won the bronc-riding event last year and she had no doubt that Jake was every bit the 'rough-and-ready' cowboy that Matt was. Now that he wouldn't be competing with his younger brother, she hoped he would show up.

Hurriedly, she finished her morning coffee and carried her cup and saucer to the dishpan, then quickly washed them, along with her father's breakfast dishes. All the while she was thinking, "I hope Charlie Wilson doesn't try to monopolize my attention again." She stopped for a moment and a smile spread across her face. "Somehow, I've a feeling that if Jake really wants to talk to me…he's not going to let Charlie get away with that again."

After finishing with the dishes, she went in search of her father. He was in his study-office, where she usually found him when he wasn't with a patient.

"Dad, Caroline and I are planning to bake cakes and cookies for the rodeo 'bake-sale'. The proceeds will go into the prize fund, along with what they make on the barbeque. She is going to spend tonight with me and we'll spend all day Friday cooking. That way we can get an early start with our baking."

Doctor Stoddard's eyes sparkled with pride as he fixed them on his only child. Carrie added, "I'm going to need more flour, sugar and eggs before I start."

He smiled indulgently. "So, you want me to hitch up the carriage?" She nodded. "If you're not too busy. I would go on the mare, but I'm afraid the packages will be too bulky and fragile to stuff into the saddlebags. I wouldn't be able to handle her and the eggs too." She smiled sweetly.

"No—Of course you can't. I'll bring the carriage around front. Are you ready to go right now?"

"By the time you get back, I will be." She stepped around his desk and placed her hands on both sides of his face. After kissing his forehead softly, she whispered, "You're the best Dad in the whole world. Did you know that?"

He chuckled, "I do now—thank you, Sweetheart."

While her father was at the barn, Carrie changed into a fresh dress and pulled her heavy tresses up into a becoming style. The weather was too hot to leave it hanging down. She frowned slightly and muttered, "Besides, I'm getting too old to run around with my hair hanging down my back."

* * *

Cooter arrived in town at mid-morning. He noted the absence of people on the streets. But that was to be expected. Most folks came in on Saturdays.

After making the rounds to creditors of The Silver Concho, he headed for Claude Porter's general store. Nearing the establishment, he perked up at the sight of Doc Stoddard's carriage parked in front.

Carrie stopped by and picked up her best friend on her way to the general store. The girls were looking forward to having a whole day to visit and giggle while they baked for the rodeo. It was always more fun to work with a friend.

They strolled down the piece-goods aisle of the store, looking over the, just arrived from St. Louis bolts of heavy cotton material. "This color would make a beautiful Christmas dress for you." Caroline smiled as she held the forest-green cloth against Carrie's face. "It would show off your beautiful eyes." Her expression became mischievous. Who knows? You may be wanting to 'show-off' for a certain handsome ranch owner by then."

Carrie stared at the cloth for a few seconds. Raising her eyes to Caroline's she whispered, "I can't 'show-off' for him unless I get to know him, and so far...." Her voice trailed off.

The bell over the store's front door had tinkled and both young women glanced toward the sound. "Oh, Carrie! That's Wade Marshall! He's Jake Galloway's foreman!" She rolled her eyes dramatically. "As you can plainly see...Jake isn't the *only* good-looking man out at the Silver Concho."

They both laughed, but quickly covered their mouths when Cooter suddenly noticed them near the fabric counter. He lifted his hat politely and started toward them.

"Oh my! Here he comes!" Caroline whispered excitedly out of the side of her mouth.

"Good morning, ladies," Cooter drawled, a big smile on his face. "You're both looking mighty pretty today."

"Hello Wade—thank you," Caroline answered. "What brings you into town in the middle of the week?"

Cooter's eyes flicked back and forth between the two pretty girls. "I'm here to help Hardtack keep the ranch hands out of his sugar barrel." He chuckled. Noting their questioning looks, he explained. "We're leaving on a trail-drive to Fort Worth this coming Monday. Hardtack told Jake the only way he can keep the men out of the sugar is to have plenty of candy to offer them." He winked. "Man does not live by bread alone."

"Then you're not planning to participate in the rodeo this Saturday?" Carrie tried to hide her disappointment, but Cooter noticed it anyway. He snapped his fingers. "You know! I plumb forgot that it's this weekend!" He pursed his lips. "I bet Jake let it slip his mind too."

Caroline jumped in. "I remember seeing Matt Galloway ride in the competition, and win. But I don't *ever* remember seeing his brother there."

"Nawh—Jake was always too busy running the ranch to have time to 'play' as he called it." Cooter's expression brightened. "The ranch has come a long way in the past three or four years. It's making a good profit now." He looked thoughtfully at Carrie. "I bet I could talk him into coming into town now."

Carrie's heart jumped. She swallowed before she spoke. "That would be good. The more the merrier, you know." She added, "Caroline and I will be baking cakes and cookies for the bake sale. The proceeds will go toward the prize-fund."

Cooter beamed at them. "You mean if we buy your cakes and cookies we get to eat 'em with you?"

The girls looked at each other and smiled. Caroline tipped her head to the side, "We...ll, that's not *exactly* how it works. Actually...you make a donation for a cake or such, then, we will slice it and everyone will share. There will also be barbecued beef and other foods for sale. No one will go away hungry, whether they can make a donation or not."

Carrie added, "And this year...each girl who contributes something to the bake sale will have the *honor*..." she raised her brows, "of awarding prizes or certificates of participation to the man who donated for her cake...or whatever."

Cooter was absorbing all this information. He'd be willing to bet Jake would be interested to hear it too. "I see," he said. "That sounds fair enough."

After a moment, he tipped his hat again. "Well, I guess I'd better pay the Concho's bill and get a bunch of candy. I need to head on back to the ranch." He smiled into their eyes. "I hope I... 'we' see you Saturday, ladies." With that, he turned and headed for the store's main counter.

Carrie muttered softly as he walked away, "We all hope so..."

* * *

Later that afternoon, Cooter reined his mount in front of the ranch house. Dismounting, he turned to loosen the leather straps that held his bulging saddlebags in place.

"Looks like you came back with Claude's whole stock of candy." Jake laughed softly from the doorway. "Do you think it will satisfy Hardtack, that his precious sugar barrel is safe from the 'night-raiders'?"

"Yeah—he'll have a whole new worry now. Who's trying to steal his candy when he's not looking." Cooter chuckled as he shouldered the saddlebags and stepped up onto the porch. "Let me give you these receipts before I take the bags to the 'ole pirate'."

Jake backed up to hold the door open. "Come on back to the kitchen. I just put a fresh pot of coffee on."

Cooter moved ahead—talking as he went. "When you hear who I ran into in town, you're gonna wish you'da went with me," he bragged.

Jake's attention keened. "Who was that," he asked—all the while hoping he already knew.

Drawing out his answer and thoroughly enjoying the anxious expression on Jake's face, Cooter teased. "After paying all the bills, I finally moseyed over to the general store. Before I ever went inside, I knew I was in for a pleasin' time cause…"

"For Pete's sake, Cooter! Get to the point!" Jake chuckled and held up a threatening fist.

Cooter pretended to back away. "Ok! Ok! Like I was saying, I spotted Doc Stoddard's surrey in front of the store."

Jake's head nodded as if to say "Go on."

"When I got inside, I saw Miss Carrie *and her* friend, Caroline Hartman." He raised his brows and added, "The two best-lookin girls in Texas."

Jake stared at him for several long seconds then groaned, "If I had any idea that you would run into her today—I would've gone into town and paid my own debts." His shoulders slumped. Cooter took pity on him.

"Well…you ain't heard it all yet. We got into a conversation about the summer rodeo this coming Saturday. Both girls asked if you and me would be takin' part in the competition. They even gave us both a *special* invite." He stopped and shook his head slightly. "That ain't quite right—they said they *hoped* we'd be there."

"Which one said that," Jake urged.

"Both of 'em," Cooter crowed to his friend. It was plain to see that he enjoyed being the one to give Jake the good news. "They also told me this year every girl who bakes a cake or pie or cookies for the rodeo bake sale will be the one who'll be awarding the prize or certificates to the man who buys her baked goods." His eyes sparkled as he continued the spiel. "That means…win, lose, or draw; all a fellow has to do to meet a certain young lady is to shell-out the biggest wad for her bakin'." Looking positively smug, he added, "They seemed real anxious for you and me to know that."

A pleased expression slowly spread across Jake's face. "You wouldn't tease me about something this important—would you, Cooter?"

THE SILVER CONCHO: LIFE IS A RUB-BOARD

The smug expression increased. "If I'm lyin'—I'm dyin'."

"Ye…haa," Jake almost shouted but quickly calmed himself. "What time does everything start Saturday?"

"The rodeo competition itself starts at ten o'clock, but I'm thinkin' we oughta get there a lot earlier—To make sure we get first bids on the baked goods."

Jake nodded thoughtfully. "It might even be a good idea to go on into town tomorrow evening and spend the night at the hotel. That way, we'll be sure to be the first ones there."

"If it was just me and you that'd be fine but, if I know Manny and Joel and the others, they'll be wantin' to go in and do some competin' too."

"I guess you're right," Jake conceded. Then he asked, "What event do you plan to ride in?"

Cooter dropped his head in thought for a moment. Eyeing his friend from beneath his lashes, he answered, "I thought maybe you and me could team-up and have a go at the 'bulldoggin'. I know you'd rather ride a bronc or a bull, but neither one of us needs to be stove-up, seein' as we'll be leavin' on a trail-ride come Monday morning." He paused and studied Jake's amused expression briefly before adding, "I'd be your hazer."

"Whatever suits you is fine with me." Jake good-naturedly clamped a hand on the cowboy's shoulder, "By the way…how are we supposed to know which baked goods are Carrie's and Caroline's?"

Cooter shrugged. "I guess they'll have 'em marked as 'made by such-n-such'. Won't they?"

"If they don't, we'll just have to buy *all* of them." Jake shook his head.

"Yeah—sure." Cooter's pained expression showed that he was remembering his almost empty wallet.

* * *

Caroline stayed Thursday night with her friend as planned. The girls arose early Friday morning and spent the day laughing and giggling as they took extra special pains with the taste and appearance of their 'culinary offerings'. Everything had to be perfect because Carrie was not ashamed to admit that she hoped to impress Jake Galloway—*if he showed up*. She did not voice her fears to Caroline, but she was afraid they both might be in for a disappointment.

Thursday night, Carrie had lain awake long after Caroline's soft, even breathing told her that the other girl was fast asleep. She prayed, "Father, why is it so important to me for him to be there? I don't *really* know him. But Lord, a voice in my heart tells me that he is worth knowing. I'm hoping the voice is Yours" Flopping over on her side, she continued the silent prayer. "Father, I confess that he is very nice looking, but it's the goodness and gentleness which I see beneath that big, rugged exterior that appeals the most to me. There seems to be a…a…*sadness* in his expression. He must be a man who is used to shouldering responsibility and taking care of those he loves. But Lord, maybe he is searching for someone to love him in return." She sighed. "That's the kind of man *every* girl looks for." After taking a deep breath, she ended her prayer, "Please give me wisdom and help me to know Your will. In Jesus' name, Amen"

CHAPTER ELEVEN
Charlie's Bid

Saturday morning, Llano was not 'awake' when Carrie drove by to pick Caroline up at her home. The girls were first to arrive at the pavilion where food would be sold and consumed. A few industrious businesses and tradesmen were up in order to prepare for a very busy day. They expected a marked increase in the number of area residents in town for the rodeo.

Jake, Cooter and the other men left the 'Silver Concho' just before daylight. After an hour and a half's ride, they stepped down out of their saddles in front of the hotel café. It was seven o'clock.

The mood was jovial and the men enjoyed joking and teasing each other on the ride into town. They all looked forward to a day of socializing with their friends and neighbors, *especially* the young, female variety. The chance to win a cash prize in the competitions also enhanced their anticipation.

"Come on in, boys." Jake announced. "I'm buying breakfast."

Manny, the good-looking, black-eyed Mexican flashed white teeth. "You eat too much 'huevos' (eggs) and 'tortillas'...you lose your breakfast, Jake. El caballo (the horse), he see to that. He throw you so hard 'up' that you 'huevos' and tortillas stay!"

The men laughed uproariously at Manny's words, but knew there was wisdom in them.

"Ok, don't eat so much." Jake answered. "The rodeo doesn't start until ten o'clock and you probably won't be doing any riding until around eleven. The kid's competitions are first; at least drink a cup of coffee."

* * *

Carrie helped to arrange the baked goods on display tables. She frequently glanced toward the entrance to the pavilion.

Mrs. Marcia Westing, an older woman in charge of the bake sale, had announced to all of the young women that she was instigating a *new rule*. All cakes, pies and cookies would remain 'anonymous'. Every item received a number.

"That way the young men won't be compelled to buy a cake or pie because he doesn't want to hurt someone's feelings. He can feel free to buy the one he actually thinks he would enjoy the most." She paused, trying to sound neutral. "You have all done such a good job that I'm sure *every*," she stressed the word, "item will be sold."

Caroline stood just out of Mrs. Westing's line of vision. She winked at Carrie and rolled her eyes. They both knew Mrs. Westing's new rule was to insure that her daughter's cake bought a good price; thus insuring the homely girl a trip to the center of the arena at the end of the day.

If Trudy Westing were an amiable, sweet-natured girl, no one would have noticed that she had far too many teeth in her mouth. However, her 'mulish' ways brought that very animal to mind when one looked at her.

Carrie and Caroline also knew Trudy couldn't, or wouldn't, fry an egg, much-less bake and decorate the beautiful, oversized, three layer cake that was labeled with a big, black number 'one' and prominently displayed in the center of table number one. Iced in frothy white with streaks of caramel marbled into the icing, the cake was quite delicious looking. Too bad Trudy was going to take credit for her mother's baking.

A few minutes later, the girls arranged *their* cakes and batches of molasses cookies on the end of table number three because Mrs. Westing had assigned them to do so.

"Well, so much for any chance that Cooter and Jake will bid on our cakes or cookies," Carrie moaned, "but it's probably just as well. If Jake should happen to buy mine and take a bite, only to turn his head and spit it out, I'd die of embarrassment."

"Why would he do that," Caroline questioned. "You're one of the best cooks around...for your age." She waggled her head and said between giggles, "I'll tell you one thing, if Wade Marshall also shows up, and *if* he should buy my cake or cookies..." Her hand went to her hip playfully. "Well...he just better *not* dare spit it out! I'd march right up to him and say, "Wade Marshall! Just for that—I won't cook for you....for the rest of your life!" The girls popped their hands over their mouths and chuckled with glee.

Carrie looked over the other goods displayed on table three. "Who made those pretty sugar-coated cookies on the other end of the table?" She pointed to a bright red, pottery bowl, which was piled high with small, white, almost round cookies. "They looked very attractive in the red, low-sided bowl."

"I think I saw that pretty senorita over there," Caroline motioned with her head, "set them on the table."

Carrie gazed at the lovely, dark-eyed, dark-haired girl. She was slim, yet womanly and Carrie judged her to be in her middle-late teens.

Turning her eyes back to her friend, Carrie huffed, "It may be a good thing Mrs. Westing made her new rule after all. With a girl that pretty around, the rest of us would be whimpering in shame by the time the men stopped fighting over who was going to buy her cookies." Her eyes twinkled, as she added, "We'd know for sure that we were *second choice*."

Caroline's attention suddenly shifted to the front entrance. She nodded in that direction without saying a word. Jake Galloway and Wade Marshall had just walked in.

At that moment, Mrs. Westing called for attention. She raised her high-pitched voice and announced: "Now girls, I don't want you standing near your baked goods. That would be cheating—wouldn't it?"

Carrie barely noticed as Caroline took her by the elbow and led her away from table three. Her eyes were riveted on the tall young man in the black hat, the band of which was decorated with nickel-size silver Conchos.

"That's fitting," she smiled and muttered, "The owner of the Silver Concho is wearing silver Conchos."

Jake was busy in conversation with Wade Marshall, but his eyes were scanning the pavilion while he talked. Before he caught her gawking at him, Carrie turned away. It took all her willpower not to fan her face with her hands.

* * *

"There they are," Cooter said in a low, but excited, voice out of the corner of his mouth. "Over there by the tables with all the cakes and stuff."

Jake said matter-of-factly, "That shouldn't surprise us—since they told us they'd be there." He waited a moment. "What do we do now?"

Cooter's expression became calculating. "Well...I don't think we ought to go runnin' over there right off, like we're stormin' the fort or somethin'. Let's just mosey over to the rodeo officer's tables and pay our entrance fees, then, we can just saunter over to the baked goods—kind of casual like." He leaned closer to Jake and whispered, "We don't want 'em to get the idea we're *too* interested."

"Maybe you don't—but, as far as I'm concerned, I can't get acquainted with Carrie quick enough! And I hope she can see with her own eyes just how '*interested*' I am," Jake countered adamantly.

"No, no, Jake!—Boy, you've been hung out on that ranch too long! That ain't the way to do things. You don't want to play too easy to get! Otherwise, she's liable to get the idea that you're not much of a prize! Take it slow." Cooter motioned with his hand as if he were running it over a soft fur.

"How slow? I don't want to be so slow and hard to get that I don't get *got*," Jake chuckled.

Cooter motioned over his shoulder for Jake to follow. "Just stick with me." He said confidently.

* * *

"Oh look, Carrie! They're not coming over here! Do you suppose they changed their minds about bidding on our cakes?" Caroline's voice sounded panicky.

"I don't think so," Carrie answered calmly. "...Just wait and see. They're probably going over to sign up for an event and then make their way over here."

Carrie had been watching the intense conversation between Jake and his foreman. She had observed Jake glancing anxiously toward the pavilion. "They weren't looking this way for nothing." She was sure she was right.

* * *

At the official's table, Seth Carson, Llano's Postmaster, greeted Jake and Cooter. The rodeo was Seth's favorite activity of the whole year. He was known for saying, "If I hadn't had my back injured during the late war, I'da been th'gall-durnedest bronc rider you ever saw." He always grinned widely and added, "I guess we'll never know for sure, will we?"

People smiled indulgently and let him have his dream.

"Wade Marshall and Matt...uh no...this is *Jake* Galloway! Good to see you boys! You planning on competing this year?"

He turned his eyes on Jake. 'How's that not-so-little, brother of yours? I always think of him at rodeo time. He sure did like to ride. *And*, he was good at it!" Carson stopped long enough to gasp a breath, then continued, "By the looks of you—you'll be good at it too. You Galloway boys sure do look alike. Are you going to bronc ride like he did?"

Before Jake could reply, the man began hurriedly sifting through his papers, looking for the bronc riding signup sheet. He yanked it out of the stack and waved it in front of the two young men. "That'll be two dollars…apiece." He looked back and forth between them. "That is…if you both want to ride."

Jake stood quietly with his thumbs hooked in his jeans pockets. He let the talkative fellow rattle on until the man finally 'wound down'. Then he leaned forward, placing both hands on the table in front of Mister Carson. Smiling easily, he said, "No. Actually, Cooter and I are going to team up for the 'Bulldoggin' competition." He straightened once again and motioned toward Mister Carson's stack of papers. "If you'll just sign us up, Mister Carson."

Carson's mouth, hung open while Jake was speaking. It snapped shut and he quickly found the right sheet of paper.

"It is two dollars *apiece* for this event also…isn't it," Jake asked softly.

"Sure! Sure!" Seth chuckled timidly and muttered to himself, "No fool like an old fool."

Carson turned the list around for Jake and Cooter to sign, received their money, and handed them a couple of numbered tags to pin on the back of their shirts.

"Number five," Cooter whooped. "Do you know what number 'five' stands for in the Bible, Jake?"

Jake shook his head. "No, but I've got a feeling I'm about to find out." His blue eyes twinkled.

"Number five," explained an authoritive sounding Cooter, "stands for 'grace'. So—by 'grace' we're gonna win that prize money today." He looked up with a playful gleam in his eyes. "And, by 'grace', I'm gonna have enough money to buy Caroline's cake."

Jake placed his hand on his friend's shoulder as they walked around the arena fence toward the pavilion. Leaning his head next to his friend, he promised softly, "Don't worry about buying that cake, Cooter. If *I've* got a nickel, *you've* got a nickel."

Cooter hunched his shoulders and replied calmly, "I think it's gonna take more'n a nickel."

Jake's chest rumbled. Cooter grinned without looking at him.

THE SILVER CONCHO: LIFE IS A RUB-BOARD

* * *

"Don't turn around, but they're coming around the fence toward us now," Carrie said in an "I told you so" whisper.

Caroline's hand shot to her hair. "How do I look? Is my ha..."

Grabbing the other girl's arm and pulling it down quickly, Carrie warned, "Don't let them see you do that! You don't want them to think we're too excited about their being here!"

Caroline laughed nervously, a pained expression on her face. "Okay, but how do I stop 'jittering'?"

"Just calm down and try to act natural. After all, there are other men looking at the displays," Carrie reasoned with her friend.

"Who cares?—If I have to stick my finger in *my* cake, Wade is going to know for sure which cake is mine." Caroline glanced in Mrs. Westing's direction,—"rule or *no* rule."

Carrie cleared her throat, warning her friend that the men were coming within earshot.

Cooter ignored the baked goods and made a beeline for the girls. He stopped directly in front of them and yanked his hat off. "I see you two made it." He looked from one to the other beaming. "I guess you got those cakes, and whatever, made; didn't ya?"

So much for being 'subtle' about it, Jake growled to himself. Standing a few feet behind Cooter, he watched the exchange, doing his best not to stare at Carrie. She glanced his way a couple of times, but swiftly averted her eyes.

Are you going to stand here like a tongue-tied fool, or are you going to speak to her, Jake scolded himself. *After all, this is what you came for— might as well wade into the water.* He breathed deeply and took a small step in Carrie's direction, removing his hat as he did so. However, before he could say anything, Cooter chimed in and bluntly asked, "Which ones did ya'll bake?"

The girls glanced at each other, a troubled look on their faces. It was Carrie who answered, "We can't tell you that, Wade, Mrs. Westing made a new rule." She raised her eyebrows. "The cakes, pies and cookies are all numbered. According to her," Carrie motioned with her head toward the woman, "it is more 'fair' to all you young men that way." She smiled prettily.

Jake stopped breathing. If he hadn't seen her smile for himself, he would never have believed that a full-grown woman could look so angelic…and sweetly pure. Not being able to help himself, he silently prayed as he had before…*Lord; please let me have a chance to win her.*

Caroline spoke up. "After all, we don't want you fellows to feel obligated." She stressed the words, "to buy any certain girl's cake, just to keep from hurting her feelings. Mrs. Westing thinks you should be able to pick the cake that looks the best to you."

Jake was thinking as she spoke, *I don't care if Carrie made a 'mud-pie' and set it on the table…I want it!*

Cooter dragged his hand down the front of his face with a groan. "You mean to tell me that one of 'em is Trudy Westing's…and we don't know which one?" He added, "Talk about fair!"

Caroline giggled and Carrie caught her bottom lip between her teeth. Her friend continued to speak for both of them, "I guess you'll just have to try to figure out whose is whose. That is, if you want to buy any certain girl's cake or cookies." It was plain to see that Caroline was enjoying Cooter's dilemma.

Jake turned his attention back to Carrie. This time, she was smiling up at him. *Now's the time!*

"Miss Stoddard, my name is Jacob Galloway. My friends call me Jake," he said, holding his hat awkwardly with both hands.

Carrie extended her small, soft hand. "I know who you are, Jake. Caroline told me." She allowed Jake to take her hand in his before saying further, "I'm glad to finally meet you."

He grinned sappishly at her. His brain turned to mush. *'She said she was glad to 'finally' meet me.'*

Several moments of awkward silence followed before Jake realized he was still holding her hand. He dropped it quickly, as if it were burning him.

Carrie stuck her tongue in her cheek and looked away.

Cooter was more than a little distressed by the idea that he and Jake might get stuck with some of the other girls' cakes; in particular, Trudy

Westing's. He blurted out to both girls. "Can't you even give us a *little* hint about which cakes are yours?" His eyes darted back and forth between the two young women. Jake listened closely.

Caroline pretended to pat her hair. "Oh…I suppose it wouldn't be too much against the rules to tell you that." She hesitated and Cooter leaned closer. "I like Blue Bonnets and Carrie likes Sunflowers." She winked.

Cooter's mouth snapped shut and he frowned. "*What*—does that mean?"

"That's all I'm going to tell you." Caroline answered with a chuckle. "You figure it out."

Unnoticed by the foursome, Mrs. Westing edged close enough to hear what was being said. When she picked up on Caroline's 'hint' that Carrie liked Sunflowers, she smiled smugly, giving a quick nod as she turned around. She moved determinedly to where her daughter was lounging lazily against one of the pavilion columns. "Trudy, give me that kerchief-collar you have on," she demanded.

The bandanna-like collar, popular as a trim to an otherwise plain dress, was dyed Ecru and trimmed around the edge with miniature Sunflowers!

Trudy's brows came together. "But Mama, you said it brings out my brown eyes."

"I don't care what I said! Give it to me, girl!" Mrs. Westing answered with a no-nonsense tone of voice. Trudy untied the knot and her mother snatched it from her hand and moved quickly in the direction of table number one.

* * *

Jake touched the brim of his hat to the girls. He pulled Cooter away to a discreet distance. Turning his back to the women, he murmured, "Cooter, there has to be some sense to what Caroline said. Let's just walk along the displays and look for something that fits the clue."

Cooter thought a moment and then exhaled as he moved toward table one. "I reckon that's *all* we can do," he moaned.

Caroline and Carrie watched them with great interest. So was Mrs. Westing. To have a man like Jacob Galloway *or* Wade Marshall buy her daughter's cake would, indeed, be a "feather in Trudy's cap".

* * *

"Here you are! I've been looking all over for you, Miss Carrie!"

Carrie whirled around to find Charlie Wilson standing there, a big, silly grin on his face.

"I'da been here sooner, but I had to fight ole man Carson for my lucky number in the bronc-riding competition. I got it though!" He waved the tag triumphantly.

"Number one! That's me!" He guffawed loudly.

Caroline watched as Carrie's hands clenched as she listened to the blowhard. Luckily, the fists were hidden from Charlie's view in the folds of Carrie's skirt.

Charlie leaned toward the girls conspiratorially. "I heard you can't tell anyone which cake is yours. So…if you'll just give me a *good* hint…I'll go make sure to make mine the highest bid." He winked.

Carrie reminded herself not to flinch.

Before she could answer Charlie, Caroline rescued her by smiling sweetly at the obnoxious man. "You know how shy Carrie is, Charlie, but I'll be glad to help you out. I have a *good* hint!"

Looking this way and that to make sure no one else was listening, she leaned toward him.

"The Bible says… 'The' first' shall be last and the last shall be' first'." Caroline deliberately stressed the word first both times.

Charlie's eyes squinted in thought. "First, huh?" He turned and walked along the line of baked goods toward the 'first' display table.

"Caroline Hartman! You deliberately misled him," Carrie scolded between soft sniggers. Caroline's look was, for a moment, wide-eyed and innocent—then she dissolved into giggles.

"That I did, Carrie,—that I did." Her expression changed to 'almost' serious. "It wasn't exactly a fib. He wanted your cake 'first' and we are on the 'last' table."

Carrie turned and walked away to keep from making a spectacle of herself.

Searching for Cooter and Jake with her eyes, Caroline saw that Wade was trying to get her attention. He pointed to a cake on table number one, raising his brows in a silent question.

Caroline followed his point to the cake he indicated. Her mouth dropped open in astonishment. It was Trudy Westing's big, white creation!... And it was setting on a *Sunflower* trimmed scarf! Recovering quickly, she looked anxiously into Cooter's eyes and shook her head slightly—no.

Cooter was puzzled. He pointed to the cake again and raised his brows again. Caroline re-signaled that it was *not* Carrie's cake.

Shrugging, Cooter turned to Jake, standing behind him. "She says that ain't Carrie's cake."

He scratched his ear. "Beats me, it's settin' on Sunflowers. I just knew that was the one; but—come to think of it—where's the Blue Bonnets?"

Jake was also surprised. He glanced at the girls and saw that Carrie had turned away. His eyes locked with Caroline's. She lifted her hands palms-up and wagged her head back and forth. "So much for clues," he murmured.

Suddenly, he was aware of eyes on him. Lifting his sights across the table, he found himself looking into a toothy smile. Trudy Westing!

Trudy dropped her eyes to the big white cake and smiled even wider.

Jake swallowed hard and grinned weakly at the homely girl. *Thank you, Caroline!*

* * *

Carrie returned to her best friend's side. "I don't think they're looking very hard, Caroline. Sunflowers and Blue Bonnets are not *that* hard to spot."

"They are when there's more than one bouquet on the table," Caroline snorted and motioned with her head. Carrie followed her nod and was shocked to see cake number 'one' setting on Sunflowers!

"Wha…How did that happen," She stuttered.

"I think a certain 'matron' around here has big ears," Caroline replied disgustedly.

* * *

Jake and Cooter moved on down the display table, licking their lips as they went. "There sure is some good-lookin stuff here," Cooter muttered.

"Not good enough—not until I see some Sunflowers and you see some Blue Bonnets," Jake said firmly.

They reached the third and last table. On the front left-hand corner of it sat a bright red pottery bowl filled with delicious looking, sugar-coated cookies.

Jake motioned to the cookies with the back of his hand. "I know those can't be Carrie or Caroline's, but if I had to settle for something else—which I have no intention of doing—those cookies could be awful tempting." He turned to his friend, his eyes gleaming merrily."No telling *what* comes with'em."

Cooter stared at the small round treats for a second, then he scanned the group of girls. "If I was a gambling man—which I ain't—I'd bet those are what's called 'Mexican Wedding' cookies…and," he motioned with his head, "that little Senorita rite yonder made 'em." Jake looked in the direction of Cooter's nod.

"Whoa now," he said softly. "That wouldn't be so hard to take—winding up with her on your arm at the end of the day."

He glanced sideways at his friend. "Except, she's too young—*and* she's not Carrie or Caroline; right?"

"Right—she's not quite seventeen and besides that, I think Joel's got his eye on her."

"Concho's Joel?" Jake sounded surprised. "Well, there's nothing wrong with his eyes."

Cooter chuckled. "Oh she's purty alright, but he knows he'll have to be *real* respectful around her. That's Manny's kid sister."

THE SILVER CONCHO: LIFE IS A RUB-BOARD

* * *

Carrie continued to watch Jake's progress along the display tables. When he stopped in front of the Mexican Wedding cookies, she held her breath. "I hope he doesn't figure out who made those," she whispered. A few moments later she saw him lift his eyes to the beautiful Mexican girl. She groaned.

Almost immediately, Jake moved on. Now he was getting near her cake and he hadn't bid on anything yet. Maybe…

Jake was discouraged. The only Sunflowers he'd seen were—he was pretty sure—under Trudy Westing's cake. He shuddered.

"What's the matter," Cooter asked when he saw Jake's small, involuntary movement.

Jake answered softly, "Somebody just walked on my Grandpa's grave." He sobered. "Looks like we're just gonna have to make a wild guess and…" Stopping mid-sentence, a broad grin spread across his lips. "Cooter, look at numbers seventy and seventy-one."

Cooter scanned the numbers lying in front of the cakes.

Number seventy was a big, chocolate-iced cake. It was setting on a round cake platter with a border of Sunflowers! Next to it, number seventy-one was a three-layered, vanilla cake with creamy white icing. It too sat on a round cake platter, but sported a border of Bluebonnets! The men looked at each other and nodded.

Looking toward the girls, Jake thought he had caught Carrie watching but she turned her head so quickly he couldn't be certain.

"Come on! Let's go put in our bids." Jake turned toward the bids table. Cooter reached out and grabbed his arm.

"Wait a minute! The girls also made cookies and I think those two plates that match the ones the cakes are on are theirs too." He looked at his friend with a sly grin. "I don't know about you but, at the end of the day, I want the whole 'enchilada'!"

Jake's smile broadened. "There's something else to think about. Charlie Wilson's down there looking the goods over. If he sees me bidding on number seventy, he'll try to out-bid me no matter how much I'm willing to spend." He worried his bottom lip with his teeth. "Let's just hold back and let him be 'first' like he brags he is. If he figures out which cake is Carrie's, I *will* out-bid him."

Cooter assented nervously, "Ok, but I sure hope he don't get the idea that Caroline's cake is Carrie's." He lifted miserable eyes to Jake. "His old man is one of the richest ranchers in these parts. *I* can't out-bid him."

Jake beamed at his friend, "Yes you can."

* * *

"*The first shall be last and the last shall be first.*"

Charlie Wilson stared at cake number one and muttered under his breath. He looked around for Caroline. She was smiling at him. "This *has* to be it. My lucky number is one and this is table one and that's cake number one." His expression changed to one of arrogance. "First!"

Marching confidently over to the small table where Mrs. Westing sat receiving bids, Charlie eyes twinkled. He announced, "I've made my choice, Ma'am. Cake number 'one' is so purty it *had* to made by the purtiest girl in Texas." He plopped down two five-dollar gold pieces. "I bid 'ten dollars' on cake number 'one'."

Mrs. Westing's mouth dropped open in surprised delight, "Mister Wilson! That is so gallant of you!" She reached for his money and deposited it in the cash box, then recorded Charlie's bid beside cake number 'one'.

Lifting her eyes coyly to a 'much-pleased-with-himself' Charlie, she added, "I'm sure you won't be disappointed."

Charlie reeled away from the table and walked straight for Carrie and Caroline.

Having observed the whole transaction, Caroline elbowed Carrie and whispered hastily, "Here comes Charlie, act pleased!"

"Miss Carrie! I told you that number one was my lucky number. You knew that when the cakes were numbered. Didn't you?" Not waiting for her response, he continued, "It's *your* lucky day too."

Then he cut his eyes at Caroline. He crowed, wagging his head as he spoke, "The first shall be last and the last shall be first." He nodded politely. "Thank you, Miss Caroline."

"Oh, you're welcome, Mister Wilson."

Charlie sauntered over to Jake and Cooter, a condescending smile on his face. "Jake! Glad to see you here this year!" He snapped his fingers, pretending to remember something. "Oh! That's right—Matt's gone! You won't have to compete with your 'little' brother—will you?"

He leaned closer. "If you're lookin' to bid on a certain purty girl's cake, you're too slow—again."

As he turned to walk away, he called over his shoulder, "I warned you that I was number one! You can't change fate."

Jake somberly watched Charlie swagger away. After a few seconds, he and Cooter looked at each other. "All I can say to that, Cooter, is…" His face positively burst into a brilliant smile. "Charlie is happy, you're happy, I'm happy and," by that time he was laughing so hard he had trouble finishing the sentence. "Mrs. Westing is *very* happy." They chuckled all the way to the bidding table.

"Mrs. Westing, if you please, I'd like to bid ten dollars 'each' on numbers seventy and seventy-two. My friend here also wants to bid ten dollars 'each' on numbers seventy-one and seventy-three."

A delighted Mrs. Westing took the money for their generous bids. This was a red-letter year for the rodeo bake sale. Yes sir—a red-letter year!

CHAPTER TWELVE
On with the Rodeo!

It was approaching the ten o'clock starting time and rodeo officials were calling the competitors to begin preparing for their events.

The rodeo official's box sat high above the bleachers where fans sat. Several large megaphones lined the window of the five by fifteen-foot room.

One of the announcers shouted into a microphone, "If you intend to compete in any or all events in this rodeo, you have ten minutes to sign-up, pay the entry fee and receive your number. Make sure your number is securely attached to the back of your shirt." He continued, "When your competition event is announced, go immediately to the chutes area. If we call your number and you are not ready—you will forfeit that round." He chuckled, "All you cowboys know how hard it is to make-up a 'zero' round." Fans and competitors alike laughed.

The rodeo band struck up a lively rendition of "The Yellow Rose of Texas".

August, in Texas, is a very hot month and 'King Sol' was living up to his reputation; but a spirit of excitement permeated the crowd and no one minded the heat.

"Here—pin my number on...then I'll pin yours on." Cooter withdrew the folded paper square from his shirt pocket. After smoothing the creases out of it by dragging it back and forth across the leg of his jeans, he held it out to Jake.

"Pin it with what," Jake asked. "I don't have a pin."

"Oh…Oh yeah…" Cooter fumbled in his pocket again. "Mister Carson had a bowl of safety pins on his table. I got us both one." He handed both of them to Jake.

Jake's big, work-calloused hands fumbled with the pin.

"Let me do that," said a feminine voice behind Jake. He turned to find Caroline smiling up at him. Carrie stood close by watching.

Caroline took the, number five square and the safety pin. She turned a grinning Cooter around and proceeded to attach his number on the back of the yoke of his shirt.

Suddenly, Carrie stepped forward. "Would you like for me to put yours on," she asked shyly. The thought of her hands on those broad shoulders did things to her insides.

Jake's smile was soft and friendly. "I'd like that very much…if you don't mind. He handed her the numbered square and a pin, then turned his back to her.

Carrie stood for a couple of seconds visualizing exactly where the number should go. She had not realized before just how tall Jake was. It would be dangerous to try to work the sharp pointed pin through the yoke of his blue chambray shirt without placing her hand between the material and his skin.

Rising up on her tiptoes, she slid her hand inside his collar. With her fingers splayed, she carefully placed the paper, which she had speared with the pin, in the right spot. She eased the point through the yoke, deliberately shielding his skin with her hand. Hooking the pin back to the outside, she secured the pin's latch and withdrew her hand.

"There; that should hold," she said softly, as she smoothed the number against his back.

Jake felt like his knees had turned to jelly. He was sweating now, and glad he could blame it on the hot, August weather.

Turning back to face her with a strained smile on his lips, he murmured, "Thanks."

Carrie dipped her honey-brown head and smiled. "Good luck today ̧ ₒd…be careful."

Jake knew he was gawking, but couldn't seem to help himself. Carrie continued to smile and Jake continued to sweat!

Finally, he reached up and touched the brim of his hat. "Come on, Cooter. We need to go stow our chaps near the chutes."

"What did you call Wade," Caroline asked incredulously.

"Who's 'Wade'," Jake teased. "Oh—you mean this fellow." He jabbed a thumb toward his red-eared friend. "I've never known him as anything but 'Cooter'. His mother calls him that." He grinned at the object of their discussion and grabbed an arm.

They could hear the girls howling with glee as they walked away.

"Did you *have* to do that," Cooter groused.

"Yep, might as well break'er in right."

* * *

The rodeo began with the band sitting on a wide-bed wagon, leading a parade around the perimeter of the arena while it played, 'Deep in the heart of Texas'.

Little 'cowboys' and 'cowgirls' led calves, goats, ponies, and a couple of show hogs behind the band, followed by the older competitors riding in pairs on horseback.

Carrie watched from the stands with Caroline. Carrie's father was the rodeo's official doctor. He positioned himself near one of the gates for easy access to the arena should the need for his services arise.

Carrie waved at participants who raise their hands while passing her section of the stands, but it was Jake that she was anxious to see.

Some of the riders were real 'clowns'. They thoroughly enjoyed whooping, waving their hats, and belting out Texas yells. "Yaaaa-hooo." Rodeos were always so much fun to Carrie, but never as exciting as this one.

There he was! She watched intently as he approached the curve in the fence near her. Not one of the rowdy ones, Jake's demeanor was one of quiet, self-assured, gentle strength. His slight, almost embarrassed smile bespoke a surprising shyness.

Carrie jumped when she heard his name called from behind her in the stands, "Hey, Jake! Win one for me!" A gale of giggles followed the bold female's demand.

Jake's face reddened, but he did not look up.

Just as Wade and Jake came directly in front of them, Carrie nearly fell off her seat when Caroline stood up waving and calling, "Go get'em, Cooter!"

Wade Marshall was *not* shy. He grabbed his hat and waved it in a circle above his head. "You got it, Caroline!" People around them roared with laughter.

Jake's deep-blue eyes locked with Carrie's. His smile widened as he tipped his black Stetson with sunlight bouncing off the silver Conchos. Carrie's breath caught. Never had she even imagined that a man could be *that* good-looking.

A few more pairs of riders had passed before Carrie received another shock. "Hey Miss Carrie," Charlie Wilson shouted, "Number one! Remember!"

He pointed to the number pinned to his shirt. Carrie smiled politely, but under her breath she muttered, "That's what you think, Charlie."

* * *

The next hour was filled with children's events. First, four youngsters ranging in age from five to eight led their goats and other animals into the arena to be bid on. Goats were not the preferred grazing animals in that part of Texas, and usually wound up on the barbeque spit at some large gathering.

However, one little six year-old boy, Travis Shooks just couldn't stand the idea of his 'Billy' being eaten. When Senor Lopez, the highest bidder, entered the arena to take possession of Billy, the child began to tug fiercely on the goat's lead-rope and back toward the exit gate. "No! No!" Little Travis screamed.

Johnny Shooks, Travis' father, ran to the little boy and knelt down beside him. "What's the matter, son?" The child was sobbing hysterically, "I don't want 'em to eat Billy! He's my friend!"

Johnny lifted his eyes to Senor Lopez. The kind old man also knelt down in the dirt beside the little boy. "You can keep the goat, Nino. I weel geeve the money to the rodeo prize even so."

Johnny extended his hand to his Mexican neighbor, "Thank you, Lopez. I had no idea Travis was that attached to the goat. I'll be bringing you a hindquarter of beef as soon as colder weather gets here. In the meanwhile, I have a good laying hen that I want you to have."

"Gracias Senor," Mr. Lopez said and looked down at the boy just as the child raised his little arms for a hug. The crowd applauded its approval of the tender exchange.

* * *

During the remaining children's events, Carrie kept recalling the feelings she had experienced when little Travis Shooks howled his reluctance to let 'em eat 'Billy'. Though she was a young, unmarried woman, she quickly recognized them as 'motherly'. Her eyes widened with the realization that someday she hoped to actually *be* a mother.

Then her capricious heart took the possibility one step further. Almost against her will, her thoughts leaped to the next question. *What would it be like to have Jake's child; a little boy that looked just like his father.* Carrie's face heated and she fanned herself with her hand. Caroline turned her head and smiled. "It is hot today isn't it?"

"Yes. It is."

* * *

Bull-riding was first on the schedule of adult events.

The combination of crowd noise, booming bass drums, yells of fans and contestants, as well as various sounds from excited animals were tremendously agitating to the huge, untamed bulls. Some of them weighed upward of two thousand pounds. It required high, strong fences to keep them from running wild. For that reason, the owners of those bulls wanted to get the bull riding over with and move their animals away from the noises.

Jake was partial to this event, mainly because it was considered to be the most exciting and most dangerous. Once the chute opened and the bull with rider aboard stormed into the arena, it became a matter of, "do-or-die", man against beast. The rider never knew which way a bull would twist or jump.

Most of the bulls had never been in an arena before. They didn't have an established reputation on which the cowboys could base their strategy. A man just hung on for dear life, trying to last until the bell sounded, then scrambled desperately to outrun the enraged monster to the safety of the fence.

All of the bulls had a "style." Some of them bucked like a bronco; others twisted in mid-air trying to unseat the spurring, bouncing, yelling aggravation astraddle their back.

Once a cowboy hit the ground, whether by choice or chance, it was anyone's guess as to what a bull would do. He might trot away angrily, or he might seek revenge for your un-welcomed attentions by doing his best to gore or stomp you to death.

Normally, Jake would have entered this event, but the upcoming trail drive demanded that he tone down his fun and choose an event that wasn't as likely to leave him too sore to travel on horseback for four or five weeks.

He watched with great interest as rider after rider did their best to last the full time limit. The crowd thoroughly enjoyed the excitement connected with the man against beast struggle. When some hapless cowboy went airborne, people gasped and watched with a sort of morbid hope that he would get up quickly and make good his escape before the bull had his way.

When the first round was completed, eleven riders had attempted, but only four had lasted until the sound of the bell. The four finalists would face four "fresh" bulls in the next round. By the expression on their faces, Jake could read a mixture of excitement mingled with dread. One of the finalists was The Silver Concho's own Joel.

"Crazy kid—he doesn't have enough sense to know he could get himself really busted up. 'He's too busy trying to impress Manny's sister."

Still…Jake had to admit to a cautious admiration for Joel's spunk. He walked over to where Joel leaned on the fence and waited for the cowboy workers to load the chutes with four new bulls.

Placing a hand on Joel's shoulder, Jake watched as a particularly big, bellowing, red bull reared and kicked and made life miserable for the handlers who were attempting to sandwich him into a narrow chute so they could get the "bull rope" around him. Without that rope, a cowboy didn't have a prayer of staying on the beast.

"Is that the one you drew," Jake asked in a low voice, without taking his eyes from the ruckus in the chute. Joel swallowed and nodded. He stared at the animal like a man watching a nightmare.

Squeezing his shoulder, Jake said, "Well, just remember—either you can, or you can't. Somebody said, 'Never was a bull that couldn't be rode.'" He laughed softly. "And besides, it's not always the biggest ones that give the roughest rides."

Joel turned his head to look at Jake. "You didn't finish that saying. The rest of it goes; '…and there never was a cowboy that couldn't be throwed.'"

"I didn't finish it because it has nothing to do with you today." Jake winked.

Joel grinned slightly. He took a deep breath as he set his sights back on the critter. "I sure hope you're right, Jake…I sure do."

***

Carrie's eyes followed Jake as he made his way around the arena. Tiny flashes of light glimmered as bright sunlight bounced off the silver Conchos on his hatband. Only a person who was watching him very closely would even notice the sparkles of light.

Her face flushed. She glanced at Caroline to see if her friend had caught her staring at Jake.

Caroline winked. "Like I told you…he's something, isn't he?"

Carrie nodded quickly, her face red. Now she knew most certainly that she had been observed gawking at the handsome Mister Galloway.

Turning her gaze back to Jake, she watched in silence for a few seconds. "The more I see, and the more I hear…the more I think so." The two friends were silent for several minutes.

Finally, Carrie murmured, "I can't believe he's been here in Llano all this time and I didn't know him…or even know 'of' him."

"That is odd," Caroline declared, "because anytime the girls around here start talking about good looking men, the Galloway brothers are always at the top of the list. Of course, Matt was the more sociable of the two; but anyone who had ever laid eyes on Jake would have settled for either one of them." She giggled, then quickly nodded in the direction of the arena fence where Jake stood watching the activity in the chutes. Her face turned a pleasing pink as she commented, "But; like I said before, Jake and his brother are not the only handsome men who live on the 'Silver Concho'. Carrie smiled. Caroline had it bad where Wade Marshall was concerned.

Caroline grabbed her arm and squeezed just as the bell sounded. An announcer's voice rose above the noise of the crowd, "At this time, the final round of the bull-riding competition will commence. The first rider will be A. J. Cox, from the 'Three C's' Ranch, on a bull called 'Ugly'." The announcer chuckled. "When you see this critter, you'll know how he came by that name."

In a moment, the bell sounded again and the gate of chute number one opened as an angry bellow announced Ugly's rage at the audacity of the young man on his back.

The gate bounced wide open and a cowboy had to dodge out of harm's way to avoid the back hooves of the kicking, jumping, twisting bull. The crowd roared in delight when A. J. swayed violently this way and that, trying to catch the rhythm of 'Ugly'.

A bull-rider's chief aim was to "feel" the animal and become one with its movements if he expected to complete the ride. A. J. had another problem—Ugly's horns. The big brindle colored animal had a pair of mismatched, crooked headgear. The right horn grew forward, then curled up and back toward the rider, while the left horn grew backward and curled under and over toward the front of the beast's head. They gave Ugly a frazzled, untamed look, and he was bent on living up to that impression. His rough, stomping, bucking, jump made for a high-flying ride.

It looked like A. J. might make the time limit, when Ugly abruptly tucked his head, bent almost double, and tossed the young cowboy straight up. The audience gasped at the sound of Ugly's backward curled horn ripping the armpit of the cowboy's shirt. They held their breath as A. J. landed in the dirt, near the bull's ear.

With lightning reflexes, the young man rolled aside and jumped to his feet before Ugly located him, then A. J. leaped wildly for the top rail of the arena fence. Hoisting himself up and out of the way, he barely made his escape as the bull swiped with the forward curled horn at the spot where he had been.

The announcer yelled over the din of noise, "That's tough luck, cowboy. But, you've got nothing to be ashamed of."

The crowd clapped, stomped their feet and whistled in agreement.

It took a couple of minutes to convince Ugly to leave the arena. When he did, he did so with a loud bellow. "That's his way of telling us how much he appreciates being called 'Ugly'," the announcer joked.

"Now in chute number two, on a bull called 'Redeye', is Joel Ream from The Silver Concho' ranch. We've seen some good riders from this ranch in the past. Let's see what Joel can do with 'Redeye'."

At the sound of the bell, the chute gate flopped open. Whereas Ugly had announced his displeasure with a bellow, Redeye tore out into the arena like a tornado touching ground. He spun and doubled-back again and again—kicking up so much dust that the crowd almost lost sight of Joel, who was doing his best to sit tight. Next, the beast ran in short circles and changed directions so quickly that Joel's head snapped around like his neck was broken. Redeye spun several times, until he was getting dangerously close to the arena fence. It was not by accident. The ton-plus animal whirled against the fence in an attempt to rake Joel off into the dust. In a split second, Redeye turned back toward the rails and kicked his back-half up into the air, pitching Joel over the fence and into the stands.

Joel landed with a humph! The cowboy didn't move.

"Doc Stoddard! You're needed in the stands. That cowboy took a hard fall."

Carrie could see her father rushing to Joel while everyone held their breaths. She watched the spot where Joel had sailed over the fence anxiously. She could see Manny with his pretty sister standing behind him. The girl stood on her tiptoes trying to see around her brother's broad shoulders.

The doctor gently probed for broken bones and examined Joel for signs of head injury. After several minutes, they helped Joel into a sitting position. Doc bent and said something to the cowboy. Joel shook his head 'no'.

Next, Carrie watched as her father motioned to Manny and another man to help Joel to his feet. It took a few seconds for him to steady himself, but Joel lifted his arm, signaling that he was ok. The crowd clapped and shouted for him.

"He's a tough cowboy, folks. Just had the wind knocked out of him," the announcer commented with relief.

A bellow punctuated the air from chute number three as the workers loaded it with another raging, antagonized animal. Six men worked to get the 'bull-rope' on it. After several minutes, they signaled to the officials. The announcer raised his megaphone once more, "Ok folks, the third bull-rider finalist is Tim Langley, from the Rocking 'R' ranch. This man has been a top contender in this event ever since he was old enough to climb on a bull. For this round, he has drawn a Brahma named 'Outlaw'. Mister Frank Mullins, owner of Outlaw, tells us he had good reason for giving the big rascal that name. It seems that Outlaw thinks that fences, rules, laws and bones were all made to be broken."

While the official was speaking, Tim was busy strapping his right hand to the bull-rope and praying that it would be enough to keep him seated long enough to finish his ride. Shifting his position for a tight seat, Tim nodded and the bell sounded.

Outlaw jumped out of the chute and twisted in mid-air. He came down to earth on all four hooves with a bone-jarring thump! Tim felt like his chest had just been stomped, but he gripped the bull-rope with determination and hung on.

In the next few seconds, Outlaw opened and poured out his whole bag of tricks. Absolutely bent on unloading the man off his back, he reared straight up and appeared to dance on his hind legs for a split-second. All the while, his massive head swung back and forth, like a grandfather clock's pendulum in double-time. The instant his front hooves were back on the ground, he kicked the back ones out behind and corkscrewed his body so that Tim was almost sitting in a forty-five degree angle. Then Outlaw continued the corkscrew motion with hard back and forth movements.

Tim was getting to the point that he was certain his brains were going to wind up like scrambled eggs before this seemingly everlasting ride was over. Just then, the welcome sound of the bell reached his listening ears and he jubilantly released his grip on the strap. Stumbling as he landed on the ground, Tim looked neither left nor right, but headed straight for the nearest fence.

The crowd came to its feet in admiration for Tim's "gutsy" performance. Once he was safely ensconced on the top rail, he grabbed his hat and whirled it back and forth over his head, shouting 'Yaaa-hoo." Other cowboys imitated him, long and loud.

From the official's box, the announcer shouted, "What can I say, folks?—It doesn't get any better than that!"

After the noise settled down, there was a pause of activity in the chutes, so the band struck up a lively rendition of "Dixie".

Carrie and Caroline were having a wonderful time clapping to the music and swaying from side to side with others in the stands.

When the music ended, Carrie glanced to where Jake had been standing and caught him gazing at her. The expression on his face caused her to blush.

He must like what he sees, she thought, because there was a lazy smile on his handsome face. He suddenly reached up, touched the brim of his hat and nodded in her direction.

Carrie's heart jumped into her throat, but she calmly inclined her head in return and smiled brightly.

THE SILVER CONCHO: LIFE IS A RUB-BOARD

* * *

She has to be the most beautiful thing I've ever seen, Jake was thinking. *In my wildest dreams, I've never even "hoped" to meet a girl like her.* He couldn't refrain from the next thing he did. Dropping his eyes to the ground, he prayed, "Lord, if You haven't already got somebody else picked out for Carrie Stoddard, would you please give me a chance to win her heart. I promise I'd be a good husband to her—That is…if…she will have me. In Jesus' name, amen"

* * *

The music stopped and the announcer called for the final bull-ride. "The last ride in this event will be Jared Daniels on the "Three C's" bull called 'Misery'. Jared is another local boy who's a tough competitor. Well, Jared, after Tim's great ride, you've got your work cut out for you. What do you say, cowboy?"

From chute number four, the crowd heard Jared yell, "Let 'er rip!"

The bell clanged loudly and the chute gate flopped open, banging noisily against the arena fence. Misery charged toward the center of the arena, looking like he was in a rocking chair. His front end dipped low and his back end kicked high, then he reversed his tactics and reared high in front, while sidestepping his hind legs. He swung his sharp-pointed, straight-out horns to his sides, as if he were trying to gouge Jared's legs. When that didn't work, Misery began bucking in earnest. Jared waved his free hand wildly and spurred the bull's haunches for all he was worth. It was plain to see that this cowboy knew his business.

The bell sounded and Jared's ride was over. He released his grip on the bull-rope and threw a leg over the bull's shoulders, scrambling top-speed toward the fence.

But, Misery was not finished with Jared. He had his own ideas. The bull spun around and raced toward the fast-moving man in the red shirt. Jared heard Misery's hooves pounding ever nearer. He zigzagged to dodge the sharp wicked looking horns. Misery was at least part

Mexican fighting bull and he was determined to deal out some "miseria" in any language.

People in the stands were, by now, on their feet shouting, "Run, Jared! Run!" They stomped, clapped and yelled, trying to get the angry "Toro's" attention. One of the cowboy helpers was a quick thinker. He scooped up a clod of dirt and threw it hard at the bull's head. Thankfully, his aim was true. The lump of dirt burst as it hit Misery between his eyes; distracting the animal just long enough to allow Jared's escape.

CHAPTER THIRTEEN
All in a Day's Work

Cooter sidled up to Jake, a big smile on his face. "I reckon you're glad I talked you into coming in today—rodeos are a good way to kill some time." He struggled to keep a straight face. "Course, there are other good ways to pass time too." Leaning closer, he said in a quieter voice, "Charlie's over yonder braggin' about how he's gonna be sitting by the purtiest girl here when we break to eat."

Jake's hands sprang out of his back pockets. "When are we going to stop for dinner?" Cooter's grin broadened, "That's the best part…Charlie is signed up for the bronc-riding. I say, let's wait until he's in the chute, then we'll go over to where the girls are getting ready to cut all the cakes and such. We can put in our bids for eatin' with 'em before pore 'ole Charlie can get done with his ride."

Jake grinned mischievously, clamping his hand on his co-conspirator's shoulder, "Cooter, you're the best foreman a man could ask for. I sure like the way you handle things."

"All in a day's work, Jake…all in a day's work."

* * *

It took about fifteen minutes to clear the bulls out of the holding pens and bring the bucking horses in. The crowd listened to the band play, "Red River Valley" while they watched a young vaquero (cowboy) named Antonio Barahona do some very fancy roping.

Mexican vaqueros are among the best riders and ropers in the world. Antonio proved his prowess with a "lazo" (lasso). He roped everything from bottles to pottery and set them down on the ground without breaking a single one. Finally, to show he was just as expert with moving objects, he roped bundles of sticks, thrown into the air by his younger brother—plucking them from mid-air before they hit the ground. Last of all, he roped a big, red rooster that was shoo-d this way and that in front of him.

Jake stood watching the young man. He couldn't help but admire the skills of Antonio. Leaning toward Cooter he commented, "When he gets old enough to hire—assuming he wants a job, hire him. We could use him in a big way around branding and roundup times."

After a few moments, he glanced toward the stands again, looking for Carrie. When he spotted her, the smile faded from his lips. Two cowboys were just sitting down immediately behind the girls. They nudged each other and spoke out of the corner of their mouths, without taking their eyes off the back of the women's heads. It was plain to see that they were intent on getting Carrie and Caroline's attention.

One of the cowboys leaned forward and said something to Carrie. Jake watched intently as Carrie cut her eyes toward her friend without turning her head. Jake held his breath.

* * *

Carrie was aware of the two young men who noisily seated themselves behind her and Caroline. The cowboys pretended to speak back and forth to each other, but it was obvious that they were actually trying to get the girls to turn around. She ignored them until one of them leaned near her ear and whispered, "Do you want to know my name?—I sure wanta know yours."

Carrie's head snapped around. "Don't be a dunce, Alan Bonds! You've known my name for over five years." She gave him a friendly smile—"Tough luck on your bull ride."

Alan looked momentarily chagrined; his cheeks and ears turning red. But he quickly regained his smile and drawled, "Well…you can't win 'em all."

The rascal refused to be discouraged from flirting. "Hey, purty girl, why don't you tell me which cake you made so I can go outbid the others before it's too late."

Carrie's eyes twinkled. "It's already too late, Alan. You might have trouble out-bidding some of the others." She widened her beautiful emerald-green eyes and raised her brows. "The bids are *very* generous this year."

Alan turned his head to his brother. "Well, I swan—that blabber-mouth, Charlie Wilson wasn't just making noise after all. He said he made the highest bid on her cake. I took a gander at the list and Charlie bid ten whole dollars!" He chuckled, "You're right, Miss Carrie—this poor cowboy can't pay ten dollars for one cake." He winked roguishly. "But deep pockets don't necessarily make the best man. Do they?"

"You are absolutely right about that, Alan. They do not," she said, and honestly meant it.

* * *

"Ok, folks, we're ready to start the first round of the bronc riding competition. Fourteen riders signed up for this event. Only those riders who go the time limit will be qualified to compete in the second round. By the way—we'll stop the first round of bronc riding at half past noon for dinner. All those riders who have not had their first round ride will pick up the first round at two o'clock." He paused and turned his head to speak to another official sitting beside him in the box.

* * *

Jake turned away from gazing at Carrie and went in search of Cooter. He found him talking to some of the cowhands who signed up to ride broncs. Manny was one of them.

Listening to Cooter teasing Manny for a few moments, he stuck his hand out. "Don't pay him any mind, Manny. We all know you're the top rider around here." He dipped his head at the young man and wished him, "Good luck."

"Maybe so—maybe no," Manny said, flashing a white-toothed smile. "I am maybe good rider, but top rider?—Maybe only because Matt ees gone. No?"

Jake thought a moment before answering, "Maybe so," he replied, laughing softly.

Manny headed for chute four to get ready for his ride.

"Cooter, we better high-tail it on over to where the girls are." He pursed his lips and looked in the direction of the stands. "We may be too late, though—I saw the Bond brothers sit down by them and, from what I could tell, those boys were trying to be real friendly."

Cooter's eyes jerked in the direction of the stands. He squared his shoulders and huffed good-naturedly. "Well, what are we waitin' for? Let's go!"

Jake wagged his head and followed along behind his feisty friend.

* * *

The announcer lifted his megaphone once again. "The first rider is well known in these parts. Charlie Wilson was last year's runner up champion in this event. Matt Galloway, who is no longer around here, was the first place champion. Matt is off at West Point Military Academy becoming a Cavalry officer. We're mighty proud to have him representing Llano there." A lusty yell went up from Matt's friends. Jake swallowed hard.

The announcer continued, "Everyone knows that Charlie favors the number one. He told me the reason he likes that number is because it takes the best to wear it and that's what he intends to prove he is with this ride. Alright Charlie; here you go…on a horse named, 'Last Chance'."

Gate one flew open and the big red roan nearly cracked the middle bar of it with an angry kick as he lunged through the opening.

Charlie reached up and jammed his hat down more snuggly onto his head. His hand flew out in a crazy motion as he yelled, "Yeee-haaaa!"

The horse bucked wildly, whirling in crow-hopping semi-circles. Next, the animal reared straight up—So straight up that Charlie all but lost his seat.

When Last Chance came back down to earth, it was only for an instant. He began kicking his rear-end so high and so rapidly that Charlie was in the air more than in the saddle. He bounced crazily; nearly landing behind the cantle just as the bell sounded.

A young cowboy on a horse rescued Charlie, assisting him to the ground. Charlie's boots hit the dirt, then he took a step toward the arena gate. However, one of his knees buckled and it looked for the world as if Charlie had been drinking.

People clapped, hooted and yelled encouragement to the man who aspired to be number one. Somehow, it just did not ring true.

* * *

Jake and Cooter stopped at the bottom of the steps that led into the stands. They watched as Charlie completed his ride. When it was over, Jake shook his head. "Was he the only other man to ride against Matt last year?" Cooter's eyebrows nearly touched his hatband. "No. There were at least nine or ten others. Why?"

"Nothing," Jake answered and started up the steps... "Amazing."

Caroline leaned over and laid her hand on Carrie's arm, squeezing it as she nodded in the direction of the steps in front of them. Carrie turned her eyes to the bottom of the steps.

In all the years Alan Bond had known the Galloway brothers, he'd never known Jake to venture off the Silver Concho except on business. Well...once or twice he remembered seeing Jake at the rodeo, but it was very rare. Now, all of a sudden, he showed up, apparently with the intention of getting to know the two prettiest girls in town. Alan bristled. He was there first...and he wasn't leaving!

Jake stopped in front of where the girls were sitting. He noticed Carrie's flushed cheeks. The thought flashed through his mind, *Could it be because I sought her out again? Or is she annoyed at me for interrupting her conversation with Alan Bond?* Jake knew a moment of confusion and intimidation.

Caroline spoke up first, "Wade, ah…Cooter," she giggled, "and Jake! Are you looking forward to your event? Too bad it won't be until this afternoon; Carrie and I are anxious to watch you compete." Jake relaxed as he watched the twinkle in Carrie's eyes.

"What event did you sign up for?" Alan butted in.

"Hello Alan, Glen—it's been a while," he said with an amiable smile to his neighbor and, it appeared, his competition. Jake's smile and outstretched hand completely disarmed Alan.

Without being invited, Cooter lifted his booted foot, and stepped over the row of seats in front of Caroline and sat down to her left. "Thanks for saving me a seat."

Caroline's mouth flew open. She was delighted. Alan was not. His eyes snapped back to Jake to see if the big rancher would be as bold as his foreman was.

Jake smiled at Cooter's antics, but didn't move. After a moment, Carrie spoke up, "Aren't you going to sit down, Jake?" She scooted a little closer to Caroline, leaving a space on the end of the bench, to her right.

"Thank you. I think I will," he said softly as he lowered himself down beside her. Carrie's cheeks became even rosier.

Alan was not going to be ignored. "I guess you didn't enter the bronc-riding—'else you wouldn't be up here. Was Matt the only good rider in your family?" he pushed.

Jake turned to look at him. "No, I didn't enter the bronc-riding. Matt *is* a good rider, but I guess you'll never know whether or not I'm any good." He stared at Alan with an amused sparkle in his eyes. "Wade and I are signed up for the bull-dogging."

Alan couldn't say anything to that. He nodded and rubbed his nose.

Cooter leaned forward to get Jake's attention and nodded toward the steps. Jake glanced in that direction. Charlie Wilson was standing with his mouth open, gazing angrily at the sight of Cooter and Jake, plus Alan and Glen Bond sitting with Carrie and Caroline.

Uh-oh—last chance! Summoning all his courage, Jake plunged ahead, "Are you girls gonna eat dinner, or will you be too busy with the cakes to eat?"

"Oh—we'll go help cut the cakes and pies; but, when that's done, we'll be free to eat with everyone else," Carrie answered quickly. "Of course, Mrs. Westing will stay with the tables to make sure none of the kids forget their manners. It will be self serve." She looked at Jake expectantly.

From the corner of his eye, Jake saw that Alan was about to say something to her. He blurted, "Cooter and I would like to buy your dinners...if you would let us." He cleared his throat.

"Miss Carrie! I'm glad I caught you before you took off to cut the cakes," Charlie's booming voice interrupted them before Carrie could answer Jake.

"I'm planning on buying *both* of your dinners." He looked smugly at Jake. "Since I bought her cake, I thought I might as well enjoy it with her." He cut his eyes at Jake. "Don't you think so, Jake?"

"I'm sorry, Charles; but Caroline and I have already accepted Mister Galloway and Mister Marshall's invitations to eat with them."

There followed a full ten seconds of angry, glaring silence by Charlie. He looked back and forth between Cooter and Jake.

Cooter grinned from ear to ear and tipped his hat at Charlie. Jake passed the back of his hand over his mouth to hide his smile.

Finally, Charlie looked at Carrie and said, "I guess you *have* to be polite, Miss Carrie." He started to turn away, but muttered over his shoulder to her, "I'll see you in the center of the arena when I collect my prize."

Carrie wanted to laugh but, at the same time, she didn't want to deliberately hurt Charlie. She answered, "Yes Charles, I'll see you in the center of the arena." As Charlie turned away, Jake shoulders were shaking with hilarity.

Alan leaned forward, chuckling as he spoke into Jake's ear, "Well, at least I lost out to the best man." With that remark, the group burst into boisterous laughter. People all around turned to look at the six young people who were laughing so hard.

***

Carrie and Caroline left the stands to go help with the cakes. Jake and Cooter watched the next six bronc-riders. At the end of the first round, there were three finalists, including Charlie Wilson. Jake was amazed.

***

The pavilion was alive with pleasant, smiling faces. The two men made their way toward the bake sale tables.

"Hello, Jake," a familiar voice said behind him. Jake spun around, a huge smile on his face. He extended his hand. "Good to see you, Sheriff—it's been a while, hasn't it?"

The Sheriff chuckled, "Yeah, I think the last time I spoke to you was at the jail about four months before Matt left. He was not a happy cowboy when you came to bail him out."

Jake grinned, shaking his head at the memory. "No, he wasn't. But you and I both know that you slapped him behind bars for his own good." His face grew serious. "Did I ever thank you for looking out for him?"

Briscoe waved his hand, dispelling the "thank you" from the young man he respected as much as anyone he knew. "No thank you was expected. Anyway, Matt would have scalped you on the way home if you had thanked me for throwing him in jail. Especially since it was for no reason. He'da thought you and I were in cahoots." Briscoe was laughing by now.

"He might have," Jake answered.

Cooter had been silent up until then, "*Might have*, nothing! You'da had a circle-saw on your hands!"

Briscoe changed the subject. "So, what made you decide to come out for the rodeo? I heard your cattle was leaving for Fort Worth this coming Monday."

Jake shifted from one foot to the other. "The question isn't 'what' but 'who' made me decide to come into town."

The sheriff stepped backwards a step, his brows rising in question. Cooter leaned closer. "Doctor Stoddard has a might pretty daughter."

It was the sheriff's turn to be surprised. "So—you *did* meet Miss Carrie. She was ask…"

Embarrassed that he had almost betrayed a confidence, he muttered, "Nothing."

"She was asking what," Jake pried anxiously.

Briscoe's facial expression said he was trapped… He smiled weakly, "Jake…as I was telling Carrie the other day, I don't make it a habit of telling all I know about folks here 'bout."

Jake stared thoughtfully at the lawman who had been a friend to him and his brother since they were kids. After a few seconds, he decided to let it go. He nodded, "Good to see you, Sheriff. Cooter and I are on our way right now to eat dinner with *that* young lady and her friend, Caroline." He said sincerely, "Say a prayer for me—that I won't spill my tea or something. She has that effect on me." He touched his hat and moved on, with Cooter right behind him. They could hear Briscoe laughing and calling out, "I'll be sure to, Jake."

* * *

Carrie hurried to the bake sale tables. She left the stands right after Charlie stomped angrily away from where she had been sitting beside Jake Galloway. She smiled, thinking smugly, *Rather, where he had been sitting beside me.* A thrill coursed through her from head to toes.

An equally excited Caroline chattered all the way to the baked-goods tables about Wade 'Cooter' Marshall.

Mrs. Westing continued to play her game of pretending to maintain secrecy as to "who baked which cake or pie". "Carrie, you and Caroline stay away from your cakes. I'll have Senorita Lopez help you at table one. Trudy and the girls who baked the goods on table one will cut those on table two, and the other girls will handle table three," she ordered haughtily. "That should work out fine."

The older woman moved on to give instruction to the rest of the girls. They went to work and, in a short time, the sweets were ready to be self-served. Just then, the rodeo announcer called for a break until two o'clock.

Carrie and Caroline stepped a few feet away from the bake sale tables, but remained in the general area. Leaning toward Carrie, Caroline whispered nervously, "We don't want Wade and Jake to think we're avoiding them, do we?"

Carrie had already spotted Jake's black, concho-banded, hat moving through the crowd toward them. She watched as he and Wade stopped to speak with Sheriff Briscoe. Remembering the sheriff's "pyrite and pure-gold" advice, she whispered beneath her breath, "Thank you for your 'honest' opinion of Jake."

Caroline looked at Carrie with her brows raised, "Did you say something?"

Carrie's cheeks blossomed again as she answered, "No—just talking to myself."

* * *

Approaching the girls, Jake removed his hat and held it loosely at his side. "Are you ladies ready to eat?"

Carrie noted that his dark, gleaming, slightly curled hair was especially curly above his ears where his hatband had been. She found herself itching to reach out and run her hand through it.

"If you're ready—we're ready," she answered cheerfully, redirecting her thoughts.

"I could eat a horse," Cooter declared, a look of mock frustration on his grinning face, "But I think we're gonna have to settle for beef, chicken, goat or pork today."

Caroline wrapped her hands around Cooter's bicep and looked up into his face, teasing him, "Oh—You don't have to settle for either one of those. I heard Mister Hazel is frying up some rattlesnake…if you would prefer that."

Cooter's brows came together, pretending to consider the rattlesnake. Caroline's eyes widened. "But let me warn you, Wade Marshall…I don't want to eat beside any man who has that on his plate!"

Cooter wasn't going to let her out do him, "You mean to tell me, woman that you'd pass up good 'ole rattlesnake meat? It tastes just like the white meat of chicken!"

She shivered. "I don't care if it tastes like peach pie! I don't want to be anywhere near it!"

Cooter cut his eyes at Jake. "Can you beat that? This female don't know what's good—does she?"

Jake chuckled, dipping his head toward Caroline. "I'm afraid I have to agree with her, Cooter. I know there are those who will eat snake, but I'd have to be 'mighty'..." he emphasized the word mighty, "hungry to even take a bite of it."

Carrie smiled up at him. "Thank heaven!—We're going to be too late to get anything if you two don't come on," she said to Caroline and Cooter. She grabbed Jake's arm and pulled him toward the barbequed beef.

Jake allowed himself to be tugged along. "A woman after my own heart."

The two couples were served huge pieces of thick-sliced barbecued beef, fried potatoes, tomatoes and corn on the cob. They had their choice of buttered cornbread or Mexican tortillas.

Jake and Cooter paid for the meals. Then, with plates in hand, they each grabbed a glass of tea or lemonade and began searching for a place to sit. The tables were all almost full, but they managed to find one that was just being vacated in the far corner of the open-air pavilion.

Cooter turned to the others after setting his plate on the table. "Do you reckon me and Jake had better go and get our pieces of cake before the good ones are all gone?"

"Might be a good idea," Jake replied. He looked down at Carrie, a soft gleam in his eyes. "What can I get for you?"

Carrie smiled; "Whatever you're having."

Caroline looked up at Cooter, whose brows were raised with the same question as Jake had asked. "Whatever you're having," she mimicked. He nodded. "We'll be right back."

* * *

The men made their way toward the desserts. Carrie gazed at Jake for several seconds, then turned to her friend. "I can't explain it, Caroline, but…" she hesitated, "You know I don't make impulsive decisions…yet I have a feeling this is one of the most important days of my life. Something 'good' started when Jake bought my cake and cookies." She raised her brows. "Don't you think so?"

Caroline reached across the table and put her hand on Carrie's. "I sure do—and, I'm hoping that goes for me and Wade 'Cooter' Marshall also." She winked, then turned to watch the men standing near the desserts. "Oh my goodness," she gasped. "Look who's getting his dessert too!"

Carrie saw that Charlie was smiling widely at Jake and Cooter while motioning toward the tables. She glanced quickly around the pavilion. "Caroline, we have to get someone to take those other two seats at our table! Charlie will ruin everything if he sits down here!" Just then, she spotted her father and Sheriff Briscoe near the serving table with their plates. "Hold our places, while I run get Dad and Sheriff Briscoe to eat with us." Caroline's head bobbed up and down.

* * *

At the desserts table, Jake was attempting to maintain a somber expression as Charlie crowed to the delighted Mrs. Westing. "Yes, ma'am, Mrs. Westing, I'm glad I figured out which purty girl made this big white cake. 'Cause it's a double prize when a girl looks like her and can cook too!"

"Oh, Mister Wilson, you're so kind. But I guess we can't argue with your reasoning."

She put a hand on his arm and leaned closer. "I'm not prejudiced when I say that you are absolutely right! The girl who made this cake is indeed a young beauty." She smiled knowingly.

Charlie turned to Jake and Cooter. "…And I get to meet her in the center of the arena, *and*," he stressed, "I'll be asking her for the privilege of escorting her home tonight." He smiled deliberately at Jake and added, "Again."

Jake nodded. "Good luck, Charlie."

Charlie's smug expression faltered for a second. That wasn't the answer he had been expecting from Jake. Pursing his lips, he shrugged as he walked away.

CHAPTER FOURTEEN
A Friend at All Times

"Dad, hurry!" Carrie was urging her father and the sheriff toward their table.

Doctor Stoddard cut his eyes at Briscoe. "What's the rush, girl? We need to get something to drink before we sit down."

Carrie looked panicky. "Ok, but hurry! Plee-eese hurry!" They chuckled at her urgency.

* * *

Carrie, the doctor and Sheriff Briscoe moved toward where Caroline stood with her hands flat on the table, guarding the two vacant spots. She watched Charlie Wilson across the pavilion. He was stretching his neck, looking around. Caroline had no doubt as to who he was looking for. She glanced again toward the dessert table, searching for Cooter and Jake. "What's taking them so long," she muttered.

* * *

Jake shook his head and pointed to the chocolate cake on table three. "No, thank you, Mrs. Westing; I'm really partial to chocolate cake…when I can get it."

The woman's mouth looked as if she had tasted something sour. She shifted her gaze to Cooter. "And you, Mister Marshall—do you prefer chocolate cake also?"

Cooter held his hat in front of his chest with both hands. "No, ma'am. Since I bid on number seventy-one, I think I'd like to taste it."

"Very well," Mrs. Westing answered primly.

"Oh yes!" Jake was almost afraid to add, "Two of each, please."

* * *

Across the pavilion, Doc Stoddard tried to hide his amusement. His daughter was certainly anxious for him and Briscoe to eat at her table. It took only a few seconds to see why.

As he and John Briscoe seated themselves, Charlie Wilson barreled toward them through the crowd. "Hey Doc,—I see you and the sheriff are gonna be eatin' at your daughter's table. Since it's not full yet, I think I'll sit with you."

"I'm sorry Charles, but I think it 'is' full. We're expecting two others." He motioned toward Jake and Cooter's plates. "They left their plates to go for desserts." He smiled. "Sorry."

Charlie refused to take a hint. "Oh, I'll just find a chair and sit at the end, near Miss Carrie; if you don't mind."

"He may not mind, but I do," Jake injected from behind. Charlie whirled around. Jake's face bore a fake smile. "Tough luck, Charlie."

Carrie's mouth dropped open and the sheriff's eyes twinkled at Doc's surprised expression. Caroline, with eyes sparkling, popped her hand over her mouth.

Briscoe leaned closer to the doctor. "That's one thing I've always admired about Jake,—you know exactly where you stand with him. He never beats around the bush."

The doctor nodded thoughtfully. "I see what you mean."

Carrie's gaze didn't leave the two young men at the end of the table. She frowned. Was this what Charlie meant when he said Jake was used to "bullying" others to get what he wanted?

After a few tense seconds, Charlie said, "You win this time, Galloway." He turned away to find another table, but not before he heard Jake say, "I plan on winning, 'period', Wilson. That was 'your' last chance."

The girls looked at each other. Caroline thought Carrie's face revealed admiration for Jake's assertiveness and there was something else there that she could not quite interpret.

* * *

At two o'clock, the bronc-riding competition resumed. There were seven riders who had not had their first round rides yet. Manny Lopez was number eleven. Jake followed Cooter around the arena fence to see Manny before his ride.

They left the girls working with Mrs. Westing to condense the remaining desserts to one table, instead of three. First come, first served.

Mrs. Westing would probably have her hands full, trying to make sure that a group of four or five junior-age boys didn't make off with all the sweets. Somehow, Carrie had no doubt that the

Matron was perfectly capable of handling the task.

Jake joked as they made their way to the loading end of the chutes, "I have a word for Manny."

Manny was strapping his chaps on when his boss arrived.

Winking at Cooter, Jake said, "Manny, I came to tell you not to get out there and mess around. You'll be representing the 'Concho'."

The handsome, black-eyed man grinned from ear to ear and jabbed a thumb at his chest. "I do that, Jake. I weel show caballo who is boss. Si? I weel say 'Meester Caballo, you are been rode already.'" He hunched his shoulders. "I hope he weel beleef me."

Jake slapped Manny's shoulder. "You just *make* a believer out of him."

"Si, boss-man."

THE SILVER CONCHO: LIFE IS A RUB-BOARD

* * *

When Manny's turn came, Jake heard the announcer say, "Rider number eleven is a first time contender in the bronc-riding event. He usually rides the bulls. I talked to Manny Lopez when he signed up this year and he explained that he wants to help maintain the reputation of the 'Silver Concho' in this event. He aims to win! Let's hear it for Manny Lopez out of chute number one on a horse called," the announcer paused, "Get this folks…Diablo!"

The crowd yelled wildly. Manny was a favorite with all who knew him. He was an amiable, easy going young man and a capable ranch hand.

Jake thought; *I'm lucky to have him out at the Concho.*

When the chute gate swung open, Manny and Diablo made a noisy entrance into the arena. It almost looked like Diablo was going to kick the chute down. He was snorting and jumping before the gate was completely out of his way. Manny spurred expertly, so that the horse would buck the harder.

When the black mustang stallion crow-hopped away from the chute, his head was down so far that Manny leaned back and his shoulders almost touched the horse's high-flying rump. Then Diablo changed his tactics and began twisting his body and kicking his back legs straight out behind. He appeared to be trying to literary 'jar' the rider off his back as he repeatedly landed flat on all fours.

The noise from fans and cowboys sitting on the fence rails was deafening. "Atta boy, Manny! Ride 'im cowboy! Hang on, give 'im something to think about! Yahoo!"

The bell sounded and, for the second time that day, a rider received a standing ovation. Manny reached out and grabbed the arm of the rescue man who had ridden his horse as close to the still bucking Diablo as possible. Manny jumped to the ground, whipped off his hat and turned to the crowd waving it over his head. "Lo locre! Lo locre! (I did it! I did it!) Bravo! Bravo," at the top of his lungs. The band broke into a lively Mexican tune.

Jake was watching and when Manny reached the arena gate, his pretty sister met him. She threw her arms around her brother's neck, laughing and kissing his cheeks. Joel Ream stood nearby smiling, a wishful expression on his face.

The bronc-riding event lasted another hour and a half. When the last round was finished, six cowboys had completed their rides in both rounds. Now the rodeo judges would decide which of the riders received first, second, and third place prizes. These would be revealed at the end of the day. Both Manny and Charlie were among the six finalists.

* * *

Carrie and Caroline finished helping with the desserts, then hurried back to the stands. They were in time to see the final round of bronc-riding.

Charlie Wilson was back on the ground after successfully completing his second ride. He marched across the arena and climbed over the rails right in front of Carrie and Caroline.

As he started up the steps toward them, triumph was written all over his face.

Carrie groaned with exasperation, "I hate to hurt anyone's feelings, but he just can't seem to understand that I wish he'd go away!"

Caroline laughed softly. "I don't think you *can* hurt his feelings; his skull is too thick."

Sure enough, Charlie came and plopped himself down beside Carrie just as the rodeo announcer was declaring the final event of the day—bulldogging.

Some of the rules and stipulations regarding size, age and weight of all animals in the event were explained. Carrie did her best to listen above Charlie's constant interruptions. This was Jake and Cooter's event. She didn't want to miss a second of it.

"Folks, this event probably takes the most brute strength on the part of the cowboy. Even though the steers cannot be over two years old, some of them can weigh upwards of nine hundred pounds. That's a handful for any man, especially when the rules say that the steer's legs must all be pointed in the same direction once he hits the ground. I guess that's the reason there are only nine teams signed up for this event.

"Unlike the other events where the cowboy is racing against the bell, in bulldogging a man is racing against himself. He has to throw the steer in the shortest length of time and he has to do it right the first time.

"Each of the bulldoggers has an assistant called a 'hazer'. The hazer's job is to keep the steer, once it leaves the chute, from running away from the horse to its left. The hazer, like the bulldogger, has to know what he is doing. One more thing, I want you to watch the horses in this event. These animals are some of the best trained in the world."

* * *

Charlie spoke up, "I'm thinking, Miss Carrie, that Jake Galloway is gonna find out that he can't always win at 'bulldoggin'—be it a steer *or* his brother."

At that moment, Carrie knew that she had been as guilty as Charlie of misinterpreting Jake's actions. Jake wasn't a bully; he was a man who had, because of circumstances in his life, learned to ignore or overcome obstacles, and to keep working toward his goals.

Carrie had had enough! She turned her head sharply toward the obnoxious, would-be suitor. "Charles, I don't know where you get your information about the Galloway brothers, but I have it from several reliable sources that Jake and Matt had a difficult time growing up, *together,* on their ranch. I also heard that Jake was a hardworking, hard-driving young man who did his best for his younger brother."

She paused, trying to calm her temper, for she was warm to her subject. "Unless you saw it with your own eyes or Matt himself told you that Jake bullied him, I wouldn't be too quick to criticize. I don't know what, if anything, happened between those brothers…and I suspect that you don't either!" She stared angrily at Charlie's shocked expression.

Charlie was speechless. He hadn't expected Carrie to know

anything about Jake or Matt. He had to think fast or risk making her so angry that she wouldn't ever speak to him again.

"Ah…ah…I'm sorry if I upset you, Miss Carrie, but I was just saying what some of Matt's friends have been saying." He raised his eyebrows. "And…Matt *is* gone."

Carrie's expression became skeptical. "Charles, real friends do not try to widen a breech between brothers. They try to help bring reconciliation. As far as Matt's being gone…it was a once in a lifetime opportunity for him to receive a commission in the U.S. Cavalry. I can certainly understand why he would want to seize it…if he is bent that way."

"Yes, Ma'am," Charlie answered meekly. He paused a moment, then rose to his feet. Without looking at her, he said, "I think I'll go offer to help load the chutes."

Carrie didn't respond as she watched him move down the steps. "Good riddance!"

* * *

Jake was doing a slow burn. He watched Carrie and Charlie Wilson from behind the fence rail near the chutes. "No telling what that blabbermouth is telling her," he muttered to Cooter.

His friend stood with his forearms resting on the top rail. "She ain't gonna be fooled by Charlie Wilson; give 'er credit for more sense than that!"

Jake didn't look at him, but stood silent for another couple of minutes. Sighing, he turned away and murmured, "Come on—let's go put our chaps on."

* * *

The first three bulldoggers threw their steers in reasonable times, thirty-two, twenty-eight, and thirty-one seconds, respectively. But the fourth young man was dealt an unlucky blow and his time wound up being much longer than those before him.

Johnny Chandler and his hazer waited on either side of the chute gate for the large animal to be released. The young bull charged out of the opening and Johnny spurred his mount into action. The hazer kept the steer in a tight glove between his horse and Johnny's, which was exactly what he was supposed to do. However, at the instant when Johnny leaned over to grab the horns, the ornery critter decided to try to use those horns. He swung his head at Johnny's mount. The horse naturally shied, causing the young cowboy to miss the left horn.

Johnny managed to hang on to the other horn, but had a hard time regaining his balance or achieving the leverage it took to throw the animal to its side. His time was a whopping forty-three seconds—too long to be a serious competitor.

Carrie straightened her back and lifted her eyes toward the chute gates. Jake and Cooter stationed their mounts on either side of chute gate number five. Her heart raced at the sight of the big, handsome man on the sturdy, paint horse. The animal stood poised in anticipation.

Jake shifted his weight slightly forward in the saddle. He reached up to settle his hat more securely, yanking it down on his forehead.

"This one's for me, Jake," the same female voice Carrie had heard yelling during the

entrance parade called out to him.

Carrie had never before experienced jealousy. In fact, she had never been interested in any particular man enough to be jealous. At that moment, she knew *exactly* what it felt like.

* * *

Jake heard the woman's shout, but did not acknowledge it. Carrie Stoddard would not make a spectacle of herself by shouting across the arena—and he wasn't concerned with anyone else.

Caroline leaned sideways and laid her hand on Carrie's arm. "I wish Trudy Westing and those other flirty friends of hers would learn some manners. Don't you?"

Carrie nodded, then commented, "It's been said, Caroline, that 'empty wagons' make the most noise." Caroline squealed in delight, "Meow, Carrie!"

* * *

"Ok, folks, the next bulldogging team is Jake Galloway, owner of the Silver Concho ranch, and his foreman, Wade Marshall. I believe it's been about four years since we've seen Jake compete. His brother Matt was a regular for several seasons before leaving for West Point. Both the Galloway brothers are competitors. They're used to getting things done. How 'bout it, Jake? Let's see what you and Wade can do."

Jake and Cooter lifted their hats toward the official's stand. A mixture of Texas yells, whistling, and flirtatious encouragements went up from the stands.

* * *

On signal, the rope barrier was dropped and a cowboy slapped the large steer on its rump. The startled beast lunged forward full-speed. Jake was ready.

He heeled his mount in the flanks; the well trained cow-horse raced alongside the fast moving steer. Cooter's horse stayed right where it should have, a mirror image on the right side of the running shorthorn.

One…two…three…four…five; on the sixth second, Jake made his move. Kicking his boot out of the left stirrup, he leaned over to grab hold of the bobbing, waving horns beneath his right knee. Six…seven…eight…seconds…

Allowing the momentum of the steer to yank him out of the saddle to the ground, Jake landed with the heels of his boots plowing up the sandy ground. Nine…ten…eleven…twelve…the steer, a large, red shorthorn, probably weighing around nine hundred pounds, did not want to lie down. Thirteen…fourteen…fifteen…sixteen…

Jake's biceps and shoulder muscles bulged as he gave a decided twist to the horns and dug his heels in even deeper. The steer began to roll toward him with its front legs buckling to the right. The back end followed and the animal flopped heavily over on its side. Seventeen…eighteen…nineteen…twenty seconds flat!

Jake's arms flew into the air. Cooter's hat came off and he waved it as he rode in a circle around Jake.

Both girls clapped with glee. Of course, neither of them had doubted the abilities of Jake and Cooter, but it was so good to have Charlie Wilson proven wrong.

* * *

Jake led Guapo through the arena exit gate to the water trough. Cooter was waiting for him. "I don't want to crow too soon, but that was good time, Jake—the best so far." He grinned, laying his hand on the other man's shoulder. "Good work."

"Well, you handed him to me on a plate," Jake answered with a smile. He turned his head back toward the arena. "How many more bulldoggers are left in this round?"

"I think I remember the announcer saying that there were nine teams signed up."

Jake gave a quick nod. "I think I'll go watch the other four." He walked toward the fence, trailing Guapo behind him.

Cooter, intending to join him, happened to glance at three men standing near the loading end of chute number one. They were listening to Charlie Wilson. Charlie's back was to Cooter.

All three men saw Jake as he passed them. Cooter had no doubt about 'who' was the subject of Charlie's jabbering.

He sucked in a deep breath and strolled quietly up behind Charlie. One of the men in the group grinned at him as he approached. Everyone in Llano knew Wade Marshall was not only Jake Galloway's foreman, but also his best friend.

"That was just a fluke, I tell you. Jake Galloway won't be able to do it again—he's all show. Ya'all remember how he rode roughshod over Matt, don't you? I bet the only reason he showed his face at today's rodeo was because, now he won't be put to shame by his brother. Matt finally got enough of Jake's bullying. He probably left to keep from killin' him…"

Cooter's hand clamped down on Charlie's shoulder and yanked Wilson around to face him. "What was that you were saying about Jake being all show and a bully?"

Charlie's face paled. His mouth dropped open and he stammered, "I…ah…"

Cooter didn't wait for Charlie to answer. Through gritted teeth, he continued, "I ain't gonna flat-out call you a liar, Charlie. I'm gonna give you the benefit of a doubt and just tell you that you're badly mistaken. Jake Galloway is neither a big show, nor a bully. Him and Matt did have some problems, I grant you; but, let me tell you first hand that the problem was Matt's—not Jake's." He stopped speaking and glared at the red-faced blowhard for a couple of seconds.

"And, let me warn you about something else—you're purty brave to talk about Jake behind his back; but you might as well know that Jake ain't likely to call your lies a mistake, like I just did. I dare you to say those things to his face—unless, he's afoot and you're sittin' a fast horse when you do it. Believe me, he'll convince you right quick that he ain't got a bluffing, bullying bone in his body."

Cooter looked at the three men who had been listening to Charlie. One of them grinned with his bottom lip between his teeth, another rubbed a hand over his mouth, and the third one nodded with a wink.

Turning to leave, Cooter suddenly spun back around. "One more thing, Charlie; I don't really think you've got what it takes to face Jake, so let *me* make you a promise. If I ever catch you runnin' your mouth about him again… As his friend, I'll be coming on to you with both fists." Cooter added, "He's a better man than you can ever hope to be."

* * *

Jake turned his head as Cooter sidled up to the fence beside him. He noted his friend's red neck and splotched cheeks. "Something wrong," he asked.

Cooter looked at Jake's raised brows and made an instant decision.

He was not going to ruin this day for his friend by relating what Charlie had been saying.

Pursing his lips, he said disgustedly, "You know, Jake… I try to like ever' body—but, some fellers just can't be liked."

Jake chuckled, "Charlie Wilson?"

"Charlie Wilson."

CHAPTER FIFTEEN
Center of the Arena

"Let's give the band a round of applause for the good job they've done today!"

The band had just finished playing, "When Johnny Comes Marching Home" to the delight of all the Civil War veterans.

People were in high spirits and, as usual, everyone had enjoyed the fellowship, good food, and friendly competition with their friends and neighbors. The crowd responded to the announcer's call for a show of approval of the band with exuberant cheering coupled with loud clapping.

"Now it's time for the final round of this last event of the day—bulldogging. By way of reminder, these cowboys are competing for the best time. When the second round is over, the competitors will take their best time of the two rounds and it will become their final score.

"The time to beat, at this point, is Jake Galloway and his hazer, Wade Marshall's score of twenty seconds flat. Next highest score is Tom Joplin with twenty-five seconds, and the third best time is Bill Gibson with twenty-eight seconds. Ok, boys. Let's see if you can beat any or all of those times."

The second round of bulldogging began with a cowboy named Aubrey 'Buddy' Johnson. Buddy's score for the first round had been thirty-two seconds. He knew he would have to beat that if he wanted to be in the money-winner's circle that evening.

When Buddy's second attempt was over, he had improved his score by four seconds and was tied for second place with Bill Gibson. On the other hand, eight more teams had a second chance coming up.

* * *

Jake and Cooter watched as three more teams tried to best the top three scores—including theirs. Bill Gibson managed to shave one second off his first-round score. He was now in second place with twenty-seven seconds.

Jake and Cooter were already in place on either side of the rope barrier when the announcer spoke, "Alright, Jake, we're all going to be watching the clock to see if you and Wade can shave any time off your already fantastic score of twenty seconds…Lots of luck, boys!"

The crowd went wild. Men shouted and whistled, women stood up and clapped and Trudy Westing and her friends chanted, "Jake's the one…. Jake's the one."

Carrie had to fight a strong urge to turn around and glare at the brazen girls. Charlie Wilson was solemn.

Cooter looked across the twelve feet of space between them and nodded. "They're right about that—you're the one, boy!"

Jake grinned, shook his head and reached up to tug his hat down. "Let's get 'er done, Cooter!"

* * *

"Yee-haw," a cowboy shouted and slapped the rump of the big cream-colored steer. This fellow, Jake estimated, weighed about eight-fifty to nine hundred pounds. It leaped forward, just as the barrier dropped.

The animal was fast and had a mind of its own. It seemed to be headed straight for the exit gate.

Cooter kneed his horse to crowd the steer, forcing it to swerve more toward Jake's mount. One…two…three…four…five…six…seven seconds passed before Jake's mount was in position for him to grab the huge, u-shaped horns.

As in the first round, he kicked his left boot free of the stirrup and leaned low to the right—seven…eight…nine…ten.

Jake stretched to get a firm grip on the right horn, barely managing to grasp both of them at the same time. The steer threw his head back, trying to loosen Jake's hold on him—'eleven…twelve…thirteen…fourteen.

Jake was yanked hard out of the saddle when the beast bowed and twisted its neck—fifteen…sixteen…seventeen.

Plowing up dirt as he hit the ground, Jake muscled the steer's right horn toward himself. The animal tried to regain its balance; however, Jake's considerable strength coupled with the kind of determination he'd had all his life won out.

Just as the steer began to topple, it butted Jake in the chest with the curve of its left horn, causing Jake to fall with the animal's huge head against his upper body.

"Humph…hh!" The wind rushed out of him in a blinding stab of pain—eighteen…nineteen…twenty.

With a gargantuan effort, Jake rolled free of the beast and jumped to his feet with his arms in the air—twenty-one…twenty-two…twenty-three seconds.

"Yeeee-haw! Yeee-haw," Cooter galloped around the arena shouting.

Caroline leaped to her feet and threw him a kiss as he rode by.

Jake reached down to pick up his battered hat from the dust. It had flown off his head when the steer's horn whacked him in the chest. He saw with dismay that it had been crushed beneath the huge animal. Jake flinched…the hat had once belonged to his father, Thomas Galloway.

Carrie watched closely as Jake more or less hobbled out of the arena amidst the shouts and cheers. She could tell, even with the distance between them, that something was wrong.

Turning to Caroline, she grasped her friend's arm. "Caroline, I'm going down there where Jake is. I think that steer must've hurt him." She looked pleadingly at the other girl. "Go with me, please! There's nothing but men down behind the chutes."

Caroline's look of surprise quickly changed to one of concern. She grabbed Carrie's hand. "Sure,—let's go!"

* * *

Jake shuffled to a sawhorse used to stow saddles. He sat down and bent forward at the waist. Grimacing with pain, he tried his best to take a deep breath. It was as if an iron band prevented his lungs from expanding. Sweat beaded his forehead and upper lip.

Cooter stood beside him, helplessly. "Jake? What's the matter, boy? You look pale. Did that ornery steer crack some ribs?"

Jake shook his head negatively. He answered with short gasps of breath, "I…just think…he knocked…the wind…out of me. I'll…be alright in…a minute."

Carrie and Caroline came skidding around the end of the chutes, their faces drawn with concern. Carrie stepped in front of Jake and bent down so she could see his face. "You're hurt; aren't you, Jake?" Her voice was breathy from running.

Jake lifted his hand, waving it back and forth. "No…I just had…the wind…knocked out…of me. Give me a….minute…and I'll…be ok."

Carrie turned her eyes to Cooter. He saw that they were bright with tears. She raised her brows in question. Cooter dragged a hand down his face and shrugged his shoulders. It was plain to Carrie that he was worried too.

"Go find Dad," she said to Caroline. The girl nodded and ran quickly to find Doctor Stoddard.

Jake shook his head, "I'll be ok…no need for…the Doc."

Cooter squatted down before him. "Well, it won't hurt to be sure. You probably just got a bad bruise, but let's make certain anyway."

Jake didn't try to answer.

* * *

"Doc…Doc, come quick! Jake Galloway is hurt," Caroline's voice quivered as she explained rapidly.

The doctor instantly grabbed his medical bag and trotted behind the girl. She raced toward the loading area of the chutes.

They arrived to find Carrie and Cooter both kneeling down in front of Jake. He was half-seated, half-leaning on a sawhorse.

The doctor motioned his daughter and Wade to back up as he squatted in front of the man.

"What seems to be the trouble, Jake," he asked, all the while visually evaluating Jake's distress.

Jake lifted his head, wincing in the process. "Just got the…wind knocked out…of me, Doc…I'll be ok."

Doc Stoddard had treated many cowboys who had been thrown from horses or stepped on by bulls. He knew the signs of simply having the breath knocked out of a man versus cracked or broken ribs.

Jake's color and the beads of perspiration on his face spoke of more than a simple short-term loss of breath. Doc scanned the area, looking for something. "Wade, drag that bench over here. This boy needs to sit up straight so I can take a *good* look at him."

Cooter hurried to pull the eight-foot, wooden bench over to Jake. One of the other young men saw him and came to help. When the cowboy realized who it was for, he stayed to watch.

Soon others noticed the group around Jake and curiously drifted over to see what was happening.

"Now Jake, I want you to sit up as straight as you can and take as deep a breath as you can." The doctor was unbuttoning Jake's shirt while he spoke. He slid both hands inside the shirt and splayed his fingers against Jake's ribs.

Jake attempted to fill his lungs but, after only a short gasp, he gritted his teeth and closed his eyes against the pain.

"That's as deep as you can breathe?" The doctor frowned and ran his fingers over Jake's ribs once more.

Jake managed to nod. "It doesn't...bother me around...my ribs, Doc. It's the middle...of my chest...that hurts."

The doctor watched his face for a few seconds. Nodding, he stood up and placed a hand lightly on Jake's shoulder. "I don't find any broken ribs, but that doesn't mean you don't have a cracked rib or two. My guess is that you're badly bruised...or a rib is cracked."

He turned to Cooter again. "Go find him a straight-back chair. I saw some in the pavilion." Turning back toward Jake, he said, "We'll seat you someplace where you can watch the rest of the rodeo. Don't move around...don't talk. Let's just see if your breathing will improve in the next little while."

Jake nodded. He was sure he would have no trouble obeying the doctor's orders.

* * *

Cooter returned with two chairs in tow. "We can put these by the arena gate. He can see everything from there."

The doctor nodded and motioned for someone to help ease Jake to his feet. Jake waved them away.

Cooter ran ahead with the chairs. He placed them strategically behind a gate near the steps which led into the stands. Doc usually sat there for easy access into the arena.

While Jake was making his way to the provided chair, men who had gathered curiously were murmuring to each other about his possible injuries. Charlie Wilson had elbowed his way into the group to see if Jake was seriously injured.

As the men dispersed, he made a disparaging remark, mostly to himself, but unlucky for Charlie, someone else heard him when he muttered, "Serves him right...he got just what he deserved."

One second Charlie was walking back toward the chutes. In the next, he was flat of his back holding his jaw, a surprised look on his face.

"What was that you are saying Senor? You geet what you deserve; No?" Manny Lopez stood over Charlie rubbing the knuckles of his right hand.

* * *

Jake sat down carefully, keeping his back straight. It seemed to be the most comfortable position. Even at that, he found it difficult to take a deep breath.

Carrie followed right behind Jake. After he sat down, she turned to look at Cooter, who didn't miss the pleading in her eyes. He understood that she was begging him to allow her to sit in the chair beside Jake.

Cooter winked at her and grinned, inclining his head subtly toward the chair. "Jake, I think I'll sit right up there on the end of the row near the Doc—just in case you need something."

Carrie's smile was grateful as she quickly lowered herself into the chair next to Jake.

Doctor Stoddard was watching the subtle communication between Wade Marshall and his daughter. Somehow, he was not surprised.

With a gesture that seemed automatic, Cooter took Caroline's hand and pulled her along with him. They found two empty seats on the end of the second row, just above where Carrie and Jake were sitting.

* * *

When the bulldogging event was completed, Jake and Cooter's best time of twenty seconds was the first place winner. Tom Joplin won second place with twenty-five seconds and third place went to Bill Gibson with twenty-seven seconds.

Carrie sat quietly, covertly watching Jake. She made a conscious effort not to say anything that would require a response. It was evident that his breathing was painful, even though he tried to hide the fact.

* * *

The clock showed the time to be a few minutes after five o'clock when the rodeo officials mounted a flatbed wagon, positioned in the center of the arena. The Band Wagon was situated to the right of it.

"It's been a great rodeo. What do you say, folks?"

THE SILVER CONCHO: LIFE IS A RUB-BOARD

The people responded, as always, with hometown enthusiasm. After a few moments, the announcer raised his megaphone again. "That's what we like to hear. As long as there are cowboys—there will be rodeos!" His comment brought another wild round of whistling and clapping. The audience finally quieted down and the much anticipated awards presentations began.

"Before we start presenting prizes, your rodeo officials want to thank all the young ladies who participated in the bake-sale this year. Another special thanks also goes to the barbeque committee for the fine job they did with the other food."

"As all of you know, any man who competes in any event of the day has an opportunity to bid on the cakes and other sweets provided for the bake-sale". This year, Mrs. Marcia Westing was in charge. She chose to add a little mystery to the bidding. Instead of posting the names of the one who made the baked goods, she numbered them. It will be interesting to see if there are any surprises when the young ladies' names are called."

The announcer chuckled and wisely added, "Of course, you fellows are in a 'no lose' situation. We don't have anything but pretty girls in these parts."

"The first event of the day, 'Bull-riding' is the dare-devil event. Any cowboy who climbs aboard one of those animals is to be commended for his 'spunk', win, lose, or draw. There were eleven contestants."

The names of the seven men who were eliminated in the first round were called along with the names of the young ladies whose baked goods they had bid on. The couples met in the center of the arena and what followed was pure delight to those in the stands.

The first two young men bowed and kissed the hand of the girl bearing his certificate of participation. The next three men, possessed of more imagination, danced toward the girls, blowing kisses. The last two each fell down on one knee and pretended to propose marriage— a foolhardy thing to do, considering the number of witnesses.

"Now for the four bull-riding finalists; the first was A. J. Cox. This young man always does a fine job, but in the second round it was his misfortune to draw a bull named Ugly. You remember, he was the critter that looked for all the world like he was coming and going at the same time," He laughed at his own description. "But A. J. won't go away empty handed. He leaves the arena this evening with a ten dollar consolation prize and pretty Miss Emily Darst on his arm."

Emily entered the area smiling. A. J. was a timid young man, but not so timid as to miss the chance to plant a quick "peck" on her cheek when she presented his prize. The audience applauded his courage.

Joel Ream from the Silver Concho ranch is the next finalist to receive a consolation prize. "Joel was unseated by an ornery bull named 'Redeye'." The announcer chuckled. "But Joel came out the winner anyway, because he bid on a big bowl of Mexican Wedding cookies baked by Senorita Reina Lopez."

Moments later, Reina stood before Joel. He took her hand, bowed slightly and kissed it. He really would have liked to kiss her lips, but her big brother and her, very proper, parents were watching. Accepting the consolation prize of ten dollars, he placed a hand on her shoulder and ushered her through the arena exit gate.

There was a pause as the announcer conferred with the other officials. He nodded and raised his megaphone once again. "The two last finalists both made such spectacular rides that our judges were unable to determine a second place winner. Officials decided to combine first and second place prize monies and split it down the middle as two 'tie' awards. Tim Langley and Jared Daniels, come on out here boys."

Tim and Jared walked toward the official's wagon with the band playing, 'Oh Susannah'. They cut smiling eyes at each other and shook hands.

"I could just hand each of these fellows their prize money," the announcer teased, "but I suspect they'd rather it came from the hand of a young lady." He waited for the noise to subside. "Tim…to present your prize money is Miss Florence White."

Carrie smiled as her friend, Florence, nervously passed by her and Jake through the arena gate. The girl's legs were trembling so that Carrie was afraid she might faint dead away before she reached Tim. Thankfully, that didn't happen.

Tim could see that the girl was shaking, so he took the prize with one hand, and stepped closer to her, placing a steadying hand under her elbow. As they walked out of the arena, he held Florence's hand firmly against his side.

"Jared, that delicious peach cobbler you bid on—I know it was delicious because I had some of it for dinner—was baked by Miss Lydia McMullin. Miss Lydia, will you come present the cowboy with his prize money?"

Jared threw his hat into the air and caught it. "Yee-haw," he yelled as the pretty, blond girl made her way toward him. She received the envelope, then turned toward Jared with it held behind her back. She shook her head "no" when he reached for it. Tapping her cheek, she leaned toward the delighted young man. He obliged her with a kiss on her cheek.

"Nothing shy about her," Carrie chuckled. But then they're engaged to be married next spring."

As uncomfortable as Jake was, he lifted his brows and smiled in response to her comments.

What did he mean by that, Carrie wondered. Her next hopeful thought sent a thrill coursing from her head down to her toes.

Jake saw the high color flood her cheeks. He smiled again weakly.

* * *

"Fourteen men signed up for the Bronc riding event; six made the final round and three finished with both rides completed."

One by one, eight cowboys received their 'Certificates of Participation' from some pretty girl or girls. Sisters and cousins were not exempt from the bake sale. A few of the men bid equal amounts on more than one baked item. They received their certificates from 'co-awarders'. It was great fun for the younger girls to be allowed to participate.

The three men who were unseated in the second round received ten-dollar consolation prizes. As it turned out, no one seemed to have been '*mystified*' by the numbers instead of names in front of the baked goods—no one except Charlie Wilson.

* * *

"Three men completed both Bronc rides…Charlie Wilson, Manny Lopez and J. D. Kidd. Gentlemen—to the center of the arena please."

"Number one, Miss Carrie; remember?"

Carrie was startled when a voice spoke into her ear from behind. Her head snapped around to find Charlie grinning at her. His expression was unmistakably 'cocky' and it was plastered across his face from ear to ear.

Charlie shifted his eyes to Jake as he commented arrogantly, "You can't win 'em all, Jake." With that, he sauntered through the gate. Swaggering toward the officials, he lowered his head and pointed a single finger skyward.

Jake commented softly, "There'll never be another Charlie Wilson."

Nodding slowly, her eyes fixed on Charlie, Carrie sighed, "Thank heavens." She added, "I can't decide if he's full of misplaced confidence or if he's just minus….something."

* * *

Charlie, Manny and J. D. moved into place before the officials' wagon.

"These men were scored for their final ride in four ways—up to five points for 'form, up to five points for 'spurring the mount', up to five points for the horses 'bucking' and finally, up to five points for 'dismount'. That's a possible score of twenty for a perfect ride." The announcer turned to the judges beside him and received a piece of paper.

"For the third place prize of twenty dollars, the judges have scored J. D. Kidd at seventeen points."

J. D's friends and family whooped loudly and cheered. There was no shame in third place…especially when the prize money was more than half a month's pay.

"Miss Sue Clark… Will you please come forward to present this cowboy's prize money to him?"

THE SILVER CONCHO: LIFE IS A RUB-BOARD

The young woman blushed prettily as she received the envelope from the judges then turned to J. D. His eyes twinkled as he winked at her then bowed and gave a loud 'smacking' kiss to the hand that held the envelope. "Stay where you are J.D. Miss Sue," the official instructed.

"Second place prize of twenty five dollars, for a score of eighteen points, goes—for the second year in a row—to Charlie Wilson!"

Charlie was more than a little surprised and disappointed. His friends and family loyally cheered for him in the stands, but, at the same time, Manny Lopez's family and all the men of the Silver Concho, including Jake and Cooter, were celebrating with the realization that Manny had won first place.

Manny stood by quietly watching Charlie's reaction. He found himself pitying the loud, obnoxious fellow, in spite of how much Charlie deserved to be embarrassed because of his blatant bragging.

Holding up a hand, the announcer shouted, "Ok, folks!—Let's get on with Charlie's prize. Since Charlie likes the number one—he bid on cake number one and for his generous bid he will receive his prize money from the hand of the young lady who made it—Miss Trudy Westing!"

Trudy's friends clapped uproariously while she moved through the arena gate.

Charlie's head whipped around toward the announcer; a huge scowl distorted his face. He marched over to the edge of the wagon-stage where officials sat and whispered, "That ain't right! Carrie Stoddard baked cake number one."

The announcer scanned the bidding sheet Mrs. Westing had given him. He looked up at Charlie and shrugged his shoulders. "You're mistaken, Charlie. It says right here; cake number one baked by Miss Trudy Westing."

Charlie looked like he was ready to panic, but did his best to smile as he turned to face the, fast approaching, Miss Westing.

Trudy did not have a shy or self-conscious bone in her body. She walked briskly between Manny and J. D. to the judge's wagon, grabbed the prize money and turned to take a stunned Charlie's hand. She yanked him forward to stand next to Manny. Then, she proceeded to slap the envelope into Charlie's hand and planted a big kiss on his open mouth.

Cooter leaned toward Caroline, "Doesn't the Bible say…'Vengeance is mine…saith the Lord'?" His shoulders jiggled up and down as he silently chuckled. "I think Charlie just got a big dose of it."

"Wade Marshall! You're bad," Caroline whispered loudly, struggling to keep the bubble of laughter in her throat from bursting forth.

"Manny Lopez is this year's champion bronc rider with a perfect, score of twenty points." Such a roar of cheering and applause erupted that the announcer was forced to wait a several seconds. "Presenting Manny's prize will be his pretty little sister, Reina. This is Senorita Lopez's second trip to the center of the arena. Her cooking received double-bids by her brother and Joel Ream."

When she heard her name called, Reina made her way through the gate past Jake and Carrie. She smiled brightly at him, but Carrie tried to appear not to notice.

Manny seized his sister, bear-hugging her and waving the envelope in the air.

* * *

"Last of all…the Bulldogger-r-r-rs," the announcer drawled.

Six of the bulldogging teams came together in the arena with twelve girls who were called to present their certificates.

A veritable square dance broke out when one of the cowboys started a hand-over-hand trip down the line of girls, kissing their cheeks as he went. Not to be out done, the other men followed suit. The band started playing, 'She'll be coming around the Mountain'.

Jake watched the free-for-all out in the arena. He tried to smile but it was strained, for every time he attempted to fill his lungs the pain increased in the middle of his chest. If he leaned forward, it hurt or if he leaned back, it hurt. His body was telling him that his problem was more than a bruised rib.

THE SILVER CONCHO: LIFE IS A RUB-BOARD

* * *

"As you all know, the three best times in the Bulldogging event this year were: first place, Jake Galloway and his hazer, Wade Marshall with twenty seconds, second place goes to Tom Joplin and his brother, Mark, with twenty-five seconds, and third place winner is Bill Gibson and his hazer, Phil Knott, with twenty-seven seconds." People in the stands applauded and cheered.

Jake could hear the Concho ranch-hands yelling, "Number one, Jake! Number one, Jake!"

His smile was an embarrassed one when glanced at Carrie. She placed a hand over her mouth, admiration twinkling in her eyes.

Cooter appeared at Jake's side. "You gonna be able to make it out there, Jake?" Jake nodded, rising to his feet. "I'll make it…or die trying."

Cooter slipped his hand beneath Jake's elbow. "Here, let me help you."

"Cooter!—You wanta get us both laughed out of the arena?" Jake realized, too late, that he had spoken harshly. He shrugged regretfully and said softly, "Sorry…but, I *have* to do this on my own steam."

Cooter studied his face for a moment. "Ok, let's go."

* * *

The one hundred foot trek to the arena's center might as well have been a mile. Jake's chest throbbed and burned with every step and his head swam from shortness of breath. True to his nature, he was determined to complete his original goal to meet Carrie Stoddard in the center of the arena at day's end.

All six men exchanged handshakes; but it took only a few seconds to see that Jake Galloway had a problem with the gesture. His barely concealed gasp and the wincing so startled Tom Joplin that he took a closer look at the big rancher and muttered, "Jake, boy you better get off your feet. You look like you're about to fall down."

Jake's head shook slightly. "I'll be ok…Tom…Thanks."

The announcer raised his megaphone. "Will the following young ladies make their way to the center of the arena when I call your names, please?

"Presenting the first place prize to Jake and Wade will be Miss Carrie Stoddard and Miss Caroline Hartman." He chuckled, "I understand that Carrie baked more than one sweet for the bake sale...and...Jake outbid everyone else on *everything* she made. Likewise, Wade outbid all others on Miss Hartman's baked offerings."

The announcer was having a good time teasing Jake and Cooter. He continued, "Take a good look at these young ladies, folks. I think you'll see why it was more than 'good cookin' that emptied these cowboy's pockets."

Manny, Joel, and the other Concho hands whooped and whistled.

Caroline grabbed Carrie's hand and held it tightly as they walked, red-faced, to retrieve the prize envelopes. They turned around immediately and went to stand before Jake and Cooter.

This is why I came today—the sole reason for participating in the rodeo. Lord, help me not to let this pain ruin it for me—or her,' Jake prayed silently. His brow was dripping with perspiration and he could barely focus on the lovely vision before him. However, he managed to smile bravely when Carrie placed the envelope in his right hand. She took hold of his left one and stepped back to stand beside him.

Wade, as usual, had no inhibitions when it came to clowning around. He took the envelope from Caroline and reached for her free hand. Pulling it straight out in front of her, he proceeded to trail kisses from her fingertips up the length of her arm, over her shoulder, and up the side of her neck. He cupped her laughing face and planted a big kiss on each cheek. Throwing his hat into the air, he gave a Texas yell, "Yeee-haaah!"

Needless to say, the officials, the people in the stands, and the other men were howling in delight by then.

Cooter swung around, bowing to everyone several times. Then, he hooked his arm through Caroline's and led her toward the gate. Jake and Carrie followed.

* * *

Trudy Westing and her friends were closely observing the couples. Trudy smirked to the girl beside her. "I don't know about you, but I don't think Jake looks very happy. I think he thought he was bidding on *someone else's* cake—don't you?" The other girl's brows shot up at Trudy's ridiculous observation.

* * *

"I'm sorry I can't really show you…what a pleasure it is…to have you presenting the prize to me, Carrie… Give me a little while…and I'll…make it up to you."

Carrie's heart wrenched at Jake's distress. "Jake, I was extremely flattered by your, more than generous, donations to the prize fund. I don't think anything else is necessary. Thank You."

They reached the gate and Jake started to open it; but Cooter beat him to the punch. He and Caroline started walking in the direction of their seats.

Turning to face Carrie, Jake said, "I have to confess…something to you…" Stopping to draw a labored breath, Jake continued, "I didn't bid on…your cake and cookies…just so I could contribute…to the prize fund." He looked down at his boots. "I was contributing to the 'Jake and Carrie' fund."

Carrie's mouth flew open and her eyes sparkled. "Jake, I…"

Jake had dropped to his knees at her feet.

CHAPTER SIXTEEN
Circumstantial Evidence

"Wade! Wade!—Dad!" Carrie shouted, sinking down beside Jake. His eyes were clinched shut and his teeth gritted against the pain. In the background, the announcer could be heard awarding more prizes.

Doctor Stoddard and Cooter arrived at the same time. Cooter's face twisted with compassion. As a friend, he was suffering also. "Doc—something's *bad* wrong! It takes a lot to put Jake down. He's hurting fierce... Help him, Doc!"

The doctor only half-listened to Cooter. He was busy watching Jake's chest rise and fall. "Is the pain much worse than a little while ago?"

Jake was motionless for several seconds, then dipped his head slightly in answer.

"Wade...round up a flatbed wagon. We're going to take him to my house—so I can get him on my examination table. He definitely has something worse than bruised ribs."

Cooter took off like a shot. He ran around to the back side of the stands where wagons parked.

Manny and some of the Concho hands met him there. They'd been watching Jake and saw him fall. When Cooter started running toward the back of the stands, they ran also.

"What ees wrong weeth Jake," Manny asked anxiously.

Cooter didn't reply, instead, he asked, "Do any of you boys know who any of these wagons belong to?"

"Si! Theese one," he pointed, "ees my Pa'pa's."

Cooter leaped up on the bench seat and untied the reins from the brake pole. "Go tell your Paw we need it to take Jake to Doc Stoddard's. I'll bring it back."

"Si!"

Cooter pulled up as close to where the doctor knelt over his friend as possible.

"You boys help Jake up onto the back of the wagon. Be careful—he can't stand any pressure on his chest." The doctor motioned to the Concho men who had arrived with the wagon.

After carefully helping Jake to lay flat on the wagon bed, Joel and the others ran for their horses. They intended to follow.

Carrie climbed in beside Jake. She bunched the tail of her skirts and made a cushion for his head—he couldn't stand to raise his head high enough for her to cradle it in her lap. Though Cooter was as careful as could be, every jostle or bump in the road brought a gasping moan from Jake's lips. They moved off the rodeo grounds and down the street.

Cooter kept glancing over his shoulder in concern. Jake was vaguely aware of soft hands and Carrie's soothing voice as they moved toward the doctor's house.

* * *

The doctor owned a stretcher, leftover from his military service days. Jake was a large man and it took great effort to transfer him from the wagon to the stretcher without causing more excruciating pain. After he directed the loading, he led the way through the house to his examining room.

Once Jake was on the table, Stoddard unbuttoned his shirt and pulled it open. He stood motionless for a moment, his brow wrinkled as he observed the contours of Jake's chest. Gently, he rested the tips of his index and middle fingers on the upper-center of Jake's breastbone and pressed lightly, walking them down it."

Suddenly, Jake cried out in pain, "Oh! That's it, Doc!"

Swiftly lifting his hand, Doc stuck his tongue in his cheek and stared at the spot. "Jake, I know it's painful, but I have to be sure…"

Jake was inhaling short puffs of air. He nodded in understanding of the doctor's warning against the sharp pain to come.

Repeating the process, Doc's fingers pressed the center of the breast bone between Jake's pectoral muscles. Jake moaned again in response.

"It's worse than I initially thought," Doc said softly. Standing over Jake, who laid flat on the table, the doctor explained, "That steer butted you pretty hard, didn't he?—Don't try to answer!" He pursed his lips in thought.

"You're in for three or four weeks of pain. But the good news is…it *will* heal."

Jake stared at the face above him. What was the doctor trying to tell him?

Turning to his daughter, who was also his nurse, the doctor said, "Go tell Wade and Manny to step in here. They need to hear this too."

Carrie hurried down the hall to the front room where Jake's men waited for word of his ondition. "Wade, Manny; the doctor wants you to come to the examination room, please."

The two men entered the room and stood at Jake's feet. Their expressions betrayed their fear for him.

"Don't look so scared," the doctor scolded gently. "He's going to be fine. But…I wanted you two in here as witnesses to the instructions I'm about to give him." He paused for effect, then added, "Because you're going to have to be more hard-headed than he is in order to make him stay home from the cattle drive."

When the doctor said, "'stay home from the cattle drive", Jake tried in vain to sit up. "I can't stay home, Doc! I'm needed to help with the cattle."

Laying a hand on Jake's shoulder, Stoddard reasoned, "I know the men would rather have you along, but you've got a cracked sternum." He waited a moment, before continuing. "It's the bone that runs down the middle of your chest. The steer's horn must have hit you like a hammer. I'm surprised you got up and walked away." He watched

Jake's expression. "The Sternum bone is a lot cartilage and heals comparatively quickly—that is…*if* you allow it to heal. You can't be lifting, jostling around, or doing anything that will aggravate the break.… In addition, believe me; you will want a pillow to hug if you should cough for a few days. There's no such thing as setting that bone—you'll just have to keep still and let nature do its job."

Jake looked to Cooter, his eyes pleading.

Jerking his head a little, Cooter said, "It won't be a problem for Manny and me to take the herd to Fort Worth." He looked at the Mexican boy beside him. "What do you say, Manny?"

Manny's grin was wide. "Si, Jake. We would rather you to go—but it is no much trouble to go weeth out you."

Jake managed a strained smile. "Doc, it looks like I'm in bad need of some friends—the ones I had just turned against me."

* * *

Ten days after Jake's accident, he lay on a quilt, flat of his back on the front porch. Jake had always been an outdoors person. He hated being cooped up in the house, even in the winter when it was fifteen degrees outside. At least, out on the porch, he could turn his head and look off down the hill at the cows grazing there. A couple of calves, too young to make the drive this time, romped around their mothers and, at regular intervals, lowered their heads to nurse. Jake smiled sadly. "Enjoy being with 'Mama' while you can little fellow. It doesn't last long."

He listened to the sounds Manny's mother, Senora Lopez and her daughter, Reina, made as they puttered around the kitchen. He was grateful for the Lopez family's willingness to see to his needs while all the hands were gone off to Fort Worth. Manny had assured him that his folks would be glad to come out to the Concho to take care of him. Their 'Rancho' was small and did not require a lot of work at the house. Senor Lopez came to take care of the barn animals and to make any necessary trips into town until the men returned. At times, Jake had to listen closely to understand the family's' broken English. He tried hard to comprehend what they said. He admired them for their efforts to add a second language to their mother tongue.

"What a time to be laid up," he grumbled. "Can't even ride into town to see Carrie."

Doctor Stoddard told Jake before Cooter reloaded him into the Lopez wagon on a mattress of blankets and straw, "Just listen to your body, Jake. It will tell you what to do—and what not to do. In other words, if it hurts…don't do it. I'll give you a few days to start healing, then I'll drive out there and check on your progress."

For the first week, Jake doubted that the doctor knew what he was talking about. It hurt to even lift a fork to eat! He could not turn over in the bed, nor even put his own clothes on without blinding pain shooting down the middle of his chest. He adamantly refused to let Senora Lopez or Reina dress him. Senor Lopez came into his room each morning to help him.

Jake's appetite deserted him, partly because of agitation at circumstances, and partly because there was no way anyone was going to spoon-feed him!

"Meester Jake, you are comfortable; no," pretty, little Reina Lopez asked as she shoved the screen door open with her hip. In her hands, she carried a tray loaded with steak, hot tortillas and refried beans. She stepped across the porch to where Jake was on the quilt. She dropped gracefully to her knees without unbalancing the tray. "You weel eat something, please," she begged.

"I'm not very hungry, Reina, but thank your Mama anyway. Ask her if there was any coffee left from breakfast," Jake answered. "Maybe I can sit in that straight-back and drink it."

"You no like Mexican cooking?" Reina looked hurt. "Mama makes thees steak especial for you."

"Of course I like your Mama's cooking. She's one of the best cooks around," Jake replied quickly. "I guess it's because I can't move around and work up an appetite. I don't seem to be interested in food these days—no matter how good the cook is."

"Perhaps your mind is on 'other' things, such as the beautiful Senorita Carrie…no?" Reina's smile was teasing.

Jake's ears turned red. "Perhaps," he chuckled.

"I too am thinking of someone, most all days," she confided. "He ees in my heart very strong."

"Joel?"

Reina clinched her teeth and her eyes widened in surprise. "You know this?—But, I did not tell any others. Maybe he ees not wanting to be for me. I would be most…em…em. How you say?"

"Embarrassed," Jake answered. "Look, Reina,—I don't want to butt-in, but I can tell you from what I saw the day of the rodeo, that Joel *does* want to be special to you. He couldn't keep his eyes off you that whole day."

"Oh, thank you, Meester Jake! I am hoping it ees so," she cried. She was silent for a minute then spoke again. "Joel saves his money for land. He ees dream of building a rancho to grow hor-caballos. I am dream also, to help him."

Jake was impressed. "Joel is a hard worker *and* he stays *at* whatever he starts. I have no doubt that he'll have his dream. And, God willing…you'll have yours."

Reina smiled brightly. "And you, Senor? What is your dreams?"

Jake grinned. Reina watched his eyes soften. "Pretty much the same as yours. 'To have someone living in this house who will help me make a happy life…and a family."

"Reina! Vengase! Come here," Mama Conchita called from the kitchen.

Reina held the tray out toward Jake once again. "You are certain you are no hungry?"

"I'm sure, thank you anyway."

The girl disappeared through the front door. Jake lay silently mulling over their conversation. Suddenly it came to him; what would he and Matt have done if there had been no 'Silver Concho' when Big Mama died? How would they have made it? The going had been tough but, at least they had a roof over their heads and a heritage to hang onto. *Thank you, Lord. Please forgive me for ever complaining.*

* * *

Two days later, Jake was out on the front porch again enjoying the morning sun. On this day, he sat in one of the straight-back, dining room chairs. His chest seemed to be improving a little at a time; though it was still painful for him lift any weight. At least, he could feed himself with very little discomfort…when he felt like eating.

The "rattle-ching" sound of trace chains drew his attention to the road leading to the house. A buggy with two women in it rounded the curve and approached the house—Trudy Westing and her mother!

Jake groaned, "Just what I need."

"It ees Senora Westing and her hija…ah daughter, Meester Jake," Reina said, suddenly appearing beside his chair. She turned to him and he thought he could read sympathy in her eyes.

"Do you want me to make the tea for your company?"

Jake stared at her, a blank expression on his face. "Tea?"

"Si, the mujeres—womens, they like the tea."

Jake shrugged. "Yeah, I guess so." He added shrewdly, "But don't make it too good. I don't want them to stay very long."

Reina shrugged with a giggle, "As you say, Senor."

The buggy arrived in a cloud of dust. "Oh, Mister Galloway, it's so good to see that you're up and about. Trudy and I were certainly distressed to hear of your accident. I trust you are mending well," the older woman gushed as she and her daughter alighted from the carriage.

"I think I'll be as good as new in a couple of weeks, Mrs. Westing, thank you," Jake answered politely. His thoughts were anything but polite *Bless their hearts…they can't help it if they're both as ugly as mud fences. Be nice, Jake.*

"Well, Trudy and I," she motioned with her hand as she spoke, "decided that you must be terribly lonely out here all by yourself. Your men *are* gone on a cattle drive, aren't they?"

You mean 'you' decided that I'd be too crippled up and sore to hide from her. "Thank you for thinking of me, Mrs. Westing, but the Lopez family was kind enough to come out here and see to my needs while my men are gone." Jake took a perverse pleasure in telling her that fact.

Mrs. Westing glanced quickly at the front door. Jake could see the wheels turning in her head. *That means that the pretty senorita is here with him.*

"Yes…well…I'm sure that was very nice of them; but you must be *starved* for some good home-cooking." Without taking a breath, she continued, "Trudy was very sorry that you didn't get any of that beautiful, delicious cake she baked for the rodeo bake sale—so she just rolled up her sleeves and made another one like it *'especially'* for you."

"That's real nice of you, Trudy. I hope it doesn't ruin before I get my appetite back. I haven't been very hungry these past two weeks."

"See! It's just as I thought. You need some *real* cooking." The woman had no manners, but she added quickly, "I'm sure Senora Lopez is a good cook, *'if'* you like *'that'* kind of food."

"I do," Jake said flatly. "It's not Mrs. Lopez's cooking; it's the soreness in my chest that's robbed me of an appetite."

The screen door opened and Reina, bearing a tray with a tea pitcher and cups came out onto the porch. Jake watched as Mrs. Westing's eyes darted back and forth between Trudy and the beautiful girl. The woman's brows came together. It was evident that she was uncomfortable with her comparison of the two young women. Recovering quickly she gushed, "Oh, Jake—may call you, Jake? How nice of you to order your servants to bring us tea!"

Jake was beginning to lose his calm. "Reina isn't a servant, Mrs. Westing; she's a very good friend." He raised his voice a little, to be sure she heard him. "And I didn't order this tea, Reina volunteered to make it for you. She said ladies enjoy tea."

"Oh well…my mistake." She turned to Trudy, "Don't just sit there, girl! Go bring that beautiful cake you made. We'll enjoy a piece of it with our tea." Turning her eyes on Reina, she said haughtily. "Bring some plates, a knife and some silverware, if you please, Reina."

"Si, Senora," Reina answered politely and disappeared through the door.

* * *

For nearly an hour, Jake endured the prattle and matchmaking attempts of Mrs. Westing. He listened, poker-faced, while she sang the praises of her "kind, talented, lovely" daughter.

Finally, the two Westings stood to leave. "Oh! Don't try to get up, Jake. I know you're still sore. Trudy and I must be on our way, but we will be back to check on you. Next time, we'll bring you a big pot of Trudy's delicious stew. I *know* you'll be looking forward to it."

Climbing up into the carriage, Trudy, who hadn't said two words the whole time, turned to him and lifted her hand. She wiggled the ends of her fingers at him, "Tootle, Jake. It was *so* nice to see you."

The good manners Big Mama had tried to instill in Matt and him came to fore. "It was nice of you to come, Trudy. Thank you for the cake."

The toothy girl giggled. "Oh you're very welcome…Jake." She drew his name out, a flirtatious tone in her voice.

Jake watched, open mouthed, as Mrs. Westing turned the carriage around and trotted it down the road toward Llano.

"Whew," he muttered. He turned his eyes to Reina. They both dissolved into laughter.

* * *

Carrie was all-ears as Caroline related the latest gossip about Trudy Westing's visit to the
Silver Concho Ranch. According to Trudy, Jake had been *most* appreciative of her attentions. He had insisted that she and her mother stay for tea.

Tea? Jake? Carrie, somehow, could not put the two together. She doubted the accuracy of Trudy's account.

Caroline was laughing hilariously, clutching her stomach, "To hear her tell it, they're practically engaged. She says he asked her to call him Jake, instead of Mister Galloway."

Carrie studied her friend's face. "How much of this do you believe, Caroline?"

Caroline rolled her eyes, pretending to study the cookie in her hand for a few moments. "Mmmm...I guess I believe the part about her and her mother going out to the Silver Concho—but not a *single* word of the rest of it. Bless her heart, Trudy is just wishing, and then telling it for the truth."

"That's what I think." Carrie was relieved to hear someone else give voice to her own opinion. Her expression changed. "Dad told Jake that he would go out there to check on him after a few days. I am hoping it'll be this afternoon or tomorrow. I plan to bake another chocolate cake for him. After all, he paid ten dollars for the other one and only got one piece." She smiled impishly. "You might want to do the same for Wade when he returns from the cattle drive."

"Carrie my dear that is a wonderful idea."

* * *

"Carrie, I plan to make a trip out to the Silver Concho tomorrow morning to check on Jake Galloway." Doc's voice was nonchalant, but his eyes twinkled. "I'd like a little company...if you don't have anything else planned."

The light in Carrie's eyes matched her father's. "Oh,—I had planned to wash my hair, but I guess I can go ahead and do it today. I wouldn't want you to have to drive all the way out there by yourself."

"Thank you, sweetheart; I thought you might feel that way." Father and daughter gazed intently at each other for a few seconds before Carrie leaped into her dad's arms, hugging his neck hard. "Thank *you*, Dad."

* * *

Jake sat on the porch day after day, reading or staring off down the road. He ate very little; so little that Reina and her mother were concerned over his weight loss. Reina decided to see if she could tempt him to eat. She would make a batch of the same wedding cookies that she had made for the rodeo bake sale. Jake had once remarked about how good they had looked to him.

All morning, Reina and her 'ma'ma' worked on the special treats. The cookies were about one and a half inches across when they came out of the oven. They rolled them in sugar and allowed them to cool before serving.

* * *

"You know I could get my feelings hurt, if I allowed myself to," Doctor Stoddard teased his daughter again. "The last two chocolate cakes you've made have been for Jake Galloway. They're my favorite too, you know."

The Stoddards were on the road to Jake's ranch. The cake was in a cheese box and balanced on Carrie's lap.

"Dad, you know very well that all you have to do is speak the word and I'll bake you a chocolate cake anytime. Jake has no one to make one for him. And...I may never have another opportunity to do this for him," Carrie pleaded.

"I suspect, if he has his way, you will." He turned on the buggy seat to look at her. "To tell you the truth, I think he's after my cook!"

Carrie was silent for a few moments, studying her father's face. "I hope so," she muttered. Doc threw back his head and laughed.

* * *

Jake got up from his chair and went into the house. He walked through the front room and turned down the hall into a room that had always served the Concho as office and library. Jake's father, Thomas, had been an avid reader of history. He had enjoyed any book that was either a downright history book, or contained adventure stories based on history. Jake inherited his father's reading tastes. Books covered one entire wall of the room. They covered many subjects. Jake read them all; but "Historical Adventures" were his favorites.

He chose a book to read. It was one he had read before, but he settled down in a big, man-sized, leather, wingback chair. The chair was soft with a straight back and most comfortable to Jake.

"Meester Jake, I have som'thing especial for you," Reina said, swinging into the room with a plate of cookies held out toward him. "I know you weel no say 'no' to thees galletas—cookies."

"Those are the same kind you made for the rodeo bake sale aren't they?" His smile betrayed the pleasure her thoughtfulness brought to him. "Reina, if I ate all the food you and your Mama poked at me, I'd be so fat I couldn't get on my horse. Especially, since I'm lying around with no exercise these days."

"Oh, but Meester Jake, these cookies are leetle. They weel no make you gordo—fat. I make them just right size so a whole cookie weel feet in you 'boca'—mouth. How can one leetle cookie be bad? Here—I show you."

Reina plucked one of the bite-sized morsels from the plate and came to stand over him. "Now open you mouth. I weel show how eesy for to eat."

Jake chuckled at the girl's antics. He turned his head from side to side, pretending to dodge the cookie she was pushing toward his mouth.'

* * *

The carriage had barely stopped rolling when Carrie, ignoring her father, climbed to the ground. She reached over the side of the buggy beneath the seat to retrieve a large box containing the cake. She spied Senora Lopez through the screen door moving around the kitchen.

Not bothering to knock, she elbowed the door open and entered. Mama Conchita turned at the sound and greeted the pretty, young lady with a smile. Her eyes dropped to the large cheese box; comprehension registered in them. She approached Carrie and grasped the girl's elbow, turning her down the hall. The Senora smiled with pleasure as she nodded toward a door at the end of it. Sounds of voices were coming from a room there.

Carrie's heart beat so rapidly that she feared she would drop the cake. She halted just before reaching the doorway and took a breath; then stepped in front of the opening. Her eyes widened in surprise and she stared open-mouthed at the scene before her.

There was Jake, chuckling, with his head tilted back and his mouth open. Standing over him, almost in his lap, was Reina Lopez! The girl was saying, "Just one leetle one. You weel like it!"

Carrie's breathing stopped and tears rushed into her eyes. She looked down at the cake in her hands then whirled around, nearly running over her father in her haste to get away from the sight she had just seen.

"Carrie! Wha…" Doctor Stoddard was stunned. "Where are you going in such a hurry girl?" Carrie shook her head and muttered over her shoulder, "I'm going to leave this cake in the kitchen." She added softly, "I'll wait for you on the porch."

Jake heard a quick gasp. He leaned around Reina in time to catch a glimpse of a petticoat, flashing from beneath the hem of a pale yellow skirt. Carrie!

Reina's head snapped around, just as Doc Stoddard entered the room. She could tell by the expression on his face that he was trying to determine what Carrie had seen. "Oh! Doc'tor! I am trying to geet Meester Jake to eet thees cookies. He ees eating nothing for two weeks. It is no good…no?" Her dark eyes flicked back and forth between Jake and the physician.

"I'm sure his appetite has diminished with inactivity, Miss Lopez. But you are right, it is not good for him to go too long without eating something." Doc shifted his gaze to Jake whose open-mouthed stare toward the open door bespoke his shock.

* * *

Carrie's sudden entrance into the kitchen startled Senora Lopez. The girl set the cheese box on the table. Quickly removing the lid, she lifted a delicious looking chocolate cake out and set it down without saying a word. Then she turned to Conchita. "I…I brought this for Ja…Mr. Galloway. Will you give it to him, please?"

Conchita Lopez was a very astute woman. She noted Carrie's red-rimmed eyes. "You are ill, Senorita?" Carrie lowered her head and shook it slightly. "No. I'm not ill, Mrs. Lopez—I...I'm in a hurry," she blurted and fled to the front porch. Conchita stared at the vacant doorway. "Que paso?"

Doctor Stoddard's mind was running in two directions. What had happened to upset Carrie...and how was Jake's sternum injury healing? Working the shirt's buttons as he spoke, he smiled at the young man. "I need to open your shirt so I can feel the bone. How much pain do you have now?" He placed his hand on Jake's sternum and pushed lightly.

Jake's expression revealed a small amount of discomfort. "I'm doing much better, Doc. Now it only hurts when I try to lift something heavier than my boots, or when I push myself up from my chair."

Doc listened closely and asked, "Can you sleep on your side yet?"

"I can, but I'm more comfortable flat on my back," Jake answered.

Stoddard's head bobbed slightly, "Sounds like you're coming along ahead of schedule. It's only been a little over two weeks. You shouldn't be able to sleep at all on your side yet. Keep on doing...whatever you're doing."

Jake chuckled as he re-buttoned his shirt, "You mean keep going nuts! I haven't been this still since the day I was born. I can't stand much more rest."

The doctor grinned. "You ought to be as good as new in about ten more days. But let me warn you, you'll probably have little 'twitches' in the middle of your chest for the rest of your life—especially when you have a cold and do a lot of coughing. It will depend on how it knits. If you do hurt...just peg it for what it is and don't worry."

Jake nodded. "Thanks Doc." He turned his eyes to the doorway. Carrie stood there with a thin smile on her lips. "Hello, Mister Galloway. I hope you are mending well. I brought you another chocolate cake." She hurried to add, "...To replace the one you paid so much for and only got one piece." Her lips tensed a tiny bit. "But I guess you prefer the delicious cookies that Miss Lopez makes. I'm sorry—I don't have that recipe."

Before Jake could unscramble his brain, she turned in a wink and was gone. He stared dumbly at the doorway. He turned slowly to Carrie's father.

Doc grinned. "Don't look at me—I don't understand them either." Retrieving his hat from the desk top, the doctor gave a small wave of his hand as he commented, "I don't think it will be necessary for me to check on you again, but in case you *do* need me, send Senor Lopez and I'll come running,"

What happened? Why did Carrie act like that? What did she 'think' she saw?

Jake was miserable. He ran a hand through his hair which, he absently thought, was in bad need of a cut. "I'm innocent! I didn't do a blooming thing! Women!"

Carrie was silent as she and her father rode back toward Llano. She stared unseeingly across the landscape. Finally, her father spoke. "Want to talk about it?"

She turned a face full of hurt to him. "Dad...how can people be so cruel as to pretend to be your friend, when they're really making fun of you behind your back?"

The doctor exhaled heavily. "Carrie, one of the worst things you can do is to jump to conclusions."

"Dad! I *know* what I saw," Carrie cried.

The doctor stuck his tongue in his cheek for a moment, then replied, "Maybe so,—maybe no; as I've heard Manny say."

CHAPTER SEVENTEEN
Unexpected Ally

"Meester Jake, weel the Concho vacqueros be here by end of next week?" Reina looked anxiously into his face.

Jake thought for a moment. "If they've had good weather and no major problems, they should be getting into Fort Worth today or tomorrow. It takes about three weeks going and one week coming back. That'll put 'em here by Thursday or Friday of next week. Why?"

Reina's dark eyes gleamed as she smiled dreamily. "I was hope it would be so." She dropped her sights to the carpet in front of her. "There ees to be a church 'pic-neek' Saturday after this coming one. Mujeres—ladies are to invite. I am so looking forward!"

"Aaahh," Jake nodded. "Joel most likely will be here by then. You probably ought to plan on it." Her bright-eyes looked so much like her brothers when she responded, "I weel do that. Gracias—thank you, Senor."

After she left the room, Jake thought dejectedly, *Guess I won't be going. If I can't be with Carrie, I don't even want to go.*

* * *

Early the following Saturday morning, Conchita called her daughter into the kitchen. "Necessito som'things del la tienda." She motioned with her hand toward Reina, "You go."

Reina smiled. She enjoyed trips to town, hoping to see some of her friends. "Si, Ma'ma'." She took the list her mother had prepared and headed for the barn. Her father would hitch up the horse and buggy for her.

In a few minutes, Senor Lopez watched Reina and the buggy disappear in a cloud of dust around the curve, a little way from the house.

* * *

Llano was its busiest on Saturdays. Reina waved to several acquaintances and even stopped to talk for a while with one of her friends. She pulled up in front of the store a few minutes later, tied the reins off and climbed down. With a small shopping basket over her arm, she entered the crowded store.

With no time for browsing, Reina went directly to the aisle where canned tomatoes were shelved. Placing three cans in her basket, she proceeded toward the cornmeal and dried bean barrels. She was about to turn out of the aisle when she overheard a familiar voice. Stopping in her tracks, unseen by the speaker in the next aisle, she listened.

"Oh yes…I've decided to let Jake escort me to the church picnic. He should be up and around very well by then. He does so like my cooking, and I just *know* he's starving to death—having to eat the Lopez woman's fare."

Reina leaned closer. She knew she shouldn't be listening, but that voice belonged to Trudy Westing. Reina knew Jake would not be apt to go with the mouthy girl to the picnic…unless Carrie Stoddard failed to invite him. She shook her head at the thought. Jake wouldn't go with Trudy even if Carrie didn't get there first!

"I'm planning on going back out to the Silver Concho this coming Monday morning to inform him that I've decided to go to the picnic with him as my escort."

Enough! Reina all but ran to the bean and meal barrels, scooped up the amounts her mother had specified and waited impatiently while the clerk took care of the customer ahead of her.

After paying for her purchases, she ran out of the store and hopped into the buggy. She untied the reins, snapped them and turned the horses around in the middle of the street. It took only five or six minutes for her to arrive on Doctor Stoddard's doorsteps.

Carrie heard a quick, excited rapping on the front door. She hurried to answer, afraid that there was an emergency. When she opened the door, her mouth dropped open in surprise. Reina Lopez, her rival, stood there with a worried look on her face.

Carrie collected her dignity and spoke to the beautiful girl, "Come in, Miss Lopez.... Is something wrong out at the Silver Concho? Do you need to see my father?"

Reina was in a quandary. How could she approach this woman, without admitting that she had eavesdropped? She twisted her hands for several seconds before speaking. "You are mistake, Senorita," she said humbly.

Carrie was puzzled. "I beg your pardon—mistaken about what?"

"About what you theenk you see when you come to see Meester Jake,"

Carrie's chin lifted slightly. "I think not...it was pretty obvious..."

"No! You theenk Meester Jake ees flirt with me, but ees not so." Reina was not to be intimidated, nor would she allow Carrie to continue to hurt over a misunderstanding.

Carrie stared at her with a shocked expression. Reina continued, "For two weeks, Meester Jake, he stare out the ventana—window. He is watch the road. He does not eat and he does not sleep well. He is look for *you* to come.

"Other muchachas—girls come; they flirt weeth him, but he has no interest in them. He ees only polite to them." She took a quick breath. "The day you and doc'tor come, I haf' made galletas—cookies. Meester Jake ees not eating his deener, so I teese him and try to make him eat my ga...cookies." She added anxiously, "It ees better than no'thing; no?

"I tell him, 'Whole cookie weel go in *you* mouth and I pretend to put one there. He is laugh." She sighed, "That ees when you are come in." Leveling her eyes at Carrie, she added, "Ees not flirt between Senor Jake and me...only friends. I am enamorado—luf weeth Jo'el Ream." Her eyes widened. "Oh!—But please, no tell him!"

Carrie's mouth dropped open. "I don't know what to say."

Reina closed the space between them and took Carrie's hand in both hers. "You must go, Senorita...today! You must invite Senor Jake to church pic-neek. I am hearing Trudy Westing say she weel go to the rancho 'Concho' to ask him to be with her at pic-neek. She weel go Monday, next! He does not weesh to be with her. He only weesh to be with you. Thees I know!"

"W...when did you hear Trudy say this," Carrie stuttered. Reina dropped her eyes. "I am in tienda—store, only one hour past. She ees there weeth her amigas—friends. They do not see me, but I am leesen. Trudy say she go weeth her ma'ma to veesit Meester Jake. They weel conveence him. You must hurry! Go today!"

"But, how do you know that Jake is interested in me? Has he said something to you?" When Carrie happened up on Reina and Jake in his office that day, she had convinced herself that she had taken too much for granted because he bid on her cake at the rodeo.

Reina's head was bobbing in the affirmative. "Si! He is speak every day to Ma'ma and me about you. He say you are most hermosa—beautiful senorita he ever see before." She smiled with a wise expression in her eyes. "All who see hees face when he ees speak of you can know he ees enamorado—luf weeth you."

Carrie's heart pounded with joy. "But what excuse would I have for going out to his ranch today? Dad is out making other calls."

"No excuse! Go as freend; to see if he ees well," Reina urged.

Carrie's face brightened. "I'll do it! I owe him *and* you an apology, anyway...for misjudging both of you." Carrie's cheeks burned as she added, "I was jealous of you, Reina."

Reina smiled sweetly. "I am most honored, Senorita; that one so beautiful as you could be jealous of me."

The girls hugged, and as Reina turned toward the door, she whirled back around, "I weel see you at the Concho today; no?" She hunched her shoulders and added merrily, "I weel no tell Meester Jake you are come."

"Thank you, Reina. I'll give you a thirty minute start ahead of me." Carrie's eyes were bright with excitement as she squeezed Reina's hand.

* * *

Jake was sitting on the front porch as usual. His sternum was healing nicely and he felt good enough to take a walk down to the barn. But he knew himself well enough to know that if he did go down there, he would find something he needed to do. Doc Stoddard had said one more week and he would be over the worst. Then, "within reason", he would be able to return to his normal activities.

Right now, the only activity Jake wanted to be involved in was to gaze at the beautiful face of Carrie Stoddard. He moaned. It wasn't likely he'd get another chance to do that. She thought he was some kind of Romeo cowboy after what she happened upon this past week. He wasn't angry with Reina. The girl was just trying to get him to eat; but he sure wished the young senorita's timing had been a little bit better.

Movement near a small copse of scrub cedar in the curve of the road that led up to the house drew Jake's attention. Just emerging around them was a buggy—his buggy. He watched as the wheels stirred up the dust of the dry road. "We sure could use a good rain," he muttered.

It was Reina, returning from her errand to town for her mother. Jake smiled to himself. Senorita Reina Lopez handled a team as if she'd been born with reins in her hands. She was a fine young woman. Joel Ream was a lucky man. *Luckier than I am it appears*, he thought miserably.

In a few moments, Reina stopped the buggy in front of the porch. She tied off the reins before climbing down. Walking around the vehicle, she reached over into the boot for the things she'd bought in town for her mama. "Ola, Meester Jake, you are feel better, Si?"

Jake grinned and nodded, "Yeah, I'm almost ready to hit the saddle again."

Reina stopped in her tracks. "Why you heet you saddle, Senor?"

Jake laughed out loud, but quickly composed himself before replying, "Reina, that simply means that I'm ready to ride my horse again." She looked at him as if she were trying to decide if he were teasing her or not. "Oh—You make the joke?" Jake's brows shot up and he wagged his head. "Well, sort of."

Reina changed the subject. "You weel eat today, Meester Jake. Ma'ma, she make especial tamales for you. They are most time for the Navidad—Christmas celebracion, but she want to make you more gordo—fat." The girl laughed at Jake's expression.

"Reina, I'm already as big as the barn," Jake chuckled.

"No, Senor. You *were* beeg as barn, but you haf lose weight. Now you are tall, but no very fat," Reina argued. "Ma'ma feex you up." She bobbed her head to emphasize the last sentence.

From the kitchen, they heard, "Reina! Vengase!" Reina glanced through the screened front door then said, "I go help Ma'ma now. You want some coffee?" Jake shook his head, no. He did not see the smile on Reina's face when she left him, heading for the kitchen.

* * *

Jake leaned his chair against the porch wall, balancing it on the back legs. His mind drifted back to the rodeo on Saturday. A smile played at his lips, remembering Charlie Wilson's bid. Poor Charlie; the man just didn't understand that "a person who toots his own horn is the only one who enjoys the music." If it had not been so funny, Jake would've almost feel sorry for Charlie when the rodeo announcer called Trudy Westing, instead of Carrie, to the center of the arena to award Charlie's prize. Almost.

The smile disappeared. He chided himself for making fun of Charlie. He had also been foolish enough to take too much for granted. He had thought Carrie was as happy to be in his company as he was to be in hers; but she sure proved him wrong this past week. She *barely* stuck her head in the door to speak to him. Why did she even come?

Just then, Jake became aware of another vehicle emerging from between the trees in the curve. His heart rate sped up when he saw that it was Doctor Stoddard's buggy. Why would the Doc be coming back out here today? Jake hadn't sent for him; it was an eleven-mile trip!

In one single instant, Jake's mouth went dry and his heart began to pound faster. It wasn't *Doctor* Stoddard, it was Carrie! He leaned forward, plopping his chair down on all four legs.

A sharp pain down the middle of his chest reminded him that he was not completely well.

His breath stopped and hung in the back of his throat as he stared pointedly at the approaching buggy. Rising to his feet, he stepped to the edge of the porch and waited.

Carrie saw Jake stand up and move to the porch steps. She chewed her bottom lip nervously. *What do I say to him? He'll think I'm as forward and bold as Trudy; coming out here like this for no reason. He's sure to mention last week, and I'm not about to admit that I was jealous of Reina!* An almost irresistible urge to wheel the buggy around and head back to town seized Carrie. She was ready to panic; then Jake raised his hand in greeting, a big smile on his face. The sight of his welcoming gesture warmed her heart and gave her courage.

Carrie pulled up on the reins and the buggy came to a stop right in front of where Jake stood. For several moments, they stared awkwardly at each other. Neither of them knew how to open the conversation.

Jake Galloway had always been a "take the bull by the horns" type fellow. He stepped to the ground and laid his hand on the buggy's side, leaning casually against it. "I thought I must have been dreaming; I didn't know angels drove buggies," he said softly. Smiling up at her, he raised his brows.

Carrie laughed softly and relaxed; pleased at his comment. "No, you're not dreaming. Having a nightmare maybe. It's me, in the flesh."

Jake's smile widened. "Yeah, I can see that." He lifted his hands, "Might I help you down?"

Carrie shook her head emphatically, "No, you cannot! It is not time for you to be lifting that much weight. I can manage nicely." She tied off the reins, pulled her leather gloves off, laid them on the seat then climbed down on her side of the buggy.

Jake met her, just as her foot hit the ground. His pulse was going wild. He was afraid she would see the front of his shirt jumping because his heart was beating so.

Clearing his throat, he said, "It's getting close to dinner time and Senora Lopez is making something special. Will you have dinner with me," he asked hopefully.

Carrie felt a wave of tenderness for Jake surge through her. He was such a sweet man. He wasn't even aware of what a handsome and desirable picture he made as he stood there with his heart in his eyes; but that was good. Carrie couldn't stand arrogance, even when it was justified.

She shrugged apologetically, "I'm sorry, Jake, but I can't stay that long. Dad will be completing his rounds about three o'clock. I need to be back home in time to have supper prepared by five."

Jake had absolutely no control over the next thought that ran through his mind. *He had better enjoy her meals while he can. If I have my way, she'll soon be cooking for me.*

None of his thoughts were reflected on his face. He grinned suddenly with mischief in his eyes. "At least let Reina make some tea. I heard ladies like tea." He was thinking of Trudy Westing and her mother's recent visit.

"Oh?... And where did you hear that?" Carrie saw the glint in his eyes and she knew the answer to her question. She wanted to see if he would confess. It was hard to admit, but Carrie took great pleasure in the knowledge that Jake had not enjoyed the Westing's visit.

Jake watched her for a few seconds, his teasing expression unchanged. "Reina told me. I had some...ah...visitors one day last week. Reina volunteered to make tea for them. According to her...ladies always enjoy a cup of tea," he shrugged, "So, we had tea."

Carrie almost cackled at the mental picture his words painted. Jake's big, manly hands trying to deal with a delicate china teacup. Carrie looked into his teasing eyes. "I suppose some of them do, but I've always enjoyed a good cup of coffee myself," she said matter-of-factly.

"A woman after my own heart," Jake said appreciatively. Carrie heard a soft sincerity in his voice.

Jake cleared his throat again then turned to call over his shoulder, "Senora Lopez, do we have any coffee made?"

"Si, Senor Jake. Reina weel bring it for you and the senorita." Jake and Carrie turned startled eyes on each other. "How did she know *you* wanted coffee too," he mumbled.

Carrie placed her hand over her mouth to muffle her laughter. After a moment, she replied, "Guess."

Jake's mouth dropped open. He glanced toward the open door then wagged his head in amazement. Suddenly remembering his manners, Jake reached for her hand." Let's sit down while we wait for our coffee. A shock vibrated up her arm when his warm, callused fingers wrapped around hers. Jake felt like he was in a daze. He could not believe this was actually happening—Carrie...here...to see him!

They stepped up on the porch together, and Jake motioned for Carrie to take the chair he had been sitting in. He raised his voice once again, "Reina! Would you bring another dining room chair out here, please?" From inside, they heard, "Si, Meester Jake, pronto—right away!"

In a moment, the screen door bumped open as Reina backed against it, half carrying, half dragging one of the heavy dining room chairs. Jake moved quickly to help her. "I'm sorry, girl; I forgot they're so heavy," he mumbled, taking the chair from her and positioning it next to Carrie. His back was toward Reina, so he didn't see the wink she sent Carrie's way.

Carrie was grateful that the younger girl had had the courage to *interfere* on her behalf. Reina would always be a valued friend...and ally.

Jake saw the secretive smile. He glanced uncertainly from her to Reina then back again. Reina schooled her features to reveal nothing. Carrie acted as if the smile was just for him. That suited him just fine. *If something is going on between those two*...he shrugged and decided that what he didn't know couldn't hurt him...he hoped.

Jake angled his chair so he could see Carrie better. She fidgeted with the ruffles running down the front of her bodice. *What do I say next? He must be wondering why I came... Lord, help me to say this right.*

"Jake, I...ah...I came out here today for two reasons. One is that I feel I owe you an apology; no, I *know* I owe you an apology." She took a fortifying breath. "The day I rode out here with Dad to check on your progress, I...I jumped to some wrong conclusions about what I saw. It was totally unfair of me." She took her bottom lip between her teeth for a moment. "I apologize."

Jake smiled warmly. "And...just what did you *think* you saw?"

Carrie squirmed a little. He was not making this easy. "I thought you and Reina were...were...interested in each other," she blurted the second half of the sentence, then added, "I was angry; mostly with myself for misinterpreting why you bid on my cake the day of the rodeo."

"What changed your mind?" Jake continued to lead her with questions. Carrie felt like a mouse that was being toyed with by a big tomcat.

"Reina set me straight...ah," her hand flew to her mouth. "Forget I said that—I didn't have permission to tell you that." Carrie's face was beet red by now.

Jake's eyes widened. "Reina," he questioned incredulously. "When did you talk to Reina?"

Carrie glanced uncomfortably toward the front door. Jake saw her gesture. "Do you like young animals," he suddenly asked, totally off the subject.

Carrie's brows came together. She cocked her head to the side trying to decide if she had heard him right. "Ah...yes, I do." Jake rose to his feet and extended his hand to her. "Come...take a walk with me down to the barn. One of my mares had the prettiest filly you ever saw, two weeks ago" His smile was inviting. "Want to see her?" He quickly added, "Senor Lopez is down there...it's okay."

Carrie gave him her hand and they stepped off the porch together. They had gone barely fifteen steps when Jake muttered under his breath, "The house seems to have ears these days." He grew serious, "I have something I want to say to you in private but first, what was the second reason you came out here today?"

Jake was fishing and Carrie knew it. She thrilled to think that he might be hoping for an invitation to the picnic from her.

Lifting her head, instead of looking where she stepped, she answered cautiously, "I... There's to be a church-wide picnic next Saturday. Ladies are supposed to do the inviting." Jake saw an impish smile spread across her face. "I heard that Trudy Westing is planning to come out here this coming Monday to invite you, "she faltered for a moment, "and...I thought it would be nice if you knew that you have more than one choice." She blurted rapidly, "So, before she asks, I'm inviting you to come to the picnic with me."

Jake threw back his head and laughed. "Trudy Westing is a 'choice'?"

He laughed softly again, a deep, rumbling, masculine sound. Abruptly, stopping in the middle of the road, he placed both hands on Carrie's upper arms. His heart was in his eyes as he spoke his next words, "I heard about the picnic from Reina. She was hoping Joel would be back from the trail drive for it." He glanced around them for a second. "Come on over here...under this tree, out of the sun. We'll go see the filly in a minute."

A large pin oak spread its limbs over the road, providing the perfect shady spot for what Jake had to say. "Carrie, I wouldn't make fun of Trudy. She's...well, she's just Trudy! But, you should know that I definitely have my eye on someone else." A calculating grin spread across his face. "You."

Carrie's pulse was racing once again. Should she tell him that she returned his interest? Would it sound too—forward? Her pride was definitely involved. Jacob Galloway was the finest young man she had ever met...and the handsomest. Still, most men wanted a woman who was a "prize". Not one who played hard-to-get, but not a man-chaser either. Her father often quoted an old Indian proverb that seemed to fit the situation, *"The fruit a man has to reach for is better than that he stoops to pick up."*

She cleared her throat. "Jake, I don't know what to say, except that you don't know me very well at all. You may change your mind after you've been around me more."

Jake was shaking his head slowly as she spoke. "Carrie, I'm from a good family; by that I mean, I had *good* parents and grandparents who loved me and my brother, Matt. Even though both my parents died when I was ten years old, they *and* my grandmother—who died four years later—taught me four things that have stood the tests of my life. They taught me to love God, to love my family, to work hard for what I want, and to be an honest man. I learned very early in life to make up my mind about what I wanted and then go after it with good, honest intentions coupled with hard work."

His cobalt-blue eyes held hers captive while he dragged the backside of his fingers along Carrie's smooth-as-satin cheek. "The day I saw you passing Abe Mills' blacksmith shop, I knew I was watching my dreams come true, in the flesh."

He looked down at his boots. "It might not be too smart of me to be so blunt, but the one thing my folks *didn't* teach me was how to play games with my feelings." Lifting his eyes once more, he spoke softly, "So, I'm telling you...honest intentions are a part of my make up." Leaning forward until their faces were just inches apart, he finished his statement, "And where you're concerned, I *do* have intentions."

By then, Carrie's knees felt as if they were made of rubber. She stared, wide-eyed, up at him. "You're amazing," she whispered. "I don't understand how it is that I've been living in Llano for over six years and yet...I had never met you." Her eyes sparkled and she added sincerely, "Jake, I think you must be the most honest...most handsome man I've ever met."

"Handsome! Girl! I didn't get you in out of the sun quick enough!" Jake's mouth was so close she could feel his breath on her cheek. He stopped abruptly; his expression changing as he swallowed and looked away, staring across the pasture for a few seconds.

Carrie waited patiently, but finally said, "Jake, what's wrong? Did I say something wrong that...." He swung his head back to look at her again. Shaking it, he denied, "No. You didn't say anything wrong. I just...I want to ask you something and I don't quite know how to ask it."

A frown creased Carrie's smooth brow. "It won't hurt to ask, Jake," she answered quietly.

Jake's eyes flickered with indecision, but he took a deep breath and plunged in, "Carrie, I haven't had much chance to be…sociable. I didn't worry about it, until now. But…" he shook his head slightly in annoyance with himself, "What I'm trying to say is…would you let me…can I kiss you?"

Carrie's mouth popped open. She wasn't shocked at the question as much as his *asking* if he could kiss her. There was no doubt whatsoever in her mind that she would like to be kissed by Jake Galloway; but in truth, Carrie had never been kissed before and somehow, in all her dreams, the man didn't *ask;* he just did it!

Jake interrupted her thoughts, "I'm sorry…I shouldn't have asked that. It's just that I've never kissed a girl before—Never really found one I *wanted* to kiss. I guess I wanted you to be the first…" his voice trailed off.

"Jake, don't apologize. Don't ruin it for me," she whispered, "You see; I've never been kissed before either. I don't take it lightly like some girls do. In all my dreams, in my first kiss, the man never had a face…until now." She stepped closer to him and turned her face up to his. Just before she closed her eyes she said, "Make it a good one."

Jake's pulse rate caused his hands to shake a little as he pulled her into his arms. Just before his lips touched hers, he murmured, "Carrie, I want you to be the *first* and *last* girl I ever kiss." His mouth came down over hers and Carrie felt like she was swirling out of control in a whirlpool of feeling.

Jake, having no prior experience with kissing girls, was not quite sure how he should handle it. Yet it turned out that the instant his mouth touched hers, nature simply took over. He tenderly explored her lips, moving his mouth subtly with an ever-increasing, possessive pressure.

Jakes senses rioted. He had known that kissing Carrie would be pleasurable, but he wasn't ready for the heart-stopping desire which accompanied it. He struggled with the determination to finally release Carrie's lips. Laying his forehead against hers, he whispered raggedly, "Forgive me, but you're so…"

Carrie pushed away so she could look into his face. "There's nothing to forgive, Jake. I also wanted that kiss."

Jake silently memorized her face. He couldn't believe that she, the most beautiful of girls, had actually welcomed his kiss. *Carrie didn't just 'let' me kiss her, Lord; she welcomed it.* He wanted to shout.

Reina watched the couple through an arched, patio window. She sighed wistfully, thinking, *I weesh it could be so weeth Jo'el and me.* She smiled to herself. *Meester Jake ees a very happy man. Thees I know.*

* * *

"Don't you think we could go see the little filly now? I really want to see her and it's almost time for me to start back to town." Carrie reached for his hand and took a step in the direction of the barn. Suddenly, her mouth flew open and she cut her eyes up at Jake, "You haven't told me whether or not you will go with me to the picnic."

He rolled his eyes skyward, pretending to think about his answer.

"Jacob Galloway! Don't you *dare* turn me down! I'd never hear the end of it from Trudy!"

Jake's eyes twinkled with pleasure. He dropped an arm around her shoulders, and bent to whisper in her ear, "Honey, where do you want me…and when should I be there?"

CHAPTER EIGHTEEN
Liver and Onions

"Oh no," Jake groaned when he stepped out of the barn just in time to see the Westing's carriage rounding the curve. Mother and daughter were both perched on the front seat of the large, fancy, black vehicle. He couldn't stop the grin that spread across his face. *Thank heaven Carrie came Saturday. I sure would hate to try to turn down Trudy's invite without a good excuse.*

It was the Monday morning following Carrie's visit. Earlier, Jake walked down to the barn to check on the little filly. Now, he stood watching the buggy as it approached the house. In a few moments, Trudy and Mrs. Westing pulled up in front. Jake saw Reina come out onto the porch and point toward the barn. He took a step forward, pretending to be just coming out of it.

Trudy's head whipped around in his direction and she raised a hand over her head, waving frantically. "Yoo hoo, Jake," the smiling, homely young woman called out, "Guess what Mother and I brought you today?"

A twinge of guilt pricked Jake's conscience. *I can't fault her friendliness, she's always been that; but she and Charlie Wilson are two of a kind. Neither one, can take a hint that someone is not romantically interested in them.* He pasted a smile on his lips and continued up the hill toward the house.

"Jake, I made my famous recipe for *liver and onions*, just for you. I know you're going to love it!" Trudy scrambled to the ground; her mother did the same. Mrs. Westing reached over into the carriage, grunting as she lifted a heavy Dutch oven from the floor of it.

Bile bubbled up into Jake's throat. Even as a child, he had never been able to stomach liver. Big Mama had tried to convince him that it was good for him—that it would make him big and strong, like his dad. Jake groaned softly to himself. *If eating liver would have made me big and strong, just how big would I be today;* considering the fact that he had reached a stalwart, six-feet, four inches tall, weighing two hundred and six pounds. *Good thing my growth was 'stunted' or I would have been another Goliath.*

"Good morning, Mrs. Westing...Trudy," he said politely. "You're out early today."

"We have a very special reason for coming so early," Trudy gushed. "I have something to talk to you about. First, let's get this Dutch oven into the kitchen so Senora Lopez can transfer this dee-licious dish into another pot. She can keep it warm for your lunch."

Just then, Reina, who had been standing near the front door listening, came to the edge of the porch to receive the heavy vessel. Struggling with its weight, she waddled with it into the house.

Jake stopped at the bottom of the porch steps. He waited for the Westing girl to speak first. He didn't have to wait long.

"Mister Galloway, ah...Jake, I guess you've heard that there is to be a church-wide picnic this coming Saturday." Jake nodded, but before he could answer, Trudy rushed on, "It's *lady's choice*." She paused dramatically, an inviting smile on her homely face. "Since you've recuperated so well, I have decided to invite you to go with me. I know you must be terribly bored with staying at home for a full month." She looked up at him expectantly.

Jake looked down at the rose bush growing beside the steps. He knew he had to be careful with the girl's feelings; no sense insulting her. "Yes, Miss Trudy, I did hear about the picnic..." Trudy's smile broadened and her mouth opened to speak, but Jake quickly continued with what he was saying.

"In fact, I had a visitor out here the day before yesterday who told me about it. She invited me to go with her also." He did his best to look repentant. "I'm sorry, but I'm afraid I've already accepted an invitation to the picnic."

Trudy's facial expression went from surprise, to shock, to anger in the space of three seconds. "Who invited you, may I ask? I made it clear to everyone that I planned to invite you myself. Who was so rude as to come out here before me, knowing *my* intentions?"

"Did you tell Carrie Stoddard that you intended to invite me," Jake asked, knowing the answer already.

"Carrie Stoddard! She...well...no...I haven't seen her since the rodeo." Trudy whirled around looking at her mother. The older woman's mouth was opening and closing like a fish out of water. "Did you hear that, Mama? Of all the nerve!"

Mrs. Westing at last regained her composure. "Mister Galloway...I don't like to talk about my neighbors, but I feel I must warn you that that Stoddard girl is chasing you. I noticed it the day of the rodeo bake sale. From the moment you walked into the pavilion, I think she set her *cap* for you." She straightened her shoulders. "I suppose you have to go with her to the picnic, since you are a gentleman. But after this, if I were you, I would avoid her."

Jake stared at the woman, saying nothing for several seconds. *We both know whose chasing men, Mrs. Westing...and Carrie doesn't 'have' to.*

"Thank you for your advice, Mrs. Westing. I'll think about what you said." *About three seconds.*

Trudy's head swung back and forth between her mother and Jake, as if expecting her mother to *un-do* Carrie's invitation. Her hands went to her hips and she huffed, "Well! In that case, I guess I made a trip out here for nothing!"

Jake bit his bottom lip in an effort not to smile as he said, "Do you want your liver and onions back, Miss Westing?" Trudy gaped at him for a moment then tossed her head, "Of course not!"

***

About ten o'clock the following Thursday morning, Jake was out in the barn again when he heard several horses approaching. He stepped to the open door and saw Cooter, Manny, Joel and the other Concho hands galloping into the barnyard, all smiles. They were glad to be home.

Cooter swung lithely out of his saddle, grabbed his hat and began beating the dust from it on the leg of his pants. "How's the invalid these days," he quipped with a grin.

"Rip, raring, and ready," Jake chuckled, extending his hand to his friend and foreman. "How did it go? Did you have any trouble? Was the market price as good as we expected?"

"Good trip, no trouble, better than expected," Cooter fired back. "Hardtack oughta be pullin' in any minute." Cooter winked at Manny, who was standing beside Jake by then. "That little sugar-hoarder wouldn't even let the boys into that candy you bought without his say-so. He claimed it would rot their teeth. You'd think he was their mama, the way he slapped their hands and hid the sugar *and* candy from them." All the men were laughing by then. Cooter said between chuckles, "I'd be willing to bet that he still has most of the candy hid away somewhere in the chuck wagon."

Jake shook his head with unbelief, a big smile spreading across his face, "Well...next trip, I'll give each man his own supply of candy for his saddlebags. If he runs out then he's on his own fighting Hardtack for more."

He tossed the currying brush he had been using into a bucket sitting beside the barn door. "You boys go get cleaned up and come on up to the house. Senora Lopez was about half expecting you for dinner. She'll feed us. That'll give Hardtack time to unload and get the cook shack settled before he has to worry about fixing anything to eat."

He cut his eyes at Joel. "If I were you, I'd hurry. There's a certain little senorita that's real anxious to talk to you about something," he said, winking at the young cowboy. Joel nodded and bolted for the bunkhouse.

"I'll be up there in a few minutes," Cooter said. He reached inside his shirt pocket to withdraw a folded piece of paper. "Here... This is burning a hole in my shirt."

Jake took the paper and unfolded it. As he expected, it was a check from a Fort Worth cattle company for 'Forty-One thousand, two hundred and seventy dollars'. Jake let out a low whistle. "That's more than I ever expected." He laid a hand on Cooter's shoulder. "Good goin', Cooter. There'll be a bonus for all of you."

The next couple of hours were spent around the dining table. Jake laughed until his sides hurt at some of the stories told by his men; tales of near-encounters with rattlesnakes, swollen streams full of fast-moving debris, and a couple of warriors who trailed the herd, hoping to pick up a stray or two. There were many other accounts of life on the trail ride.

"I figured...since we was trailing our herd through their old buffalo huntin' grounds—we owed those Indians a beef or two. So I told the boys to purposely let two steers drop behind like we didn't notice," Cooter said solemnly. "I was purty sure you'da done the same thing."

"That's *exactly* what I would have done," Jake assured him. "It probably saved you men some trouble. It's better to giv'em the cattle than to have them out-right steal them."

All the time the men were seated in the dining room, Reina flitted in and out on any pretext of serving she could think of. She paid special attention that Joel's glass was never empty. Each time she left the room, the men teased Joel about the preferential treatment he was receiving. Their joking didn't seem to annoy him in the least. He just grinned and said to Manny, "I'll tell you the secret to my success sometime."

Manny's usual wide grin split his face, "Secret! There ees no secret, Jo'el. My seester's eyes done tell you secret; no?" Joel dropped his head, his ears turning red.

* * *

"I guess you know about the "lady's-choice" picnic, Saturday," Jake asked Cooter later that day. The other men had gone to the bunkhouse. They were dog-tired from the trip and wanted nothing more than to lie in bed and sleep for sixteen hours straight.

"Yeah... Before I left, Caroline told me that it would be the third or fourth Saturday in September. She informed me that I was going with her." Cooter shrugged, his eyes full of mischief. "I decided that there was no use arguing with her, so...I guess I'll go." He hesitated a moment, then asked, "Are you planning on going with...someone?"

"Not just "someone", I'm going with Carrie Stoddard," Jake answered proudly. Cooter whooped, pounding his friend's back. "Hey! How did this come about?"

Jake took great pleasure in telling Cooter all about both of Trudy Westing's visits. He told of how Carrie had misunderstood Reina's attempt to get him to eat her cookies, and of the little senorita's intervention on his behalf. Laughing so hard that he could hardly finish, he reported on Trudy's visit the past Monday morning and of her 'bribe' of liver and onions.

Cooter nearly doubled over, his eyes dancing. "Liver and onions: it's a wonder you didn't take that shotgun by the front door after her, if she was trying to poke that stuff at you."

Jake was a little chagrined, "I sort of felt sorry for the girl, so I let her down easy. I pretended the only reason I was going with Carrie was because she asked me first." His expression changed and he asked quickly, "Why don't we go in the big buggy—it has two seats. I could drop you off at Caroline's house Saturday morning, go on out to the Stoddard's and pick Carrie up and come back by to pick you and Caroline up."

Cooter rubbed the back of his neck thinking. After a few seconds, he said, "I was kind of planning on borrowing one of the buggies. Wouldn't you rather have Carrie all to yourself at the end of the day?" He hurriedly added, "The four of us will be together all day, but there's something real pleasurable about taking your girl home, when it's just you and her—don't you think?"

Jake cocked his head to one side, a pleased expression on his face. "You just might have something there, Cooter." They laughed, agreeing to leave at the same time and meet at the picnic grounds at ten-thirty.

* * *

"She's not here? But, she was supposed to go with me to the picnic today." Cooter's voice showed his disappointment.

Mrs. Hartman, Caroline's mother, took pity on him, "Yes, I know, Wade. She said to tell you to pick her up at Carrie's. She spent the night over there last night."

Cooter's smile returned immediately. "Thank you, Ma'am, so much!" He bounded down the front steps and leaped into the buggy parked out front of the Hartman home.

* * *

"Carrie, he's here!" Caroline dropped the edge of the curtain that she had been peeking behind and turned to Carrie with a puzzled look. "But he's by himself. Do you suppose Cooter forgot that this is the day?"

Carrie shook her head slowly back and forth. "I don't see how he could with Jake coming after me this morning. I hope he's not sick or something."

Just as she completed the sentence, a knock sounded on the door. The girls looked at each other with big smiles. Caroline gave her friend a hasty hug. "He's the "stuff" dreams are made of... Good luck, girlfriend!"

Carrie patted her hair nervously. Caroline had worked for over an hour on it; combing and pushing the golden-tawny mass of curls up on top of Carrie's head. Loose, wispy tendrils hung near her face and a ribbon of the same fabric as her dress circled around the base of the curls on top. Carrie had chosen a pale green cotton print with little yellow flowers sprinkled over it. The colors combined to compliment her emerald green eyes. Taking a deep breath, she opened the door.

Jake's look of appreciation let her know that she looked just right. "Come in, Jake. Caroline and I were just putting everything into the picnic basket." She motioned toward a couch, "If you'll be seated just a few minutes, we'll be right out with it."

Jake removed his hat and stepped inside. "Cooter must not have known that Caroline would be here. He's in the other buggy at her house right now," Jake commented.

"Oh, I told mother to send you...him over here. I thought you would be together," Caroline said lightheartedly. "He'll be along by the time we're ready to go."

Jake nodded, saying nothing, but was thinking. *I hope they are willing to go in both buggies. I was looking forward to the ride home with Carrie this evening.*

"Would you like something to drink while you wait," Carrie asked sweetly.

"A glass of water, if you don't mind," Jake answered and sat down.

The girls disappeared down a hall. In a moment, he could hear the muffled sound of their voices. Caroline reappeared with his water. "When Wade gets here, please let him in," she said, smiling.

"Sure."

* * *

"We'll meet you at the picnic grounds," Carrie waved over Jake's shoulder at Cooter and Caroline in the other buggy.

"Don't you worry about that...you've got the food," Cooter teased. He flicked the reins and the buggy lurched toward town. Caroline hooked her arm through his and leaned her head dreamily against his shoulder. "I'm so...oo glad you made it back in time, Wade. I dreaded the thought of going with anyone else today."

Cooter leaned forward to look down at her, a frown on his handsome face. "You mean you *would* have gone with someone else if I hadn't made it back?" There was hurt in his voice. Caroline turned her face up to him and leaned so close that their lips almost touched. "I'm afraid so... Mama said, if you didn't get back in time, I had to take my little brother." She smiled invitingly. Cooter could not resist the temptation; he brushed his lips across hers ever-so-briefly and whispered huskily, "Sorry, little brother."

Jake and Carrie were behind Cooter's buggy. They saw the kiss.

Cooter's got the right idea, Jake thought, enviously. *But the day has just started. My time will come.*

* * *

The annual church-wide picnic was held near the church on the outskirts of town, at a small spring-fed pond. Cottonwood trees, common to that part of Texas, surrounded the pond. A small open-air tabernacle had been constructed by the men of the community on the shore of the pond. It was used for many of the smaller, outdoor gatherings, such as, family reunions, birthday celebrations, summer revival meetings and the annual church picnic.

When the two couples arrived, there were already nearly two-dozen buggies and wagons parked around the perimeter of the area. They pulled their vehicles up beside the tabernacle in order to unload Carrie and Caroline's food. Tables had been set up under the structure and, as usual, all the food would be combined for a huge 'pot luck' picnic lunch.

After placing her last basket, filled with fresh rolls, on the table, Carrie turned to Jake, "Have you picked out a spot for us to spread our picnic blanket yet?" Jake had been too busy admiring Carrie as she efficiently moved to help arrange the food. His startled expression at her question told her that his mind had been elsewhere. She smiled, "We better hurry and get settled. The best spots are filling up fast." She pointed to a large tree on the top of a little knoll near the water. "That looks like it needs four people...like it was made for us," she said, looking up at him and wrinkling her nose adorably.

Before Jake could gather his senses, Cooter grabbed Caroline's hand and started pulling her in the direction Carrie had pointed. "You two put your blanket on one side of the tree and we'll spread ours on the other. That way, we'll have some privacy." He wiggled his brows at Jake. Jake chuckled. "All the privacy in the world; broad-daylight with only two-hundred people around us...real private."

Abe Mills, the blacksmith, was also a deacon of the church. His love for young people made him volunteer when Brother Keller asked for "someone" to be in charge of the picnic this year. He made his way to the tabernacle about eleven-thirty, to announce that the food was ready to be served. "Everyone serve yourself. When we're through eating, a good time is planned for the afternoon. The Redding sisters have prepared two or three special songs, Cole Jones will play the guitar for us, and several others have agreed to present a talent during the afternoon. There will also be a 'couples' three-legged race and a 'mixed' horseshoe tournament. At the end of the day, we will have a sunset sing-a-long. Have a good time...and *no* onlookers—everybody participates," he instructed with a chuckle.

The whole day was enjoyable. Jake couldn't remember ever having had an opportunity to spend this much time "doing nothing" but having fun. His entire young life had been spent trying to keep the Silver Concho in solid financial condition.

His greatest pleasure of the day was derived from the fact that Carrie was always in his sight....*And to think...she's been in Llano for over six years. I'm sure glad Matt didn't get to know her well...it wouldn't do for brothers to be in love with the same woman.* He smiled at the thought.

Carrie glanced up and saw his smile. "What are you thinking about," she asked with a suspicious look in her eyes. Jake's smile widened, "Oh, I can't tell you—if a person tells their wish, it won't come true." His eyes darkened as he leaned closer, "And I *was* making a wish."

Carrie tilted her head to one side; a half smile turned her pretty mouth up in one corner. "When it comes true, will you tell me?"

Jake gazed tenderly into her eyes and nodded slowly, "You'll be the *first* to know."

Cooter pointed across the pond, "Looky yonder—that's Joel and Reina ain't it?—If I've ever seen a feller in 'hog heaven', he's him. That little senorita is a mighty purty girl." The four of them watched as Joel helped Reina to her feet and the couple started strolling around the pond hand in hand.

"Joel's not any happier than she is—I have it on good authority, "Jake said solemnly, his eyes never leaving the young lovers.

After the sing-a-long, Carrie and Caroline went to the tabernacle to retrieve their baskets and platters, while the men went for the vehicles.

CHAPTER NINETEEN
To Be Sure

"Carrie, don't look now, but Trudy Westing is coming this way. Pretend you don't see her." Caroline warned out of the corner of her mouth.

Carrie moaned under her breath, "I hope she doesn't make a scene."

Trudy came straight toward Carrie, ignoring Caroline's presence. Carrie braced herself for whatever the mean-spirited girl would have to say.

Stopping within three feet of Carrie, Trudy's hands went to her hips. "I just wanted to let you know, *Miss* Carrie Stoddard that, even though you took advantage of your father's position as Jake's physician." She took a breath, "...And, even though you sneaked out to his ranch before me; knowing that I was planning to ask him to the picnic; and, even though you tricked him into bidding on your cake instead of mine... Jake Galloway has made it crystal clear that he is interested in me—not you. So, back off! Let this be the last time you try to horn-in on our relationship." She tossed her head in finality.

Caroline was listening to the girl with a pitying smile on her face; but, with the last remark, she stepped around Carrie, ready to do verbal battle on behalf of her friend. Carrie grabbed the back of Caroline's skirt, pulling her back. "Don't bother to say anything, Caroline. The bible says that we're not to argue with f...people like her."

She smiled sarcastically and said, "Trudy, when Jake—not you—makes it 'crystal clear' to me that he is interested in you instead of me, you won't have to rave or threaten me. I will honor his wishes and he'll not see me again." She waited a moment, and then asked, "Agreed?"

Trudy stared hatefully at Carrie. Her mouth worked soundlessly—a mannerism the Westing women were famous for when frustrated. Caroline raised her brows and glared stoically at the malicious girl.

After flicking her blazing eyes back and forth between the other two young women, Trudy tossed her head and spun away, commenting loudly, "I should have known it would be impossible to reason with you, Carrie Stoddard; you're just that sort of person!"

"Well, don't come around trying to 'reason' with me either about Wade, "Caroline enjoined firmly.

They watched Trudy stomp angrily toward the group of, wallflower girlfriends and young male cousins that she had dragged to the picnic with her, mostly to make herself look popular.

As she watched Trudy and her companions across the small field, Carrie's expression was a mixture of anger and hurt. Caroline observed her friend's face and sent a silent prayer heavenward. *Lord... Please forgive me for behaving no better than Trudy. I confess that I shouldn't have butted in with my mouth blazing. Help me, Lord, to learn to be sweet to those that I don't think deserve it. I know I don't deserve Your kindness either, but, Father, please help Carrie to ignore or forgive—whichever You want—the hateful things Trudy said. Carrie didn't deserve it...and I know You know it. Thank You, Father for hearing this prayer. In Jesus' name.*

The clatter of buggy wheels on the rocky ground brought both girls out of their musings. They turned around to find Jake and Cooter hopping to the ground in order to load the picnic baskets. "It sure has been a real pleasant day," Cooter drawled. His eyes sparkled as if he had a secret. "...and now it's mine and Jake's chore to get you two safely back home."

Caroline swatted his arm and answered in mock anger, "You don't *have* to do any such thing, Wade Marshall. I'm pretty sure Carrie and I could get some other fellows to do your 'chore'."

Cooter saw that the pretty, dark-eyed girl wasn't going to be bested.

He swung his head back and forth, looking here and there. "You just let 'em try to take you two away from us." He looked over his shoulder at his friend, "Ain't that right, Jake?"

Jake's chest rumbled and he shook his head. "Cooter, you talked yourself into this corner: you talk your way out. I never said a thing about it being a chore. I'd rather think of it as a pleasure." He winked at Carrie. She smiled back at him.

* * *

The Stoddard's home was about one and a half miles from the picnic grounds. Jake wanted the ride to last as long as possible, so he deliberately held his buggy team to a walking pace.

Carrie sat beside him on the padded, high-backed, bench seat. She wasn't nearly as close as Jake would have liked. He frowned, recalling that she wasn't as close as she had been on the way *to* the picnic. Was something amiss? Had he inadvertently said or done something to annoy her? His mind replayed the day's events, but he couldn't think of a thing that would have offended Carrie.

You took advantage of your father's position… You sneaked out to his ranch before me… You tricked him into bidding on your cake instead of mine. These thoughts troubled Carrie as she rode in silence beside Jake. Looking back, she admitted to herself, *I 'did' take the opportunity to go out to his ranch with Dad…and I 'did' rush out there last Saturday, knowing that Trudy intended to invite him…and I ' did' allow Caroline to give Jake and Wade a hint that practically pointed to our cakes.*

Shaking her head, the thoughts continued to trouble her. *Am I chasing Jacob Galloway—and, am I taking advantage of his lake of social experience?* She groaned.

"Did you say something?" Jake leaned forward, anxiously, so he could see her better. Carrie lifted her eyes timidly to his. "Oh…no, Jake," she lied, "I'm just tired."

Her answer relieved Jake and he grinned devilishly. "Then why don't you scoot over here next to me and lean your head on my shoulder?" His smile widened, "I'm just dying to help you."

She smiled feebly. "I know you are, Jake. You're the kindest, most unselfish man I've ever known, but…"

"But…?" Jake was bewildered.

Carrie stared at his handsome face for a few seconds, then muttered, "Nothing… I'll tell you about it sometime…maybe." She looked away—and she didn't scoot any closer to him.

Jake decided not to push her for more.

* * *

The Sun had dropped behind the distant mountains. It was that time of day when everything was seen as deep purple in color. The first evening stars were making a twinkling appearance and a soft night breeze ruffled the loose curls at Carrie's neckline and temple. It was a perfect time for romance.

Jake glanced at her from the corner of his eye. My…but she was a pretty thing.

Lord, You know I don't have much experience with women; but I'm absolutely sure that I'll never find another one that suits me better than this girl beside me. Besides being the prettiest thing I've ever seen, she's gentle and kind, without being mousy. She's a real Christian lady. He cleared his throat with the next thought.…*and she'd make a fine mother for my children.*

Carrie turned her head when Jake cleared his throat. He smiled wistfully down at her. She did move closer to him then, and hooked her arm through his. Laying her other hand on his forearm, she whispered up to him with a sigh, "Jake Galloway, you're just too good to be true."

"Who's been telling all my secrets?" he teased. "Whoever it is, I hope they keep talking. Where you're concerned—I can use all the help I can get."

* * *

They fell silent the rest of the way to Carrie's home, each with their own thoughts. When the buggy came to a stop in front of the

Stoddard's front gate, Jake tied off the reins and jumped down. He came around to her side, lifting his arms to help her down with his heart in his eyes.

Carrie leaned toward him and placed her hands on his shoulders. As he gently lowered her to the ground, he was in no hurry to let go of her. Looking deeply into her eyes, he spoke softly, "Would it be alright if I kiss you goodnight?"

Carrie's heart thundered in her chest as she lifted her face up to his and answered meekly, "If you really want to."

If I really want to… I think I'd die of longing on the way home if she said no. Jake moaned deep in his chest as he captured her soft lips with his. Though the kiss was tenderly soft and sweet, Carrie could sense restrained possessiveness in it.

When Jake's hands left her waist, he pulled her into a tighter embrace against his chest; moving his mouth over hers with unspoken longing for more. He lingered for a long time, for he had no wish to break away from her.

Jake forced himself to release her soft lips. Carrie's whole body would have melted at his feet had he not been holding her against himself. She swallowed and pushed at his muscular chest.

Jake noticed that she refrained from making eye contact as she muttered, "Will you please get the baskets for me?" He hesitated for an instant, but quickly complied.

Setting the baskets on the edge of the porch, he turned back to her. "I had a wonderful time today, Carrie. I hope you did too." His sincerity tugged at Carrie's heart like so many things about this wonderful man.

She nodded and smiled; but Jake could detect a troubled look behind the smile. She stepped up onto the porch and turned back to hold out one of her hands toward him. He took it and waited for her to say something.

"Good night, Jake. Thank you for going with me," she offered quietly and went inside.

Jake gazed after her for several moments. "Good night, Carrie," he whispered then turned back to the buggy and left without looking back.

* * *

Cooter was in a whistling mood the next morning. Jake watched him with a humorous expression. The Segundo fairly danced across the kitchen, poured himself a cup of coffee and turned back to face his boss and friend.

"I take it you and Caroline had a nice ride home last night," Jake chuckled.

Cooter came to the table where Jake was sitting, spun one of the ladder-back chairs around and straddled it; all the while, sipping his coffee. "I'm telling you…" he said, as he lowered his cup to the table, resting his elbows on the top rung of the chair's back. "Nice…don't get it! I had a 'larrapin' good time. That Caroline fits in my arms like a new pair of leather gloves," he crowed. He picked up his coffee cup and asked over the rim of it, "How 'bout you and Carrie?"

Jake dropped his eyes to his hands, which were resting on the table. "I had a real good time,—but Carrie seemed to be troubled about something."

Down went Cooter's cup again. "Jake, didn't Carrie tell you what Trudy said to her at the tabernacle while we were going for the buggies?"

Jake's brows came together. "No—she didn't. I noticed she was real quiet on the way home; but I had no idea why. Did it have something to do with Trudy?"

Cooter exhaled, "Could be… Caroline told me that Trudy said some pretty mean things to Carrie about her and you."

"Exactly, 'what' did that… 'girl' say?"

Cooter studied his friend's face before continuing, "Caroline said Trudy marched up to Carrie and told her in no uncertain terms that she—Carrie—was buttin' in on your and Trudy's 'courtship'. She accused Carrie of takin' advantage of the fact that her Pa was your doctor, just so she could see you. Then she went on to declare that Carrie tricked you into bidding on her cake instead of Trudy's."

Jake's expression went from surprise, to incredulous, to an

approaching thundercloud in the space of time that Cooter was speaking. "And Carrie believed her?"

Cooter shrugged. "Caroline didn't seem to think so, but you know women. No telling how much of it Carrie took to heart after she got to thinking about it."

Jake's mouth was by now gaping. He snapped it shut. "Huh! What am I supposed to do with that?"

"I don't know about you, but if it was my girl, I'd go straighten her out about who she needs to be listenin' to…and I'd do it quick," Cooter answered, almost angrily.

Jake looked at him without really seeing him. Suddenly, he slapped the table. "This is Sunday and Brother Keller's in town; I'm going to church. And…if I have my way, I'll be spending some time this afternoon at the Stoddard's."

Cooter hopped up. "I'm comin' with you; only I won't be following you to the Stoddard's after church," he joked.

* * *

The sermon was, as usual, directly from the Bible. Jake appreciated the fact that Keller didn't short-change his people by talking about everything except God's Word from the pulpit.

Even though he listened intently to the preacher, Jake's eyes strayed continually to the back of Carrie's head. She and her father sat on their regular pew, near the aisle. Jake thought smugly, *and no Charlie Wilsons in sight.*

* * *

Standing at the foot of the church's entrance steps, Jake watched Carrie and the doctor as they came through the doors. She smiled pleasantly at him as he reached up to help her to the ground; though she actually needed no help.

Doc stuck out his hand, "Well, Jake, I'm guessing you've completely recuperated. You look fine."

Jake grinned at the gentlemanly man, "Thanks to you Doc," he said, returning the handshake. Turning his attention back to Carrie, he began, "Carrie, I…"

"Oh Jake, there you are! I was afraid you might get away before I had a chance to invite you to have lunch with me and my family," Trudy's pretentious falsetto whined as she practically ran out of the church building.

"I'm sorry, Miss Westing, but I've already been invited to eat at the Stoddard's," Jake said without taking his eyes from Carrie's.

Father and daughter's brows shot up at his declaration. Neither one said anything, but their surprise was evident.

Trudy pivoted toward Carrie, her mouth working, but no sound came forth. After a second, she noticed Carrie's father watching her solemnly. "Well!" She huffed, glancing from the doctor to Jake and back to Carrie. "I guess you win…again!"

She turned and flounced across the yard to her waiting mother. Their heads went together and Mrs. Westing lifted her eyes to Carrie. Her lips became a thin line.

Doctor Stoddard observed all this, and turned his attention back to Jake, who was watching Carrie with a "bull-headed" look on his face.

Carrie's tongue came out to lick her pink lips, her eyes silently scolding Jake for his fib.

Jake was not to be put off, "Well! I *am* invited,—I invited myself." His expression became anxious. "I need to talk to you; Carrie…and it can't wait."

Doctor Stoddard watched Carrie's merrily twinkling eyes. They were both forced to press a finger to their lips in order to avoid making a laughing spectacle of themselves.

"Jake, I had every intention of inviting you to dinner. You just beat me to it," Carrie chuckled.

Jake relaxed. "I'll side you home."

* * *

The meal was the usual Sunday fare: fried chicken, mashed potatoes and gravy, with green beans and slices of the cake leftover from yesterday's picnic.

Jake was sure it must be good, but he was so intent on speaking to Carrie privately that he hardly tasted a thing.

When they finished, Carrie rose from her chair at the dining table and announced, "Jake, if you and Dad will go on into the front room, or out on the porch, I'll have the table cleared in short-order and then we can have that talk."

Jake nodded as he and the doctor pushed away from the table and stood. They left the dining room, heading for the front porch. It was mid-September in Texas and the temperatures made "porch-sitting" pleasurable.

Once they were settled into the two white rockers, Doc spoke, "Well, Jake, how good was the market for your cattle this time? Did you come out satisfactorily?"

Jake smiled. "Yes Sir, we came out even better than I hoped. It seems those easterners are depending more and more on Texas cattle…and…are willing to pay for them."

They talked for a few minutes about raising cattle and the best time to sell. Next, the conversation turned to Llano's recent growth and its future. Doc shared with Jake his dream of building a small hospital to meet the needs of Llano and the surrounding areas.

They fell silent at one point. Jake could hear faint sounds coming from the kitchen. He decided to make his move with Carrie's father. Taking a deep breath, he jumped in, feet-first.

"Sir, I wanted to talk to you as well as to Carrie about something. Is now a good time?"

The older man nodded. He felt that he knew what was coming, but tried not to show it.

"Sure; what did you have to say?"

Squirming a little in the rocker, Jake said, "Well Sir…it's like this…I haven't ever done this before," *I should hope not*, the doctor thought. "…and maybe I ought to talk to her first, but either way, you have to know sooner or later."

"And, what is it that I need to know," the doctor asked calmly with barely controlled mirth.

"Well, Doc…you might as well expect…" Jake exhaled nervously, "as soon as I can talk her into it..." Then he blurted, "I want to marry your daughter." He nervously added, "She doesn't know yet."

I suspect she does. The doctor smiled and the two men stared at each other for what seemed to be an eternity for Jake. *Why doesn't the Doc say something?*

At that moment, they heard Carrie's footsteps coming down the hall from the kitchen. Doctor Stoddard leaned forward in his rocker, putting him closer to Jake. "Well Son, if you can *talk* her into it...you have my blessing."

Jake wanted to yell, but held it in check. Carrie pushed the screen door open and stepped out on the porch. She turned to Jake. "...Want to go for a walk down by the river? I'd like to show you my favorite spot."

Jake had risen to his feet. He motioned toward the front gate with his hand, "Lead the way."

* * *

Carrie, more or less, held her breath as they silently walked hand in hand toward the river. When they were about fifty yards from the house, Jake spoke softly, "Carrie, I'm not positive, but I think I'm disappointed in you."

Carrie gasped, "Whatever for, Jake? What did I do?"

Jake stopped walking and turned to look into her eyes. "From the way you acted on the way home last night, you chose to listen to Trudy Westing's meanness instead of remembering what I told you the day you came out to the ranch to ask me to the picnic.

Carrie's eyes flared open wide then she dropped them to the ground. "Where...who...how did you know," she stumbled over her words.

Jake cocked his head and reached for her chin. Lifting it so that she was forced to look directly at him, he answered, "Cooter and Caroline talk to each other, Carrie." He sighed and dropped his hand. "...Like I wish we would learn to do."

Carrie's beautiful green eyes filled with tears. "Oh Jake,—I'm so sorry. I would never hurt or disappoint you on purpose. But I couldn't help it. After Trudy said what she did yesterday, I started remembering some things." She looked miserable as she continued. "Jake, I *did* allow Caroline to give you a hint about my cake. That was unfair to the other girls…and I *did* use Dad's trip out to your ranch as an excuse to see you again. I also invited you to the picnic knowing that Trudy was planning to do so." She lifted a hand, palm-up, in a pleading gesture. "Don't you see? All of a sudden, I was throwing myself at you," she trailed off.

Jake shook his head. "Carrie, just because I didn't take time to go to social events, or just because I've never singled out one certain girl, doesn't mean I haven't been 'girl-watching' all these years. I know more about women than you give me credit for."

He grinned. "I know that women are softer than men, that they are more tender-hearted, and they are a whole lot prettier. I know that, without a woman in it, a house is just a house." He stopped talking and placed both his hands on Carrie's arms, just below her shoulders. "And…I want you to know that I've been waiting for a special young woman to make the Concho into a home. I knew exactly what I was looking for." His blue eyes softened as he added, "I've found her."

Carrie stood very still. Her eyes solemnly searched his face. Finally, she murmured, "We'll see." Grabbing his hand, she tugged him along toward the river.

"Come on, I want you to see what a pretty old cottonwood I found. It's the biggest one I've ever seen. I go down there when I want to be alone."

Jake stopped and pulled her around to face him. He tried to look serious as he asked, "Do you want to be alone right now?"

Carrie's chin hiked and she started walking again. "Alone with you."

Jake reached for her, but she skittered out of the way and veered off the road onto a winding narrow trail. She was heading for a short bend in the river just a few yards ahead. Jake trotted after her, shaking his head at her antics.

It took just few moments for Carrie to stop beneath the giant cottonwood tree. She leaned back against its trunk and motioned for him to join her. "See what I mean? Isn't it pretty here?"

Jake glanced at the tree, then toward the river. The Llano River, with its sandstone-strewn banks, ran clear and, for the most part, shallow. Only after a heavy thunderstorm was it too deep for a horse to wade. The spot was very peaceful.

Looking back at Carrie, he found her watching him. Their gazes locked and Jake's pulse went crazy. He stepped closer, propping one hand against the tree's trunk, next to Carrie's head.

Without taking his eyes from hers, he lowered his head and claimed her lips once again. Unlike the kiss of the night before, this one was urgent, almost demanding. Jake dropped his hand to circle her waist and pulled her full-length against himself. He groaned and deepened the kiss.

Carrie relished the feel of Jake's rapidly beating heart beneath her hands against his chest as his lips moved pleasurably over hers.

Lifting his mouth from hers, he trailed short, breathy, kisses over her forehead, hairline and neck. Swallowing hard, he looked into her eyes, "How long, Carrie? How long do I have to wait before I can ask you to be my wife?"

Carrie's mouth moved, but nothing came out. Her heart was beating so fast, she could not speak. She reached up with one hand and traced his soft lips with her fingertips. "…Until you're absolutely sure."

A smile leaped across his handsome face. "Then I'm asking you right now, this very moment. Carrie Stoddard…will you marry me?"

Carrie circled his waist with her arms and laid her head against his broad chest. She whispered sincerely, "How can I say anything but yes when I love you so."

Jake lifted her chin again, "Ah, Carrie." He kissed her tenderly, while tears of joy trickled down his cheeks. When their lips parted, he spoke with renewed excitement, "Will you marry me today…tomorrow," he frowned, "…next week?"

Carrie gave him a "you're a bad boy" look. "Jake, we're both adults. You know as well as I do that, if we rush to the altar, people like Trudy Westing and her mother would have a glorious time with speculation as to why we were in such a hurry. I don't want to give them ammunition for gossip."

She patted his cheek, her eyes twinkling. "Besides, I want to have a while to enjoy being the envy of every grown female between here and yonder, after our engagement is announced."

Jake exhaled, "Alright, but you still haven't told me when you're gonna marry me."

Hooking her arm through his, she looked up adoringly at him, "How does New Year's day sound?"

When she saw that he was about to balk, she rushed to say, "It's only a little over three months." Before he could consider that, she said, "Come on... I want to go tell Dad. He'll be so surprised!"

* * *

"Three months," Jake complained, but started toward the house with her. Under his breath, she heard him mutter, "He won't be surprised." He looked down and winked playfully.

* * *

One hundred and ten days until Carrie would be his for all time. Jake numbered and checked the days off on the feed store calendar hanging on the kitchen wall. During the next few weeks, he filled the days with work and, as often as possible, passed the evenings sitting on the Stoddard's front porch. When the weather became too chilly to sit outside, he and Carrie moved into the parlor, where they played checkers. Sometimes, Jake would bring a favorite book and Carrie would read to him as they sat side by side on the couch.

More than once, Carrie's father came to the parlor door and cleared his throat; signaling that it was time for Jake to leave.

On the Sunday in October when Brother Keller was in Llano, the couple decided to announce their engagement. Of course, Doctor Stoddard claimed the honor.

After the sermon, when the Pastor called for announcements, Joseph Stoddard rose to his feet with a wide smile on his face. "Pastor Keller," he said and turned to glance around the congregation, "It is my great pleasure to announce the engagement of my daughter, Carrie, to be married to Mister Jacob Galloway."

The people gasped, grinned and clapped collectively. The doctor went on to say, "They have set the date for the nuptials as this coming January 1st." Applause broke out in earnest this time.

Jake reached for Carrie's hand and squeezed. He leaned closer and whispered, "I'm the happiest man in the world, Carrie." Carrie's face beamed up at him and she mouthed silently, "And I'm the happiest woman."

After the congregation was dismissed and everyone had filed outside, people came to congratulate Jake and wish Carrie happiness. Trudy and her mother watched forlornly from a distance. The Westings turned toward their buggy and Trudy sighed, "Well… I guess there's always Charlie Wilson." Her mother chuckled as they climbed into their buggy.

CHAPTER TWENTY
Cooter's Dilemma

October and November flew by and, at the same time, dragged by for Jake. He had never been so contented, nor more anxious for time to hurry along. The one hundred, ten days dissolved into twenty-nine on the first Sunday in December.

Carrie received a shower, for her hope chest, by all the women of the church. Another shower, for her wedding night lingerie, was hosted by her closest girl friends. They giggled and teased as they swooned over Jake all afternoon. Carrie took it all in stride, knowing they were right; Jake was enough to make any girl swoon.

When he arrived on the Stoddard front porch just as the shower was breaking up, the girls passed him batting their eyelashes and blushing to the roots of their hair as they twittered by.

He was at a loss as to the reason for their behavior, but when he asked Carrie about it, she just smiled and said, "I'll tell you all about it…after we're married."

Jake winked. "Then I can't wait to hear *all* about it." It was Carrie's turn to blush.

Changing the subject, Jake took Carrie's hand and pressed his lips against her palm, then looked up seriously. "Carrie…the Silver Concho will be your home after January first. You'll be the 'lady' of the house." He took a short breath and looked away for a brief moment. "I was wondering…what I mean to say…," he faltered again.

Carrie frowned with puzzlement. "Jake, is something bothering you about that?"

"No, no, no…not bother; but I want the house to be just like *you* want it. I…" He reached up and rubbed the back of his neck, then dropped the hand to his side. "What I'm trying to say is…I wanted to know if you'd like to come out to the house, to see what changes you'd like to make." He rushed on, "My mother and Big Mama, my grandmother, had their turns. Now, I think it's only fair that you have yours. I'll tell Mister Porter to let you have anything you want and put it on my bill."

Carrie leaped into his arms. "Oh Jake, you're so wonderful!"

* * *

Jake got up from the bench where he sat working inside the barn and walked to the door. He peeked outside.

"Jake, you'll never get that cinch fixed at the rate you're going," Cooter remarked good-naturedly. "The girls will be out here before noon; just like they said they would. Doc even sent word that he would bring 'em to make sure Sunday night's rain hadn't messed up the roads too bad."

Jake turned back and looked at his friend, an uncertain expression on his face. "I know, Cooter, but…what if she doesn't like the house? It *is* over thirty-five years old and she's never seen anything but the porch, kitchen and the back hallway. Oh, and she got a brief glimpse of the library." He rambled on, "What if she can't be happy in stucco, ranchero-type house…and…it's over eleven miles from town."

Cooter continued to shake his head in denial of all Jake's worried comments. "Jake, believe me, any woman in her right mind would like that house! All the rooms are big, and it's cool in summer and warm in winter. It has those purty, shiny, red tile floors…and the arched windows with the walled-in patio and garden make it look like some sort of Spanish castle." His voice trailed off as he added softly, "There ain't very many men who can offer a new bride such a house."

* * *

Suddenly, Jake stared at his best friend. Cooter's head was down.

How could I be so blind? Here I am worrying about whether or not Carrie will like my big, sprawling Hacienda, when Cooter is worried that he has nothing to offer Caroline. A shock of realization caused Jake to understand why Cooter had not yet asked Caroline to marry him.

Have I been so selfish and wrapped up in my own happiness that I couldn't even see my best friend's misery? Jake felt a shame like he had never experienced before.

Clearing his throat, he said, "I think we need to talk, Cooter. Something's bothering you and I'm bettin' I know what it is…I'm sorry I didn't see it before."

Cooter lifted his eyes. "What do you think is botherin' me?" he asked softly.

Jake raised a brow and replied, "Before I answer that, I want to ask you a question. Why haven't you asked Caroline to marry you? Don't you love her?"

"I…I just don't think the time is right," Cooter hedged. "Our situation is different from yours and Carrie's—a lot different."

"How's that?" Jake was not going to let him out of admitting the truth. *I love him too much for that.*

Cooter heaved a sigh. "Jake, you've worked hard to hang on to your and Matt's heritage, and you've done a good job. I'm happy for you…truly happy." He shook his head slightly, "I've worked hard too…all my life. I'll also have an inheritance…someday." He continued, "The difference is…my Pa, thank God, is only fifty-four years old. He's in good health and I hope he lives to be a hundred." Taking a deep breath, he continued, "That means I'll probably be an old man before I have control of my own piece of land."

Jake winced at the misery he had not noticed before in his friend's eyes. Cooter's voice sounded soft and hesitant, "Don't you see, Jake; I *can't* ask Caroline to wait that long and I *sure* can't ask her to marry me and live in the house with Mama and my pa. She's from a purty well-off family; what with her Pa being a lawyer and all." Dropping his head once more, he twiddled his thumbs nervously.

"I see," Jake answered quietly. Only, he did not see. *If I'm any judge of character at all, there's more to Caroline Hartman than a girl who only loves a man for what he possesses in land and houses.* Jake was sure of it.

As if he had read Jake's thoughts, Cooter said flatly, "In case you're thinking that I'm short-changin' Caroline; I ain't. I know she's not some kind of gold-digger. She'd live with me in a tent with a dirt floor if I asked her to…if she really loves me." Cooter sounded defensive, even to himself.

"Well…have you asked her if she loves you?—And have you told her that you love her," Jake pushed. *Cooter's the finest man I know…with or without land and houses.*

"She knows I love her. I can see the way she looks at me. I just haven't let our conversations get to the point of talking about marriage," Cooter huffed, "And I ain't!—I'm not gonna do that to her. I guess I'm a coward…or I would've already walked away, so she could find somebody with a future."

Jake thought carefully before he spoke again, "Cooter, you've always encouraged me to pray about everything, I mean *everything*. There aren't very many decisions you will make in life as important as who and when you marry. I hope you take your own advice and really talk to the Lord about this. I believe He wants you and Caroline both to be happy. After all, you're both His children."

Jake smiled and laid a hand on his friend's shoulder. "I also remember hearing Brother Keller say…in the Bible it says; when two or three agree on anything, they can ask and it will be done. Right?"

Cooter nodded, but without enthusiasm.

Jake was warm to his subject, "Then let's pray right now, and keep praying until God works things out for you." Jake bowed his head and Cooter followed suit.

"Heavenly Father, we know You are interested in everything about us as Your children. I'm not coming to you to try and tell you what's best for Cooter and Caroline, but I *am* coming to You asking that You help Cooter to look to Your power and love for the answer to his situation with her. You see, Lord; Cooter is in love with that sweet girl and he wants to ask her to be his wife. But he doesn't feel like he can do that in his present financial state. So, I'm asking You to take charge. If it's Your will for these two fine people to become a family, make it possible in a way that Cooter can provide for her needs and comfort." Jake could hear Cooter snuffing tears. "I ask all these things in the name of my Savior, Jesus Christ. Amen."

Jake finished the prayer and lifted his head to look at Cooter once again.

* * *

They heard Doctor Stoddard calling from the front porch of the house, "Jake…can you hear me, boy? I brought not one, but two, of the prettiest sights you'll ever see this side of Heaven."

Jake and Cooter nearly stumbled over each other as they rushed to the barn door and leaned out to wave at the threesome on the porch. "We'll be right there, Doc. Go on in and make yourselves at home," Jake shouted.

They quickly stowed their work and trotted up the hill with their breaths clouding the cold air.

The next two hours, Carrie and Caroline moved from room to room with pencil and paper in hand, making notes of the changes Carrie wanted to make in the house's décor. The men were at the kitchen table, drinking piping hot coffee.

"Of course, I won't change a thing if I don't think Jake will like it," Carrie confided. "Even though he gave me permission to do as I please, I think it would be selfish and insensitive of me not to check to see if he has some sentimental attachment to certain things."

She beamed at her friend, "Isn't he wonderful to even *suggest* that I remodel the house to my tastes?"

"He certainly is," Caroline sighed. Carrie noted the wistfulness in the other girl's voice. Her brows came together, but Caroline did not see the expression.

* * *

In the kitchen, the men laughed and talked, enjoying each other's company while they waited for the women to complete their rounds throughout the house.

"Well, I think I have some really exciting ideas, Jake," Carrie announced as she swept into the room waving her list.

She came around to stand behind Jake's chair then leaned over his shoulder and kissed his cheek. "Of course, I want you to agree before I do a thing. After all, this will be *our* house."

She skipped around him and sat down in the chair next to his. Placing the sheet of paper on the table in front of them both, she smoothed it flat. Turning her sparkling green eyes on him, she was about to speak when Jake stopped her by pressing his index finger to her lips. "Honey, I've already told you…if you like it, I'll like it. Just having you here with me will make this the most beautiful house in the world. You can't go wrong. I trust you completely."

Carrie gazed at him for a moment, then asked, "But Jake, isn't there anything you absolutely want left as it is…in memory?"

Jake shook his head negatively. "The whole house, the whole ranch is a reminder of my folks…I don't care what color you decide to make the curtains or paint the walls. I just want you to be happy." He touched the end of her nose with his knuckle. "Understand?"

Carrie nodded with tears in her eyes. She still could not believe that Jake was real. He was just too good to be true.

Caroline had been watching Cooter's face during the tender exchange. He face revealed a mixture of both happy *and* sad. She also detected a wishful expression there. *Will Wade ever love me the way Jake loves Carrie?*

* * *

A few days after the girls' visit, Jake rode into town to see Carrie. His heart was heavy for Cooter and Caroline. He wondered what Carrie would think. Smiling to himself, he dismounted in front of the house.

THE SILVER CONCHO: LIFE IS A RUB-BOARD

After all these years of not having anyone to talk to about things like this, it feels good to know that...from now on, she'll always be there.

He knocked and in a few moments Carrie's sweet face appeared in the round window of the door. Her mouth flew open and she called through the closed door. "Just a minute, Jake, I have to clear out the front room before you can come in!"

Jake heard rustling noises and then Carrie's hurried steps as she ran down the hall to her room.

Suddenly, the door opened. Doctor Stoddard pulled it open wide and stepped back as he motioned for Jake to enter. He called over his shoulder, "Carrie! Are you trying to give your groom pneumonia, two weeks before the wedding? It's cold out there, girl!" He shook his head and chuckled as Jake side-stepped him into the warm room.

Carrie appeared in the doorway, her cheeks pink with embarrassment. Jake thought she had never looked more beautiful. "I'm sorry, Jake; but I couldn't let you see my wedding dress." Her eyes twinkled mischievously as she added, "Yet."

Jake laughed softly. "I'm looking forward to seeing it." His expression turned serious and he motioned toward the sofa with the sweep of his hand. "Can we sit down for a few minutes? I need to talk to you about something important."

Carrie stared at him for an instant and then she complied. "What's wrong?"

"Oh, nothing is wrong exactly. I just wanted to know what you think about Cooter and Caroline." He lifted his eyes to his future father-in-law, who was standing near the door to the hall. "I'd like to hear what you think too, Sir."

Doc nodded and seated himself in a big overstuffed chair. "Have those two had some kind of falling-out? I hadn't heard."

"They haven't had a falling-out...yet; but I'm afraid that's where it's headed if I can't figure out a way to help Cooter," Jake answered solemnly. "You see, Cooter has it in his head that he can't ask Caroline to marry him unless he can offer her a nice home with a secured future." He glanced at Carrie and back to the doctor and sighed, "You see, he keeps comparing his situation to mine."

Carrie leaped to her feet. "But that's crazy! Caroline knows that most young couples start out with nothing. It's part of being in love. You work together and just being together is enough. He must think Caroline is an awfully shallow girl."

At that point, Carrie's voice had reached an angry pitch. "He certainly had better not let her know that he thinks so little of her love for him...because she just might show him the gate."

"Now Carrie," the doctor soothed, "Caroline knows that Cooter is a fine person, and that he just wants what's best for her. Of course, you and I know that his pride is involved. That's true of all men. We won't be helping either of them by criticizing his motives."

Carrie eased back down on the sofa beside Jake. Her cheeks were burning with shame. "I know, Dad. Wade Marshall is one of the finest men I know; but it seems so unfair to Caroline for him to think that." She turned to Jake. "Don't you agree, Jake?"

Jake reached to take her hand in his and then pressed it to his lips. Lifting his head, he reasoned, "Carrie, you mean to tell me that it means nothing to you to know that we won't have scratch and scrape for a living...and our kids," he looked at Doc quickly, "...will come into this world with a nice home?"

"Jake! Of course I'm delighted that you have a nice home and a paying ranch. But let me tell you right now...if you didn't have the proverbial 'pot' and we had to live in Daddy's barn, I would love you just as much."

"And I would love you just as much...but I would feel miserable and guilty if I had to put you through that." He added softly, "I understand what Cooter is feeling...I just don't know how to help him." Shaking his head sadly, he murmured, "I was hoping you two might."

They sat silently, each with their own thoughts for several minutes. Finally, Doctor Stoddard said, "Carrie, I need a nice, hot cup of coffee; would you mind making some for us?"

Once Carrie was out of the room, the doctor turned to Jake. "Jake, I do have a suggestion—for what it's worth. It all depends on how close you and Wade are. Do you want to hear?"

THE SILVER CONCHO: LIFE IS A RUB-BOARD

* * *

Carrie carefully balanced the heavy tray; loaded with cups and a plate of cookies on her right hand. She held the coffeepot with the other in her left. Without taking her eyes from it, she handed the pot to her father as she set the tray on a small table at the end of the couch. Retrieving the coffeepot she said, "I hope I made it strong enough for you two. I brought a few molasses cookies as a peace-offering in case I…" she paused, "Where is Jake?"

The Doctor tried his best to look innocent. "Oh, he decided to go see Adam Hartman"

* * *

Jake rapped softly on the front door of the Hartman home and hugged himself against the icy temperature. He shuffled from one foot to the other in an effort to stave off the cold while he waited for someone to answer his knock.

A few moments passed and he heard from within, "I'll get it Mama!" He smiled, recognizing Caroline's voice. The door opened narrowly and the girl's face brightened at the sight of him. "Jake! What in the world…" she exclaimed. Then, remembering how cold it was outside, she reached around the door, grabbing his coat sleeve and pulled him inside.

"Are you ok? Nothing's wrong with Wade…is there?" she asked anxiously.

"No. Nothing is wrong, Caroline. I know it is after his office hours, but I need to see your father. Will you ask him if he can give me a few minutes?"

Caroline was relieved by Jake's assurance that nothing was amiss; nevertheless, she was instantly aware that Jake's expression was serious.

"Oh… Sure." She motioned toward a small, but cozy room, "You just go on into the parlor and I'll let him know you're here."

An hour later, Jake left the Hartman's home, his heart warmed by the satisfaction of a mission accomplished.

CHAPTER TWENTY-ONE
Eternally Yours

The Stoddard-Galloway wedding ceremony was set for ten o'clock on New Year's morning. Jake, Cooter, and all the men of the Silver Concho spent the night at the hotel in Llano. A reception was to be held at the community center, immediately following the wedding.

Jake arose at the crack of dawn, for this was his wedding day and he was most anxious for it to begin.

* * *

January 1, 1871—Llano, Texas

The sky appeared threatening. Ominous, dark gray, heavy-looking clouds were moving in from the northwest. The temperature plunged dramatically as families of the area arrived in their buggies and wagons.

Pulling up in the Llano churchyard, men quickly jumped down to assist their wives and daughters to the ground. No one tarried outside; not even the young, single men, who usually took every opportunity to socialize with the unmarried girls of the community.

Despite the weather, spirits were high. No one would have dreamed of missing this wedding. It was the highlight of the long, cold, Texas winter of 1871.

THE SILVER CONCHO: LIFE IS A RUB-BOARD

* * *

'This is it," Jake whispered to no one in particular. His heart overflowed with joy at the certain hope of making Carrie his wife on that very day. Ignoring the weather, he saw the day as the brightest, most wonderful day of his life. With wonder in his voice, he whispered repeatedly, "Mrs. Jake Galloway... Carrie Galloway...my wife...mine...eternally."

Heretofore, Jake had reverently held his thoughts in check with regard to the coming night. Now, as he waited in the pastor's study for the music to begin, he couldn't help but relish the feelings brought on by the promise of being a bridegroom on his wedding night.

Cooter glanced up just then and realized that Jake's neck and cheeks were flushed. "You ain't *scared*...are you boy? This is what you've been livin' for ever since you first laid eyes on that girl."

Jake cut his eyes at his best man. Sticking a forefinger in his collar, he pulled it away from his neck. "No, Cooter. I was thinking about...tonight," he replied frankly.

"Oh," Cooter answered. Immediately a light of understanding appeared in his eyes and his lips spread in a wide grin. "First things first—okay? Let's get you two married then *all* your dreams can come true."

Jake turned his head, directing a troubled look at his best friend. "Cooter...is it wrong for me to be thinking those thoughts? I mean...is it disrespectful to Carrie?"

Cooter slapped his leg and chuckled, "Not at this late date. There'd be something wrong with you if you didn't think about that on your wedding day."

Jake nodded and grinned. "I guess I'm just guilty of being a man."

Brother Keller stuck his head in the door and whispered, "Now's the time, Jake. You ready for this?"

"I'm more than ready, Preacher."

"I thought so... Come on."

***

A temporary screen had been erected in the back corner of the small church building. It was too cold for the bride and her father to wait outside for the signal to begin their procession down the aisle. The building's entrance vestibule was not large enough to accommodate the two bridesmaids and Carrie in their long, full dresses, plus her father.

Doctor Stoddard patted Carrie's hand, resting nervously on his forearm. "You're not nervous, are you, Honey," he asked sympathetically, "Today is the day you've been dreaming of since Sheriff Briscoe compared Charlie Wilson to pyrite and Jake to pure gold."

Carrie's beautiful green eyes twinkled as she replied impishly, "Actually Dad, I think I knew Jake was the one the moment I saw him standing in front of Abe Mills' shop gawking at me."

She sighed, "He was…and is…the humblest, kindest, sweetest, most handsome, unselfish man I've ever seen," she winked, "besides you."

Just then, they heard the sound of a throat being cleared and the processional music began. Jake turned and faced the front entrance to the sanctuary. His anticipation knew no bounds as Carrie's maid-of-honor, Caroline, stepped out from behind the screen and made her journey down the center aisle of the little church.

The color of her emerald-green, satin dress reminded Jake of Carrie's eyes. It boasted a long bouffant skirt, which was drawn up in a large, tucked V, revealing a ruffled, white-lace underskirt. A matching narrow, green satin, bow was tied in the back of her long, dark hair; its streamers flowing down the same length as her beautiful tresses.

In her hands, Caroline held a bouquet of violets surrounded by the same lace as in the underskirt.

Jake fleetingly wondered where the violets came from at that time of the year. Then he remembered that Caroline's mother prided herself in successfully raising those flowers in the east-facing, closed in, multi-windowed, porch of the Hartman home.

THE SILVER CONCHO: LIFE IS A RUB-BOARD

Glancing at Cooter, he saw that his friend was staring like a man frozen. The expression on Wade's face was one of pure rapture. Jake grinned and nudged him, whispering softly, "You're next."

Jake almost lost the joy of the moment when a pained expression immediately spread over Cooter's face.

Caroline's eyes were fixed on Wade. She saw the troubled expression suddenly spread across his face and her heart plummeted. *Why would Wade look so…disappointed?*

Jake felt almost guilty, because he knew something Cooter didn't…yet. Everything would work out for his best friend…and the woman Cooter loved. Jake had already seen to that.

* * *

Mrs. Keller watched intently while she expertly played for Caroline and her little sister, Grace to complete their trek down to the front of the podium.

Once they were there, she lifted her hands dramatically and increased the volume of the music to signal the beginning of the actual bridal march.

Everyone in the sanctuary, including Doctor Stoddard, wore a huge smile as he stepped from behind the screen with his stunningly beautiful daughter on his arm. He patted her hand as he escorted her regally down the aisle to her waiting groom.

Carrie's wedding dress was made of soft, milk-white velvet with insets of lace that matched that in Caroline's dress. The fitted bodice bore a high neckline and a five-inch lace waistband which 'peaked' beneath her bosom. The "Queen-Anne" tapered sleeves also had lace peaks just above the wrists. The skirt was split down the front. Ruffled tiers of the lace underskirt were visible as Carrie moved gracefully forward.

Her golden, fawn-colored, hair was pulled up and back, with curls falling softly from the "up-do" at the crown and a few small, wispy, ones at her temples. Her waist-length veil with its train of the same lace was secured in her hair by pearl-ladened, silver combs.

The bride's bouquet was composed of white satin rosebuds, interspersed with violets from Mrs. Hartman's in-house garden; and surrounded by lace and pale-lavender, satin streamers.

* * *

"If I'm dreaming, Cooter, don't you *dare* wake me up," Jake muttered out of the corner of his mouth. His cobalt-blue eyes sparkled intently as he watched the beautiful girl of his dreams gliding toward him beside her father.

Swallowing several times in an effort to rid his throat of the lump that had formed there, Jake thought, *Lord, you sure knew what You were doing when You put that girl together...and to allow me to have her as my wife...is more than I can understand. I promise to praise you, Father, for the rest of my life. And I ask that You help me to take care of her...treasure her...eternally.*

Carrie did her best to keep her lips from quivering. She smiled bravely and sought Jake's eyes for encouragement. She found those eyes watching her, a light of pure love shining out of their dark-blue depths. He smiled softly.

Just a few more steps, Carrie thought, leaning on her father's arm.

* * *

"I now pronounce you man and wife," Brother Keller declared. His lips split with a smile that encompassed his whole face. "Jake, you may now kiss your bride."

Jake grinned like a besotted fool. He fumbled with Carrie's veil, but managed to lift it over the back of her head without destroying her hairdo. Without taking his eyes off Carrie's lips, he said, just before he lowered his head, "I thought you'd never get to this part, Preacher."

The kiss went on and on until, finally, the minister cleared his throat, "Jake, I think you better put that kiss on hold. The weather looks bad and you've got to get your *wife* home before dark."

The entire congregation of guests howled in glee.

Jake released Carrie and winked, "We'll finish this conversation out at the Concho tonight." He turned in the direction of the front door then placed her hand on his forearm.

Brother Keller announced to all, "I present to you, for the very first time, Mr. and Mrs. Jacob Galloway."

When they reached the front door, Jake placed his hand on Carrie's waist and pulled her close to his side. The couple ran out of the church and across the yard to the side door of the community building, laughing as they went.

Once inside, Jake drew Carrie against himself, pushing the door shut with his foot. He kissed her passionately and hungrily until the crowd started beating at the door shouting, "Come-on, Jake; it's cold out here!"

Carrie sighed in his arms, "Jake, we can't let everyone catch pneumonia...open the door."

He gave her one more, quick kiss, then swung the door open. "Sorry. I forgot you folks were there," he joked with a grin.

* * *

Everyone transferred from the church to the community building with teeth chattering and beating their arms against the cold. The clouds continued to darkened, even more than before the ceremony began. It looked like a "blue-northern" was on the way.

Once inside, the building was warm and no one wanted to hurry away from the event; though common sense said they should.

Carrie was sensitive of the dangerous weather. After about a half-hour, she leaned against Jake and whispered for his ears alone, "Jake, I don't want to put a damper on our wonderful day, but unless you want to spend the night at Dad's house, we'd better hurry things along." She added, "We have to consider our guests also."

Jake panicked at the very thought of spending his wedding night under the roof with his father-in-law. He gazed at her upturned face and answered playfully, "Sweetheart, I'm ready to leave right now. I can't wait to get you all to myself. And I promise you that I'm *not* gonna spend our wedding night at the Doc's house!"

His expression changed abruptly and he asked, concern evident in his voice, "Are you afraid to drive in this weather? If you are, we can stay at the hotel for a couple of days until the weather clears."

She shook her head vigorously, "No. I'm not afraid. I want to go home…our home."

His smile was grateful, but Carrie detected an apologetic waver in his voice when he answered, "But there are a couple of things we have to see to first." He winked adorably, "Are you with me, *Mrs.* Galloway?"

"Forever," she whispered.

* * *

Caroline and Wade had stationed themselves at the beginning of the reception line with the bride and groom in the center, followed by Doctor Stoddard at the end.

The wedding guests wasted no time as they filed in from the cold and congratulated the young couple. When the last person had passed by, Carrie motioned to Caroline and Mrs. Hartman. They came immediately, anxious to help.

"Mrs. Hartman, Caroline, as you can see, the weather is worsening by the minute. Jake and I agree that we should speed the reception up in order to give everyone time to reach home before travel becomes dangerous. Would you mind if we make a few statements of gratitude and an announcement that Jake has planned and then get on with the cake, punch and sandwiches? I really hate to rush things, but this will be something we can tell our kids." She blushed rosy-pink at her reference to children. Caroline glanced at her mother and chuckled.

The two women were in complete agreement with her concerning a reason to hurry. They went directly to the beautifully decorated table which held the cake and other foods and prepared to serve when Carrie gave signal.

THE SILVER CONCHO: LIFE IS A RUB-BOARD

* * *

Jake raised his hands to quiet the guests.

After a moment, he cleared his throat nervously and said, "Folks, Carrie and I want you to know how thankful we are that you came today. Your presence makes this an even more special occasion."

He pulled Carrie snuggly to his side and looked tenderly down at her, "…if that's possible." The group chuckled in unison.

Jake cleared his throat again. He was not comfortable with public speaking, but knew that this was something he had to…no…was *glad* to do.

CHAPTER TWENTY-TWO
My Friend...Through Thick and Thin...

"I'm not very good at this sort of thing, but, I wouldn't count myself as much of a man...or a friend, if I didn't take this opportunity to open my heart to you."

Jake shifted from one foot to the other. "Once in a lifetime...maybe twice...a man is blessed by the Almighty with a real true friend; a person who knows the worst things about you, yet sticks by you anyway through 'thick and thin.' That person might be a relative, a brother, or just someone who chooses to be your friend for no particular reason...not because he *has* to.

"As for me, Wade Marshall has been a friend that stuck closer than a brother." Drawing Carrie nearer to his side, Jake lifted his hand and motioned for Cooter to come forward. Cooter's eyebrows shot up, but he complied.

Jake was unaccustomed to expressing himself in public, but he pushed ahead. "Ever since I can remember, Wade 'Cooter' Marshall has been my friend. He was always there, helping Matt and me through good and bad times. A lot of times, he sacrificed his own plans to help us."

Jake looked around, searching for Cooter's parents. When he spotted them behind some of the other guests, he said softly, "By the way, I want to thank his parents for allowing and, most of the time, encouraging him to be there for Matt and me."

"Another thing," he swallowed, "I could always depend on him to tell me the truth...even when I didn't want to hear it."

"Cooter has been one of the biggest Christian influences in my life. He constantly encouraged me to look to the Lord about everything." Jake smiled down at Carrie. "...Everything." By that time, Cooter's ears and neck were very red in light of Jake's praise.

"Cooter, I want you to know that I prayed for some way to show you how much I appreciate you. I know I could never repay you for all the years you've stood by me...I wouldn't even try; but I think I've found a way to even the score...in a small way."

He ran a hand inside his coat pocket and withdrew a long envelope. Reaching out to grasp Cooter's hand, Jake placed the envelope in it.

"This is from Carrie and me...and I know Matt would want it too." Cooter accepted the envelope. With an expression akin to wonder, he stared down at it.

"Well, don't just stare at the thing...open it," Jake admonished softly.

The wedding guests held their breath. They were more than a little touched by Jake's speech. What could a friend give another in order to show appreciation? Money—certainly not! That would cheapen the relationship. Jake wouldn't do that. So they waited with anticipation as Cooter stuck a finger under the flap and opened the envelope.

Removing the document, he unfolded it and read silently for a few moments then lifted suspiciously bright eyes. "Jake...I...I don't know what to say," he stuttered.

"Don't say anything. Just get-on with your life," Jake answered sincerely.

"What's in there?" Charlie Wilson called out.

Cooter looked at his parents, whose curiosity matched everyone else's. "It's a deed to a whole section of Concho land, adjoining my folk's place. That increases our holdings, Pa, to two whole square miles of land...Twelve hundred and eighty acres!"

He turned back to Jake, who was grinning from ear to ear. Jake said, loud enough Cooter's parents to hear, "I'm giving orders to the Concho hands to brand half of the new Spring calves with the Marshall brand. There'll be no fences between us...unless *you* put them up."

Cooter stared at his friend for several seconds. Dropping his eyes to hide the tears, he spoke in a voice hoarse with emotion, "Jake, I always regretted that I was an only child. I watched you and Matt through the years and wished I had a brother, too. 'But you just made me realize that I *do* have a brother…two brothers."

He leaned closer to Jake, with a silly grin. "I know why you did this…and I can never thank you enough."

Jake's eyes twinkled with pleasure.

* * *

The bride and groom shared the first piece of cake. They laughed and teased, kissing away crumbs from each other's face. The watchers were delighted to see Jake Galloway—big, serious, Jake Galloway—behaving like twitter pated fool.

Doctor Stoddard watched with amusement glowing in his eyes. Anyone who happened to glance at the good Doctor could easily tell that he was pleased for his beautiful daughter. Jake was a prize son-in-law.

After half an hour, people began to come expressing regrets to the couple for leaving but, considering the weather, it was necessary. Jake and Carrie certainly understood.

Carrie said, "But…let me throw my bouquet before all the girls leave!" The girls lined up, giggling and pushing good-naturedly, vying for the best position.

When Carrie let it fly, Caroline jumped up and snatched the bouquet from the air. She laughed smugly when the other girls teased that the catch had been rigged.

* * *

Cooter had waited as long as he could. He approached Caroline from behind and whispered to her, "Can you spare a minute, right now, for me?"

She whirled around, a wide smile on her lips. "I can spare more than a minute. In fact, you can have all the time you want."

He led her to a secluded corner of the room and looked deeply into her dark eyes; then he said softly, "This might not be the right time and place to do this, but I can't stand it any more."

Caroline was quivering with excitement. She had been wondering how long it would be before Cooter worked up his nerve to approach her.

"I think you already know that I love you; but, in case you haven't figured it out, "he chuckled, "I love you, Caroline Hartman. I have for a long time. I just couldn't tell you because I didn't have anything to offer you."

Caroline interrupted him at that point, "Wade Marshall, you're all I want...or need. It doesn't matter to me what you have or don't have. I could almost be angry with you for thinking it would." She cupped his face with her soft hands, "You see...I've loved you for a long time too."

"I kinda figured you did," he whispered. "But I couldn't ask you to live like I would have been able to provide...until today."

He continued softly, "I wish I had you off some place by ourselves to do this; but...in a couple of years, working real hard; I know I can save enough to build us a house. It'll be a small house to start with, but I'll build it so it will be easy to add onto." Taking a deep breath, he said in a rush, "Will you marry me then?"

Caroline smiled secretly while he spoke. She didn't answer him for several moments. Finally, Cooter said in exasperation, "Caroline!—Will you?"

"No, Cooter, I won't marry you in a couple of years," she said, with mock seriousness.

Cooter's mouth flew open to protest, but Caroline stopped him with the heel of her hand against his lips. "But I will marry you this coming June. I think six months is enough time to build our house."

With a pained expression, Cooter pleaded, "But, Caroline, you don't understand. I don't have..." Caroline was having fun. She interrupted him in mid-sentence, "Oh yes you...we do!"

She jumped into his arms, still talking, "Three days ago, my daddy, your daddy and Jake came to me and gave me a 'letter of intent'. It says that, at a time to be named by me, they promise to furnish all the materials and labor to build a house for us." She quirked her lips, "So, ask away...and I'll give the word!"

Cooter whooped as he circled her waist with his arm and swung her around. Suddenly, he lowered her to the floor. "Why didn't you tell me this before?"

Caroline placed her hands on her hips and leaned toward him from the waist, her face just inches from his. "Because I didn't want you marrying me for my house, like I didn't want to marry you for yours!"

Cooter stared at her. What did she just say?

* * *

The men of the Silver Concho, Adam Hartman and his wife, and Doctor Stoddard watched with enjoyment as both couples, at opposite ends of the room, sealed their vows and promises with kiss after kiss.

After giving them what he felt was a reasonable amount of time, Doc cleared his throat, "Alright, all you love birds, we all need to get out of here. The weather is getting worse and you should have already been headed for the Concho."

He winked at Adam Hartman, "Unless you and Carrie want to stay with me tonight." Jake's men chuckled.

That was all Jake needed to hear. He grabbed Carrie's hand and headed for the door. He had driven his lightweight, covered, two-seater carriage into Llano the day before. Manny was responsible to see that it was waiting outside the community building door.

Catching Carrie by the waist, he swung her up into the boot of the buggy and jumped in beside her. Yanking a heavy blanket from behind the seat, he packed it snuggly around his bride, stole a quick kiss, and dropped the leather curtain on her side of the buggy.

Reaching down under the seat, Jake retrieved a pair of leather gloves. After pulling them on and taking the reins, he leaned forward to scan the skies. A frown stole across his face, "Manny, you all stay close by on the way out to the ranch. I don't want to take any chances."

"Si, Jake. We steek to you very near," Manny replied, giving a quick, worried glance at the approaching clouds.

* * *

When Jake closed the curtain on her side, Carrie suddenly experienced an overwhelming sense of security. His loving act of protectiveness reconfirmed to her that Jake would always be a husband that would put her and her comfort before his own.

She sat quietly as they hurried toward the ranch, not wanting to distract him. She smiled to herself and promised in her heart that his selfless love would never be one-sided.

Gazing at the big, handsome man…her husband, she sighed and watched with admiration while he expertly sawed the reins and pushed the horse to maintain a steady pace against the increasing cold, northwesterly, winds.

CHAPTER TWENTY-THREE
Sweet Promises

Manny, Joel and the other Concho hands rode on either side and behind Jake's buggy. They watched for possible windblown obstacles ahead and were ready to keep the lightweight vehicle from tilting during hard gusts of wind.

About six miles out of Llano, a sudden blast of wind brought a splattering of sleet mixed with rain. The icy mix increased in intensity until the men were forced to bend forward in their saddles, holding their hats down to shield their faces and eyes.

Seeing that Jake was having the same problem, Carrie leaned from behind the protective curtain and reached up to place her hand on top of his hat, holding it securely in place for him.

Jake's heart was warmed by her selfless act, but he said, "I don't want you to get too cold. I wish you would get back behind the curtain. I can manage."

Carrie smiled up at him, a lovingly tender light in her eyes, "I know you can...but I want to help. I'll be alright. We're in this together...from now until forever. Remember?" She sighed, "Isn't it wonderful, Jake?"

Jake's thoughts were filled with wonder, *Lord, what a remarkable woman—no "wife"-You've given me.*

Despite the difficulty he was having with the horses, which balked against the wind and pelting ice, he switched the reins to his left hand and cupped the back of her head with the other. Pulling her toward him, he kissed her urgently. "You'll never know what that means to me, Carrie."

Releasing her, his eyes changed and a no-nonsense gleam appear behind his smile, "But right now, please—get back behind the curtain. I don't want you to get sick...on your wedding day...night, Mrs. Galloway."

Carrie giggled, "Have it your way, *Mister* Galloway."

She scooted behind the leather barrier and snuggled deeper into the blanket around her shoulders.

* * *

The top of the small carriage was beginning to bow with the weight of sleet that had collected there and turned to solid ice as they rounded the curve in front of the Concho ranch-house.

Manny pulled his horse over, near to Jake's side of the buggy. Speaking against the howling wind, he yelled, "Jake, Hardtack has the house nice and warm for you and Mees Carrie. You take her inside, pronto. I weel put the buggy a-way."

He smiled warmly, adding, "Congratulations, mi amigo."

Jake nodded gratefully, touching his hat in acknowledgement.

* * *

The vehicle stopped directly in front of the porch steps. Manny dismounted quickly to grab the reins from Jake.

Jumping to the ground, Jake went hurriedly around to Carrie's side of the buggy. She, in the meanwhile, disengaged herself from the blanket and pushed the curtain aside. Her smiling groom stood there worshipfully with his arms up. Gathering her skirts, she draped her arm around his neck as Jake scooped his bride up, then swung around to step onto the porch. She hung there for a moment, waiting for him to lower her feet to the floor. Instead, Jake moved to the door and motioned with his head for her to turn the doorknob, "I know this isn't the first time you've been across this threshold, but it *is* the first time since you became the woman of the house. It is my pleasure to carry you across it...Mrs. Galloway."

Carrie delighted in the sound of her new name. She laughed softly and reached down to turn the knob. "Please do... 'Mister Galloway'."

Jake, mindful of the billowing skirts of her wedding dress, lifted her high in his arms as he stepped through the doorway and closed it behind them with a shove of his heel.

He looked down at the beautiful woman in his arms, an expression of possessive wonder in his eyes. "Do you have any idea of how much I love you, Carrie?" he whispered.

Carrie laid her head on his shoulder. Looking up into his eyes, she answered softly, "The longer I know you, Jake Galloway, the more I *think* I understand." She put her free hand behind his head and pulled it down so she could kiss his lips tenderly. "Thank you, Sweetheart," she sighed.

Jake smiled, the romantic light in his eyes growing brighter by the moment. "I don't want to put you down in here. I think it's more appropriate to set you down in our bedroom." He paused, smiling tenderly, "I have a couple of things that I want to talk to you about, that need to be said in there."

Carrie's pursed her lips, trying to look amused... She leaned away from his chest to get a better look at his face. "Jake...what are you up to?"

Jake didn't answer, but kept walking down the hall to their bedroom. Once inside, he, once again, kicked the door closed behind them. It was not necessary for they were completely alone in the big, rambling house.

He lowered her gently to the floor, then dropped his hands. For what seemed a long time to Carrie, he just watched her face.

She could tell that he was rehearsing something in his mind. "What?" she finally asked, not able to wait any longer.

Jake said nothing, but took her hand and moved to the bedside. He pulled her down beside him as he sat down on the edge of it. Carrie was amused; yet semi-wary. What was he so serious about?

THE SILVER CONCHO: LIFE IS A RUB-BOARD

"Carrie, my momma told me that Dad made her some promises on their wedding night. She said, no matter what came their way through the years, those promises gave her strength to keep going in tough times. They were the foundation of their marriage...and my folks had a wonderful life together," he winced, "...short as it was."

His cobalt-blue eyes captured her emerald green ones, a loving expression in them. "I'm going to make the same promises to you, Sweetheart...

"They are not just foolish promises that I might not be able to keep—such as wealth, health, or freedom from trouble and heartaches. Those things, I won't always be able to control. But there are things that I *know* I can promise you...like the fact that you will be the 'only' woman I will ever love. I will keep my vow to forsake all others. When we have a quarrel, as all couples occasionally do; no matter how angry we may be at each other, I promise that I will never seek comfort, counsel—or anything else from any woman but you."

She leaned against him and laid her head against his chest. He continued to hold her hand as he spoke, "I'm a big man, Carrie," Carrie smiled in agreement. "...but, you will *never* know meanness—physically, or by words, from me. I would give my life, if necessary, to stop anyone else who might try to harm you...or the kids we hope to have."

He ran his thumb over the top of her soft hand, "Maybe I should have said this first—I promise to try to be the 'spiritual leader' in our family. I believe it is my responsibility as husband *and* father to see that Christ is the center of our home. He will be the guide for every decision I...we...make together."

I could never possibly doubt you, my darling, Carrie was thinking as he spoke.

"The third promise is that...I have never been a lazy person, so I promise to work hard and do my best—even if it kills me—to provide all you need and, hopefully, all you want—that goes for our children, too."

He shifted on the bed, watching her expression. "Next, I think you need to know that this ranch is half Matt's. I'm hoping that, someday, he will want to come back and claim his part. In the meanwhile, I split profits and expenses right down the middle. I have an account, in his name, in Llano. It'll stay there until he dies…or until he comes back.

"If he never claims his half of everything, I've made provision that his wife and children will inherit what is rightfully his."

He looked almost sheepish as he added, "I'm not bragging, Carrie, but the Concho is a big place. Matt and I could split it right down the middle and still come out with two of the biggest spreads around here." He stopped speaking and watched for Carrie's reaction to the things, he had just said to her.

She gazed at her husband without say a word—she didn't have to speak, her eyes were saying it all. "Jake, it was wonderful to *hear* you promise those things, but I already know in my heart, that you're the kind of man who would do them, with or without any spoken promises.

Like your mother, I'll hold them dear to my heart all our lives… And, even after death, I believe I'll somehow know that I spent my life with the most wonderful man anywhere in the world."

Carrie breathed in, "My turn—I also have some promises to make to you… I promise that our problems will remain just that—'our' problems. I will talk to you and no one else, when…if…I ever have a grievance with you. I will be slow to get angry, and quick to forgive. I will not pout or act childish and I won't ever try to 'get even' with you."

Her eyes were twinkling. She reached up to cup his handsome face once again, whispering, "…And I don't want us to ever…ever go to bed angry." She kissed him long and passionately.

When, at last, Jake lifted his head, he whispered huskily, "Are you ready to get started on that family, Carrie Galloway? He winked, "I'm anxious to do *my* part."

Carrie stood up, laughing softly, her face red as a beet, but she was determined to 'never' be shy with Jake. "Well…we *all* have to do our part," she giggled.

Turning her back to him, she whispered over her shoulder, "Will you…help me out of this dress?"

Jake eagerly complied.

CHAPTER TWENTY-FOUR
Full Circle

Five years...has it really been five years? Jake got to his feet and stretched. He looked down at his friend, who still sat on the edge of the creek. "We're two of the most blessed men I know, Cooter. God is good."

"You got that right, boy," his friend responded, scrambling to his feet. "I thank Him every day for landing our families in this corner of Texas together." Chagrinned by such talk between men, he continued, "He knew we would need each other."

Both men grinned at each other, a little embarrassed.

Jake didn't say anything for a while, but looked out across his land to the south. Cooter chunked rocks at a palmetto bush on the other side of the creek.

Finally, Jake spoke, "When Matt took off for West Point, I don't think I could have stood it if you hadn't kept insisting that God was in control and He would bring good out of my situation."

"I admit, my faith was weak...and I thought you were just trying to fill me with hope to keep me from buckling. It wasn't until I got that letter from Dimple that I began to really believe that what you had been saying all along was true—that the Lord was working it out for my...and Matt's good."

Jake stared at nothing, but in his mind he was reliving the morning, last September, when Matt and Dimple galloped across the bridge and rounded the grove of trees in sight of the Concho ranch house.

* * *

Of all people, little Collin was out on the front porch and was the first to see them. He had stationed himself there every day, all day, from the moment he had been told that 'Unca' Matt was coming.

The two year-old had never seen the mysterious soldier-uncle, and wasn't really sure what the excitement was all about. But, he had instantly decided that he wanted to see the "so'jer" suit his Unca Matt would be wearing.

In his young mind, a "so'jer" must be a very important person for Jake to be so anxious for him to come.

About eight-thirty that morning, Jake was sitting at the kitchen table watching Carrie as she moved around the room. They were discussing all they wanted to do when Matt and Dimple arrived.

Like Collin, Carrie wasn't quite sure what to expect. Of course, she had seen Matt from a distance four and a half years ago. She knew that he was very much like Jake in appearance and mannerisms. However, Matt had left home in anger. It had taken a young Christian woman to help him see his need to yield that anger to God. *Will Matt be different now? Maybe so; he's had a lot of training in self-discipline. Will that military training make him a stern, distant, un-friendly man, or will he be a warm, caring person like Jake?*

Carrie kept her questions to herself. She determined to not do, or say, anything that might dampen Jake's excited anticipation.

Suddenly, through the open front door, they heard their little son's voice, "I see 'em, Daddy! I see Unca Matt's 'so'jer' suit!"

The child scrambled down the porch steps as fast as his short legs would allow. Running several steps in the direction of the approaching couple, he stopped suddenly—intimidated by the big, black stallion his uncle was riding.

He stood perfectly still, a chubby forefinger stuck in his mouth and watched in wonder with wide, blue eyes.

"Look at that," Dimple breathed, when she and Matt spotted the darling little boy standing a few feet in front of the house, watching them solemnly.

"Isn't he the most beautiful thing you've ever seen?" she cooed.

Matt nodded, but said nothing. His eyes had teared and his throat tightened at the sight of his brother's son. *Jake's boy—my nephew.*

The screen door popped open. Jake and Carrie came rushing out onto the porch, hand-in-hand. She was smiling brightly, but Dimple noted that Jake appeared to be apprehensive. Matt understood Jake's uncertainty, for he too was at a loss as to how this first meeting would go.

Dimple glanced from Matt to Jake. At the same time, Carrie looked from Jake to Matt. Then the two young women looked at each other, understanding, and tears gleaming in their eyes.

Reining Breeze and Mimi to a halt, Matt and Dimple dismounted. Matt's heart was thundering. *What can I say? How do I make him understand how much I love him; after the way I left?* Fixing his eyes on the child, who had inched toward him, Matt squatted down and extended open hands to the boy. To his surprise, Collin flew into his embrace and wrapped his baby arms around his uncle's neck. Matt closed his eyes in rapture.

Pushing away so he could look into his uncle's face, the little rascal said boldly, "Hi, Unca Matt—I'm Collin. I want a 'so'jer' suit like yours." All four adults laughed hilariously and the tension was broken.

Dimple held her hands out, beckoning Collin to come to her, "Hello, Collin, I'm your Aunt Dimple. I don't have a 'so'jer' suit, but I sure do love little boys. May I hold you?"

Collin looked her over somberly for a moment. He decided that she was pretty, like his mother, so he leaned toward her with his arms raised. Dimple hugged him warmly and kissed his soft cheek.

Carrie came forward, her hand held out to Matt, "Matt, I don't expect you to remember me, but I used to watch you ride in the weekend rodeos. I'm Carrie 'Stoddard' Galloway. Welcome home."

Matt took her soft hand and raised one brow. "How could I 'not' remember you? Every cowboy in the state was trying to get your attention." He motioned toward Jake with his head, "My brother must've done some fancy talking to get your attention. He really got lucky, pretty lady."

Carrie was pleased with his greeting. Then she turned a warm smile in Dimple's direction. "I feel like I already know you, Dimple, and I am looking forward to us becoming *very* good friends. After all, we're 'family' now."

Dimple's cheeks showed the famous indents as she smiled widely and reached out to hug Carrie.

Wedged between them, Collin looked back and forth between the two women as they squeezed him for a moment, then he stretched out with his short, chubby arms and encircled both their necks, pulling their faces against his on either side.

"Did you ever see a prettier sight," Matt said with a grin.

No…I never did. Jake grinned without comment.

Standing at the foot of the porch steps, Jake had shoved both hands into his back pockets. He watched the others silently, like a man in a dream.

The Galloway brothers turned similar blue eyes on each other and froze. Neither one knew exactly what to do, but after several seconds, Jake pulled his hands from his pockets and stepped in Matt's direction. Matt met him halfway as Jake reached out to embrace his younger brother…hugging him fiercely.

Drawing a ragged breath, Jake said against Matt's neck, "Welcome back, little brother."

Matt reached up and put one of his hands behind Jake's head. He turned his face and rested his forehead against his brother's. "I'm sorry for being such a jerk. I love you, man. Even when I pretended otherwise, I knew better—you're my brother. Thank you for forgiving me," he whispered huskily.

Collin was watching with a puzzled expression. *Was his daddy crying? Nawh…Daddy didn't cry.*

The whole bunch locked arms and filed into the house with Collin riding on his "Unca" Matt's shoulders.

Hallelujah! Matt was home again!

1875

"Well, I guess I'd better head to the house…to see what Carrie's been up to in the kitchen," Jake said as he climbed the bank. Picking up Guapo's reins, he swung easily into the saddle.

Cooter chuckled, "I know what Caroline's been up to. Nothing. We're supposed to go over to her folks to stay the night and tomorrow. It'll be the last time we spend the night at their house until I get back from the cow-drive."

He slipped his boot into the stirrup and slung his leg over the saddle. Waving his hat as he rode away, Cooter gave his famous Texas yell, "Yeeee…haaa!"

* * *

The closer he came to home, the more thankful Jake's mood became. He had the world by the tail. There was not another thing he would ask God for than what he had already been blessed with.

He squinted against the late afternoon Sun as he approached his home. "Lord…in case I haven't told You lately, I want to thank You again for all Your blessings on me and Carrie. I also want to apologize for those times when I doubted You. I was walking by sight and not by faith—wasn't I, Lord? Thank You for Your mercy, patience, and understanding," Jake prayed in a low, sincere, voice, as he rode.

CHAPTER TWENTY-FIVE
Some People Never Learn

Two weeks after Jake, Cooter and the ranch hands left the Silver Concho, heading for the Fort Worth cattle market, Reina drove into Llano to Mr. Porter's general store. She stopped in front of the long, low, two-windowed building and, using the wagon wheel spokes, climbed to the ground. Reaching over the side of the wagon, she retrieved her shopping basket. Ma'ma was making fresh tortillas and needed more maza—cornmeal. Reina was always happy to go shopping for her Ma'ma, because it meant she would see her friends in town.

She pushed the door open and stepped into the cool interior of the store. Mr. Porter was talking to some customers, but lifted his eyes when she entered. "Reina, how's it going out at the Concho with everybody gone on the trail ride?" he asked in his usual friendly manner.

Reina walked to the counter, nodding at the others there as she spoke, "The Concho ees,—how you say—muerto—dead—weethout the vacareos. Ma'ma and Pa'pa are take care of the animales in the b— barn. No one else ees there. Meese Carrie and the leetle one are stay weeth her Pa'pa, the doc' tor', unteel Meester Jake is come home. But, I am enjoy being at the rancho. It is bee-u-ti-ful casa, house."

Mr. Porter and the others smiled at her accent. She was such a lovely, sweet girl and a delight to know.

THE SILVER CONCHO: LIFE IS A RUB-BOARD

Unheeded by others in the room, a big, scruffy looking man was sitting at the end of the counter eating crackers and cheese. It was Mr. Porter's custom to have a large barrel of soda crackers and a round of cheese positioned there for travelers or anyone looking for something to eat. He charged ten cents for all one could eat. The man ate quietly, but listened intently. *Jake Galloway stole twelve years of my life from me. He's gonna pay...and pay dear; the young smart-aleck. I wonder, jest where is the doctor's house. There weren't no doctor here when I was in these parts before. He musta come here after the War. I a'magine that most folks could tell me where he lives though.*

* * *

On the sixteenth day of the cattle-drive, the herd had just passed the half-way mark and Jake was riding as point-man. The blistering hot day made the cattle tired and thirsty. Young bulls testily resisted being driven. Jake knew that the situation was primed for a stampede if his men failed to be careful to not spook the animals.

At noon, Jake's stomach told him it was time to eat. He raised his hand high over his head as a signal to the other riders to stop the cattle's forward motion. Then he guided Guapo off to the right where he knew Hardtack trailed along-side the herd, attempting to avoid the trail dust.

As he neared the rattling, bouncing chuck wagon, Jake spotted a familiar figure approaching from the opposite direction. "What in the world is he doing here," he muttered. He raised a hand in acknowledgment of the lawman.

Briscoe was waiting beside the cook's wagon with a cup of coffee in his hand when Jake arrived. "Good to see you, boy. It looks like you're making good time. How many head are you pushing on this trip," he asked with a slow, Texas drawl.

"Good to see you too," Jake responded, "We're doing better than expected with this size herd. I have two thousand head in the bunch, Cooter has fifty, and Mr. Cagle has two hundred and fifty. I don't think we've lost any, so that means there's around twenty three hundred total."

"Whew! That's quite a handful. Any trouble?" The lawman was always concerned about rustlers or Indians.

"No—no trouble. What brings you here," Jake questioned as he reached for the cup Hardtack was passing to him. "You're sort of out of your jurisdiction, aren't you?"

The Sheriff grinned, then turned serious. "You remember that Clancy kid who got mixed up with the Waylon bunch, awhile back? Well—he was caught up around Waco. The Marshall over there sent word for me to come make a positive identification of him before they send him to Huntsville." He shook his head, "I sure hated to do it—it nearly killed his mama when he got in trouble. She's a good woman." He took his hat off and scratched his head. "What makes a youngster go off like that? He had good raising."

Jake didn't reply. What could he say?

John Briscoe stayed around for a while and had dinner with Jake and the hands. He laughed and joked with them the whole while. Briscoe was thirty-nine years old and had known most of the Concho hands since they were youngsters. He became sheriff of Llano when he was twenty three years old. In Jake's opinion, he had been a mighty fine one. Briscoe tried to be a friend to most of the people he served.

The Sun indicated that it was nearing one o'clock; Briscoe motioned with his head for Jake to come aside. Jake, puzzled, followed him to the shade of a small pen oak tree.

"Jake, I don't want to worry you none, but while I was at Waco, the marshal told me that Joe Washington got his freedom papers a couple of weeks ago. The warden at Huntsville told the marshal that the 'yard' scuttlebutt is that Washington is still shootin' his mouth off about how he's gonna get even with you for costing him twelve years of his life. The warden said it's probably just a blow-hard's talk—the man's always been a coward you know. The marshal knew that you are a friend of mine."

Releasing a long breath, Briscoe continued, "Anyway, I want you to know that I'll be keeping my eyes open. If he comes anywhere around Llano; I'll run him off."

Jake listened thoughtfully. Nodding, he replied, "Thanks for the warning, Sheriff. I'll get this cattle drive over as quick as I can and get on back to Carrie and my boy. I don't like the idea of that no-good being within a hundred miles of them; especially when he's still carrying a grudge against me."

The sheriff left, headed for Llano. Jake was irritable for the rest of the journey. Even though he was dog-tired at night, he found it impossible to rest. When Cooter questioned him, Jake told him the truth and both men determined to push the cattle even harder toward Ft. Worth.

* * *

It had been the longest three weeks of Carrie's life. She missed her husband terribly. Doc Stoddard did his best to keep his daughter occupied, but he could tell that Jake was never off her mind.

One morning, Doctor Stoddard suggested that they pack a picnic lunch and walk down to the Llano River. Collin could play and splash around while wading in the shallow clear water. Carrie eagerly agreed. She always enjoyed relaxing under her favorite cottonwood tree at the edge of the river.

The tot chattered excitedly as they walked along the trail that led to the picnic spot. "Mama, I'm gonna catch you and papaw a big," (he held out his arms to show how big), "fish for our supper."

Doc and Carrie glanced at each other, smiling indulgently, "You catch me a big fish, and I'll sure cook it for us tonight," she said, her eyes wide as if she really believed it would happen. Collin's little head bobbed as if that settled the matter.

They spread their lunch on a huge flat rock at the very edge of the water. The day was very warm, but the shade of the huge tree shielded them from the direct sunlight. Collin was having a wonderful time, splashing around in the six or seven inches of water. He kept a sharp eye out for the fish he intended to catch. The adults, who sat at the edge of the flat rock with their bare feet dangling in the water, played the game with him and pretended to look for a fish also.

Collin bent down and grabbed a handful of small pebbles from the shallow water at his feet. He had started toward them with his little hand outstretched to show them his treasures, when he stopped and stared at something behind them. Carrie and her father twisted at the waist to see what the child was looking at.

There, leaning against the cottonwood tree, was a big, dirty-looking man. He had been watching them silently for a few minutes. *Jake Galloway has a mighty fine lookin' woman, and I a'magine he's shore proud of that little'un too. Her paw, the doctor, ain't as old as I had expected him to be. I reckon I'll have to catch her by surprise…when he ain't around. Then I'll make Galloway pay for the past twelve years.*

Doctor Stoddard called out to him, "Do you need something? Can I help you?"

Joe glowered in response. "Nawh…I reckon not." He turned and disappeared into the woods behind them. Grabbing the reins, Washington swung up onto the back of his long-legged black mule. He still preferred mules to horses.

* * *

Ft. Worth was in sight and Jake was elated that the drive was almost over. He couldn't wait to get the cattle sold so he could head back to Carrie and Collin. Cooter was happy too; he had fifty head in the bunch and they represented the beginning of real financial independence for him and Caroline. Also, the money from the sale of their cattle would be the 'go-a-head' for starting a family; something Cooter and Caroline both wanted dearly.

It took two days to complete the sale, but Jake finally had the check in his pocket. He and Cooter and the others would leave at the crack of dawn the next morning. Jake called his men together that evening and gave them an early draw on their pay. He would give them the rest of it when they got back to Llano.

"Manny… Cooter and I will be hightailing back to the house as quick as we can. You heard about the possibility of Joe Washington coming around my family. I want to get back pronto and so I want you and the others to ride along with Hardtack and the chuck wagon. Make sure he doesn't have any problems. I'll see you when you get back to the Concho."

Manny nodded, "Si, Jake. I understand."

* * *

"Ma'ma... I weel go this morning to see Mees Carrie. I am wanting to know if she has heard from Mr. Jake. Jo'el weel also be regresando—returning weeth Senor Jake." Reina hurried down to the barn and asked her father to saddle a horse for her. He chuckled when she told him where she was going. "You are anxious for Jake to come home—no?" Reina grinned. She knew her father understood that it was Joel, not Jake, she was anxious to see.

* * *

Caroline was just arriving from her father's house when Reina rode into the doctor's front yard. The girls greeted each other warmly. Caroline said, "I can guess why you're here. We're both hoping to hear if Carrie's had word from Jake and Cooter about when they'll be home." Reina jiggled her head vigorously. "Si—I am most anxious."

Carrie heard them speaking from inside the house. She stepped to the screen door and was about to push it open when Collin scooted past her and ran out onto the porch. "Hi Aunt Caroline... Aunt Reina. Mama is taking me down to the river to play in the water. It's fun! Do you want to go too?"

Caroline held the front gate open for Reina, all the while talking to the energetic little boy, "I sure do! I love to wade in the water. It's so hot today, I just might sit all the way down in the water," she answered with a decided nod of her head. Collin giggled. He loved his *Aunt* Caroline and *Aunt* Reina.

Carrie, still holding the door, said, "Let me get us a blanket to sit on—those rocks at the riverbank are so sandy. She disappeared for a few moments and then came back with a blanket draped over her arm. "Come on—he's been after me all morning to take him down there."

A short time later, the young women sat on the blanket at the water's edge. They laughed and talked about their men and of plans for the future, all the while keeping a protective eye on Collin who was playing in the water.

Reina told her friends, "Jo'el says thees is last cattle drive for him. He weel begin his rancho de caballos." She dropped her head shyly, "We are comprometido—ah—how you say…engaged. It ees my hope that we weel be married by summer next."

"Oh, Reina!" the other girls cried in unison. "That's wonderful!"

"You are such a beautiful couple. I know you will both be very happy together," Carrie gushed sincerely. "Your kids will be so handsome."

"Thank you, Mees Carrie. I am hope they will look like their pa'pa'."

"I am *sure* Joel is hoping they look like you—you're so beautiful," Caroline said positively Reina smiled prettily, "You are most kind, Mees Caroline; eet is good to haf friends such as you."

Collin was busy stacking small flat rocks near the edge of the water. Out of the blue, the child said, "Mama, I need a boat so I can float it in the water."

Caroline smiled at the tot and said, "I saw a big leaf off that cottonwood behind us, lying near the base of the tree. It would make a good boat." Cottonwood leaves are often as big as a dinner plate, especially from a tree the size of that one.

Collin took off hurriedly up the incline behind them as they continued talking about the projected time for Jake and the Concho crew to return home.

* * *

Unknown to the women, Joe Washington had been observing them and the child for several minutes. Hidden behind the giant cottonwood tree, it was easy for him to grab the child when Collin bent over to pick up his boat-leaf. Placing his huge, rough hand over the little boy's mouth, he hurried away from the area before he was detected. Yanking Collin up onto his mule with him, he kicked the animal in the flanks and followed the river's edge until he found a shallow place to ford it.

Then, he turned northwest, heading for the rough, dry-gully, cactus strewn country. Collin kicked and squirmed with all his might, but to no avail against such a large man. Tears flooded from his eyes and ran over the hand that threatened to smother him.

* * *

After a minute or two, when Collin did not return with his "boat", Carrie turned at the waist to look for him. He was not there! Jumping to her feet, she said to the others, "Collin is not in sight. Come on, I have to find the little rascal."

Thinking that Collin had decided to look for another leaf or stick to use for a boat, she ran to the big cottonwood. Caroline and Reina were right on her heels, calling, "Collin…Collin…where are you sweetie? You don't need to go out of your mother's sight!"

Carrie had reached the foot of the tree first. She scanned the dirt beneath it for tiny footprints, hoping to see in which direction he had moved. She popped her hand over her mouth when she spied the huge boot print directly behind her son's small one. "Oh… Oh…" she gasped and pointed to the boot print.

Caroline and Reina both paled when they saw what Carrie was pointing at. "But…who…we see or hear no'thing," Reina exclaimed.

Carrie's mind was racing back to the day when she and her father had seen a big, scruffy-looking man watching them. She thought his reaction to her dad's offer to help him had been odd. Now she knew why. Who was he? Had he taken her son? Why?

Wasting no more time, she turned to her friend, "Caroline, someone has taken him. Go right now, as fast as you can; get the sheriff and my dad. Tell them what happened. And tell them I am going to follow the tracks as best as I can." She started to moved toward her father's barn, but Reina reached out and grabbed her shoulders. "Mees Carrie! Thees man weel be most peligro…dangerous! Please wait; let you pa'pa' and the sher'eef go for tu nino…you leetle one."

Shaking her head forcefully, Carrie answered, "No. I can't wait! I have to catch the person who took him. Collin needs me!" She turned once again, running to saddle a horse.

Carrie's friends moved swiftly to retrieve the buggy and Reina's horse. As they ran, Reina said to Caroline, "I know the way...the trail Meester Jake weel come. I weel ride to meet him; to tell him of thees trouble."

Caroline responded, "That's a wonderful idea, Reina! Bring them as quickly as you can." They hurried away to complete their own charge.

* * *

"Do you see what I see, Cooter," Jake asked with a satisfied grin. He was referring to the north bend of the Llano River.

"Yea boy, I do," Cooter responded. "A couple or three more hours and we'll be looking at the purtiest sights in Texas." He winked at Jake, "I sure hope Caroline is ready to go on home this evening, 'cause I don't want to stay at her folks' house tonight—if you get my drift." Jake chuckled. The men had set a hurried pace all day, but now they were allowing their tired horses a breather.

"I think I'm gonna take Carrie and the boy, *and* the doc to the hotel dining room this evening for a celebration dinner." Jake said, thinking out loud. "I want them to share in how good the Lord has been to us, financially, on this trip...and to Matt and Dimple."

He turned in his saddle to look at his friend. "Cooter, you should have seen Matt's face last fall when I told him that I had been splitting the profits between us all these years. When he heard how much he had in the bank, I thought he was gonna faint. He couldn't speak for a full minute. Then he asked, 'Jake, have we really got that much...each?' I told him we had and he muttered... 'That's enough to build another house...and then some. Shoot!—That's enough to build ten houses!' I laughed and asked, "What are you gonna do with *ten* houses?" He just grinned, but I was hoping that he was thinking about coming home and doing that very thing."

"Looky yonder," Cooter said, pointing to a rider coming toward them in a big hurry. "Wonder, where he...she's headed in such a....

That's Reina!" They kicked their horses into a gallop and met Reina half-way.

"Girl, where are you going in such a hurry," Jake said, reaching out to take hold of her horse's bridle. The horse danced to the side, but Jake held on tight.

"Meester Jake, you must come quickly to Doc'tor Stod'dards' casa. You are needed by Mees Carrie and you leetle one."

Jake's heart slammed against his chest wall. "What's wrong, Reina? Is Carrie hurt...or Collin?," he asked anxiously. Reina was crying; this scared Jake even worse. "What is it girl! Tell me!"

"Oh, Meester Jake, we are by the ree'ver. We watch the leetle one play. He ees wanting to find a cottonwood leef to use for a lancha...boat. He ees find it by the beeg tree. But, when we look to see him, he is no there. Beeg man's bota...boots print ees there. Boy ees gone!" She leaned across the distance between them and grasped Jake's shirtsleeves. "Mees Carrie, she ees go to catch the hombre who take her leetle one. Hurry Meester Jake...ees much pelegro...danger for them!"

By that time, the Concho hands had gathered around them. Joel moved his mount next to Reina's. "Ride like a madman, Jake. We'll be right behind you."

Neither Jake nor Cooter heard Joel's last sentence. They had already kicked their horses and were flying toward Llano. Both men were praying fervently, "Lord, please take care of Carrie and the baby, 'til we can get to them."

* * *

Caroline went straight to the sheriff's office, only to find out that he and Doctor Stoddard had ridden out together; to check on an Indian family with the chicken pox. The disease was much more serious for Indians than for whites. Briscoe and Doc were not expected back before sundown.

Hearing that, Caroline turned her buggy around swiftly in the street and drove to her father's house at the other end of Llano. When Adam

Hartman heard what had happened to Carrie and the boy, he quickly saddled a horse and rode out toward the Indian family's home.

* * *

Carrie had no experience following trails, but the mule's big-footed tracks were not hard to see. She found where it had crossed a shallow place in the river and was now traveling west-northwest. The terrain was becoming increasingly rugged. Small, scrub cedars and cactus dotted the area, strewn with narrow gullies and ravines. Her skirts snagged constantly on Cat-claws, a desert bush with odd-looking, claw-like spurs at the end of its limbs. From the corner of her eye, she saw something slither down a hole in the sand. Kicking her horse in the side, she moved quickly away from the spot to keep from screaming.

* * *

Joe Washington was the worst kind of man—a brutal coward. He attacked only those over whom he was sure he had the upper-hand. The little two year old boy sitting on the saddle in front of him crying softly was a prime example. After weighing his options between snatching the child or the mother, he chose the child simply because Carrie would be more capable and more likely to defend herself.

He had not yet definitely determined what he was going to do with the boy. A number of devices ran through his mind. Perhaps he would just turn the child loose in the wild, rough country and let nature kill him. Or, he could take the little blue-eyed, blond headed tike down to Mexico and sell him. Some of the wealthy families there would pay a big price for a little 'orphan' with hair that color. The child was too young to tell them the truth about what really happened to his folks.

In all his musings, the thought never occurred to Joe that he was unleashing a veritable "freight train." Jake Galloway would never give up looking for his son, no matter how long it took to find him, and heaven help the man who had perpetrated the crime.

The sun was going down in the west and Joe started looking for a campsite for the night. He felt sure that Jake would not hear of his son's disappearance for two or three more days, so he was not concerned about stopping for the night. That would give him time to dispose of the boy and disappear down into Mexico.

He came upon a little grove of scrub cedar at the edge of a small ravine and decided make his camp in the middle of it. The trees would offer a little shelter from the cooler night winds.

CONCLUSION
Do unto Others

Carrie's eyes were red, burning and swollen from crying, but she kept on riding. Every so often, she found it necessary to dismount for a closer look at the ground...or risk losing the trail. It was getting very late in the day, and she knew that spotting the mule's tracks after dark would be impossible. She might totally miss the signs of the animal's passing.

If darkness overtook her before she caught up with her son's abductor, she would be forced to stop for the night. Her heart wrenched at the thought of her dear, sweet, little Collin in the hands of that monster at night. She knew he was a monster because only a monster would do such a thing.

* * *

It was late afternoon when Jake and Cooter came roaring into Doctor Stoddard's barn. Reina and Manny were not far behind them. But by the time they arrived, Jake and Cooter had already been down to the river and the big cottonwood. Thankfully, the tracks were still visible. Jake found where Carrie's horse's tracks intersected those of a much larger-footed animal—probably a mule. A mule...Joe Washington always rode mules!

"Jake, let's switch mounts; we don't want to kill ours. No tellin' how much longer we'll be riding," Cooter warned.

"Alright, but let's make it fast—daylight is burning," Jake replied. They hurriedly returned to Doctor Stoddard's barn and threw their saddles on two of his horses.

Manny, Joel, and three other Concho hands arrived. They had changed mounts at the livery in town. "Where are we to go, Jake," Manny asked anxiously.

"I found tracks leading down the river a ways. Carrie is right behind whoever took the boy," he added, his lips tight. "I found her tracks also." He looked at Manny and the others; a combination of pain and hard determination emanated from his dark-blue eyes. "I'm sure I know who did this…and nothing can help him when I catch him."

"You think it's Joe Washington—don't you," Cooter asked, though he already knew the answer.

Jake nodded and swung into the saddle. He warned the others, "Let me go first. Stay behind me a few yards; it won't do for us to trample the tracks." The others said nothing, but drew back a distance of about thirty feet behind him.

* * *

Joe tossed a small piece of stale cornbread in front of Collin. "Here, you little scamp—I don't know why I'm botherin' to feed you. Being as yo're pa is Jake Galloway, you ain't worth feedin'."

Collin had no idea what the man was saying or why he had brought him out into this dark place. But he heard his father's name and asked innocently, "Are you my papa's friend?"

"Friend! I don't even like yo're pa," the foul-mouthed man barked. Collin flinched and began to cry.

"You shet yo're mouth! I ain't puttin' up with no whining!" Joe stood up from his perch on a large rock that lay in the small clearing. He lumbered toward the boy, who only howled louder in terror of the huge, dirty man.

From the corner of his eye, Joe saw movement. He whirled as a woman immerged from the dark shadow of the trees surrounding the campsite. "Mister, I don't know who you are or why you took my child, but you're not taking him any further. Come here, Collin." Carrie bent and held her hands out. She had been listening to the conversation between Joe and her son.

Collin ceased crying immediately at the sound of his mother's voice. He scrambled to his little feet and ran toward her, but Joe Washington reached out and grabbed him by the arm. He leered at Carrie, yanking the boy behind himself. "You don't have much to say about where I take him, Missy. You ain't 'man enough' to stop me." He chuckled wickedly at his own crude joke.

Carrie was shaking with fear for her child, but tried not to show it. "Who are you? Why are you doing this?"

"'Cause that smart-aleck husband of yours cost me twelve years in the pener'tentry. He weren't no more'n a boy, but he still cost me hard time in that stinking hole in Huntsville. I aim to make him pay for what he done," Joe growled.

A light went on in Carrie's head. Jake had related the story of a no-good named Joe Washington who attempted to rustle Concho cattle back when Jake was a very young man. Sheriff Briscoe intervened and together they caught the thief.

"If your name is Joe Washington, my husband told me about your attempt to steal his cattle when he was only seventeen. How can you possibly blame him when you were the thief!" Carrie wasn't going to let him get away with blaming someone else, especially Jake, for his own meanness, or for the consequences of his deeds.

Joe did not bother to defend himself. Instead, he started in her direction with his arms spread wide, intending to catch her. She skittered to the side of the clumsy oaf and ran to Collin. Sweeping him up in her arms, she darted toward the gully. When she reached its edge, she hesitated. It was dark down in the small ravine and she had no idea what she might encounter.

The sound of Joes' grunting and cursing, as he approached from behind, forced her to descend the side of the bank. With Collin in her arms, she could not afford to stumble; that slowed her progress.

Reaching the bottom, she moved carefully along near the embankment, in an effort to be less visible in the dark shadows. A place to hide—she must hide; for she knew it would be only the matter of a few seconds before Washington caught them.

To her left, Carrie saw what appeared to be a dark hole. It was a small, cave-like indention in the side of the gully-wall. She clutched Collin against her breast and backed into it. Grabbing desperately at branches of a small bush growing beside their hiding place, she pulled them down in front of the entrance and squatted down.

Hugging her little boy tightly and stroking his back in effort to comfort him, she whispered, "Don't cry, honey. Be quiet... Daddy will come for us. We have to hide where that bad man can't find us until your papa gets here." Collin's heart was beating rapidly, but the brave little tot embraced his mama's neck fiercely and said nothing.

Just then, Carrie heard the loud snapping noise of a breaking limb, then a yelp of fear that was followed by crashing sounds and a curse. She stiffened, afraid to move.

The branch Joe Washington clutched, as he tried to follow Carrie down the decline, suddenly snapped and he fell headlong until his body smashed against a pile of large rocks at the bottom of the gully. When he finally stopped tumbling, the middle of his back struck a sharp, fist-sized rock, and excruciating pain shot upward between his shoulder blades. "Ohhhhhh...." he screamed; then cursed at full volume.

* * *

Jake became aware of a man shouting...and cursing. Even though it had been twelve years since he last heard Joe Washington, he recognized the voice. Dropping off his horse, he stealthily made his way toward the small fire he could see in the center of some trees. Cooter was right behind him, followed by Manny and the others. They were uncertain as to where the voice was coming from, and why the outlaw was shouting and cursing. They proceeded as quickly and quietly as possible.

The darkness of night prevented Carrie from seeing very far. A half-moon afforded some light, but there were some clouds and the gully was deep. She heard Joe's yelping. Was the man really hurt or was it just a trick to get her to reveal her position? After listening for several minutes to the thrashing, wailing and cursing, she made an anxious decision to try to make it back up to the top of the ravine to her horse.

She cupped her hand over Collin's ear, "We're going to try to climb back up to where my horse is…so we can go home…away from that bad man. You'll have to keep on being a brave boy…be very quiet." She kissed his cheek, tucked his head against her chest, and ventured back out of the cave. Moving as softly as she could, careful not to disturb loose rocks, she retraced her earlier path as best as she could.

Joe peered into the darkness at the faint noise to his right. "Woman! Don't you go off and leave me here in this fix," He shouted. "I'm hurt! And it's yo're fault."

Carrie ignored his demand and began climbing as fast as she could manage. She fell to her knees at one point, and Collin squealed in fright. "It's okay, baby. We're not hurt. Be quiet."

She regained her footing and managed to reach the top of the embankment. As her feet stepped up on level ground, suddenly big, rough hands grabbed her shoulders and she was yanked into a crushing embrace. She and Collin both screamed in fright.

"Hush, Sweetheart…it's me, Jake. You're both safe now," Jake said softly. His heart was running wild and his eyes filled with tears of joy.

"Jake? Papa," Carrie and Collin spoke in unison. Jake was kissing both of them all over their faces. After a moment, he ceased, "Yes, it's me."

Jake turned and handed his family into Cooter's arms. "Take care of them; I've got a rat to kill," he said grimly. "Oh, Jake—be careful! He may be hurt, but that doesn't mean he won't have a gun," Carrie warned.

"If he does have one; he's gonna eat it!" Jake called over his shoulder as he boldly decended into the darkness.

Cooter smiled nervously at Carrie and the boy. "Carrie, I'm gonna follow him…back him up. Okay?" She nodded quickly. Cooter spoke to Manny, "Here, Manny; get her and the boy back to where the horses are. If there's any shootin', we don't want them in the line of fire."

Jake reached the bottom of the gully at full speed. His anger at Joe Washington was so hot that his judgment had become reckless.

"Is that you, woman? I need you to brang my mule down here—I don't thank I can climb that hill," Joe yelled. He had heard gravel tumble as Jake's boots skidded in places.

"You're not gonna need a horse, Joe," Jake replied into the darkness. He still hadn't located the outlaw. "I've got a gun and a rope. Which one do you prefer?"

Startled, Joe called out, "Wha...who is that?" Then he remembered that Jake was no longer a boy—the man's voice speaking to him now had to be Galloway's. He became deathly still. Maybe Jake wouldn't find him in the dark. But in that instant, a match flared. In it's light, Joe was staring into the face of the man he had three-times wronged; a face full of anger, disgust, and...revenge. The match burned out.

Hoping to play on Jake's sympathy, Joe whined, "I...I'm hurt. I can't feel my legs." Jake wasn't touched. "Then I guess I'll be doing you a favor to put you out of your misery." With that, he drew his gun with his right hand and struck another match with his left.

"I want you to see the face of the man who has had all he's gonna take from you, Joe. You've been bothering me and my family, including my brother, for over twelve years, off and on. Your first mistake was when you showed up at the Concho thinking you could ramrod two kids out of their ranch. The second was when you stole our cattle. But the biggest mistake you've *ever* made was putting your filthy hands on my wife and son. I would have beat the daylights out of you for messing with my property, but I'll *kill* you for touching Carrie and Collin." Jake rocked the hammer back on his gun.

Cooter was standing behind Jake about ten feet. He spoke out of the darkness, "Jake, I know how you feel; the man's dirt. But you can't do this. You've *got* to think of Carrie and the boy."

"I am thinking of them," Jake yelled.

"Let the law take care of this filth, Jake. Kidnapping a woman and child is a hanging offence in Texas. You don't want to live with his blood on your hands—even though you're justified in killing him," Cooter continued to coax.

Jake struck another match, his gun still pointed at Joe. He vacillated between, *Listen to Cooter* and *the law would give you a medal for killing Joe Washington.*

Joe stared in horror at the barrel of Jake's weapon. After several tense moments, Jake slowly lowered the gun. "Go get his horse and a blanket. We'll make a travois to take him back to Llano. But you and Manny are gonna load him onto it. I don't want to touch him," Jake spat.

* * *

Two weeks later, Jake and Carrie were sitting on the front porch. Jake had Collin on his lap. The child was leaning against his father's chest with his thumb in his mouth…something he had not done before his experience with Joe Washington. "Will he get over this…thumb sucking," Jake asked his wife. Carrie replied, "Dad says it will pass as soon as he's absolutely secure again."

Jake's heart clenched with the thought that his little son was still afraid. He would do anything to assure Collin that he was completely safe now. He tightened his arms around the child and whispered in his ear, "You know I love…don't you, Son? That man will never touch you or your mother again. I promise." Collin nodded his little head solemnly, but the thumb stayed where it was.

"Jake, look; there comes Sheriff Briscoe," Carrie announced. They watched as the lawman approached. He reached the house and dropped down off his horse in front of the porch steps.

"Howdy Sheriff. Come on up and make yourself comfortable," Jake said, pointing to a big rocking chair. "Would you like something cool to drink? I have some lemonade," Carrie offered cheerily.

"That sounds mighty nice, Carrie. I believe the weather has cooled off some, but it's still hot as blue-blazes out in the open," the sheriff responded gratefully. He dropped his horse's reins, knowing the animal would not wander any farther than the nearest patch of grass.

THE SILVER CONCHO: LIFE IS A RUB-BOARD

Briscoe eyed Collin for a moment while he took the offered chair. "How are you doing, little man?" To their surprise, Collin took his thumb from his mouth and squirmed down out of his father's lap. He walked straight to the sheriff and lifted his arms to be held. Briscoe's brows went up and he looked a Jake with surprised pleasure in his eyes.

Once he was settled in the lawman's lap, they discovered the reason for Collins' actions. He turned to face the star pinned to Briscoe's vest and began stroking it with his small hand.

"Do you think we might be looking at Llano's future sheriff?" Briscoe was delighted by the boy's action.

Carrie returned with three tall glasses of lemonade on a tray. They drank the refreshing liquid and talked amiably about various things for several minutes.

Jake wasn't fooled. John Briscoe did not ride eleven miles in the hot sun for a glass of lemonade.

A few minutes later, Briscoe proved him right. The sheriff looked at Carrie apologetically, "Mrs. Carrie...do you mind if I have a word with Jake, alone?" Carrie stared at the man. "Ah...oh, sure," she stammered. She picked Collin up and disappeared into the house.

* * *

"Jake; the reason I rode out here, is to find out if you want to go ahead with the charges against Joe Washington," the sheriff explained.

Jake was shocked by the question. "Do I want to go ahead? I thought the law took over when I brought him in. He kidnapped my family, Sheriff." He raised his brows, "What else do I have to do?"

The sheriff released a long, heavy breath before he spoke again. "Jake... Doc Stoddard says that Joe Washington will never walk again. He's paralyzed from the waist down. It can't be reversed with surgery." He looked expectantly at Jake.

"Is that supposed to make me feel sorry for him, John? He got what he deserved...but he still ought to hang," Jake declared adamantly.

John Briscoe was not only a just man; he was a merciful man also. He turned his head and stared down the hill toward the barn for a few moments. Looking back at Jake, he spoke, "Jake, will you do me a favor?"

The question surprised Jake, but he answered his friend, "Well...sure...what do you need?"

"I don't need anything. I want you to do something." He paused, "I want you to study Mark 11:25-26, and then Matthew 7:12. Take a good look at both those passages tonight.

"Tomorrow, if you still feel the same way...come see me, and I'll get a trial set up for Washington."

For the first time since he had known John Briscoe, Jake bordered on being angry with him. Why would the man ask him to look at the Bible in connection with Joe Washington's guilt? Joe was as guilty as sin.

Jake was silent for so long that Briscoe thought he was going to refuse; but after a long minute, Jake said, resignedly, "I don't know what difference it will make in what I think, but...because you are a friend, I'll do it."

"Good," the sheriff said.

* * *

That night, Jake was sitting on the side of his bed reading the scriptures Briscoe had mentioned. Mark 11:25-26—"And when ye stand praying, forgive, if ye have ought against any; that your Father also which is in heaven may forgive you your trespasses. But if ye do not forgive, neither will your Father which is in heaven forgive your trespasses." Jake frowned.

He flipped his Bible back to Matthew 7:12—"Therefore all things whatsoever ye would that men should do to you, do ye even so to them; for this is the law of the prophets."

After reading the second passage in Matthew, Jake muttered, "If I had stolen someone's wife and child, I'd expect to get my head blown off. Joe Washington should have *expected* to be hung for what he did. So I'm not asking the law to do anything I wouldn't expect to be done to me."

"What did you say?" Carrie rolled over sleepily on her side of the bed and stared at Jake's back. Her eyes widened when she realized that Jake was reading his Bible...that late at night. She whispered so she would not disturb Collin who slept in the middle of their bed these nights. He had been ever since his frightening experience with Joe.

"I said I don't know why Briscoe wanted me to read these verses of Scripture. They don't say a thing that would make me change my mind about Joe's guilt." Jake had raised his voice and Collin squirmed. Carrie pressed her finger to her lips as a signal to lower his voice. Jake glanced at his son and nodded.

"Which verses did he ask you to read?" Carrie was wide awake now.

Jake read the verses to her in a subdued voice. When he finished, he asked, "Do you see anything in those verses that says I should change my mind about Joe Washington's guilt?"

Carrie smiled with understanding. "Jake, I don't think the sheriff wanted you to change his guilt—he wanted you to change his sentence."

"What do you mean...change his sentence? I'm not the one who will be sentencing him—the law will do that," Jake defended himself.

"But Jake, if you forgive him—he won't be sentenced. You have to press charges in order for him to even be indicted for the crime."

"Carrie! You mean you want me to just let him get away with it?" Jake asked incredulously.

Patiently, Carrie reasoned, "He didn't get away with anything, Jake. Don't you realize that the man is crippled for the rest of his life? Collin and I were frightened, but we were not harmed. God knew you would get there in time to protect us... Don't you see that?"

She scooted closer to him, careful not to disturb Collin. "Jake, all of us deserved to die for our sins against God, yet He stood ready and willing to forgive us of everything we had ever done. We didn't have to pay the price for our sins...Jesus did that for us."

She took a deep breath—this was important. "The Lord is willing to forgive us—no matter what. So shouldn't we do the same for each other?"

"He don't deserve it," Jake fumed.

"Neither do we. We commit the same sins over and over; yet He never refuses us." Carrie laid a hand on his arm, "Now read those verses again and put *your* name everywhere it says 'you'."

Jake slowly turned back around. His eyes dropped to his Bible once more. "And when *Jake* stands to pray, forgive, if *Jake* has ought against any—Joe Washington—that *Jake's* heavenly Father may forgive *Jake*, his trespasses."

He turned back to Matthew once more. "Therefore all things whatsoever Jake would that men should do to him, do, Jake, even so to them...."

Carrie was watching her husband's broad back as he read. There was not a man around as sweet and pure-hearted as Jake Galloway. She knew he would do the right thing.

After a moment, Jake turned at the waist and looked at her solemnly. He gave her a strained smile, laid his Bible down, and turned out the light. Carrie could hear him sigh in the darkness, a moment later.

* * *

Sheriff Briscoe was just coming out of Joe Washington's cell with the morning's breakfast tray when Jake and Manny came through the door into his office.

"Good morning, Jake, Manny," the sheriff said with a smile. "I guess you're here to let me know what to do about Joe Washington. Right?—But before you tell me, I want to know if you did as I asked you to last night?"

Jake nodded. "Yeah—between you, those verses of Scripture and Carrie, I guess I've decided not to press charges."

"Good! Good! I knew you'd do the right thing, Jake. Not for Joe's sake as much as for yours."

Jake cocked his head at the wily lawman, "Last night, I got to thinking about how Matt was willing to forgive me for all the wrong I'd done him...and how I didn't deserve it. I realize now that I would have to be pretty selfish not to forgive someone else."

Briscoe shook his head, "Jake, there's no comparison between what Joe Washington did to you and your family, and the trouble between you and Matt. But the need to forgive is the same, no matter what the trespasses, as the bible calls them, are." He laid a hand on Jake's shoulder and added, "As far as Joe receiving punishment…well, all I can say is he's in a prison of his own making now. He'll never use his legs again. I don't know what to do with him…how's he gonna get along?"

"I have the answer to that question," Jake responded. "I had Manny drive the wagon in behind me this morning. We'll load him up, go by Doc's house to see about how to get a wheel chair for him; then he can live out at the Concho for the rest of his life. He can still use his arms and there are a lot of mending jobs I can give him to do. Hardtack can probably use him in the cook-shack too."

Briscoe's mouth was hanging open. "Well… I'll be." He shook his head in amazement, muttering, "Well…I'll just be."

The three men stepped through the door that separated the office from the prisoner's cells. Briscoe shoved the key into Joe's cell door lock and said in a friendly voice, "Joe, we're moving you to your new home today. I have two men here to help me load you onto their wagon."

Joe jumped at the sound of Briscoe's voice and he opened his eyes groggily. "What'd'ya mean, my new home? I ain't got no home but this cell."

"You do now. And you've even got a job mending tack and peeling spuds or whatever else needs doing out at the Silver Concho," the sheriff informed him.

Joe's eyes widened. "The Concho! B…but that's Jake Galloway's ranch. Why would he want to hire me…or even let me around his place?"

Jake stepped around the lawman, into Joe's line of vision. "Because someone forgave me for my meanness one time, Joe. I'm just passing that forgiveness on to you."

Joe stared at Jake with unbelief on his haggard-looking face. When he closed his eyes a tear ran down the side of his cheek. He nodded, but said nothing.

Manny looked at Jake, admiration shining in his expression. "Why, Jake?"

"Do unto others…" was Jake's reply.

THE END

GRANNY'S LESSON

Andrew chuckled, "Granny…I guess Jake learned the hard way, didn't he?"

Granny nodded, "Sometimes. But his heart was good, and he was willing to learn. Jake Galloway must have been what all *real* men aspire to be. He was selfless, hard-working, loving, brave and humble; all rolled into one, big, handsome man." She continued, "I think the lessons to be learned from Jake are; that we must be willing to admit our mistakes and strive not to make them again; we must stay open to learning from God and apply what we learn to our lives."

Andrew thought a moment. "I think his greatest strength was in his willingness to think of others first. I hope I can be that kind of person."

"That's an admirable goal for anyone," she answered with pride for her grandson shining in her eyes.

Andrew reached out and hugged his grandmother. "Thanks for sharing that story with me." Next, he said, "I'll be coming home again at Christmas; will you have another story for me?"

Granny smiled secretively, "I've already promised to tell your sisters about the "Crocheted Button" in my button box. Don't miss it!"

also available from publishamerica

THE FIRE THAT NASA NEVER HAD
by Colonel B. Dean Smith

This book is an account of Colonel B. Dean Smith's flying activities in support of research and development of the United States' Ballistic Missile program and the space exploration of NASA from Cape Canaveral (Kennedy), Florida. Included is a report of a test done for NASA that examined space suits for the Gemini project. During this project, the author and another pilot experienced a disastrous fire in a simulator containing 100% oxygen, nearly taking both their lives. Five years later, in 1967, NASA's Apollo I capsule was consumed by a similar 100% oxygen fire, taking the lives of three astronauts, Gus Grissom, Ed White and Roger Chaffee. The author takes the reader through an account of the preparations made before his test flight and fire. He then makes a comparison of the two fires and the subsequent NASA investigation report of the Apollo I incident and draws conclusions regarding the lessons learned.

Paperback, 270 pages
6" x 9"
ISBN 1-4241-2574-X

About the author:

Colonel B. Dean Smith graduated from the US Naval Academy in 1953, commissioned in the Air Force. After pilot training, he served numerous flying tours and administrative positions. He earned an MBA from GW University, and served a tour in Vietnam, retiring from the Joint Chiefs of Staff on July 1, 1974.

available to all bookstores nationwide.
www.publishamerica.com